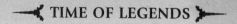

*Book Two of the Sigmar Trilogy*

# EMPIRE

*The Legend of Sigmar*

## Graham McNeill

*This one is for Sawney, the newest recruit.*

**A BLACK LIBRARY PUBLICATION**

First published in Great Britain in 2009 by
BL Publishing,
Games Workshop Ltd.,
Willow Road, Nottingham,
NG7 2WS, UK

10 9 8 7 6 5 4 3 2 1

Cover illustration by Jon Sullivan.
Map by Nuala Kinrade.

A CIP record for this book is available from the British Library.

ISBN 13: 978-1-84416-688-6

Distributed in the US by Simon & Schuster
1230 Avenue of the Americas, New York, NY 10020.

See the Black Library on the Internet at
**www.blacklibrary.com**

Find out more about Games Workshop
and the world of Warhammer at
**www.games-workshop.com**

Printed and bound in the US.

THIS IS A DARK age, a bloody age, an age of daemons and of sorcery. It is an age of battle and death, and of the world's ending. Amidst all of the fire, flame and fury it is a time, too, of mighty heroes, of bold deeds and great courage.

AT THE HEART of the Old World lie the lands of men, ruled over by bickering tribal chieftains.

IT IS A land divided. In the north, King Artur of the Teutogens surveys his rivals atop the mighty Fauschlag Rock, whilst the berserker kings of the Thuringians know only war and bloodshed. It is to the south that men must look for succour. At Reikdorf dwell the Unberogens, led by the mighty King Björn and his fated son, Sigmar. The Unberogens seek a vision, a vision of unity. The enemies of man are many and if men cannot overcome their differences and rally together, their demise is assured.

TO THE FROZEN north, Norsii raiders, barbarians and worshippers of Dark Gods, burn, slay and pillage. Grim spectres haunt the marshlands and beasts gather in the forests. But it is in the east where dark forces are moving, and the greatest threat lies. Greenskins have ever plagued the land and now they march upon the race of man in their numberless hordes with a single purpose – to eradicate their foes forever.

THE HUMAN KINGS are not alone in their plight. The dwarfs of the mountains, great forge smiths and engineers, are allies in this fight. All must stand together, dwarf and man for their mutual survival depends on it.

# Our Land in the time of Sigmar

Salzenhus

FOREST OF SHADOWS

Brass

Fauschlag Rock

REST ROAD

Battle of the
Berserker King

THURINGIANS

Count Otwin's
Castle

U

THE
FO

JUTONES

Jutonsryk

GR. NORTH ROAD

TEUTOGENS

BRETONII

Reikd

Astofen

Marburg

ENDALS

UNBEROGENS

PALE
SISTERS

GREY MTNS.

# BOOK ONE

## Empire of Hope

*Then all chiefs made an oath
To stand together, united as men,
And a crown was fashioned
By Alaric, runesmith of the dwarfs,
Placed by Ulric, the priest,
Upon noble Sigmar's brow.*

## ✦ ONE ✦

# The Last Days of Kings

THE SHADOWS WERE long as the Hag Woman stepped from the misty hilltop overlooking the city of Reikdorf. She had walked many miles from her home in the Bracken-walsch, and her limbs were aching from the long journey. The poultices and tisanes of Spiderleaf and Valerian were no longer able to keep the crystals in her joints from causing her pain, and she rested for a moment upon a long staff fashioned from the wood of the rowan tree. The staff's top was hung with talismans of protection and shrouding, for the Summer Solstice was a time when the eyes of the gods were turned on the world, and it did not do to attract unwanted attention.

The Hag Woman set off down the hill towards the city that shone like a beacon in the gathering darkness. Torches had been set on the new walls of stone and light poured from the city, illuminating the landscape around it in a warm, safe glow.

The Hag Woman knew that safety was illusory, for this was a dangerous world, an old world, where monstrous beasts lurked in the sprawling forests, and warlike green-skin tribes raided the lands of men from their mountain lairs. Nor were these the only dangers that pressed close to the light: things unknown and unseen gathered their strength in the darkness to assault mankind.

A shiver travelled the length of the Hag Woman's spine, and she felt the clammy embrace of the grave in its chill. Her time in this world was nearing an end, and there was still so much to do, so many courses yet to steer, and so many fates to thwart. The thought made her pick up her pace.

The ground was soft underfoot, warm and still damp from earlier rain. Though a stone-flagged road wound its way towards the open southern gate of the city walls, the Hag Woman kept to the grass, preferring to feel the life of the world beneath her feet. To walk barefoot was to feel the power that dwelt in the earth, and to know that streams of uncorrupted energy still existed in the sacred places of the world.

That such places were becoming ever fewer was a source of great sorrow to the Hag Woman. Every road, every hall of stone and every step taken on the path of civilisation took mankind further from his connection with the land that had birthed him. The advancements that allowed men to survive in this world were the very things divorcing them from their origins and their true strength.

The city walls reared up before her, tall and strong, constructed from blocks of dark stone. They were at least thirty feet high, and she recognised the teachings of the mountain folk in the precisely cut blocks. A pair of stout towers flanked the open gateway, and she saw the gleam of firelight on armour behind their saw-toothed battlements.

She reluctantly stepped onto the roadway and limped through the gateway, past rows of bearded Unberogen warriors armoured in fine hauberks of gleaming mail and bronze helmets with horsehair plumes.

None of the warriors so much as glanced at the Hag Woman, and she smiled at how easily men were fooled by even the simplest of enchantments.

Reikdorf opened up before her, and though it had been many years since she had come to Sigmar's city, she was nevertheless shocked by how much it had changed. What had once been little more than a simple fishing village on the banks of the Reik had grown to something huge and sprawling. Despite herself, she was impressed by Sigmar's achievements.

Buildings of stone clustered tightly together in a warren of streets and alleys that reeked of life and unfettered growth. Granaries and storehouses loomed over her, and shouted oaths drifted from reeking taverns. Even this late in the day, metal clanged on metal from a nearby forge, and runners darted through the crowds carrying messages between merchants. The streets were thronged with people, though none save children and dogs spared her more than a glance. As she made her way through the city, men made the sign of the horns for no reason they could adequately explain, and women pulled suckling babes tighter to their breasts.

She could see the longhouse of the Unberogen kings ahead, a magnificently constructed hall fashioned by dwarf hands in gratitude for the rescue of King Kurgan Ironbeard of Karaz-a-Karak from greenskin marauders. The heavy timber shutters were thrown open, and yellow light spilled from within, carried on the sounds of great mirth and raucous merrymaking.

A host of banners was planted before the longhouse, a riot of colours and devices that had once signified division, but which now spoke of unity and shared purpose. She saw the raven of the Endals, the rearing stallion of the Taleutens, the Skull Banner of King Otwin of the

Thuringians and many others. She frowned at the one notable absence, and shook her head as she made her way towards the longhouse, to where the lord of the Unberogen tribe and soon-to-be Emperor gathered his warriors.

Wide doors of iron-banded timber led inside. Before them stood six warriors in thick wolfskin cloaks with heavy hammers of wrought iron. As before, none paid her any attention as she passed between them, fogging their minds and memories of her presence. The guards would go to their graves swearing on their children's lives that not a single soul had passed them.

The smell of sweat and free-flowing beer assailed her inside the longhouse, along with the vast heat of the fire pit at its centre. Sturdy tables ran the length of the building, and hundreds of warriors filled it with songs and laughter. Smoke from the fire gathered beneath the roof, and the rich aroma of roasting pork made her mouth water.

Though she had passed unseen through the streets of Reikdorf, she kept to the shadows, for there were minds close by that were sharper than those of ordinary folk. Kings, queens and dwarfs had gathered in Reikdorf and would not be so easily fooled. She made her way to the rear of the longhouse, far from the empty throne at the other end of the hall that sat beneath a series of grisly battle honours.

War banners hung from the rafters, and the Hag Woman was gratified to see tribesmen from across the Empire moving through the hall with an ease only shared by brothers-in-arms. These warriors had fought and bled at the Battle of Black Fire Pass, against the greatest horde of greenskins the world had ever seen. That incredible victory and shared horror had forged a bond as unbreakable as it would be enduring.

Endal pipers played martial tunes, and dwarf song-smiths told tales of ancient battles in time to the skirling music. The atmosphere was festive, the mood joyous, and the Hag Woman felt a moment of guilt for intruding on this day of celebration.

She wished she could have brought the new Emperor a gift of joy on his coronation night, but that was not the way of the world.


HIGH ABOVE REIKDORF on Warrior Hill, Sigmar knelt before his father's tomb, and scooped a handful of soil into the cup of his palm. The earth was dark, rich and loamy. It was good soil, nourished by the ancient dead. Looking at the great slab of rock that sealed King Björn's tomb, Sigmar wished his father could see him now. He had achieved so much in his time as king, yet there was still much to do.

'I miss you, father,' he said, letting the earth pour between his fingers. 'I miss the strength you gave me and the earned wisdom you freely offered, though too often I heeded it not.'

Sigmar lifted a foaming tankard of beer from the ground beside him and poured it onto the earth before the tomb. The smell of it stirred a thirst in Sigmar as he drew his hunting knife from its sheath at his belt. The weapon was a gift from Pendrag, and the workmanship was exquisite, the blade acid-etched with the image of a twin-tailed comet. Even King Kurgan had grunted that the blade was serviceable, which was about as close as a dwarf ever came to a compliment on the metalworking skills of other races.

With one swift motion, Sigmar drew the blade across his forearm, allowing blood to well in the cut before turning his arm over to let the ruby droplets fall to the ground. The dark soil soaked up his blood, and he let it flow until he was satisfied that he had given enough.

'This land is my one abiding love,' he said. 'To this land and its people, I pledge my life and my strength.

This I swear before all the gods and the spirits of my ancestors.'

Sigmar stood and turned his gaze further down the hillside, where countless other tombs had been dug into the earth. Each contained a friend, a loved one or a sword-brother. The day's last light caught on a pale stone lying flush against the hillside, its surface etched with long spirals and garlanded with wild honeysuckle.

'Too many times have I sent my brothers into the hillside,' whispered Sigmar, remembering the climb to roll that boulder across the darkened sepulchre housing Trinovantes's body. It seemed inconceivable that sixteen winters had passed since his friend's death. So much had happened and so much had changed that it was as if the time when Trinovantes had lived belonged to some other life.

Painful memories threatened to surface, but he forced them down, not wishing to tempt fate on the day his grand dream of empire was finally coming to fruition.

A cold wind flayed the summit of the great Unberogen burial mount, but Sigmar did not feel its chill. A dark wolfskin cloak was pulled tightly about his shoulders and a padded woollen jerkin kept him warm. His blond hair was pulled tight in a short ponytail, his forelocks braided at his temples. Sigmar's features were strong and noble, and his eyes, one a pale blue, the other a deep green, carried wisdom and pain beyond his thirty-one years.

Sigmar stood and brushed his hands clean of earth. He took a deep breath, and looked out over the landscape as dusk cast its purple shadows eastwards. Reikdorf shone with torchlight below him, but it was possible to see spots of light in the far distance, each one a well-defended town with a strong body of armed men to protect it. Beyond the horizon of forest, hundreds more villages and towns were spread throughout his domain, all united under his rule and sworn to the cause of a united empire of man.

The year since Black Fire Pass had been a bountiful one, the fields providing much needed grain to feed the returning warriors and their families. The winter had been mild, the summer balmy and peaceful, and the recent harvest had been among the most plentiful anyone could remember.

Eoforth claimed it was a reward from the gods for the courage shown by the warriors of the empire, and Sigmar had been only too pleased to accept his venerable counsellor's interpretation. The years preceding the battle had been lean and hard, the land ravaged by constant battle against the greenskins. Mankind had been on the verge of extinction, but the flickering candle-flame had survived the darkness, and, now, burned even brighter.

'Winter coming soon,' said Alfgeir, standing a respectful distance behind him.

'A fortune teller are you now, old friend?' asked Sigmar, gripping the handle of Ghal-maraz, the great warhammer presented to him by King Kurgan Ironbeard.

'Don't need to throw the bones to feel winter on this wind,' said Alfgeir. 'And less of the "old" thank you very much. I'm barely forty-four.'

Sigmar turned to face the man who was both his Marshal of the Reik and personal bodyguard. Standing tall and proud in his gleaming bronze plate armour, Alfgeir was the very image of a proud Unberogen warrior. His face was scarred and craggy, yet Alfgeir wore his age with great dignity, and woe betide any young buck who sought to humble the old man during training on the Field of Swords. Once, his hair had been dark, but now it was streaked with silver.

Like Sigmar, he wore a long wolfskin cloak, though his was white and had been a gift from King Aloysis of the Cherusens. A longsword of cold iron was belted at his waist, and his eyes constantly scanned the landscape for enemies.

'There's nothing out there,' said Sigmar, following Alfgeir's wary looks.

'You don't know that,' replied Alfgeir. 'Could be beasts, goblins, assassins. Anything.'

'You're being paranoid,' said Sigmar, setting off down the path towards his city. He pointed towards the tribal camps beyond the city walls to the west. 'No one would try to kill me today, not with so many armed warriors around.'

'It's having so many warriors around that makes me nervous,' said Alfgeir, following Sigmar towards Reikdorf. 'Any one of them might have lost a father, a brother or a son in the wars you fought to win their kings to your cause.'

'True enough,' agreed Sigmar. 'But do you really think any of the great kings has brought someone like that to my coronation?'

'Probably not, but I do not like to take chances,' said Alfgeir. 'I lost one king to an enemy blade. I'll not lose an emperor to another.'

King Björn had fallen in the wars to drive the Norsii from the lands of the Cherusens and Taleutens, and the shame of his failure to protect his liege lord had broken Alfgeir's heart. When Sigmar became king of the Unberogen, he had all but destroyed the northern tribe in the following years, pushing their armies into the sea and burning their ships. His father had been avenged and the Norsii cast out from the empire, but Sigmar's hatred remained strong.

Sigmar stopped and placed his hand on Alfgeir's shoulder.

'Nor shall you, my friend,' he said.

'I admire your certainty, my king,' said Alfgeir, 'but I think I'll be happier keeping my guard up and my sword sharp.'

'I would expect nothing less, but you are not a young man anymore,' said Sigmar with a grin that robbed the comment of malice. 'You should let some of the younger White Wolves assist you. Perhaps Redwane?'

'I don't need that young pup hounding my heels,' snapped Alfgeir. 'The lad is reckless and boastful. He irritates me. Besides, I told you, I am barely forty-four, younger than your father was when he took the fight to the north.'

'Forty-four,' mused Sigmar. 'I remember thinking such an age to be ancient when I was young. How anyone could let themselves grow old was beyond me.'

'Believe me, I don't recommend it,' said Alfgeir. 'Your bones ache in winter, your back gets stiff and, worst of all, you get no respect from youngsters who ought to know better.'

'I apologise, my friend,' chuckled Sigmar. 'Now come on. We have honoured the dead, and now it is time to greet my fellow kings.'

'Indeed, my Emperor,' said Alfgeir with a theatrical bow. 'You don't want to be late for your own coronation, eh?'

'You ARE DRUNK,' said Pendrag.

'That I am,' agreed Wolfgart, happily taking a bite of roast boar. 'I always said you were the clever one, Pendrag.'

Wolfgart drained his tankard and wiped his arm over his mouth, smearing a line of beer and grease across his sleeve. Both men were dressed in their finest tunics, though Wolfgart had to admit that Pendrag's had survived the preliminary festivities rather better than his.

His sword-brother was dear to him, and they had shared adventures the likes of which would make great sagas to tell his son when he was born, but he did so love to nag. Pendrag was solid and immovable, the perfect build for an axeman, where Wolfgart had the wide shoulders and narrow hips of a swordsman.

Pendrag's flame-red hair was worked in elaborate braids, and his forked beard was stiffened with black resin. Wolfgart had eschewed such gaudy adornments, and simply restrained his wild dark hair with a copper circlet Maedbh had given him on the anniversary of their hand fastening.

Serving girls threaded their way through the heaving mass of celebrating tribesmen, bearing platters stacked high with meat and tankards of foaming beer, while fending off the attentions of amorous drunks. Wolfgart reached out and swept a beaten copper ewer of beer from one of the girl's trays and slurped a noisy mouthful without bothering to pour it into his tankard.

Most of the foaming liquid went down his front, and Pendrag sighed.

'You couldn't stay sober tonight?' asked Pendrag. 'Or at least not get so drunk?'

'Come on, Pendrag! How often does our childhood friend get to be crowned Emperor over all the lands of men? I'll be the first to admit, I thought he was mad as a Cherusen Wildman when he told us his plan, but Ulric roast my backside if he didn't go and do it!'

Wolfgart waved his tankard at the hundreds of feasting tribesmen gathered around the long fire pit. Wild boasts and happy laughter passed back and forth, pipe music vied with songs of battle, and the rafters shook with the sound of great revelries.

'I mean, look around you, Pendrag!' cried Wolfgart. 'All the tribes gathered here, under one roof and not fighting each other. For that alone, Sigmar deserves to be Emperor.'

'It is impressive,' agreed Pendrag, taking a refined sip of Tilean wine. King Siggurd had brought six barrels of the stuff, and Pendrag had acquired quite a taste for it.

'It's more than impressive, it's a damned miracle,' slurred Wolfgart, using his tankard arm to encompass the entire longhouse. 'I mean, the Cherusens and Taleutens have been fighting over their border territories for longer than any of us have been alive, and here they are drinking together. Look over there... Thuringians swearing blood oaths with thems as used to be Teutogens! Bloody miracle is what it is, a bloody miracle.'

'Aye, it's a miracle, but it'll be a greater miracle if you're able to walk in a straight line when the time comes to take the king's march to the Oathstone.'

'Walk. Stagger. What's the difference?' asked Wolfgart, lifting the ewer once again.

Pendrag reached over to restrain him from pouring another drink, and Wolfgart felt the cold metal of his friend's silver hand. A Thuringian axe had taken three of Pendrag's fingers during the Battle of the Berserker King, and Master Alaric of the dwarfs had fashioned the new gauntlet for him. Pendrag claimed that the mechanical fingers functioned as well as his old ones, but Wolfgart had never been able to get used to them.

'You will shame Maedbh if you cannot stand up,' pointed out Pendrag. 'And do you really want that?'

Wolfgart stared hard at Pendrag for a moment before upending the ewer.

'Damn, but you always cut to the bone, friend,' he said, reaching instead for the largely untouched jug of water. 'I slept with the horses for three days the last time I came home drunk.'

Wolfgart took several gulping draughts of water, rinsing his mouth of the taste of beer and spitting it over the straw-covered floor.

'Civilised as always,' said a voice beside Wolfgart as a warrior, armoured in iron plate painted a deep red lowered himself to sit next to him. 'I thought Reikdorf was the light of civilisation in the world these days, and that the northerners were supposed to be the crude barbarians?'

'Ah, Redwane, how the young misunderstand the ways of their elders and betters,' said Wolfgart, smiling and throwing an arm around the White Wolf. Like Pendrag, Redwane's copper-coloured hair was elaborately braided, and his handsome features were open and friendly. Some called them soft, but those who had seen Redwane fight knew that nothing could be further from the truth.

'In the south, it is a sign of good breeding to behave like a lout from time to time,' said Wolfgart.

'Then you are the most civilised man I know,' said Redwane, adjusting his wolfskin cloak around his shoulders, and setting down his hammer before lifting an empty mug.

Wolfgart laughed, and Pendrag poured Redwane a beer.

'Welcome, brother,' he said. 'It is good to have you back in Reikdorf.'

'Aye, it's been too long,' agreed Redwane. 'Siggurdheim is a fine place, with cold beer and warm women, but I'm glad to be home.'

'How come he gets to drink beer, but I don't?' demanded Wolfgart.

'Because Ulric has blessed me,' said Redwane, patting his flat stomach. 'My guts are lined with trollhide, and, unlike you milksops, I'm able to consume more than a flagon before falling down dead drunk.'

'That sounds like a challenge to me,' said Wolfgart, reaching for the beer.

'Leave it,' ordered Pendrag. 'Save it until after the coronation.'

Wolfgart shrugged and threw his hands up, saying, 'Ulric deliver me from these mother hens, one of them barely seventeen summers!'

'How was your journey?' asked Pendrag, ignoring Wolfgart's exasperation.

'Uneventful,' said the warrior, 'more's the pity. Since Black Fire the roads have been quiet, no bandits or greenskins to speak of. Even the forest beasts seem cowed.'

'Aye, it's been a quiet year,' agreed Pendrag.

'Too quiet,' grumbled Wolfgart. 'My sword's getting rusty above the fireplace, and I've not killed a greenskin in two seasons.'

'Wasn't that the point?' countered Pendrag. 'All the years of war were to keep our lands safe and protected. Now we have done that, and you complain because you do not have to fight and risk your life?'

'I am a warrior,' said Wolfgart. 'It's what I know.'

'Maybe you can learn a new trade?' said Redwane, winking at Pendrag. 'With the land safe and the forests being cleared for new settlements, Sigmar's empire will need more farmers.'

'Me, a farmer? Don't be foolish, boy. I think that southern air has rotted your brain if you think I'll be a farmer. Just because we slaughtered the greenskins at the pass doesn't mean they won't be back. No, I'll not be a farmer, Redwane. I'll leave that to others, for this land will always have need of warriors.'

Redwane laughed.

'I expect you're right,' he said. 'You would make a terrible farmer.'

Wolfgart smiled and nodded. 'You have the truth of it. I've not the patience to work the land. I fear I am more suited to ending life than bringing it forth.'

'That's not what I hear,' said Redwane, elbowing Wolfgart in the ribs. 'The talk is that you are to be a father in the spring.'

'Aye,' said Wolfgart, brightening at the mention of his virility. 'Maedbh will bear me a strong son to carry on my name.'

'Or a daughter,' said Pendrag. 'Asoborn women beget girls more often than not.'

'Pah, not on your life!' said Wolfgart. 'With the strength of my seed, the boy will climb out himself, you mark my words.'

'We shall see in the spring, my friend,' said Redwane. 'Whatever form your heir takes, I will help you wet its head in beer, and sing the songs of war through the night with you.'

'I'll be happy to let you,' said Wolfgart, clasping the White Wolf's wrist.

SIGMAR'S BROTHER KINGS were waiting for him at the base of Warrior Hill, resplendent in robes of many colours and armour of the highest quality. Each carried a golden shield upon one arm, and a line of flaming brands was set in the ground before them. The firelight cast a warm glow about them, the most powerful warriors in the lands of men. Together they had saved their people from annihilation, and now they had gathered to bear witness to a singular event in the history of the world: the crowning of the first Emperor.

This night would seal their pact to preserve the safety of every man, woman and child in the empire. Sigmar loved them all, and mouthed a silent prayer of thanks to Ulric for the honour of standing shoulder to shoulder with such heroes.

King Krugar of the Taleutens, a broad-shouldered warrior in a gleaming hauberk of silver scale, stood at their centre, flanked by King Henroth of the Merogens and Markus of the Menogoths. Both southern kings were smiling, though Sigmar could see the great sorrows they carried. Their kingdoms had suffered terribly in the wars against the greenskins, and little more than a thousand of their people had survived the years of death.

Sigmar's eyes were drawn next to Queen Freya of the Asoborns. The flame-haired queen was clad in shimmering mail that looked as though it had been woven from golden thread. A torque of bronze and silver encircled her graceful neck, and a winged crown of jewel-studded gold sat on her high brow. A cloak of vivid orange hung from her shoulders, but did little to conceal the smooth curve of her limbs and the sway of her hips as she turned to face him.

Sigmar felt himself responding to Freya's primal beauty, recalling the night of passion that had sealed their union with a mixture of pleasure and remembered pain. He quickly suppressed his feelings and concentrated on greeting the rest of his allies.

Next to the Asoborn Queen stood Adelhard of the Ostagoths, his drooping moustache waxed to gleaming points, and his chequered cloak of black and white echoing the trews and shirt he wore beneath it. Ostvarath, the sword of the Ostagoth kings, was sheathed at Adelhard's side. Adelhard had offered to surrender this sword to Sigmar in return for his aid in battle against the orcs. Sigmar's warriors had fought alongside the Ostagoths, but he had declined Adelhard's sword, claiming that so mighty a weapon should remain with its king.

Aloysis of the Cherusens was a lean, hawk-faced man with dark hair tied in a long scalp-lock. In the manner of his fiercest warriors, he had shaved his beard and adorned his face with curling tattoos of blue and red, and his bright red cavalry cloak flapped in the wind. The laconic king give Sigmar a respectful nod.

King Aldred of the Endals wore a fur-lined robe of brown wool, edged in black and gold thread. The symbol of his kingship, the elf blade Ulfshard, was belted at his side, and Sigmar remembered Aldred's father hurling the blade to him at Black Fire Pass. The weapon had saved Sigmar's life, but Marbad had died moments later. Sigmar saw the bitter echoes of Marbad's death in his son's eyes.

The kilted warrior next to Aldred was King Wolfila of the Udose, a gruff king of reckless bravery and great warmth. His clansmen had fought the Norsii for many years, and his pale skin shone with a healthy glow in the torchlight. A great, basket-hilted claymore was sheathed over his shoulder, longer even than Wolfgart's monstrous blade. Wolfila grinned like a loon, and his pleasure at the night's events was clear.

Sigmar smiled to see that King Siggurd had outdone himself, appearing in a rich array of purple and blue robes, edged in ermine and bedecked in enough gold to make a dwarf's eyes gleam with avarice.

Given his last observation, Sigmar was not surprised to see that King Kurgan Ironbeard of the dwarfs stood next to Siggurd, though his oldest ally wore almost as much gold as did the Brigundian king. Clad in a shirt of runic gold plate with silver steel pauldrons and a gold helmet, Kurgan seemed more like one of his people's ancient gods than a mortal king. Alone of all the gathered kings, Kurgan's weapon was bared, a mighty axe with two butterfly-winged blades enchanted with runes that shone with their own spectral light.

King Otwin of the Thuringians stood slightly apart from the others, though whether that was his choice or theirs was unclear. His crown was a mass of golden spikes hammered through the skin of his head, and he wore little more than a loincloth of dark iron mail and a cloak of deepest red. The Berserker King's bare chest heaved, and Sigmar saw the wildroot juice staining his lips.

Myrsa of the Fauschlag Rock, dazzling in his armour of purest white, looked uncomfortable in the company of kings but, as the master of the northern marches, he had earned the right to be part of this fellowship. A long-handled warhammer was slung at Myrsa's belt, but it was no imitation of Sigmar's weapon, for this hammer was designed to be swung from the back of a charging steed.

Only one tribe was not represented, and Sigmar quelled his anger at the absence of the Jutone king. That was a reckoning for another day.

He squared his shoulders, and glanced round at Alfgeir, who gave a barely perceptible nod.

Sigmar took a deep breath and began to speak.

'Never before has this land borne witness to such a gathering of might,' he said, unhooking Ghal-maraz from his belt. 'Even on the barren plain of Black Fire Pass we were not so proud, so strong or so mighty.'

Krugar of the Taleutens stepped from the ranks of kings and drew his sword, a curved cavalry sabre with a blade of brilliant blue steel.

'Have you honoured the dead, King Sigmar?' he asked. 'Have you made offerings to the land and remembered those men from whence you came?'

'I have,' replied Sigmar.

'And are you ready to serve this land?' asked Siggurd.

'I am.'

'When the land is threatened, will you march to its defence?' demanded Henroth.

'I will,' said Sigmar, holding Ghal-maraz out before him.

'Then it's to the Oathstone!' shouted Wolfila, swinging his enormous claymore from its scabbard. 'Ar-Ulric awaits!'

# ⫷ TWO ⫸

# Rise an Emperor

SIGMAR LED THE kings from Warrior Hill into Reikdorf. Word of their coming had spread, and the city's populace came out to greet them. Hundreds of people lined the streets, carrying torches to dispel the darkness, and cheering as the procession of kings passed. Warriors spilled from the longhouse, banging their swords on their shields as they came. Endal Pipers ran to the front of the procession and led the way to the Oathstone, their lilting music speaking to the heart and filling the blood with fire.

He saw Wolfgart and Pendrag in the crowd of warriors, and smiled at their joy. To have come so far and achieved so much was incredible, but Sigmar knew he could not have done it without his friends. What he and his sword-brothers symbolised was the empire in microcosm; individually men were strong, but together they were mighty.

The kings of the land marched alongside Sigmar with their heads held high and their weapons resting on their shoulders. Tribesmen from all across the empire yelled and whooped to see their kings so honoured.

Banners waved in the air in a dazzling array of rearing stallions, mailed fists, golden chariots and snarling wolves. Oaths and promises of fealty in a dozen different dialects were shouted as every warrior gathered offered his sword to the king of the Unberogen. As Sigmar watched their faces, ecstatic in the reflected glow of firelight, he felt the weight of their expectations settle upon his shoulders.

To have won this land was only the first part of his journey.

Now he had to keep it safe.

The procession wound its way through the cobbled streets of the city, past great halls, stone dwellings and timber-framed stables. Children in colourful tunics ran wild, playing with barking dogs, their innocent laughter a welcome counterpoint to the martial shouts of warriors.

The procession emerged into the open square on the river's northern bank, where the sacred stone carried from the east in ages past by the first warriors of the Unberogen was set in the earth. This had been the centre of the original settlement of Reikdorf, back when it had been little more than a collection of wattle and daub huts huddled by the side of the river. The settlement had grown immeasurably since those long ago days, but its heart was ever this place.

The pipers peeled away, taking up positions beside Beorthyn's forge. Sigmar smiled. The irascible old smith had been dead for ten years, yet the forge still bore his name.

Perhaps a thousand people filled the square, pressed against the buildings at the square's perimeter. Torches were planted in a circle around the Oathstone, and a huge figure stood within the ring of firelight beside a vast cauldron of black iron.

Clad in wolfskin and glittering mail that shimmered with hoarfrost, the figure's breath gusted from his mouth as though it were the darkest winter night instead of the last days of summer. He carried a staff of polished oak, hung with long fangs and topped with a wide axe blade that glittered like ice. His face was obscured by a wolf-skull mask, and a thick pelt of white wolfhide hung from his shoulders.

Taller and broader than any warrior Sigmar had ever seen, this was Ar-Ulric, the high priest of the god of battles and winter, a warrior who wandered the wilds with the snow and wind. Generations might pass without any sign of Ar-Ulric, for he had little to do with the affairs of mortals. Ulric was a god who expected his followers to fend for themselves. At his side were two enormous wolves, one with midnight-black fur, the other of purest white. Their fur stood erect, as though frozen, and their eyes were like smouldering coals.

The pipers ceased their music, and the warriors filling the city fell silent as Sigmar entered the circle of torches. His fellow kings took up positions around the circle as Sigmar stood before the enormous cauldron. Dark water filled it, and ice had formed on the surface.

The wolves slowly padded forward and began circling Sigmar. Their fangs were bared and thick ropes of saliva drooled from their jaws. Ar-Ulric remained unmoving as the wolves growled and sniffed him. Sigmar felt the cold of their gaze upon him, knowing he was being judged by a power greater than that of mere beasts.

Cold waves radiated from the wolves, and their icy touch entered Sigmar's bones. Endless winter swept through his flesh in a moment, as though his blood had turned instantly to ice. A vision of vast, unending tundra, eternally roamed by packs of slavering wolves, flashed into his mind. Sigmar glanced at his fellow kings gathered at the ring of torches. None appeared to be feeling the dreadful cold. The breath of Ulric touched only him.

The wolves completed their inspection, and the vision faded from Sigmar's thoughts as they returned to their master's side. Their orange eyes never left Sigmar, and he knew their gaze would always be upon him, no matter where the paths of fate led him.

Apparently satisfied with his wolves' judgement, Ar-Ulric came around the cauldron to stand before him. Like the wolves, the high priest carried the chill of unending winter, and Sigmar saw that the blade of his axe was indeed formed from a jagged shard of ice.

Sigmar knelt before the priest of the wolf god, but kept his head held high. He honoured Ar-Ulric, but he would not show fear before him.

The mighty priest towered over him, a primal presence that spoke of devotion beyond measure and a life of battle in realms beyond mortal ken. Where Sigmar had served Ulric faithfully in battle, Ar-Ulric was the very embodiment of Ulric. This warrior's power was enormous, and for him to emerge from the icy wilderness was a great honour.

'You seek Ulric's blessing,' said Ar-Ulric, his voice hoarse, like a blast of winter wind and just as cold. 'By what right do you think you are worthy of the lord of winter's favour?'

'By right of battle,' said Sigmar, fighting to stop his teeth from chattering in the cold. 'By my blood and sacrifice I have united my people. By such right, I claim dominion over the land, from the mountains to the seas, and all who dwell there.'

'A good answer, King Sigmar,' replied Ar-Ulric. 'Ulric knows your name and watches you with interest. How is it that Ulric should care for the fate of a mortal such as you?'

'I passed through the Flame of Ulric and was not burned,' said Sigmar.

'And you think that is enough?'

Sigmar shrugged.

'I know not,' he said, 'but I have fought every battle with Ulric's name on my lips. I could have done no more.'

Ar-Ulric reached down and took hold of Sigmar's head. The priest's fingers were sheathed in wolf claws, and Sigmar could smell the blood on them. 'I see into your heart, King Sigmar. Your lust for immortal glory sits alongside your devotion to Ulric. You seek to rival his mighty deeds and carve your name in the pages of history.'

Defiance flared in Sigmar's heart.

'Is that wrong?' he asked. 'To desire my name to live beyond my time in this world? Lesser men may be forgotten, but the name of Sigmar will echo into the future. With Ulric's blessing, I will forge the land into an empire that will endure until the end of all things.'

Ar-Ulric laughed, the sound as brittle as ice and as cold as the grave. 'Seek not immortality through war, for it will only bring you pain and death. Go from here, sire sons and daughters, and let them carry your name onwards. Seek not to match the gods in infamy.'

'No,' said Sigmar. 'My course is set. The life of hearth and home is not for me. I was not made for such things.'

'In that you are correct,' said Ar-Ulric. 'There will be no soft bed to pass away the last breath of your dotage, not for you. A life of battle awaits you, Sigmar, and this pleases Ulric.'

'Then you will bless my coronation?'

'That remains to be seen,' said Ar-Ulric. 'Stand and call forth your sword-brothers.'

Sigmar forced himself to his feet, his limbs cold and muscles cramped. He turned towards the ring of firelight and scanned the crowd for his sword-brothers. At last, he saw them just beyond the ring of firelight.

'Wolfgart! Pendrag!' he shouted. 'Come forth and stand with me.'

The kings parted to allow the two warriors through their ranks. Both were dressed in long tunics of red, with wide leather belts from which hung daggers and wolf-tail talismans. Pendrag's attire was clean, where Wolfgart's was crumpled and stained with grease and beer spills. Both looked pleased to be asked to come forth, but Sigmar could see their unease at being in the presence of the hulking priest of Ulric.

'Damn, but I wish I was drunk,' hissed Wolfgart, his gaze never leaving the burning eyes and bared fangs of Ar-Ulric's wolves.

'You already are, remember?' said Pendrag.

'Drunker then.'

A low snarl from the black wolf silenced them both.

'My sword-brothers, Wolfgart and Pendrag,' Sigmar told Ar-Ulric. 'They have fought at my side since we were youngsters, and are bonded to me in blood.'

Ar-Ulric's wolf-skull mask turned towards them, and Sigmar heard sharp intakes of breath as the full force of his frigid gaze swept over them.

The priest nodded and waved Sigmar's sword-brothers forward.

'Disrobe him,' he said, 'until he is as he came into this world.'

Sigmar handed Ghal-maraz to Wolfgart, and, piece by piece, his sword-brothers removed his clothing until he stood naked before the cauldron. His body was lean and muscled, with a host of pale, ridged scars snaking their way over his arms and across his chest and shoulders.

'This is the Cauldron of Woe,' said Ar-Ulric. 'It has been used for centuries to determine the worth of those who seek Ulric's blessing.'

'The Cauldron of Woe?' asked Wolfgart. 'Why's it called that?'

'Because those found unworthy do not survive its judgement,' said Ar-Ulric.

'You had to ask,' snapped Pendrag, and Wolfgart shrugged.

'How does it judge my worth?' asked Sigmar, fearing he already knew the answer.

'You must immerse yourself in its waters and if you emerge alive, you will have proved your worth.'

'That doesn't sound so hard,' said Wolfgart. 'It looks cold, sure enough, but that's all.'

'Do you want to try it?' asked Sigmar, already imagining the freezing temperature of the icy water in the cauldron.

'Oh no,' said Wolfgart, putting up his hands. 'This is your day after all.'

Sigmar gripped the cauldron's edge, feeling the intense cold of the water through the iron. The ice on the surface was solid, but there would be no help in breaking it. He took a deep breath and hammered his fist upon the ice. Pain and cold flared up his arm, but the ice remained firm. Again, he slammed his fist down, and this time a spider-web of cracks appeared.

His hand was a mass of pain, but again and again Sigmar punched the ice until it broke apart beneath his assault. His chest heaved with painful breaths and his fist was covered in blood. Sweat was freezing on his brow, but before he could think of how cold the water was going to be, he hauled himself up and over the lip of the cauldron, and plunged in.

The cold hit Sigmar like a hammer-blow, and the breath was driven from him. He tried to cry out in pain, feeling his heart batter against his chest, but freezing water filled his mouth. Bright light, like the dying sun of winter, flashed before his eyes.

Sigmar sank into the darkness of the cauldron.

\* \* \*

THE DARKNESS BENEATH the surface of the water was absolute, unending and unyielding. Cold seared his limbs, the sensation akin to being burned. Strange that such icy water should feel like that. Sigmar sank deeper and deeper, far further than the cauldron's size should allow. His body tumbled in its icy depths, lost in the endless night of winter.

His lungs were afire as he tried to hold his breath, and his heart's protesting beat sounded like the pounding of orc war drums in his head. Images flashed before him in the darkness, scenes from his life replayed before him as they were said to do before the eyes of a drowning man. Sigmar watched himself lead the charge at the Battle of Astofen, feeling the savage joy of breaking the greenskin horde, and the numbing sorrow of Trinovantes's death.

He saw the fight against the forest beasts, the slaying of Skaranorak, the battle against the Thuringians and the wars he had fought against the Norsii. A rippling face drifted into view, cruelly handsome with lustrous dark hair and eyes of seductive malice.

Hate swelled in his breast as he recognised Gerreon, the betrayer who had slain his own sister and Sigmar's great love, the wondrous Ravenna. In the wake of his treachery, Gerreon had fled the lands of men, and none knew what had become of him, though Sigmar had always known there was blood yet to be shed between them.

Gerreon's face vanished, and Sigmar saw a great tower of pearl in a mountain valley, long hidden from the sight of men. Atop this tower, he saw a crown of ancient power, and the loathsome creature upon whose skeletal brow it sat. This too drifted from sight, and was replaced with a vision of a towering pinnacle of rock set amid a sprawling, endless forest. A city was built upon this rock, a mighty city of pale stone, and above its towers and spires was a shimmering vision of a snarling white wolf.

Sigmar recognised the Fauschlag Rock, but not as he knew it. This city was old and time-worn, groaning at the seams with centuries of growth. Mighty causeways pierced the forest canopy, immense creations of stone that defied the eye with their enormous proportions. They soared towards the summit of the rock, and a host of warriors garbed in strange, slashed tunics held them against attack.

An army of cruelly malformed horrors, each a hideous meld of man and beast, fought to destroy the city on the rock, but the courage of its defenders was unbreakable. Warriors in bloodstained armour of brazen iron gathered around the city in vast numbers, and the forest burned with sacrificial pyres to their Dark Gods.

The tide of beasts and warriors broke against the city's defences as a warrior clad in a suit of brilliant white armour sallied forth to break the charge of the hideous attackers. The warrior's face was obscured by the visor of his winged helm, but Sigmar knew that whatever the identity of this warrior, his life was tied to that of the city. If he fell, the city would fall.

Before Sigmar could see more, the vision of battle faded as he sank deeper into the cold depths of the cauldron. His strength was almost spent and his lungs cried out for air.

Was this how his dream of empire was to end? Was this how the greatest warrior in the lands of men was to die, frozen within the Cauldron of Woe and judged unworthy?

Anger lit a fire in Sigmar's heart, and fresh strength flooded his limbs. He swept his arms out with powerful strokes, determined not to die like this..

No sooner had he formed the thought than a shaft of light pierced the darkness, and Sigmar twisted in the water's icy embrace to seek its source. He saw a circle of brightness above him, and twisting spirals of red sank down through the water towards him.

Warmth and the promise of life were carried with the light, and he kicked upwards, swimming through the frozen water towards it. With each stroke, the light grew brighter, and the promise of life surged in his veins. Bursting for air, his head pounding with fiery agony, Sigmar swam through the descending trails of red liquid. He recognised it as blood, but knew not who or what had shed it.

The light shone like the new sun of spring, and with one last desperate heave, Sigmar broke the surface of the water.

SIGMAR ERUPTED FROM the cauldron, drawing in a huge, gulping breath. His vision swam, and he gripped the rim of the cauldron for support as he drew one tortured gasp after another. Cold water ran from his body in a torrent as he held himself upright, determined that he would stand tall before all who witnessed his icy rebirth.

He felt the presence of warm bodies around him, and blinked water from his eyes. Standing around the cauldron were Sigmar's fellow kings, each with bared arms that bled from deep cuts in their flesh. He looked down and saw the water was red with their blood. Ar-Ulric stood behind him. Sigmar swung his legs over the side of the cauldron, and stood naked before his people, holding himself upright with a supreme effort of will.

The cold presence of Ar-Ulric moved closer, and a heavy wolfskin cloak was set upon Sigmar's shoulders. The pelt was warm and soft, and the aching cold of his immersion vanished in the time it took to fasten the leather thong at his neck.

'Kneel,' said Ar-Ulric, and Sigmar obeyed without hesitation.

The Oathstone was on the ground before him, and Sigmar placed his hand upon it. The stone was rough to the touch, red and streaked with gold veins unlike any other stone hewn from the rock of the mountains. It felt warm to the touch, and he heard a keening wail in his head, as though the stone itself was screaming. It was a scream of joy, not of pain, and Sigmar smiled at this affirmation.

He looked up to see if anyone else could hear this scream of elation, but it was clear from the faces around him that the sound was for him and him alone.

Kurgan Ironbeard stepped from the circle of kings, a crown of wondrous design in his hands, a rune-inscribed circlet of gold and ivory set with precious stones. Sigmar lowered his head as the dwarf king handed the crown to Ar-Ulric. The mighty priest stood before him, but his freezing aura did not trouble Sigmar, the icy cold kept at bay by the magic of the wolfskin cloak.

Ar-Ulric raised the crown above his head for all to see. The glow of the torches reflected from the ivory and jewels like starlight on silver, and Reikdorf held its breath. 'The cauldron judges you worthy. You are reborn in the blood of kings.'

'I was born in blood once before,' replied Sigmar.

'Serve Ulric well and your name will live on through the ages,' said Ar-Ulric, setting the crown upon Sigmar's soaking head.

It was a perfect fit, and as the crown settled on his brow the people of Reikdorf erupted in wild cheers, and the music of the pipers began anew. Drums beat and horns were blown as men and women of all the tribes roared their approval, dancing and singing, and beating swords on shields as the mood of jubilation spread throughout the city.

Kurgan Ironbeard leaned forward and said, 'Wear this crown well, Sigmar, for it is the work of Alaric.' The dwarf king winked. 'He wanted to present it to you himself, but I am keeping him busy forging those swords I promised you.'

Sigmar smiled.

'I will wear it with pride,' he said.

'Good lad,' said Kurgan, as Wolfgart came forward, holding Ghal-maraz out to him.

Sigmar grasped the mighty warhammer, feeling the immense power the ancient craft of the mountain folk had wrought into its form. The hammer's grip fitted his hand as never before, and Sigmar knew that this moment would live in the hearts of men forever.

'Arise, Sigmar Heldenhammer,' cried Ar-Ulric, 'Emperor of all the lands of men!'

ONCE AGAIN, THE longhouse was filled with kings and warriors. Wolfgart was enjoying himself immensely: he had bested warriors from the Thuringians, Cherusens and Brigundians in feats of strength, and had put a Menogoth under the table in a drinking contest. Galin Veneva, the Ostagoth warrior who had carried word of the greenskin invasion from the east, now challenged him to a fresh drinking game with a spirit distilled from fermented goat's milk.

'We call it *koumiss*,' said Veneva. 'Is good drink for toasts and games of drinking!'

Wolfgart loudly and graciously conceded defeat after one mouthful of the stuff.

'It's like drinking molten lead,' said Wolfgart, slapping Veneva on the back, his eyes streaming at the liquor's potency. 'But then I'm not surprised you eastern types like your drink so strong, I've seen your women. You'd need to be blind drunk to sleep with them.'

Pendrag led him away from the good-natured jeering of the Ostagoth fighters, steering him through the scrum of painted, armoured and sweating bodies. Tonight, the kings of men feasted with their warriors, and the smoky atmosphere in the longhouse was one of good cheer and battle-earned brotherhood.

At the end of the longhouse, Sigmar sat on his throne, speaking with Kurgan Ironbeard of Karaz-a-Karak, and the gold of his crown shone as if with an inner fire.

Clad in dwarf-forged plate, a mighty gift from King Ironbeard, the Emperor shone like a god. Alfgeir stood to one side, while Eoforth, Sigmar's venerable counsellor, sat on a bench to his left. The dwarf king leant on his axe as he conversed with Sigmar, taking great gulps of ale between sentences.

Wolfgart waved, and Sigmar nodded in his direction with a broad smile.

'Look at that, eh?' said Wolfgart. 'A bloody emperor! Who'd have thought it?'

'He did,' said Pendrag simply.

Wolfgart looked over the fire pit, seeing Redwane standing on a table and swinging his sword as he recounted tall tales of his heroics at Black Fire Pass to an audience of smiling girls.

'Someone won't be sleeping alone tonight,' said Wolfgart.

'He never does,' replied Pendrag. 'Why spend coin on a night maiden when you can just seduce a pretty serving girl?'

'Good point,' laughed Wolfgart. 'Though, as a married man, I need do neither to wake up next to a warm woman.'

'You are married to an Asoborn woman,' said Pendrag. 'Maedbh would cut off your manhood if you behaved like Redwane.'

'Again, a good point well made,' said Wolfgart, laughing as he spied a familiar face amid the mass of celebrating tribesmen.

Wolfgart pushed through the crowded longhouse, scooping up two unattended tankards of beer from a nearby table on the way. Pendrag followed him as he approached a warrior in black armour, who stood close to the stone walls of the longhouse with his arms folded across his chest.

'Laredus, you old dog!' shouted Wolfgart. 'How in Ulric's name do you fare?'

The man turned at the sound of his name. He wore a winged black helmet and a dark cloak over his similarly black breastplate. Older than Wolfgart by a decade, Laredus was a warrior of the Raven Helms, the elite guards of the Endal Kings since the tribe's earliest days.

'Wolfgart,' said Laredus warily.

'I haven't seen you since before Black Fire,' said Wolfgart, thrusting a tankard towards Laredus.

The Raven Helm warrior shook his head, saying, 'No. Thank you, I won't.'

'What?' exclaimed Wolfgart. 'Take a drink, man! Tonight of all nights!'

'I cannot,' said Laredus. 'King Aldred has commanded us not to partake of any strong drink.'

'Ach, you'll be fine then,' said Wolfgart, looking into the mug. 'I think it's Merogen beer. I've pissed stronger stuff than this. Go on, take a drink!'

'No,' repeated Laredus stiffly. 'My king has spoken, and I must obey his orders.'

'Then sit with us awhile,' demanded Wolfgart, irritated at the Raven Helm's refusal to drink with him. 'Tell us of what's happening in Marburg these days.'

Laredus's jaw was set and he bowed curtly to Wolfgart and Pendrag.

'If you will excuse me, I must see to my men,' he said.

Before Wolfgart could reply, Laredus turned on his heel and marched away.

'Ranald's balls, what was the meaning of that?' said Wolfgart, turning to Pendrag.

Pendrag didn't answer, and Wolfgart watched as Laredus joined a group of cloaked Endal tribesmen gathered around their young king.

'I don't understand,' said Wolfgart. 'I wintered in Marburg after Astofen, and fought alongside Laredus against Jutone raiders. We were like brothers, and this is how he treats me! Damn it all, the bugger was friendly enough when last he came to Reikdorf.'

'Aye,' said Pendrag, looking warily at the Endals and their grim-faced king, 'but Marbad was king of the Endals then.'

'You might be onto something there, my friend,' agreed Wolfgart, not liking King Aldred's hooded gaze one bit. Alone of all the kings, he and his warriors sat apart from the celebrations, their eyes cold and aloof. Wolfgart drained the tankard he had offered to the Raven Helm, and then tossed into the fire pit, making sure the Endals saw him do it.

'Come on, leave it. It's not worth starting trouble tonight,' warned Pendrag, taking hold of his arm.

Wolfgart nodded, more hurt than angry at being snubbed by Laredus.

It made no sense. Brotherhood between warriors was a precious thing, a bond that those who had not risked death facing the enemy would never understand. To break such a bond was sure to anger the gods, and Wolfgart spat into the fire to ward off the bad luck that such a deed would attract.

He shrugged off Pendrag's arm.

'I'm fine,' he said. 'I'm not going to do anything stupid. If Laredus won't drink with us, then let's go find someone who will.'

'I'll save you the hunt,' said a gruff, northern voice behind them. Wolfgart laughed, his ill-temper forgotten as he turned to face the Warrior Eternal of the Fauschlag Rock.

'Myrsa! Gods, man, it's grand to see you,' cried Wolfgart, sweeping his friend into a crushing bear hug. Myrsa was clad in his ubiquitous white plate armour, and hammered his palm against Wolfgart's back. Wolfgart grunted at the strength of the man. He released Myrsa, who took Pendrag's wrist in the warrior's grip.

'It's grand indeed to see you too, my friends,' said Myrsa. 'You fare well?'

'We do all right,' said Wolfgart. 'Nothing a good battle wouldn't cure.'

'Indeed we do,' put in Pendrag. 'Reikdorf grows every day, our people have enough food and the land is at peace. We can ask for no more.'

'Aye, there's truth to what you both say,' agreed Myrsa, lifting a tankard of beer from a passing serving girl's tray.

The three friends took seats at a nearby table, and Wolfgart procured them a long platter of roast boar and steamed vegetables.

'Pendrag's getting soft in his old age,' said Wolfgart, chewing on a succulent rib. 'Spends all his time with Eoforth in that storehouse of books and papers. He's a scholar now, not a warrior.'

'Is that right, Pendrag?' asked Myrsa. 'You hung up that big axe of yours?'

'Wolfgart exaggerates,' said Pendrag, helping himself to some cuts of meat. 'But, yes, I have been spending a great deal of time gathering instructional texts and setting down all that the dwarfs taught us. After all, what use is peace if we do not make use of it to learn new things? How will we pass on that knowledge to future generations?'

'Pendrag has convinced me, Wolfgart' said Myrsa. 'Perhaps we should all become men of learning?'

'Would that the world would let us,' said Pendrag, slapping a hand on Myrsa's pauldron, 'but enough of this mockery. You played your part in Sigmar's crowning well.'

'Aye,' said Wolfgart. 'When Ar-Ulric cut you over that cauldron I thought you were going to bleed ice water. Almost like a proper king, eh?'

A shadow crossed Myrsa's face.

'Do not say that,' he answered. 'I am no king and do not wish to be one. I am charged with leading the warriors of the Fauschlag, but am forced to delegate command more and more often as the business of running Middenheim consumes my every waking moment. It is a nightmare, my friends, a living nightmare. I am a fighter, not a ruler!'

'Middenheim? Is that what they're calling that mountain city of yours?' asked Wolfgart.

Myrsa nodded. 'Our scholars decided that it was time we had a proper name for the city, and they chose the name of the original settlement built around the Flame of Ulric. Supposedly, it comes from an old dwarf word, "watchtower in the middle place" or something like that.'

'Poetic,' grunted Wolfgart.

'And you would know,' smiled Myrsa. 'After all, "town by the Reik" is a name of lyrical beauty.'

Wolfgart was spared from thinking of a suitable response by the arrival of Redwane. The White Wolf was escorted by a statuesque woman in a long green dress, whose skin was pale where it was not decorated with colourful, winding tattoos. She was tall, with broad shoulders and blonde hair wound in a long ponytail that reached to the small of her back.

She cuffed Redwane over the back of the head.

'Maedbh, light of my life and queen of the bedchamber,' cried Wolfgart. He wrapped his arms around his wife and pulled her tight, careful to avoid the new swelling of her belly.

'Husband,' said Maedbh. 'I am returning this lusty dog to you before some jealous warrior sticks a knife in his heart. If he has one, that is.'

'Causing trouble again, Redwane?' asked Myrsa.

'Me? No, just a slight misunderstanding,' protested the White Wolf. 'Christa was feeling faint from the heat, and

I was simply taking her outside for some fresh air. I can't help it if Erek thought my intentions towards his woman were anything other than honourable!'

'That rod of yours will get you in real trouble one day,' said Wolfgart, though he admired the youngster's nerve in making a pass at the notoriously sharp-tongued Christa. 'And my wife won't be there to pull your arse out the fire when it does.'

Redwane smiled and shrugged before sitting on the edge of the table and helping himself to some of Pendrag's food.

'Don't you worry about me,' said Redwane, patting the worn, leather-wound grip of his hammer. 'I can handle any trouble that comes my way.'

'It's not you we're worried about, you dolt,' said Pendrag. 'It's any poor fool who dares challenge you. I don't want you killing a man in an honour duel just because you fancied a tilt at his woman.'

Redwane nodded, but Wolfgart saw that Pendrag's words had made no impression on the volatile young warrior.

'Ah, what's the use?' hissed Pendrag. 'You'll hear no words I say. Only bitter experience will teach you the lesson you so badly need to learn.'

'Always the teacher, eh, Pendrag?' said Wolfgart. 'You see, Myrsa? I told you he was a scholar now.'

Myrsa nodded and drank some more beer as the pipe music filling the hall was silenced and the chaotic hubbub of voices died down. Wolfgart looked towards the end of the longhouse. Sigmar had risen from his throne, and his iron gaze swept the assembled warriors.

'What's happening?' asked Redwane.

'When a new king is crowned, it is traditional for him to dispense favours to those who supported him,' said Pendrag. 'I assume it will be the same for the crowning of an emperor.'

'Favours? What sort of favours?'

'Land, title… That sort of thing.'

'Ah, so lots of kings get more land and fancier titles,' said Redwane.

'Something like that,' agreed Pendrag. 'Don't worry, lad, it won't be anything that affects the likes of us.'

## ✦ THREE ✦

# Reckonings

SIGMAR CLOSED THE door to his bedchamber at the rear of the longhouse and sighed with exhaustion. Two of his White Wolves stood guard on the other side of the door, but if they saw any sign of his weariness, they did not show it. Alfgeir had trained them well. His three hounds lay on his bed in a lair of bearskins, basking in the sullen heat from the banked fire. Their heads bobbed up as he entered. Ortulf, the eldest of the three, bared his fangs, but bounded from the bed upon catching Sigmar's scent. Lex and Kai quickly followed him, all three inordinately pleased to see their master once more.

The hounds had been a gift from King Wolfila of the Udose in the aftermath of Black Fire Pass. Udose warhounds were vicious beasts, difficult to train and temperamental, but once their allegiance had been won, they were loyal to their master unto death. Much like the Udose themselves, reflected Sigmar.

He knelt, ruffled their fur and threw them some strips of roast boar he had taken from the feast hall. They scrapped amongst themselves for the food, though Lex and Kai were careful to allow Ortulf the choicest cuts. As the hounds devoured the boar meat, Sigmar rubbed his eyes and yawned. It had been a long day and he wished for nothing more than a good night's rest.

Sigmar removed the wolfskin cloak around his neck and reached for the clasps securing his magnificent silver armour. Kurgan Ironbeard had presented him with the armour as a coronation gift, and, as Sigmar unbuckled each piece, it felt like he had worn it all his life. Each plate was worked with a skill and craftsmanship known only to the dwarfs, the burnished metal carved with runic script and flawlessly finished to a mirror sheen.

The breastplate was lighter even than the lacquered leather chestguards the Taleuten horse archers wore, moulded to his physique and embossed with a twin-tailed comet of gold at its centre.

No mortal man had ever worn so fine a suit of armour.

He removed the armour quickly and hung each piece on a rack in the corner of the room. Clad only in his tunic and crown, he lifted Alaric's gift from his brow. Like the armour, the crown was a thing of beauty, and Sigmar sensed the ancient power bound to it in the gold runes worked upon the metal.

Sigmar placed the crown in a velvet-lined casket next to his bed and closed the lid. Ghal-maraz he set on an iron weapons rack alongside his leaf-bladed sword, an Asoborn hunting spear and his favourite Cherusen dagger. He sat on the edge of the bed, listening to the raucous celebrations from the great hall of the longhouse, knowing they would continue long into the night.

Though hundreds of warriors were close by, Sigmar felt strangely alone, as though his elevation to Emperor had somehow isolated him from his fellows. He knew he was still the same man he had always been, but something fundamental had changed, though he could not yet fathom what it was.

He thought back to his pronouncements in the longhouse, and the deafening cheers that greeted each one. In the weeks leading to his coronation, Sigmar had thought long and hard about what boons to grant those that had sworn loyalty to him. His allies were proud men and women, and would seek rewards for the blood their people had shed to make him Emperor.

Sigmar's first act had also been his grandest.

He abolished the title of king, declaring that no one who called himself a king should be subject to another's rule. Instead, each of the tribal kings would take the title of count, retaining all their lands and rights as rulers over their people. Their sword oaths still bound them to Sigmar, as his did to them.

The land of each of the counts was entrusted to them for all time, and Sigmar swore on Ghal-maraz that they and their descendants would remain his honoured brethren for so long as they upheld the ideals by which their realms had been won and made safe.

One land, one people, united under a single ruler, yet still able to retain their identities.

With the biggest proclamation made and accepted, Sigmar had then turned to individual honours. He named Alfgeir Grand Knight of the Empire, and entrusted him with the protection of Reikdorf and its people. Sigmar presented the stunned Alfgeir with a glorious banner woven from white silk acquired at fabulous expense from the olive-skinned traders of the south. Depicting a black cross with a wreathed skull at its centre, Sigmar declared it would forever be borne by those who fought in defence of Reikdorf.

Amid wild cheering, Sigmar had declared that Reikdorf would be the foremost city of the empire, his capital and seat of power. It would become a beacon of hope and learning for his people, a place where warriors and scholars would gather to further man's knowledge of the world in which he lived.

To this end, Sigmar announced the building of a great library, and named the venerable Eoforth as its first custodian. The canny Eoforth had served as Björn's counsellor for more than forty years and, together with Pendrag, had amassed a vast collection of scrolls written by some of the wisest men in the empire.

Eoforth would be entrusted with the gathering of knowledge from all across the lands of men, bringing it together under one roof so that any who sought wisdom might find it within the library's walls. Sigmar placed the grey mantle of a scholar upon Eoforth, seeing Pendrag's anticipation as he awaited a similar position within this new institution.

But Sigmar had a greater destiny in mind for Pendrag.

He smiled, picturing Pendrag's face as he was appointed Count of Middenheim, entrusted with the rule of the empire's northern marches. The shock on Pendrag's face was mirrored by the relief on Myrsa's, and Sigmar knew that the decision was the correct one.

Warriors from all the tribes were honoured for their courage at Black Fire Pass, Maedbh of the Asoborns, Ulfdar of the Thuringians, Wenyld of the Unberogen, Vash of the Ostagoths and a score of others. The longhouse shook with the sounds of swords and axes banging on shields, and with his duty to his warriors fulfilled, Sigmar had left them to their revelries.

Tired beyond measure, Sigmar slid beneath the bearskin covers of his bed, his three hounds curling together on the Brigundian rug at the centre of the room.

He longed for sleep but, as the hours passed, slumber would not come.

\* \* \*

THE HEARTH-FIRE had burned low, casting a dull red glow around his chamber. Though the room was warm and his covers thick, Sigmar suddenly felt the lingering soul-chill of his near-drowning in the Cauldron of Woe.

He shivered as fleeting glimpses of the things he had seen beneath the icy water returned to him. What did they mean and how should he interpret them? Were they visions of the future granted to him by Ulric or mere phantasms conjured by his air-starved mind to ease his passage into death? When the days of feasting were over and the counts had returned to their lands, Sigmar resolved to task Eoforth with researching the meaning behind his visions.

Ortulf and Lex lifted their heads from the rug, growling softly at some unidentified threat, and Sigmar was instantly alert. Without appearing to move, he slid his hand beneath the covers for the punch dagger hidden in a secret pocket within the bearskin.

Opening his eyes a fraction, Sigmar scanned the room for anything out of place. All three hounds were growling now, though he could hear their confusion. Something had alerted them, but they could not identify what.

A shadow detached itself from the corner of the room, and Sigmar's fist closed around the bronze hilt of the punch dagger.

'Put down your weapon, Child of Thunder,' said a loathsome voice that Sigmar had hoped never to hear again. 'I mean you no harm.'

'I wondered when you would show your face,' said Sigmar, propping himself up and keeping his grip firm on the hilt of his dagger.

'You sensed my presence?' said the Hag Woman, limping across the room. 'I am impressed. Most men's minds are too concerned with their desires to notice the truth of the world around them.'

'I sensed a foulness on the air, but knew not what it was,' said Sigmar. 'Now I do.'

The Hag Woman chuckled mirthlessly and moved towards his bed using a staff of dark wood for support.

'So that is to be the tone of our discussion,' she said. 'Very well, I shall speak no words of friendship or congratulation.'

Sigmar's hounds bared their fangs, muscles tensed and hackles raised. The Hag Woman spat a curse in their direction, and the dogs whimpered in fear, slinking away to the furthest corner of the room.

'The beasts fear me, even if men do not,' she said wistfully. 'That is something at least.'

She sat on the end of Sigmar's bed, and he could see the weight of years upon the woman. Her skin was loathsomely wrinkled, like weathered leather, and what little remained of her white hair was lank and thin. For a moment, Sigmar was moved to pity. Then he remembered the misery she had allowed to enter his life and his heart hardened.

'You truly knew I was in Reikdorf?' she asked.

'Yes,' said Sigmar. 'And now I wish you gone. I am weary and I am not in the mood for words of doom.'

The Hag Woman laughed, the sound like winter twigs snapping underfoot.

'Alaric's crown gives you perception,' she said. 'Beware you do not seek to replace it.'

'What is that supposed to mean?'

'A piece of advice, nothing more,' said the Hag Woman. 'But that is not why I am here. I come with a warning and a request.'

'A request?' said Sigmar. 'Why should I grant you anything? All you have done is bring me misery.'

A shadow of anger passed over the Hag Woman's face, and Sigmar recoiled from her cold fury.

'You hate me,' she said, 'but if you knew all I had sacrificed to guide you, make you strong and prepare you for what is to come, you would drop to your knees and grant me my heart's desire.'

'Why should I believe you?' demanded Sigmar. 'Your words bring only death.'

'And yet you have your empire.'

'Won by the courage of warriors,' said Sigmar, 'not the wiles of your scheming.'

'Won by your lust for death and glory,' snapped the Hag Woman. 'Most men's desires are simple and banal: food in their belly, a home to shelter from the cold, and a woman to bear their sons. But not you... No, Sigmar the Heldenhammer is a killer whose heart only sings when death is a hair's-breadth away and his bloodstained hammer is crushing the skulls of his foes. Like all warriors, you have darkness in your heart that *lusts* for violence. It is what births the urge to kill and destroy in men, but yours will consume you without balance in your heart. Temper your darkness with compassion, mercy and love. Only then will you be the Emperor this land needs for it to survive. This is my warning to you, Child of Thunder.'

The Hag Woman's words cut like knives, but Sigmar could not deny the truth of them. The clamour of battle *was* when he felt truly alive, when his enemies were broken and driven from the field of battle in a tide of blood.

'You call it darkness, but it allowed me to defeat my enemies,' said Sigmar. 'I need it to defend my lands.'

'It is ever my curse to be unappreciated,' sighed the Hag Woman, 'but my time in this world is short, and I have only this one chance to pass on my knowledge of things to come.'

'You have seen the future?' asked Sigmar, making the sign of the horns.

'There *is* no future,' said the Hag Woman. 'Nor is there a past. All things exist now and always. It is the blessing of mankind that they do not perceive the whole of this world's infinite structure. Existence is a complex puzzle, of which you see but a single piece. It is my curse to see many such pieces.'

'You do not see them all?' asked Sigmar, intrigued despite himself.

'No, and I am grateful for that small mercy. Only the gods dare know everything, for it would drive men to madness to know the full truth of their destiny.'

'You have delivered your warning,' said Sigmar. 'Now make your request and begone.'

'Very well, though you will be pleased that this time I speak of life, not death.'

'Life? Whose?'

'The man named Myrsa,' said the Hag Woman. 'You call him the Warrior Eternal, and it is a well-chosen title. The people of the Fauschlag Rock harken to an ancient prophecy, one that warns of their city's fall without such a warrior to lead their armies in times of war.'

The Hag Woman laughed. 'A false prophecy delivered by a conniving soothsayer to advance his idiot son's ambitions, though now it seems it has a measure of truth to it. More by accident than design, I suspect. In any case, you must not allow the Warrior Eternal to die before his time.'

'Before his time?' asked Sigmar. 'What kind of request is that? How can any man know when it is his time to leave this world?'

'Some men know, Child of Thunder,' said the Hag Woman. '*You* will know.'

Once again Sigmar made the sign of the horns.

'A curse on you, woman!' he said. 'Speak not the words of my death! Now leave or by Ulric's blood I will kill you where you sit.'

'Be at peace,' said the Hag Woman. 'I do not speak of your death.'

'Then what do you mean?'

'No,' said the Hag Woman with a knowing wink. 'That I *choose* not tell you, for it is the uncertainty of life that keeps it interesting, don't you think?'

Anger flared in Sigmar's heart, and he slid from the bed, his blade extended before him.

'You torment me with your mysteries, woman,' he said. 'Well, no more! If I see you again, I will cut your throat before that vile tongue can utter another curse upon my head.'

'Fear not, Child of Thunder, for this will be the last time we speak,' promised the Hag Woman sadly. 'Yet we will see one another again, and you will remember my words.'

'More riddles,' spat Sigmar.

'Life is a riddle,' said the Hag Woman, rising from the bed with a smile and turning her gaze upon the smouldering fire. 'Now sleep, and do not forget what I have said, or everything you have built will be destroyed.'

The hearth erupted with flames, and the dagger dropped from Sigmar's hand as he collapsed onto his bed. Great weariness descended upon him, and the sleep that had previously eluded him dragged him down into its warm embrace.

SIGMAR AWOKE WITH the dawn, warm and refreshed beneath his bearskin. There was no sign of the Hag Woman and his hounds were no worse for the encounter, though the same could not be said for Sigmar. Her words hung like chains around his neck, and throughout the rest of the week of feasting and celebration, he found his eyes darting to the shadows lest her dark form should emerge from them.

Over the next six days, the warriors of the empire gorged themselves on the fruits of their victory: mountains of food and lakes of beer. Counts from the far corners of the empire brought wines and fiery spirits from beyond the mountains to the south, and tribal dishes were prepared by the womenfolk of every land. Unberogen beer, a powerful ale flavoured with bog myrtle was consumed by the barrel-load, and crate after crate of Asoborn wine was unloaded from the docks and dragged to the longhouse.

Cherusen beef was served on platters with Menogoth pork, and every king enjoyed new and exotic dishes from across the empire. Truly, it was a feast that none gathered in Reikdorf would ever forget. Nor was it only the warriors who were honoured with such largesse; Sigmar commanded his granaries to be opened, and for the duration of the coronation, free bread was distributed to every family in Reikdorf and beyond.

Eoforth bemoaned the expense, but Sigmar was not to be dissuaded, and his name was praised from one end of the land to the other.

Custom dictated that the Emperor spent his coronation day as an aloof and magisterial ruler, but for the rest of the week he resolved to be simply Sigmar the man. Wolfgart and Pendrag had approached him almost immediately on the second morning, and Sigmar knew exactly what his banner bearer was going to say.

'I cannot do this, Sigmar,' said Pendrag. 'Ruler of an entire city? It is an honour, but there must be others more suited to the task.'

Wolfgart shook his head, and said, 'He's been like this all night, Sigmar. Sort him out.'

Sigmar took his old friend by the shoulders and said. 'Look at what you have done with Reikdorf: stone walls, new schools, forges and regular markets. You have made it the jewel in my crown, and you will do the same for Middenheim, I know it.'

'But Myrsa... It is his city,' protested Pendrag, though Sigmar saw that the thought of applying his ideas to a new city appealed to him. 'The honour should be his. He will feel slighted.'

Sigmar shivered, recalling the Hag Woman's words as Wolfgart said, 'I think Myrsa will be only too happy to have you take charge. What was it he said last night? "I am a fighter, not a ruler!" I don't think you need worry about Myrsa's feelings, my friend.'

'For a man who's been up all night drinking, Wolfgart speaks sense,' added Sigmar. 'But keep Myrsa close, for he knows the city and its people. He will be a staunch ally in your rule.'

'I am not sure–'

'Trust me, my friend, you will make a grand count of Middenheim. Now go, enjoy yourself and get drunk!' ordered Sigmar.

'First sensible thing I've heard this morning,' said Wolfgart, leading Pendrag away.

Over the following days, Sigmar mixed with his subjects and conversed with his counts about what needed to be done to secure the peace they had won. Sword oaths were renewed and plans laid to defend the east and north, while expeditions were planned to learn more of the lands far to the south.

Many called for war against the Jutones, and the sentiment found much support amongst the counts. King Marius, safe in his coastal city of Jutonsryk, endured thanks only to the great victory others had won. All agreed that a reckoning was due, and that Marius must be brought to heel or destroyed.

Queen Freya of the Asoborns was Sigmar's constant shadow throughout the feasting, and he endured countless tales of her twin boys, Fridleifr and Sigulf, who were gods amongst men if their mother's stories were to be believed. Freya's desire for him was undimmed and her disappointment was clear when he gently rebuffed her offers of carnal pleasure.

Krugar of the Taleutens and Aloysis of the Cherusens both tried to broach the subject of their shared border, each claiming that the other was sending raiders to violate their lands. Sigmar forestalled such disputes until the spring; this was a time for unity, not division. Neither count was happy with his judgement, but both bowed and withdrew.

Of all the counts gathered, Sigmar enjoyed the company of Wolfila the most. The Udose count was a garrulous guest, and seemed to have a limitless supply of energy with which to feast and partake in games of strength and skill. None who fought him in mock duels could best him, until Sigmar put him flat on his back with one punch.

No sooner had he regained consciousness than Wolfila dragged Sigmar into the longhouse to break open a bottle of his finest grain spirit, a bottle said to have been laid down in his grandfather's time. The two men drank long into the night, cutting their palms and becoming bloodbrothers while devising ever more elaborate means to solve the evils of the world.

On the morning of the fourth day of feasting, Wolfila introduced Sigmar to his wife, Petra. Swathed in a patchwork dress of many colours, Petra was petite and slender, though she had fought in battle since becoming Wolfila's wife. From the swelling of her belly, it was clear that she was with child, her first, though this had not stopped her from eating and drinking her share of the feast platters.

'He'll be a bonny lad,' said Wolfila, patting his wife's belly. 'A hellraiser and a warrior to be sure. Just like his father.'

'Whisht,' scolded Petra. 'Away with you, it's a girl, as sure as night follows day.'

'Don't be foolish, woman,' cried Wolfila. 'A boy, didn't old man Rouven say so?'

'Rouven?' snapped Petra. 'Ach, the man couldn't predict rain in a thunderstorm!'

The Udose were renowned as an argumentative tribe, whose clannish family groupings fought with one another as often as they battled their enemies. Though

Wolfila and Petra loved each other dearly, Sigmar soon learned that they would argue over the smallest thing, and that it was best to leave them to it. The strange thing was that they seemed to enjoy it.

As well as the rulers of each tribe, Sigmar spent a great deal of time with the warriors of the tribes, listening to their tales of courage and heartbreak from the field of Black Fire Pass. A Thuringian warrior broke a table as he re-enacted his killing of a gigantic troll, a pair of Asoborn spearmen ran circles around their listeners as they explained the tactics of a chariot charge, and shaven-headed Taleuten horsemen sang songs of how they rode down fleeing greenskins at battle's end.

With every account, Sigmar's awe for these men and women grew deeper and his gratitude more profound. Most moving of all were the words of a Menogoth warrior named Toralf, who tearfully begged Sigmar's forgiveness for his cowardice in running.

'We tried,' sobbed Toralf, showing a monstrous scar in his side where a great barb had pierced him. 'We killed the wolves and marched into the teeth of the spear throwers. We didn't know… We didn't know… Hundreds of bolts let fly at us, thick as a felled tree they were, and each one killed a dozen men, skewered like pigs in a row. I lost my father and both brothers in the time it takes to nock an arrow, but we kept going… We kept going till we couldn't go no more… And then we ran. Ulric forgive me, but we ran!'

Sigmar remembered the dreadful fear he had felt watching the Menogoth ranks breaking under the horrific onslaught of orc spear throwers. The greenskins had poured into the gap and savaged the flanks of King Henroth's Merogens before Sigmar had led his Unberogen sword bands forward to hurl the orcs back.

'There is nothing to forgive,' he told Toralf. 'No warriors could have held firm under such an attack. There is no shame in fleeing from so grievous a slaughter. What matters most is that you came back. In every battle, there are those who flee for their lives. Fewer are those who find their courage and return to the fight. Without the strength of the Menogoths, the battle would have been lost.'

Toralf looked up with wet eyes and dropped to his knees before Sigmar, who placed his hand on the man's head. All eyes were upon him as Toralf received Sigmar's blessing, and a palpable sense of wonder filled the longhouse as the hearts of the Menogoths were healed.

Though he favoured no count over another, Sigmar found that he spent almost no time at all with Aldred. This was not for lack of effort on Sigmar's part, for it seemed the Endal count deliberately kept away from the new emperor. King Marbad, Aldred's father, had been one of Sigmar's staunchest allies, and it grieved him to feel the distance growing between him and the count of the Endals.

No sooner had the feasting come to an end on the seventh day than the Endals mounted their black steeds and rode through Morr's Gate, Reikdorf's westernmost entrance. Sigmar watched them go, the Raven Helms surrounding their master as they followed the course of the river towards Marburg.

One by one, the counts of the empire returned to their homelands, and it was a time of great joy and melancholy. With the celebrations done and the warriors departed, Reikdorf felt strangely empty. Autumn was coming to an end, and the cold winds howled over the northern hills with the promise of winter.

Soon darkness would cover the land.

THE SEASONS FOLLOWING Black Fire Pass had been mild, but the winter that fell upon the empire in the wake of Sigmar's coronation was as fierce as anyone living could remember. The land was blanketed in white, and only the most foolhardy dared venture far from the warmth of hearth and home.

Blizzards sprang from nowhere, raging southwards to bury entire villages beneath the snow and wipe them from the map. Only when the snows retreated in the spring would many of these settlements be rediscovered, their frozen inhabitants huddled together in their last moments of life.

Days were short and the nights long, and the people of the empire were left with little to do but press close to their fires and pray to the gods to deliver them from the bitter cold. Harsh as the winter was, the Unberogen passed it with relative ease, for the granaries were well stocked, even after Sigmar's generosity at his coronation.

The ground was like iron, and work ceased on the forest clearances as well as the wide roads running between Middenheim in the north and Siggurdheim in the south. The workers were glad of the respite, for the hungry forest beasts made it too dangerous to venture beyond the walls of a settlement for any length of time. Work would resume in the spring, and fine roads of stone would link the great cities of the empire.

The danger of the forest beasts was illustrated only too clearly when a pack of twisted monsters raided the village of Verburg, burning it to the ground and taking the inhabitants captive. Though savage winds howled around Reikdorf, Sigmar had gathered a hunting party to track the beasts and rescue his captured people. His head scout, Cuthwin, found the beasts' trail a mile east of Astofen, and the Unberogen riders had fallen on the creatures as they camped above a frozen lake.

The slaughter had been swift, for the beasts were starving and weak. Not a single rider fell in the fight, but the captives were already dead, butchered to feed the hungry pack. Dispirited by their failure to rescue the villagers, the

Unberogen rode back to Reikdorf without the soaring pride that would normally accompany the slaying of so many of their enemies.

Two days later, Sigmar still brooded on the deaths of his people, and it was in this mood that his friends found him as they came to discuss the spring muster.

THE FIRE IN the centre of the longhouse burned low, yet the dwarf craft in the hall's construction was so precise that no cold seeped in through the windows or doors. Sigmar sat upon his throne, Ghal-maraz lying across his lap and his faithful hounds curled at his feet.

Behind him stood Redwane, one hand on the grip of his hammer, the other on a polished banner pole of yew. With Pendrag in Middenheim, the honour of bearing Sigmar's crimson standard had gone to the strongest warrior of the White Wolves. Alfgeir had advised Sigmar to choose a warrior of greater maturity, but he had seen great courage in Redwane and would not change his mind.

The doors to the longhouse opened, and a malicious gust of wind scattered the dry straw spread across the floor. Eoforth limped inside, swathed in thick furs and flanked by Alfgeir and Wolfgart. The cloaked warriors helped Eoforth to a seat by the fire, and Sigmar descended from his throne to sit with his closest friends.

'How goes work in the library?' asked Sigmar.

'Well enough,' nodded Eoforth, 'for many of the counts brought copies of their foremost scholars' work with them in autumn. The winter has given me the chance to read many scrolls, but the business of organising them is never-ending, my lord.'

Sigmar nodded, though he had no real interest in Eoforth's books. The first hints that winter was loosening its grip were in the air, and he was eager to make war once more.

As promised at his coronation, there were reckonings to be had.

He turned from Eoforth and spoke first to Alfgeir.

'How many men do we have under arms for the spring muster?' he asked.

Alfgeir glanced at Eoforth.

'Perhaps five thousand in the first raising,' he said. 'If need be, another six when the weather breaks.'

'How soon can they be gathered?'

'Once the war banner is unfurled, I can send riders out, and most of the first five thousand will be here within ten days,' said Alfgeir. 'But we will need time to prepare food and supplies before ordering such a gathering. It would be best to wait until the snows melt.'

Sigmar ignored Alfgeir's last comment and said, 'Eoforth, draw up a list of everything the army will need: swords, axes, spears, armour, wagons, war-machines, horses, food. Everything. I want it ready by tomorrow evening and I want us ready to raise the war banner as soon as the roads become passable.'

'I will do as you command,' said Eoforth, 'though the planning of so large a muster should be given more time than a single day.'

'We do not have more time,' said Sigmar. 'Just make it happen.'

Wolfgart coughed and spat into the fire, and Sigmar sensed his friend's confusion.

'Something troubles you, Wolfgart?' he asked.

Wolfgart looked up and shrugged.

'I'm just wondering who you're in such a rush to go and fight,' he said. 'I mean, we killed the beasts and burned their corpses didn't we? The others of their kind will get the message.'

'We are not riding out to kill beasts,' said Sigmar. 'We march to Jutonsryk. The coward Marius must be called to account for deserting us at Black Fire.'

'Ah… Marius,' said Wolfgart, nodding. 'Aye, well he needs to be dealt with, right enough, but why so soon? Why not wait until the snows break properly before ordering men to leave their homes and loved ones? Marius isn't going anywhere.'

'I thought that you of all people would be eager for this,' snapped Sigmar. 'Were you not complaining that big sword of yours was getting rusty?'

'I'm as eager for battle as the next man,' said Wolfgart, 'but let's be civilised about this and fight in the spring, eh? My old bones don't like marching in the snow or sleeping rough in the cold. War's hard enough as it is, there's no need to make it harder.'

Sigmar stood and circled the fire, Ghal-maraz held loosely across his shoulder as he answered Wolfgart.

'Every day since I threw his ambassador from Reikdorf, Marius has been fortifying Jutonsryk, building his walls and towers of stone higher. His ships bring grain, weapons and mercenaries from the south, and every day we sit like old women around the fire, his city grows stronger. The longer we wait to take the fight to Marius, the more men will die when we attack.'

Sigmar and Wolfgart locked eyes, and it was his sword-brother who looked away.

'You're the Emperor,' said Wolfgart. 'You always did see things bigger than me, but I wouldn't go haring off to Jutonsryk without making sure my back was covered first.'

'What are you talking about?' asked Sigmar, stopping in front of Wolfgart.

'Aldred of the Endals,' said Alfgeir.

'Aldred?' asked Sigmar. 'The Endals are our brothers, Sword Oath sworn and bound to us for generations. Why would you dishonour a man who has sworn a sword oath with me?'

'That's just it,' said Wolfgart. 'His father did, but he hasn't.'

'And you think Aldred would dishonour his father's memory by turning on us?' demanded Sigmar, angry that his sword-brother would suggest such a thing.

'He might. You don't know Aldred's heart.'

'I think what Wolfgart means is that the Endals are something of an unknown quantity,' said Eoforth hurriedly. 'King Marbad was your father's greatest friend and a proud ally of the Unberogen, but Aldred...'

'I grieved with Aldred when we set Marbad on the pyre,' said Sigmar. 'He knows I honoured his father.'

'We all grieved for Marbad,' said Alfgeir, 'but I agree with Wolfgart. It makes no sense to face one enemy with potentially another behind us.'

Wolfgart rose from his seat and stood face-to-face with Sigmar. 'I watched the Endals the whole time they were here, and I didn't like the looks of that Aldred one bit. The way he stared at you, well, it was as if you'd rammed that spear in his father's chest yourself.'

'You're saying that he blames me for his father's death?'

'You'd have to be a blind man not to see that,' said Wolfgart. 'Even Laredus was like a stranger, and it wouldn't surprise me if we saw less and less of the Endals as time goes on.'

'You agree with this?' Sigmar asked Eoforth.

'I think it is worth considering,' said Eoforth. 'As Alfgeir says, it's sensible to make certain of the loyalty of the warriors behind you before laying siege to Jutonsryk. Be sure of Aldred, win him to your cause, and *then* take your anger to the Jutones.'

Sigmar wanted to rage against their words, but he had seen the bitterness in Aldred's eyes and had known it for what it was. Marbad had been dear to Sigmar, but he was Aldred's father too. Nothing could assuage Aldred's knowledge that, had his father not been compelled to hurl the blade Ulfshard to Sigmar at the height of the battle, he might have lived.

Sigmar took a deep breath.

'You are right,' he said. 'My anger towards Marius and my frustration at the deaths of my people is blinding me to the wisdom of my friends. I saw the hurt in Aldred's eyes, but I chose to ignore it. That was foolish of me.'

'We all make mistakes,' said Wolfgart. 'Don't worry about it.'

'No,' said Sigmar. 'I am Emperor, and I cannot afford to act so rashly or people will die. From hereon, I will make no decisions of magnitude without speaking with you, for you are all dear to me and this crown weighs heavy on my brow. I will need your honest counsel if I am to make wise decisions.'

'You can count on me to tell you when you're being an ass,' said Wolfgart. 'You always could.'

Sigmar smiled and shook Wolfgart's hand.

'So do you still want to order the spring muster?' asked Alfgeir.

'No, not yet,' said Sigmar. 'Our reckoning with Marius will need to wait.'

'Then what are your orders, sire?'

'When the snow breaks, assemble a hundred of the White Wolves,' said Sigmar. 'We will pay a visit to Count Aldred in Marburg and see what truly lies in his heart.'

## ◄ FOUR ►

# City of Mist

THE COLUMN OF riders made its way along the muddy track that served as a road through the sodden lands of the Endals, a hundred warriors in red armour, all carrying long-handled hammers. Sigmar rode at the head of the column, with Redwane alongside him holding the emperor's standard aloft. The crimson banner hung listlessly from the crosspiece, for there was no wind and damp air had saturated the fabric.

The journey from Reikdorf had begun well, the snows breaking swiftly and spring's warmth arriving earlier than had been predicted by the bones of old men. That fortune had lasted for the first three days, as the riders made good time along the stone roads leading from Sigmar's capital.

Then the road ended and the rest of the journey had been made along muddy trails, forest tracks and rutted roadways. Wolfgart had travelled this way before, and though he was reluctant to leave Maedbh so near to the birth of his child, he insisted on riding with Sigmar.

Alfgeir remained in Reikdorf as Sigmar's regent. Though the Grand Knight of the Empire understood the honour of being appointed the city's guardian, he chafed at the thought of allowing others to protect the Emperor. At Alfgeir's insistence, Cradoc had accompanied the riders. In lieu of Alfgeir, the finest healer in the Unberogen lands would have to suffice in safeguarding the Emperor's life.

Sigmar looked over at Redwane. The young warrior was only two summers older than he had been when he first rode to war. The young White Wolf sensed the scrutiny and glanced over, his youthful face alight with excitement and anticipation.

Sigmar could barely remember being so young and brash, and he suddenly envied the young man's outlook on life, seeing the world as new and alive with possibility.

'How far is it to Marburg, Wolfgart?' asked Redwane.

'Gods, boy!' snapped Wolfgart. 'I'll tell you when we're close. Now stop asking me.'

'It's just I thought we'd be able to see it by now.'

'Aye, you'd see it yonder if not for this damn mist,' replied Wolfgart, winking at Sigmar. 'It's the noxious wind of the daemons that live in the marshes around Marburg, so don't breathe too much of it in lest you become one yourself.'

'Truly?' asked Redwane, trying to keep his lips pursed tightly together.

Cradoc stifled a laugh as Wolfgart continued, 'Aye, lad, for the daemons of the mist are cunning beasts. King Björn fought them before you were born. Rode to Marburg just like we're doing, and marched into the mist to face the daemons with King Marbad at his side. A hundred men went in, but barely a handful came out, the rest dragged to their deaths beneath the dark waters of the bogs.'

'Gods! That's no way for a warrior to die!' cried Red-wane.

'That's not the worst of it, lad,' continued Wolfgart, looking warily to either side of the road, as though the daemons might be lurking within earshot.

'It isn't?'

'No, not by a long way,' said Wolfgart, and Sigmar saw he was enjoying tormenting the White Wolf immensely. 'Some say the souls of those dead men linger beneath the marsh, and when the Dread Moon waxes, they rise from their watery graves to feast on the living. Horrible things they are, lad: a single deathly eye, needle teeth and grasping claws ready to pull you under the water to join them forever.'

Sigmar's father had told him of the mist daemons that haunted the marshes around Marburg upon their return from Astofen Bridge. Wolfgart was exaggerating that tale, but like the best storytellers, he was weaving his embellishments around a core of truth.

'Daemons, eh?' said Redwane. 'I've never fought a daemon before.'

'Then you are lucky,' said Sigmar, remembering the desperate fight against a host of daemonic beasts in the Grey Vaults, the bleak netherworld between life and death. His father had crossed over into Morr's realm to rescue him, giving up his life to save his only son. A lump formed in Sigmar's throat at the thought of his father's sacrifice.

'Ulric's teeth, what I wouldn't give to fight such a beast,' continued Redwane. 'Imagine it, Wolfgart. You'd have the pick of the maidens after a kill like that.'

'Trust me, Redwane,' said Sigmar. 'I have fought beings from the dread realms, and you should pray to all the gods that you never face such a creature.'

Wolfgart looked curiously at him. 'When did you fight a daemon? And why wasn't I beside you?'

'Do not ask me that,' said Sigmar, unwilling to be drawn on the subject. 'I will not speak of it, for evil like that is drawn by such talk. There are daemons enough in this world without summoning more to us.'

Wolfgart shrugged, and a stern glance silenced the question Sigmar saw on Redwane's lips. A thin rain began to fall, and the riders journeyed in silence for perhaps another hour before the mist began to thin and the land began to rise. Sigmar saw villages huddled in the distance, their waterlogged fields worked by mud-covered farmers and sway-backed horses.

This land was drained of life and colour, the sky was leaden and thunderous above the vast mountains to the south. Everywhere Sigmar looked, he saw tones of a dull and muddy brown. This was not what he had expected to see. Around Reikdorf, the land was green and golden, fertile and bountiful. Though life was hard and demanding, a sense of pride and purpose filled the settlements in Unberogen lands.

Sigmar saw none of that here, and a gloomy solitude settled upon him.

Several times during this last stage of the journey, the riders left the road to make way for rattling corpse-carts piled high with the dead. Each wagon was escorted by grim-faced knights in black and dark-robed priests of Morr, their monotone chants and dolorous bell-ringing muffled by the fog. Wailing mourners followed the carts, tearing at their hair and mortifying their flesh with knotted ropes hung with fishhooks.

The White Wolves covered their mouths with their cloaks, and made the sign of Shallya to ward off any evil vapours as each procession passed. Sigmar rode alongside Cradoc as the old man stared into a cart where the ties binding the canvas covering had come loose. Stiff and cold bodies looked out with bulging eyes that spoke of terrible fear and agonising pain.

'Looks like lung rot,' said Cradoc. 'Don't worry, it's not infectious, but the air here has turned bad. Something has stirred a miasma from the depths of the marsh to infect the air.'

'That's bad, yes?' asked Redwane.

'Oh yes, very bad,' said Cradoc. 'Over time, fluid builds up in the lungs, draining your strength until you can barely move or even speak.'

'Then what happens?' asked Wolfgart.

'Then you drown in your bed.'

'Shallya's mercy,' hissed Sigmar, covering his mouth. 'Should we take any precautions?'

'Not unless you plan to live here,' said Cradoc, riding away from the corpse-cart.

At last the sodden road led the riders through a wilting stand of trees of bare branches. Topping a rise shawled in wiry gorse, Sigmar caught the scent of sea air and saw Marburg. The city of the Endals sat atop a jagged bluff of volcanic black rock that reared from a desolate landscape of fog-shrouded heaths and endless marshland. This was where the mighty Reik reached the sea, and its sluggish waters were frothed with patches of ochre scum.

The black promontory of Marburg glistened in the rain, and an uneven band of pale blue stone rose to a height of about six feet from its summit, almost as though it had grown out of the rock. This was all that remained of an outpost built by an ancient race of fey folk who were said to dwell far across the ocean.

Even from here, the great skill of the stonemasons was evident, the joints between the blocks barely visible, and the curving sweep of the walls elegantly fashioned. Where dwarf-craft was solid, straightforward and had little in the way of subtlety, the remains of this structure were as much art as architecture.

Vast earthen ramparts of all too human construction were piled high upon the pale stone, and sadness touched Sigmar to see such a noble outpost so reduced. For a moment, he pictured it as it might once have looked: a glittering fastness of slender towers of silver and gold, arched windows of delicate glass and a riot of colourful flags.

The picture faded from his mind as he saw thick logs with sharpened ends jutting from the muddy ramparts, as much to reinforce the earth as to deter attackers. Black banners hung limply from a pair of flagpoles, rising from the stone towers built to either side of a wide timber gateway. Both towers were built from the same black stone of the rock and each was shaped in the form of a tall raven.

Trails of smoke rose from the city, and the tops of buildings roofed with grey slate could be seen over the walls. Flocks of dark-pinioned birds circled the winged towers of the Raven Hall at the heart of Marburg.

Beyond the city, the ocean's dark expanse spread towards the horizon. Grey banks of fog clung to the surface of the water and a few ships bobbed in the swells. Fishing nets trailed from their sterns, though Sigmar had little appetite for any fish caught in such sombre seas.

'Gods, have you ever seen anywhere so depressing?' asked Redwane, waving a hand in front of him. 'It stinks worse than an orc's breath!'

'Wasn't like this when I was here,' said Wolfgart. 'Marburg was a fine town, with good beer and food. I don't recognise this place.'

Sigmar wanted to rebuke Redwane and Wolfgart, but there was little point, for there was no denying the pall of misery that hung over Marburg. The entire land of the Endals was soaked in despair.

'Come on,' said Sigmar. 'I want to find out what's at the heart of this.'

THEY RODE TOWARDS Marburg, the widening road laid with timbers to ease the passage of wagons and horses. The raven sculpted towers loomed above them, dark and threatening, and a chill travelled down Sigmar's spine as he entered their shadow. The city gates were open, and Endal tribesmen in brown and black made way for the mud-spattered horsemen.

Sigmar knew they made an impressive sight, for their horses were powerful beasts, the product of years of careful selective breeding on Wolfgart's lands. Long ago, Wolfgart had promised to breed horses capable of wearing iron armour, and he had set to the challenge with as much determination as Sigmar had set about achieving his dream of an empire.

As a result, Unberogen horses were the biggest in the land, grain-fed mounts of no less than sixteen hands, with wide chests, strong legs and straight backs. By any reckoning, Wolfgart was a wealthy man, for his stallions were much sought after by those whose coin was plentiful, and several had been requested by Sigmar's counts upon seeing them at the gallop.

The White Wolves were no less impressive: tough, capable men who were equally at home fighting from the back of a horse as they were on foot. Their armour was of the finest quality, though they eschewed the use of shield or helmet, and their red cloaks were arranged carefully over the rumps of their horses. There was no give in them, and their long hair and beards were deliberately wild and barbarous.

Sigmar led the White Wolves through the gateway and into a cobbled courtyard. Warriors in black breastplates and helmets lined the courtyard, each carrying a long, bronze-tipped lance. Sigmar was instantly alert, for this was not the welcome an Emperor might expect. It felt more like the arrival of a tolerated enemy.

A warrior in a black, full-faced helm and a man dressed in flowing robes of green wool stood in the centre of the courtyard. Sigmar angled his course towards them. The warrior was powerfully built, while the robed man was old, his beard reaching almost to his waist. A long, curved blade hung from a belt of woven reeds, and he carried a staff of pale wood, its length garlanded with mistletoe.

'Why do I feel like there's an arrow aimed between my shoulder blades?' whispered Wolfgart.

'Because there probably is,' replied Redwane, nodding upwards.

Sigmar saw warriors peering down from the raven towers and nodded, knowing there would indeed be archers above them with arrows nocked. Aldred would not be so foolish or bitter as to have him killed, but still his senses were warning him of danger.

'Stay alert,' he hissed, 'but do nothing unless I do it first.'

The warrior in the black helmet stepped forward and bowed curtly to Sigmar. He removed his helmet and tucked it into the crook of his arm.

'Laredus,' said Sigmar, recognising the warrior of the Raven Helms. 'Where is Count Aldred? He cannot come to greet me himself?'

'Emperor Sigmar,' said Laredus, 'you honour us with your presence in Marburg. Count Aldred sends his regrets, but the health of his brother deteriorates daily and he fears to leave his side.'

'His brother is ill?' asked Sigmar, dropping from his horse to stand next to Laredus. If archers were going to shoot, he would give them a choice of targets.

'Indeed, my lord. The sickness from the marsh claims pauper and prince alike,' said Laredus.

'And who is this?' asked Sigmar, indicating the robed man beside Laredus. 'I do not know him.'

'I am called Idris Gwylt,' said the man with a short bow, his voice lilting and unfamiliar. His skin was the colour of aged oak and his hair was the pure white of freshly fallen snow. Pale green eyes regarded Sigmar with curiosity, and though there was no hostility in them, neither was there welcome.

'You'll address your Emperor as "my lord" in future,' snapped Redwane.

Sigmar waved Redwane back and said, 'What is your role, Idris Gwylt? Are you a priest, a healer?'

'A little of both, perhaps,' said Idris, with a wry smile. 'I am counsellor to Ki... Count Aldred on matters spiritual and worldly.'

Sigmar turned from Idris Gwylt and addressed Laredus. 'My men have travelled far and require food, lodgings and hot water. We shall also require stabling and grain for our mounts. When I have washed myself clean of mud, you will take me to Count Aldred, sick brother or not.'

'As you wish, my lord,' said Laredus coldly.

THE GUEST LODGINGS in Count Aldred's royal apartments were functional and clean, though no fire had been set in the hearth in anticipation of their arrival. A meal of fish and steamed vegetables came quickly, though it took an hour for enough water to be heated to allow Sigmar to bathe. Such treatment broke all the rules of hospitality that existed between allies, but Sigmar kept his temper in check, for he could ill-afford two enemies in the west.

With the journey washed from his body, Sigmar followed Laredus and a handful of cloaked Endal warriors through the streets of Marburg towards the Raven Hall. Dressed in a robe of crimson and a long wolfskin cloak, Sigmar marched at the head of Wolfgart, Redwane and an honour guard of ten White Wolves. Though outwardly calm, their hands never strayed far from their weapons.

Sigmar's crown glittered upon his brow, and he carried Ghal-maraz at his belt, holding the haft tight against his leg as he looked in horrified wonder at the dismal city surrounding him.

Water and human waste sluiced the streets of Marburg, and a sickly oily sheen coated the cobbles where it had seeped into the cracks. The rancid smell of spoiled meat and grain hung on the air, hemmed in by buildings that crowded together and loomed over the few wretched people abroad in the streets. A forsaken air hung over the city, as though its inhabitants had long ago fled its darkened thoroughfares for the lands left by the Bretonii.

The buildings were predominantly constructed from warped, sun-bleached timbers, with only the lower portions of each structure built from stone. Damp blotched the walls, and runnels of black water fell from leaking eaves. Windows and doors were shuttered, and through those that were ajar Sigmar heard little sign of life, only soft weeping and muttered prayers.

'Look,' said Wolfgart, nodding down a reeking alleyway to where another corpse-cart was pulling away from a thatched house. A black-robed priest of Morr painted a white cross upon the door as a hunched man wearing a grotesque mask with glass eyes and an elongated nose nailed a wooden board across it.

'Plague?' said Redwane. 'They must have breathed the daemon air!'

'Be quiet,' hissed Sigmar, though he reached up to touch the talisman of Shallya that he wore around his neck.

'Redwane is right, the city is cursed,' said Wolfgart. 'The carrion birds circle this place as if it were a fresh corpse. We should leave now.'

'Don't be foolish,' replied Sigmar. 'What manner of empire would I have forged if I turn my back on the suffering of my people? We stay and find the cause of this.'

'Very well,' shrugged Wolfgart, 'but don't say I didn't warn you when you're coughing up your lungs and drowning in your own blood.'

Sigmar put such concerns from his mind as the Raven Hall came into sight. The ancestral seat of the Endal rulers was a towering miracle: a majestic hall carved from a mighty spire of volcanic rock and hollowed out to form the rearing shape of a vast raven. Black pinions of glistening stone swept from the tower's flanks, and a great balcony was formed within the jutting beak at its summit.

Sigmar caught a flash of movement on the balcony, and saw the slender form of a woman clad in a long black dress with shoulder-length hair of golden blonde. No sooner had he spotted her than she vanished inside the tower.

'Ulric's bones,' said Redwane. 'And here's me thinking Siggurdheim was impressive.'

'Aye, they did something special here,' agreed Wolfgart. 'You can see almost all the way to the hills around Astofen when the mists roll back.'

'It's amazing,' said Sigmar, his anger with Aldred retreating in the face of this wondrous creation. Far to the north, the Fauschlag Rock dominated the landscape for miles around, but its towering form had been shaped by the fist of Ulric; The Raven Hall was the work of men. Countless years of toil and skill had gone into the Hall's creation, and it was a thing of dark, majestic beauty.

Laredus led them into the tower through a gateway formed between two giant claws and guarded by more Raven Helms. Now that he was closer, Sigmar saw the intricate detail worked into the tower's walls, the glassy stone carved with feathers that looked almost real.

The corridors within the tower were black, and torchlight rippled on the stonework like moonlight on water. Laredus led them deep into the heart of the tower, eventually reaching a carved stairway that led up into darkness. Sigmar wanted more time to explore this fabulous place, but Laredus lifted a torch from a sconce at the foot of the stairs and set off upwards.

Sigmar followed the Raven Helm, running his fingers over the smooth walls. The stone felt like polished glass, and was slightly warm to the touch, as though the fire of its vitrification still lingered deep in its heart. The stairs rose high into the tower, following the outward curve of its walls, and Sigmar's legs were soon aching.

'Does this damn tower ever end?' asked Redwane. 'It feels like it goes on forever.'

'You've been spoiled in Siggurdheim,' chuckled Wolfgart. 'Too much soft living has made you weak. You youngsters might have the edge in years on a veteran like me, but you've no stamina.'

'That's not what your wife says,' joked Redwane.

Even in the torchlight, Sigmar saw Wolfgart's face darken with anger. Wolfgart gripped Redwane's tunic and slammed him against the wall. His knife hissed from its leather sheath to rest against Redwane's throat.

'Speak that way about Maedbh again and I'll cut your heart out, you little bastard!' he said.

Fast as quicksilver, Sigmar's hand shot out and gripped Wolfgart's wrist, though he did not remove the blade from Redwane's throat.

'Redwane, sometimes your stupidity surprises even me,' said Sigmar. 'You insult the honour of a fine woman, wife to my sword-brother and shield maiden to a queen.'

'I'll kill him,' snarled Wolfgart. 'No man claims I wear the cuckold's horns and lives!'

'You will not,' stated Sigmar. 'Kill him and you will be a murderer. The boy's words were foolish, but he did not mean them. Did you, Redwane?'

'No, of course not!' cried Redwane. 'It was just a jest.'

'Make such jests at your peril,' hissed Wolfgart, putting up his knife and stepping away from the White Wolf. Though Redwane's life was no longer in immediate danger, Sigmar knew that Wolfgart would never forget those poorly-chosen words. He glanced over to where Laredus had been standing, but the Raven Helm had already gone ahead. Sigmar knew Aldred would already know of this altercation, and he cursed.

'Pull yourselves together and follow me,' said Sigmar, setting off after Laredus. 'And if either of you behaves like this again, I'll have you flogged and stripped of those wolf cloaks you prize so dearly.'

COUNT ALDRED'S HALL was a great domed chamber at the very summit of the tower. It was lit by twin shafts of yellow light that speared in through windows that formed the eyes of the Raven Hall. From its position in relation to the windows, Sigmar guessed that a curtain of red velvet led to the balcony he had seen from the outside. Scented torches formed a processional route towards a dark throne, and Sigmar guessed that they were lit to disguise the stench of the city below as well as to provide illumination.

Count Aldred awaited them clad in his father's armour, a bronze breastplate moulded to resemble a muscular physique and a tall helm with feathered wings of black that swept up from angular cheekplates. His long dark cloak spilled around a throne of polished ebony with armrests carved in the form of wings and legs shaped like black talons. The Raven Banner was set in a socket in the backrest of the throne, and Sigmar remembered the pride he had felt watching that same banner carried into battle at Black Fire Pass.

Laredus and Idris Gwylt stood behind Count Aldred, and two thrones of similar, but smaller design sat to either side of the Endal ruler. One of these thrones was empty, while upon the other sat the golden-haired girl that Sigmar had seen from beyond the tower. She was perhaps sixteen years old and pretty in a thin kind of way, though her skin had an unhealthy pallor to it, much like everyone else Sigmar had seen in Marburg. She looked at Sigmar with a haughty expression for one so young, yet he saw the interest behind her veneer of indifference.

Sigmar marched towards Aldred's throne, keeping his smouldering anger chained tightly within. He had come to the realm of the Endals to learn what lay in Aldred's heart, but seeing the count told him all he needed to know. The scent of the torches caught in the back of Sigmar's throat, and suddenly he knew what to say to Aldred.

'Count Aldred,' he said, 'your lands are in disarray. Pestilence blights your city and a curse lies upon your people. I am here to help.'

Sigmar hid his amusement at Aldred's surprise, and pressed on before the young count could reply, 'King Marbad was as a brother to my father, and he saved my life upon the field of Black Fire Pass. I shed tears as we sent him to Ulric's Hall, and I pledged to you that we would also be brothers. I have come to Marburg to make good on that pledge.'

'I do not understand,' said Aldred. 'I asked for no aid.'

'When the lands of my counts are threatened, I do not wait for them to ask for my help. I bring a hundred of my finest warriors to your city to help in whatever way we can.'

Idris Gwylt leaned down to whisper something in Aldred's ear, but Sigmar could not hear the words over the sound of the wind playing about the tower. Before Aldred could say anything in response to Gwylt's counsel, Sigmar took a step towards the throne.

'Count Aldred, tell me what troubles your city,' said Sigmar. 'As well as warriors, I bring my healer, Cradoc, a man who saved my life when I lay at Morr's threshold. Let him try to ease your people's suffering.'

Idris Gwylt stepped forward, and Sigmar breathed in his earthy aroma. Gwylt carried the smell of freshly turned soil and ripened crops, as though fresh from a field of sun-ripened corn. The feeling was intense, and Sigmar felt the power of the man, as though something vital coursed through him, a pulse of something old beyond imagining.

'The curse that afflicts us is beyond the power of your warriors to defeat, Emperor Sigmar,' said Gwylt. 'The daemons of the mist grow strong once more and their evil flows from the depths of the marshes. It spreads through the earth and corrupts all that it touches. Disease strikes our people and the life drains from the land, washed into the ocean with all our hopes. Hundreds of our tribe are dead and even my noble count's brother, the gallant Egil, has been struck down.'

'Then let Cradoc help him. There is little he does not know of the ways of sickness.'

'Egil is beyond the help of men,' said Idris Gwylt. 'Only the healing power of the land can save him now, and it wanes as that of the daemons waxes. Only by offering the daemons our most valued treasure can Egil's life be saved.'

'That is foolishness,' stormed Sigmar, addressing his words to Aldred. 'This man speaks of offering tribute to daemons as though you are their vassals. Daemons are creatures of darkness and can only be defeated with courage and strong sword arms. What say you, Aldred? Rally the Raven Helms to your banner and join me in battle. Together, we can cleanse the marshes of their evil forever. My father and your father fought these creatures, so let us finish what they began!'

'Our fathers failed,' said the young girl seated beside Aldred. 'The daemons drove them from the marshes and killed most of their warriors. What makes you think you can triumph where they could not?'

Sigmar lifted Ghal-maraz from his belt and held it out to her.

'I have never met a foe I could not defeat,' he said. 'If I go into those marshes to fight, I will be victorious.'

Her eyes blazed with anger.

'You are arrogant,' she said.

'Perhaps I am,' admitted Sigmar. 'It is my right as Emperor. But you have me at a disadvantage. You know who I am, but I do not know you.'

'My name is Marika,' she snapped, 'daughter of Marbad and sister to Aldred and Egil. You speak of battle as though it is the only way of ending our troubles, but not every curse can be lifted with killing. There are other ways.'

'Oh, like what?'

'It is not for me to say,' said Marika, the anger in her eyes replaced with sadness. Sigmar saw her glance towards Idris Gwylt.

'Then how would you end this curse, my lady?' asked Sigmar.

'By appeasing the daemons,' said Idris Gwylt.

'I was not asking you,' said Sigmar.

'Such daemons cannot be defeated by mortal men,' replied Gwylt, ignoring Sigmar's displeasure. 'The earth has been corrupted by the touch of the mist daemons, and we cannot restore its goodness with swords.'

'Does this man speak for you, Count Aldred?' demanded Sigmar. 'I appointed *you* to rule these lands, not some old man who speaks of appeasement. Good gods, man, you do not invite the fox into the hen house, you root him out and kill him.'

'Gwylt enjoys my full confidence,' said Aldred. 'We hold to the ways of our ancient forebears in Marburg, and it is in them that we will find salvation. Idris Gwylt is a priest of a power older than the gods, a servant of the land, who knows its ways and the means by which we may restore it. His words are wise beyond the understanding of most mortals, and he has done much to ease the suffering of my people. I trust him implicitly.'

'You may trust him, but I do not,' said Sigmar, understanding the source of Gwylt's strange and powerful aura. 'I thought the Old Faith died out a long time ago.'

'So long as the land bears fruit, it will endure,' said Gwylt.

Sigmar glared at the robed priest. 'In Reikdorf we put our faith in the gods.'

'This is not Reikdorf,' replied the priest.

SIGMAR AND HIS warriors spent the next three days secluded in the royal apartments. Though they were free to roam the city and its environs as they pleased, the sickness that ravaged the population kept most of them indoors. Sigmar spent the first day walking the fog-shrouded streets of Marburg to see how its population fared, and when he returned to his chambers there was a shadow on his soul.

The city of the Endals was a grim and melancholy place, not at all like the vibrant, cosmopolitan coastal city its old king had once told raucous tales of. Noxious mists coiled in from the marshes to drain the city of colour, and its inhabitants moved through the streets like ghosts. Despair came on those mists, a smothering blanket of misery that coiled around the soul and leeched it of vitality. Immediately upon his return, Sigmar bade Cradoc do what he could for the population of Marburg.

The old healer appropriated two score of the White Wolves to be his orderlies, and day and night Cradoc did what he could for the sick. Those whom the sickness had touched were too often beyond the power of his remedies. Families were found dead in their homes, faces spattered with crusted mucus and eyes swollen and red as though filled with blood. Despite Cradoc's best efforts, the priests of Morr led more and more corpse-carts on their sad journeys from the city.

It was thankless, heartbreaking work, but that did not stop Cradoc from trying to help those he could, and his poultices of lungwort and vinegar were freely distributed among the sick. It did little to halt the terrible pestilence, but until the source of the sickness was defeated it was all that could be done.

On the evening of the third night, frustrated at the lack of action from Count Aldred, Sigmar and Wolfgart sat outside their apartments on a high terrace overlooking the cliffs and marshes to the north of Marburg. They talked long into the night, drinking from a clay jug of southern wine and eating platters of salted fish. They told tales of battles won and friends in far of lands, enjoying a rare moment of companionship.

Though the talk was ribald and flowing, Sigmar sensed sadness in his friend that had little to do with too much wine. As Wolfgart finished telling the story of his fight against a particularly large greenskin in the opening moments of the battle at the crossing of the Aver, he sighed, his face melancholy.

'It has been too long since we talked like this,' said Sigmar.

'That it has,' said Wolfgart, raising his goblet. 'Life gets busy as we get older, eh?'

'That it does, old friend, but come, say what's on your mind. Tell me what troubles you.'

At first he thought Wolfgart would dismiss his invitation to speak, but his sword-brother surprised him.

'It's what Redwane said when we were going to see Aldred,' he said.

'You didn't take him seriously? The lad is young and foolish and he spoke out of turn, but you know Maedbh would never betray you like that.'

'I know that,' said Wolfgart, 'but that's not what I meant.'

'Then what is it?'

'I reacted to him like a stag in heat, as though he was a rival or something. I know he's not, but I pounced on him as if I was going to kill him. I would have done if you hadn't stopped me. I should have kept my temper in check, for I shamed you in front of Laredus.'

Sigmar shook his head and drained his goblet.

'Aye, we could have done without the Endals seeing us at each other's throats,' he said, 'but what's done is done. I don't hold it against you.'

'Maybe not, but I should have known better,' said Wolfgart. 'I've been around you long enough to know that I need to think before I act, but when he said that about Maedbh... Well, you saw how it affected me.'

'I'm just glad Maedbh didn't hear it,' said Sigmar with a smile.

Wolfgart laughed and said, 'True enough. She'd be wearing Redwane's balls for earrings by now.'

'You are a man of high emotion, Wolfgart, you always have been,' said Sigmar. 'It is one of the reasons I love you. Pendrag is my conscience and my intellect; you are the voice of my passions and my joys. I must be an Emperor, but you are the man I would wish to be were I not. By all means think before you act in future, especially when I must be seen to be the master of the empire, but never lose your fire. I wouldn't have you any other way, and you would not be Wolfgart without it.'

His sword-brother finished his wine and smiled. 'I'll remind you of this the next time I lose my temper and embarrass you. You know that, don't you?'

'I know that,' said Sigmar, reaching over to pour more wine. 'I think the drink must be getting to me.'

Wolfgart lifted his goblet and took a long swallow.

'You might be right,' he said. 'You never could drink as much as me. This wine's not bad, but it's not a mug of Unberogen beer. Too weak.'

'Drink the rest of the jug and tell me that.'

'Don't tempt me. I'm that sick of waiting for something to happen, I might as well spend my time here drunk. How much longer do you think they'll make us sit on our backsides?'

'I do not know, my friend,' said Sigmar with a shrug. 'But for Idris Gwylt, I think I could have persuaded Aldred to march out with us.'

'He's a sly fox that one, he needs watching,' agreed Wolfgart. 'I heard those that followed the Old Faith used to sacrifice virgins to let the purity of their blood bless the earth, or something like that.'

'So they say, but stories of old religions are almost always exaggerated by the faiths that replace them to make people glad they are gone. It's like the stories you hear as a child about ancient heroes who bestrode the world like giants only to vanish and have their people claim that they will one day return when the world needs them most.'

'Why do you think that is?'

'Because people need hope when things are at their darkest,' said Sigmar. 'Of course, none of these heroes ever do return. Most likely they got a knife in the back or fell from a horse and broke their neck, but who wants their legends to end like that?'

'Not me,' said Wolfgart, letting loose an almighty belch. 'I want my heroes to be gods among men, warriors able to level mountains with a single blow, rescue beautiful maidens from monsters without a second thought, and turn back armies with a word.'

'You always were a dreamer,' said Sigmar, laughing.

THE MOON HAD risen, lighting the sky with its pale glow as Sigmar opened his eyes. He blinked, realising he'd fallen asleep. He groaned, feeling the beginnings of a thumping headache. Wine had spilled down his tunic, and he saw that Wolfgart had passed out with his head between his knees. A puddle of vomit stained the flagstones of the terrace. Sigmar ran a hand through his hair. His eyes ached and his mouth felt as though he'd drunk a barrel-load of bog water.

'Now I remember why I do not do this,' he groaned, pushing himself to his feet. 'I need to get to bed.'

A cold wind was blowing in from the darkened ocean, and Sigmar lurched towards the wall of the terrace, resting his palms on the cool stone and taking several deep breaths. It was foolish to try and blot out problems with strong drink, for they only returned all the more troublesome the following morning.

He looked down at the city gates below the terrace, surprised to see they were open. In Reikdorf, the gates were shut fast as night fell and did not open until the dawn. More corpse-carts no doubt.

Sigmar sighed, knowing that he was going to have to order Aldred to march alongside him to end the threat of the daemons. He was Emperor, and it was time to flex his imperial muscles.

'I had hoped to avoid coercing you, Aldred,' he whispered. 'What brotherhood does not create, force will not correct.'

The night was clammy and still, but the fogs had cleared enough to reveal a portion of the marshes stretching off into the distance. It was not an inspiring view, for the land around Marburg's walls was desolate and uninviting, and the gibbous moonlight made them all the more threatening.

Looking northwards, all Sigmar could see was treacherous mist-wreathed bogs along the line of the coast. Nothing lived in those bogs, nothing wholesome at least, and Sigmar spat a mouthful of bitter phlegm over the edge of the terrace.

He was about to turn away when a column of cloaked figures emerged from the city, but this was no solemn procession of corpse-carts. Sigmar recognised Idris Gwylt at the head of the column, his white hair and beard dazzling in the moonlight. Behind him went twenty Raven Helms with the bronze-armoured Count Aldred leading them. Ulfshard shimmered in Aldred's grip, wreathed in ghostly blue light like a frozen bolt of northern lightning.

The Raven Helms escorted what looked like a captive in their midst, and Sigmar's eyes narrowed as he saw that it was Aldred's sister, Marika, her willowy form and golden hair unmistakable.

The column turned from the road and made its way into the marshes. The mist closed around them, and in a heart-stopping moment of realisation, Sigmar understood the nature of the offering that Idris Gwylt intended to make to the daemons.

# — FIVE —

# Daemon Moon

THIRTY OF SIGMAR'S warriors marched through the gates of Marburg with purposeful strides, their faces set and determined. The moonlight made their wolfskin cloaks glow, and reflected from the few pieces of armour they had been able to put on as Sigmar roused them from their beds. Wolfgart and Redwane followed Sigmar as he splashed from the roadway onto the boggy ground at its side.

He stopped, feeling the cold water seeping through the worn leather of his boots. Beyond the road, the marsh was shrouded in ghostly mist. Sigmar shivered as he remembered the last time he had seen such a desolate, soulless landscape. It had been ten years ago, when he had lain close to death and his soul wandered the barren wastelands of the Grey Vaults.

The souls of the damned haunted that netherworld between life and death, and these marshes would be little different. The mist writhed and coiled around itself, an opaque wall of grey with distant flickering lights bobbing in its depths.

'What in the name of Shallya's mercy is going on?' asked Redwane. 'Why are we here?'

'Aye,' said Wolfgart, still clad in his stained tunic. 'It's bad luck to fight beneath the dread moon, especially when it's full. No good can come of it.'

'We are here to save an innocent life,' said Sigmar, hefting Ghal-maraz in both hands. The runes worked into its haft shone in the moonlight, as though energised by the thought of wreaking havoc against creatures of darkness once more.

'What are you talking about?'

'You remember telling me about the Old Faith and their sacrifices of virgins?' asked Sigmar.

'Vaguely,' replied Wolfgart.

'Turns out they're not just stories after all. I saw Aldred lead the Raven Helms into the marsh with Marika as their prisoner. Idris Gwylt means to offer her to the mist daemons.'

'Bastard!' snarled Redwane. 'I'll break his skull open with my hammer and tear his damn heart out!'

Sigmar was surprised at the strength of Redwane's anger, but was pleased to see the outrage on his warriors' faces as word of what was happening spread amongst them. He turned to face the White Wolves, knowing that some might not survive the night. Wolfgart was right, it *was* bad luck to go into battle beneath the spectral light of the dread moon, but they had no choice if they hoped to save Marika's life.

'A deluded old man seeks to murder an innocent girl!' Sigmar cried, though the mist seemed to swallow his words, throwing back strange echoes as if to mock him. 'I will not allow this to happen, and I need your strength to stop it. Are you with me?'

As one, the White Wolves raised their hammers and roared their affirmation, as Sigmar had known they would. Though the thought of entering this terrible marsh was a fearful prospect, the Wolves would never dream of letting their Emperor go into battle without them.

Sigmar nodded and set off into the mist, splashing through sucking mud and icy pools of stagnant water the colour of pitch. He had no way of knowing exactly where the Endals had gone, for brackish water poured into every footprint and erased it in seconds. Sigmar wished he had thought to bring Cuthwin to Marburg, but wishes were for fools and children, and they would need to find the Endals without their finest tracker.

The mist closed around the Unberogen as they forged a slow, stumbling path into the marsh. Their passage was lit by the sickly glow of lifeless moonbeams, and strange burping and bubbling sounds gurgled from the bog. A whispering wind dropped the temperature, but did not stir the heavy mist.

Nightcrawlers wriggled in the reeds and flies buzzed low over the ground. Sigmar saw an enormous dragonfly droning softly as it hunted in the hungry glow of the moon. His skin crawled and the hairs on the back of his neck itched as though a clawed hand was poised to strike him. This marsh was not like the Brackenwalsch, which wore its dangers openly. It was a haunted place where death crept up on a man and took him unawares.

'Look!' shouted Redwane. 'Over there!'

Sigmar turned to where Redwane was pointing, and his eyes narrowed as he saw bobbing lights in the distance, like hooded lamps borne by weary travellers. He tried to remember if the Endals had carried such illumination. He thought they had, but couldn't be sure.

Still, he was wary. The old men of Reikdorf spoke of such lights in the Brackenwalsch. They called them doom-lanterns, for the treacherous illumination they provided was said to lure men to their deaths with the promise of safety. Pendrag had told him that such lights were merely ignited swamp gases or moonlight reflecting from the feathers of night owls, but neither explanation gave Sigmar much comfort.

If these lights were indeed those of the Endals, then they had to follow them.

'This way,' called Sigmar, setting off after the lights. 'Keep watch on the ground!'

Once more the Unberogen plunged deep into the marsh, the ground becoming progressively softer and wetter underfoot. Flies buzzed around Sigmar's head and he saw yet more of the lights surrounding them, flickering like dancing torches. Bubbles burst around his feet, sounding like the mirthless laughter of dead things.

Time ceased to have meaning, for the thick fog made it impossible to judge the moon's passage across the night sky. Sigmar looked up, wincing as the dread moon's leering face seemed to stare back at him. Ill-favour followed those who turned their faces too long to that malevolent orb, and Sigmar hurriedly made the sign of the horns.

He started as he felt something brush his legs, and jumped back, seeing a pale shape, like a darting eel beneath the surface of the water. Sigmar lifted his boot from the sucking marsh, the fine leather stained and ruined. A filmy residue of reeking ichor, like pale syrup, dripped from the buckles. Once they got out of the marsh, he would never wear these boots again.

Sigmar heard a dreadful cry, followed by a heavy splash behind him. He spun to see a group of men holding out their hammers to a fallen warrior who thrashed his arms in a hidden pool of murky water. Sigmar recognised him as Volko, a man who had fought at his side in the charge to rescue the Merogen flank at Black Fire.

Volko was waist-deep in the bog, but his armour was dragging him down swiftly. He reached for the outstretched weapons, but the marsh was not about to release its victim. Volko's head vanished beneath the surface of the water as he drew breath to scream, leaving only a froth of bubbles in his wake.

'Ulric save us,' said Wolfgart, stepping back from the water. 'I knew this was bad luck.'

Sigmar fought his way through the mud and water to the bog where Volko had died. Tendrils of fog gathered around the legs of every warrior, and it was next to impossible to tell solid ground from deadly bog.

'Move out,' ordered Sigmar. 'Check every footstep and stay close to your comrades.'

'What about Volko?' demanded Redwane. 'No warrior deserves to die without hearing the sound of wolves.'

Sigmar risked a glance into the darkened sky. 'You're right, lad, but this is a night when the wolves are silent and only the moon howls.'

'So we're just going to leave him?'

'We will mourn him later,' said Sigmar, setting off once more.

He had no way of knowing which way to go, but felt a slight pull to the north-east, as though Ghal-maraz knew better than he in which direction its enemies lay. Sigmar put his trust in the craft of the dwarfs and followed the wordless urging.

Wolfgart came alongside him, his eyes flicking from left to right.

'None of us are going to make it out of here alive,' he said.

Sigmar felt his fear, but said, 'Let none of the men hear you say that.'

'It's true though, isn't it?'

'Not if I can help it,' said Sigmar. 'We are Unberogen and there is nothing we cannot do.'

Wolfgart nodded, visibly controlling himself.

'You know we might have to fight the Raven Helms to save the girl,' he said.

'I know,' nodded Sigmar, keeping a close eye on the ground. 'And if that's what it takes, then so be it. I drove the Norsii from the empire for such barbarism, and I'll do the same to the Endals if that's what's needed.'

'Aye,' said Wolfgart. 'It's wrong is what this is. Utterly wrong.'

Sigmar halted and raised his hand. His warriors stopped with a series of splashes and curses. Ahead, more of the doom-lanterns were moving through the dark, but this time it appeared as though they were borne by indistinct, shadowy forms.

'Unberogen! Stand ready!' shouted Sigmar.

The White Wolves swung their hammers to their shoulders and formed a ragged battle line as best they were able.

The lights drew closer and the mist parted as the ghostly figures came into sight.

Idris Gwylt, eyes wide with surprise, halted at the sight of Sigmar. Laredus stood beside the priest of the Old Faith, supporting the weeping form of Count Aldred. The Raven Helm's face was grim and etched with regret. Of the twenty warriors he had led into the marsh, Sigmar counted only a dozen left alive.

Of Count Aldred's sister, there was no sign.

Redwane surged forward and lifted Gwylt by the throat.

'Where is Marika?' he roared. 'What have you done with her?'

SIGMAR SAW THE Raven Helms reach for their swords and knew that this desolate stretch of marshland might become a battleground in a matter of moments. It was madness, and he would be damned if this one moment would undo the long years of sacrifice spent in building the empire.

The Raven Helms looked to their ruler for orders, and Sigmar marched over to him. The tension racked up a notch, but instead of words of rebuke Sigmar said, 'Count Aldred, where is your sister?'

Ulfshard dropped from Aldred's hand, landing point down in the water with a soft splash as the lord of the Endals sank to his haunches. He buried his head in his hands and sobbed aching tears.

'We left her.' he cried. 'Ulric forgive me, we left her there.'

'Where?' asked Sigmar, kneeling next to Aldred. 'Tell me where and we will get her back. You and me both. This is wrong, Aldred, you know that.'

'It had to be done!' cried Aldred. 'A plague ravages my people and my brother is dead!'

Sigmar was shocked.

'Egil is dead?' he asked.

Aldred nodded, tears cutting clean lines through the mud on his cheeks. 'A few hours ago, and now my sister will join him in Morr's realm. It was the only way to save my people.'

'You are wrong,' said Sigmar.

Aldred wiped his sleeve across his face.

'What choice did I have?' he asked. 'Everything was being taken from us and only the sacrifice of a pure and noble born maiden could save us.'

Sigmar took Aldred by the shoulders and forced him to meet his gaze.

'You have been deceived,' he said, looking over his shoulder to where Redwane stood with his hammer poised to smash Idris Gwylt's skull to shards. 'Did he tell you that?'

'The daemons demanded a sacrifice!' shouted Gwylt, struggling in vain to free himself from Redwane's iron grip. 'And the girl went willingly! She knew that the land must be nourished by virgin's blood, as it was in the elder days. Aldred, you know I speak only the truth!'

'Shut your mouth, you dog,' snarled Redwane, squeezing Gwylt's throat.

Sigmar stood and snatched Gwylt's staff. He broke it over his knee before hurling the shards into the marsh. The Raven Helms still gripped their swords and the White Wolves were braced to meet their charge. With the wrong word, Sigmar could have a civil war on his hands.

'All of you listen to me!' he shouted. 'And listen well, your lives depend upon it. This is a black day for the Endals, for you have heeded the words of a madman. You are warriors of honour and this act shames you. Leading a young girl to her death in this evil place is a vile deed, and if she dies, I will damn your names for all eternity. This curse, if curse it is, will only be lifted if we seek out these daemons of the mist and destroy them. Now I am going to find Marika, and I am going to bring her back to Marburg. You can either come with me and regain your honour, or you can slink back to your homes and live the rest of your lives known forever as cowards and nithings, to be cast out and shunned by all men.'

Sigmar turned from the warriors as Aldred pushed himself to his feet. The count of the Endals rubbed the heels of his palms against his face, as though waking from a dreadful nightmare, and Sigmar saw the strength he had seen in Aldred's father.

'Aye,' said Sigmar, gripping Aldred's hand. 'Take up your sword, brother. We will get her back, I swear.'

Aldred lifted Ulfshard from the water, the blade's ghostly glow banishing the darkness with its brilliance. No trace of the foul marsh-water stained its blade.

'When my father died, light fled from our lives,' said Aldred, his voice choked with emotion. 'Since then I have lived in darkness. It has been so long that I cannot remember the light.'

'Help me rescue your sister and the light will return,' said Sigmar.

Aldred nodded, and a fierce determination shone in his eyes. He turned his gaze upon Idris Gwylt and said, 'Aye, and this old fool will lead us back to their domain or I will cut his throat.'

THE LAIR OF the daemons sat upon a large hill that reared from the heart of the benighted marsh. Banks of fog gathered at its base as the Unberogen and Endal warriors crept up its rocky slopes. Towering menhirs carved with spirals, circles and one-eyed monsters punctured the sodden gorse of the hill, like jagged teeth growing from within the body of the mound.

Nearly fifty warriors darted between the grotesque monuments as they approached the summit, keeping as low and silent as possible. The deadening qualities of the mist worked in their favour, and the clatter of plate and mail was muffled.

Sigmar kept his eyes upon the ridge at the top of the hill, feeling Ghal-maraz tingling in his grasp. The ancient weapon knew that evil creatures were near, and the urge to split their skulls coursed through Sigmar's veins. Count Aldred climbed next to him, while Wolfgart and Redwane followed close behind. The young White Wolf kept a tight grip on Idris Gwylt.

They were almost at the summit, and Sigmar halted, moving forward on his belly to a jagged, rock-crowned ridge that overlooked the daemons' lair. Looking through a gap in the rocks, he saw the top of the hill was in fact a vast crater, and the breath caught in Sigmar's throat at what lay within.

Colossal blocks of pale, moonlit stone lay scattered throughout the crater, all that remained of a city raised in a forgotten age by unknown hands. It covered an area at least the size of Reikdorf and Marburg combined, and Sigmar could only imagine the scale of the beings that had lived here if the size of the streets was any indication.

'Ulric's bones,' hissed Wolfgart, as he reached the ridge and saw the city. 'What is this place? Who lived here?'

'I don't know,' said Sigmar. 'Aldred?'

'Gwylt took Marika through the mist to the top of the hill. I know nothing of this place.'

'It looks like it was built for giants,' said Redwane.

'Then let's hope they're as dead as their city,' said Wolfgart.

All thoughts of the city's builders fled from Sigmar's mind as he saw a flash of golden hair below them in what looked like a crude arena. Marika was bound to one of the soaring menhirs, and Aldred cried out as he too saw her.

'Blood of my fathers!' swore Redwane. 'Daemons!'

Sigmar felt his blood chill as monsters emerged from the darkness. A host of vile creatures hauled themselves from lairs carved beneath the arena, and even from a distance they were repulsive.

There were around a hundred of the pallid-fleshed daemons, their bodies hairless and hunched. Bronze shields strapped to their torsos protected their wasted bodies, and barbed tails swayed beneath kilts of tattered mail. Each daemon carried a rusted weapon, either an axe or a spiked club, and beak-like snouts filled with savage, needle-like teeth snapped and gnashed as they closed on Marika.

Each of the daemons saw the world through but a single eye, and such a hideous aberration of form left Sigmar in no doubt as to their diabolical nature. More hideous than even the worst of the daemons was the loathsome creature that lurched and shuffled at the centre of the pack. Though shaped like its lesser brethren, this monstrous cyclops was much larger, the height of three tall men. Its limbs were bloated and its distended belly was like that of a woman on the verge of giving birth. Lank hair hung from this creature's skull like tarred ropes and two shapeless dugs of withered flesh hung from its breast.

Was this some form of abominable daemon-queen?

The vast creature advanced on Marika, and Sigmar's stomach turned as he saw a vile lust in its cyclopean features.

There was no time for subtlety here, only action.

Sigmar shouted, 'Into them!' and surged over the ridge with Ghal-maraz raised over his shoulder. The hammer's runes shimmered in the weak light, and the daemons let loose a gurgling shriek of warning at the sight of him.

The mass of Unberogen and Endal warriors charged after Sigmar, ululating war cries splitting the dead air with their ferocity. Wolfgart and Aldred charged alongside Sigmar, and the wiry count of the Endals pulled ahead of him, the desperate need to redeem himself and save his sister lending his tired limbs fresh strength. Redwane ran with a look of hatred twisting his young features. The daemons shambled from the arena towards them, brandishing their rusted weapons and answering the war cries of their enemies with hoarse roars of their own.

Sigmar sprinted downhill towards the arena, vaulting a fallen monolith and bellowing the name of Ulric. There was no way he could reach Marika before the daemon-queen tore her to pieces, but if nothing else, he would avenge her.

The running warriors struck the daemons in a clash of iron and bronze. As horrifying as the creatures were, they died as any creature of flesh and blood could die. Wolfgart's huge blade clove through three of the monsters with a single blow, while Aldred spun through the daemons with the elegant sweeps of a fencing master. Redwane killed with brutally precise hammer-blows, the heavy, wolf-shaped head spinning around his body in devastating arcs.

Sigmar fought to keep up with Aldred, smashing a daemon from its feet with a chopping blow from Ghal-maraz. The beast howled in agony as the runes on the dwarf weapon seared its flesh and crushed its bones. Another monster came at him, but Sigmar ducked a skull-crushing sweep of its axe and slammed the head of his hammer against the creature's midriff. Its belly split open and a bubbling gruel of stinking fluids spilled onto the hillside. Dank mist began forming in the bowl of the arena, and the vile smell of rotten meat increased on every stale breath of wind.

Sigmar pushed onwards, killing a daemon with every blow, but too many of the beasts were between him and Marika. All around him the battle raged, and the courage of his warriors, both Unberogen and Endal, was a thing of rare magnificence.

White Wolves fought with a brutal directness, always pushing forward with chopping blows from their hammers. Such weapons were designed for swinging from the back of a charging steed, but such was the skill of the Unberogen warriors that it made little difference to their tally of kills.

The Raven Helms fought to expunge the shame of leading their princess into the marsh, and each man cut into the daemons with no thought for his own defence, their swords stained with the blood of their enemies. The months of misery and suffering caused by these daemons were repaid in full, as the Endals vented their hatred and grief in every blow.

The daemons fought with equal ferocity, their axes and clubs landing with dreadful strength that smashed plate armour asunder, and tore through mail as though it were woven from cloth. Their limbs were wiry, but they were strong and brutal, and many a warrior had marched into this battle without armour.

Thick banks of mist rolled out from the enormous daemon at the centre of the horde, flowing up the hill in an unnatural tide. The stink of it was like a midden at the height of summer and it coiled through the battle like a host of wet grey snakes. Soon the entire hillside was wreathed in mist, and every warrior fought his own battle in the smothering fog, unable to tell friend from foe.

Blood stained the hillside as men and daemons hacked into each other. The Endals and Unberogen still pushed forward, but the greater number of their inhuman foes was beginning to tell. Their courageous charge slowed and finally stopped.

Sigmar caught up to Aldred, the Endal count's glowing sword blade a beacon in the obscuring fog. The mist seemed reluctant to close around Sigmar and Aldred, as though kept at bay by the magic of their weapons.

Redwane fought towards them.

'The girl!' he shouted. 'Get to the girl!'

Sigmar saw the hideous beast rear over the Endal princess. It reached for the struggling girl and let out a screeching, gurgling cry of triumph. Aldred cried out in despair, but no sooner did the daemon-queen touch Marika, than it recoiled as though burned. It loosed a hideous shriek, its monstrous features twisted in revulsion, as though disgusted by the young girl before it.

Aldred fought at Sigmar's side. Together they cut a path through the daemons, parting the mist before them with their enchanted weapons. Side by side, Emperor and count slew their foes, each protecting the other, and each fighting as though they had trained together since childhood. Their weapons wove killing arcs, and Sigmar sensed a kinship between these wondrous artefacts, as though they had slain creatures of the dark together in ages past in the hands of their makers. Though forged by craftsmen from very different races, oath-sworn pacts of ancient days still bound the fates of the weapons.

The moment passed, and Sigmar felt stone beneath his boots as he stepped onto the marble-flagged floor of the arena. He killed another monster as Aldred slew the last of the daemon-queen's protectors and ran to his sister. Marika still screamed and wept in terror, sagging against the chains that bound her to the menhir.

'So much for willing, eh?' said Redwane, coming alongside Sigmar.

The daemon-queen backed away from them, though it hissed and spat in Marika's direction. The sounds of battle still raged on the hillside above, but Sigmar knew that the daemons' curse would only be ended with the death of this monster.

'Let's finish this,' said Sigmar.

'Gladly,' agreed Redwane.

The two warriors charged towards the daemon-queen, but they had travelled no more than a few yards when the ground underfoot transformed from solid marble to sucking mud and water. Redwane stumbled, and Sigmar sank to his calves.

'Sorcery!' cried Redwane, hauling himself from the mud and pushing on. Sigmar extricated himself and splashed over the boggy ground after Redwane. Columns of yellow fog boiled from the suddenly marshy ground, and a powerful stench like rotten eggs assailed him. He gagged on the acrid mist, feeling his guts rebel at the foulness. In seconds, he was as good as blind.

A shadow moved in the fog, and Sigmar threw himself to one side as a huge clawed arm slashed towards him. He splashed into the stinking water as filth-encrusted talons flashed over his head, a hand's span from decapitating him. He tasted the rank marsh water the daemon-queen had conjured.

Sigmar coughed and spat the black fluid clear, rolling in the mud as a huge, clawed foot slammed down. He swung his hammer, and the creature shrieked as the ancient weapon struck its wet and spongy flesh.

Redwane's hammer tore into the creature's side, and a froth of blood and lumpen matter spilled from the wound. That matter flapped and writhed as though alive, but thankfully sank into the swamp before Sigmar could see its true nature. The White Wolf's hammer was a blur of dark iron, slamming home again and again into the daemon-queen's flesh.

Sigmar struggled to his feet in the slippery mud, feeling the desire of the swampy ground to suck him down to his death. The beast lurched towards Redwane, faster than its bulk would suggest, and its clawed arms plucked him from the ground. The mist closed in around the combat, and Sigmar heard Redwane roar in pain, before his cries were suddenly silenced. A heavy splash sounded, and Sigmar swung Ghal-maraz up to his shoulder.

A bloated shape moved in the mist, and the daemon-queen loomed over him, its lank hair whipping around its head as it snapped at him. Sigmar threw up his hammer, holding it above his head with both hands, and the creature's beaked jaw snapped down on the haft.

The force of the bite drove Sigmar into the sodden ground, and marsh water sucked greedily at his body, pulling him deeper into the mire. The monster's foetid breath enveloped him, and gobs of stinging drool spattered him as it tried to bite through Ghal-maraz. Mud rose past his waist, and bubbles burst around him as he sank even further.

A flash of movement caught Sigmar's eye as a dark shape leapt to the attack.

Sigmar's heart leapt as he saw Redwane. The young warrior's mail shirt was shredded, splintered links falling from him like droplets of silver. Blood soaked his side where the daemon-queen had torn his flesh, but the fury of battle was upon him and no force in the world was going to stop him.

Redwane yelled, 'Ulric give me strength!' and brought his hammer down over his head.

The weapon thundered against the side of the daemon-queen's head, and its lower jaw was smashed from its skull. Greenish-brown blood spattered Sigmar, and the pressure on his arms vanished. He wrenched Ghal-maraz free, and swung it one-handed over the splintered remains of the monster's chitinous beak. All his strength was behind the blow, and the head of the rune hammer slammed into the daemon-queen's eye.

It burst like a ruptured bladder, showering Sigmar and Redwane in reeking gelatinous fluids, and the daemon-queen howled in agony. The enormous beast crashed down, its flailing arms clutching its ruined socket. Blood squirted from the wound, and the mists that cloaked it began to fade as its life bled out. The monster convulsed in its death throes, and it vomited an enormous slick of wriggling things that flopped and thrashed like landed fish.

Sigmar struggled to free himself from the sucking marsh, as he felt the ground begin to solidify around him. He had no wish to be trapped when the magic that had transformed the stone to swamp was exhausted.

'Need a hand?' asked Redwane. His face was deathly white, and Sigmar saw how deeply the daemon-queen had cut him. Bright blood flowed from his side and drenched his leggings.

'If you can,' said Sigmar.

'I think I'll manage,' said Redwane, taking hold of Sigmar's wrist and pulling. Though his face contorted in pain, Redwane hauled Sigmar free of the mud without complaint. Sigmar got to his feet, feeling that the ground beneath him was solid stone once more.

'Right,' whispered Redwane, 'I think I'll lie down now.'

Sigmar caught the youth as he fell, and laid him down gently before lifting the torn mail from his body. The skin was ashen and slick with blood, three parallel scars running from Redwane's ribs to his pelvis.

'I need water!' shouted Sigmar,

'Damn, but that stings,' hissed Redwane. 'The bitch was quicker than she looked.'

'These?' asked Sigmar. 'Ach, they're nothing, lad. I've had bigger scars from the bites of Ortulf's fleas.'

'That old dog must have some damn big fleas,' said Redwane, gritting his teeth against the pain. 'Perhaps Wolfgart should throw saddles on them and we'll fly into battle.'

Sigmar smiled and looked uphill to where Wolfgart and the White Wolves stood triumphant with Laredus and the Raven Helms amid a field of corpses. Daemons and men lay scattered across the hillside, for it had been a battle won with the blood of heroes. The dead would be mourned in time, but for now, the victory belonged to the living.

'Here,' said a voice at Sigmar's side. 'Water.'

Sigmar looked up into Aldred's battle-weary face. The Count of the Endals and his sister stood over Sigmar. Aldred held out a leather canteen. Sigmar took it and poured clear liquid over Redwane's wounds.

'Will he live?' asked Marika, dropping to her knees beside Redwane.

'His wounds are wide, but shallow,' said Sigmar, trying not to think of the filth encrusted on the daemon-queen's claws. 'So long as the wounds do not fester, I believe he will live.'

'That's good to know,' hissed Redwane.

'He will receive the best care in Marburg, my emperor,' said Aldred.

'I will nurse him myself,' promised Marika.

Aldred offered Sigmar his hand and said, 'I have been a fool, my friend. I doubted your vision, and my father's death blinded me to its truth. Idris Gwylt fanned the flames of that doubt and his dark faith almost cost me the life of my sister.'

'He promised my sacrifice would save our people,' said Marika, and Sigmar was impressed at how quickly she had recovered her composure after so close a brush with death. Clearly Endal women were as hardy as those of the Unberogen. 'His lies had me convinced that only I could save us, that I should walk into the marsh and let that... thing devour me.'

'Aye, and for that he will pay with his life,' said Aldred. 'I will curse his soul to eternal torment with a thrice death in the waters of the marsh.'

'It is no more than he deserves,' said Sigmar.

Marika rose from Redwane's side and Aldred took her by the hand, holding it as though he meant to never let go.

'The mists are lifting,' said Aldred. 'I think the journey out of the marshes will be happier than the journey in.'

'Indeed it will,' agreed Sigmar, 'but we should move quickly. It will be dark soon.'

Aldred nodded and led Marika away as Wolfgart came over to help him with Redwane.

'Well, lad,' said Wolfgart. 'You have fought daemons now. Was it all you hoped for?'

'Oh yes,' snapped Redwane. 'I've always wanted to be mauled by a fat daemon bitch.'

Wolfgart grinned, tearing strips from the lining of his cloak to use as bandages.

As Wolfgart bound Redwane's wounds, Sigmar looked over at the mouldering corpse of the daemon-queen, picturing how the creature had recoiled from its intended victim.

'There is one thing I don't understand,' said Sigmar. 'Why did the beast not kill Marika? I thought daemons hungered for the blood of virgins.'

'Trust me,' said Redwane with a sly grimace. 'That lass is no virgin.'

## ━◄ SIX ►━

# Troublesome Kings ·

COUNT ALDRED RENEWED the Sword Oath of his father in the main square before the Raven Hall, dropping to one knee and lifting Ulfshard for the Emperor to take. Cheers echoed from one end of Marburg to the other as Sigmar took the ancient blade and then handed it back to Aldred, thus sealing their pact of confraternity.

Dawn had been lighting the eastern horizon when the battle-weary but elated warriors emerged from the marsh. They bore their dead but, after the noxious reek of the swamps, the sweet smell of clean, sea air banished any thoughts of grief.

All through the journey back to Marburg, bodies had floated to the surface of the swamp, as though the defeat of the daemons had freed them to return to the world above. The unique properties of the bog water had preserved the bodies remarkably, and in time they too would be recovered and sent into the next world with honour.

Within days of Sigmar's return, Cradoc reported a marked drop in new cases of lung rot, and soon it was clear that the worst had passed. The number of corpse-carts leaving the city dwindled, and those that had fled to the country to avoid the pestilence now returned to their homes. The city came back to life, and the oppressive gloom that had hung over it for so long was banished as light and wonder returned. The indefatigable human spirit, which had been on the verge of being snuffed out, had held on, and now bloomed stronger than ever.

Sigmar and his warriors remained in Marburg for another week, hailed as saviours and showered with gifts from a grateful populace. As she had promised, Princess Marika nursed the wounded Redwane personally, but Sigmar ensured that Cradoc was never far away. When Redwane complained about such a prudish chaperone, Wolfgart settled the matter by pointing out that Redwane would need to keep his hands to himself or take Marika as his wife, for Aldred would be well within his rights to kill him if he ever found out that his sister had been taken advantage of. Having heard the gruesome details of Idris Gwylt's execution, Redwane was in no mood to count on Aldred's forgiveness, and his complaints ceased.

Gwylt had suffered the hideous fate of a thrice death, and even Sigmar had blanched when he heard the details. The priest had been fed a broth laced with poisonous white mistletoe berries, and then led in chains to the edge of the marsh. A slaughterman then broke his crudely-shaven skull open with three precisely measured blows from an iron-tipped cudgel. Barely alive, Gwylt was dragged into the sucking bogs of the swamp, where Aldred slashed Ulfshard across his throat. Poisoned, dying from numerous skull fractures and with his lifeblood pouring from his neck, Laredus completed the execution by holding Gwylt beneath the marsh water until his feeble struggles ceased.

With so many 'deaths' inflicted upon the priest in quick succession, his soul would not know when to flee the body until it was too late. Gwylt's flesh would never decay in the depths of the swamp, and his soul would remain trapped in the corpse for all time.

The priests of Morr had protested at such a harsh punishment, for to deny a soul its final journey went against the sacred tenets of their faith. Their pleas for clemency fell on deaf ears, for the Endals had practised this form of execution for centuries, and no one could deny that such a painful death was richly deserved.

The Unberogen left Marburg in high spirits, despite bringing nine mounts back home without their riders. They travelled through a realm that was coming to life once more, the last remnants of the mist daemons' curse lifting as the strength of the land emerged resurgent from its imprisonment.

Two months to the day after setting out for the city of the Endals, Sigmar led his warriors back across the Sudenreik Bridge and into Reikdorf.

SIGMAR PINCHED THE bridge of his nose between his thumb and forefinger, and sipped the herbal infusion Cradoc had prepared for him. His head hurt, though he had suffered no injury to make it ache. Rather, it was the incessant demands on his time that caused this headache. Uniting the tribes of men had, it turned out, been the easy part of forging the empire.

He sat in his private chambers, reclining on his bed with Ortulf, Kai and Lex curled at his feet. A freshly banked fire crackled in the hearth and the soothing aroma of wood smoke helped ease the pain behind his eyes. Since returning from Marburg, the business of gathering his warriors for an expedition to Jutonsryk had occupied his every waking moment, though there had been some good news to lighten Sigmar's days.

As spring's goodness blessed the land with warmth and life, Maedbh of the Asoborns gave birth to Ulrike, who came into the world with a lusty war cry on her lips. The joyous Wolfgart paraded his daughter through the city streets with tears of wonder spilling down his cheeks, and the people of Reikdorf had showered them both with handfuls of grain, earth and water.

Wolfgart and Maedbh honoured Sigmar by asking him to be Ulrike's sword-guardian, a role traditionally filled by the closest friend of the parents. Sigmar accepted the great responsibility and solemnly swore to protect the child should they die.

At the child's birthing ritual, held on a hillside to the east of Reikdorf, a priestess of Shallya named Alessa lit a fire and anointed Ulrike's head with three drops of water taken from a nearby spring. As each droplet fell, she recited the Blessing of Welcome. 'A little drop of the sky on thy little forehead, beloved one. A little drop of the land on thy little forehead, beloved one. A little drop of the sea on thy little forehead, beloved one.'

Alessa then placed a heart-shaped locket of silver around Ulrike's neck and said, 'The heart of Shallya to shield thee from the fey, to guard thee from the host, to cloak thee from the wicked, to ward thee from the spectre, to surround thee and to fill thee with grace.'

With Ulrike protected against dark sorcery, Alessa then immersed her in the cold spring with a silver and gold coin in each hand to honour the powers of the moon and sun. Wolfgart held the crying child in the fast-flowing water as the priestess filled her palm with earth and rubbed it over the child's belly, arms and legs while singing a prayer of protection and health.

With the father's duties complete, Wolfgart handed Ulrike to Maedbh, who completed the ritual by taking Ulrike and touching her forehead to the ground as she recited a prayer to Morr. This last act was to ask the god of the dead to seal the gate between the previous world and this one, for no others should cross the threshold of life.

With the correct rites observed, Ulrike was handed to Sigmar, who lifted her towards the sky, for to move a child downwards would forever doom it to remaining lowly in the world, never able to rise to distinction or wealth.

This had been a rare moment of joy in a spring that brought ill news to Reikdorf every week. A haphazard pile of rolled parchments sat on a table beside Sigmar, each one a letter from his counts that bore news of their lands and people.

They made for grim reading.

In the north, Pendrag and Wolfila sent word of increasing raids by Norsii Wolfships, the dark-armoured Norsemen marauding settlements many miles inland as well as those on the coast. The Norsii were attacking with ever more frequency, and the cunning of their leaders was all too apparent in their choice of targets. Most of the raids had come at a time when the majority of the menfolk were gathering for sword musters in distant towns, and Sigmar sensed more than simple luck in the Norsii's timing of their attacks.

Survivors of the raids carried south the names of two warlords, names that spoke of the naked brutality of the Norsii. Cormac Bloodaxe was said to be a towering warrior in black armour, who fought in a frenzy with a mighty twin-bladed axe of red fire, while Azazel was a lithe swordsman with dark hair, who delighted in cutting his opponents apart a piece at a time.

So far, the raids had been confined to the northern coastline, though Pendrag warned that it would not be long before the Norsii grew bolder.

That was a problem for another day, for the greenskins on the eastern mountains were once again daring to venture from their mountain lairs to raid and kill. Amid the tall tales of her sons' achievements, Freya of the Asoborns warned that a growing number of settlements in the foothills of the Worlds Edge Mountains were being raided by orcs. Scouts who had ventured into the mountains found no sign of any greenskin forces of any great size, though Sigmar knew it was only a matter of time before a powerful leader emerged and sought to weld the tribes together once more.

Further west, progress on the stone roads linking Reikdorf with Middenheim and Siggurdheim had slowed considerably. Attacks from forest beasts were an almost daily occurrence. Sigmar had tasked more men to patrol the roads and protect the work gangs, as well as increasing their pay to tempt others to volunteer for the roads' construction. Alfgeir had urged him to put those who broke the law to work, but Sigmar was loath to use such labour. He wanted men to work with pride, and to feel that they had participated in something worthwhile. Men forced to work under the lash would never build something worthwhile, and Sigmar did not want his empire to be built on the backs of criminals.

In the south, Count Markus spoke of his people's attempts to reclaim their tribal domains, for the orcs, trolls and twisted vermin-beasts from beneath the mountains had grown bold of late. During the wars against the greenskins, many of the Menogoth hill forts had been destroyed, and their people slaughtered or taken beyond the eastern peaks as slaves. The Menogoths had been on the verge of extinction, and taking back their ancestral lands with so few warriors was no small challenge. Markus was a canny leader of men, and the Menogoths a hardy, pragmatic tribe, and not even dark rumours of the dead rising from their mountain tombs dissuaded them from the task.

Sigmar sighed, sipping his herbal infusion and wondering if the world would ever allow him to be free from protecting his people. No matter how many warriors he could call upon, there was always a threat building somewhere, if not from beyond his lands then from within them. Sigmar's thoughts darkened as he thought of the audience with Krugar and Aloysis earlier that afternoon.

With the looming threat of extinction lifted, the counts of the empire were free to turn their gazes on ancient grudges and long-standing feuds with neighbouring tribes. Both Krugar and Aloysis had sent bleating letters, once again claiming the other was sending masked raiders across their borders to harass their people's settlements, burning crops, killing livestock and stealing grain. Of course, both counts denied they were doing any such thing, citing years of border disputes and blaming the other for their woes.

In the end, Sigmar had summoned both counts to Reikdorf to put an end to the matter.

THE ATMOSPHERE IN the longhouse was tense, the crackle of the fire and the distant noise of the city beyond the only sounds to disturb the brooding silence. Sigmar sat upon his throne at the far end of the hall, his crown glittering upon his brows and Ghal-maraz laid across his lap. A wolfskin cloak spilled around his shoulders, and the foulness of the emperor's mood was obvious.

Alfgeir stood behind Sigmar, his bronze-bladed sword unsheathed and held with its point resting on the floor. Eoforth sat to Sigmar's left, with a long, rolled-up length of hide parchment laid across his lap. Neither man looked at the counts, and disappointment was etched into both their faces.

Aloysis, lean and immaculately presented, was a hawkish man with a closely trimmed beard and hooded eyes. The Cherusen count was precise in movement and thought, the very antithesis of his people, who were wild and rough foresters proficient with axe and bow. His robes of crimson and emerald were richly appointed, and a golden chain with a silver eagle at its centre hung

around his neck. A vivid yellow cloak was thrown rak-
ishly over one shoulder, and a long Cherusen dagger with
a beautifully inlaid scabbard of mother-of-pearl was
sheathed at his hip.

Across from Aloysis was the grim-eyed count of the
Taleutens. Krugar was a wild-bearded giant of a man in
gleaming scale armour, formed from intricately carved
leaves of silvered iron. Sheathed in a plain scabbard of
dark leather was Utensjarl, a curved cavalry sabre said to
have been forged by Talenbor, the first king of the
Taleutens. Krugar had the bow-legged stance of a seasoned horseman, and when the Taleutens made war, he
rode with the Red Scythes, the lancers who had broken
the orc line at the Aver. Krugar's cheeks and neck were tattooed with jagged lines of red and gold, and his gaze
smouldered with long-burning anger.

Neither count deigned to look at the other, and Sigmar
knew this dispute would not be settled without angry
words. Sigmar nodded towards Aloysis, and the count of
the Cherusens did not hesitate to speak.

'This situation is intolerable, my emperor,' began Aloysis. 'Taleuten riders regularly cross the Taalbec river and
spread terror and destruction amongst my people.
Already nine Cherusen villages have suffered at their
hands, losing grain and precious supplies for the winter.'

'Pah,' sneered Krugar. 'If my riders were crossing into
your territory to raid, your people would not have food
to last them a week. Taleutens know how to pick the land
clean.'

'You see?' cried Aloysis. 'The braggart admits his crimes
before you! I demand justice!'

'I admit nothing, you fool,' roared Krugar, gripping the
hilt of his sabre. 'It is you who sends axemen across the
river! Your logging gangs hack down trees from land that
is not theirs and float them down-river to Cherusen lum-
ber yards in the Howling Hills.'

'A fool, am I?' roared Aloysis, the veins standing out on his neck as his hand flashed to the engraved hilt of his dagger. His eyes bulged, making him look like one of the painted Wildmen of his tribe. 'I'll not suffer your lies and insults any longer, Krugar.'

'Lies? You are the one poisoning the air with falsehoods!'

'Enough!' roared Sigmar, rising from his throne. The two counts ceased their bickering as he strode towards them. He glared first at Aloysis and then at Krugar, his expression softening in regret.

'It saddens me how soon you forget the brotherhood we forged in blood,' said Sigmar. 'Can you not remember how your souls soared at the Pass when the orcs broke and ran? Has the golden memory of that shared victory faded from your thoughts?'

'Never, my lord!' said Aloysis. 'I will take the glory of that bloody day to my grave.'

Krugar drew his sword and held it before Sigmar. The silver blade was etched with the dwarf rune for Black Fire Pass. 'Each time I unsheathe Utensjarl, I am reminded of that great battle!'

'That day brought us together,' said Sigmar, 'all men joined in unity and fighting as one race. We stood before the largest army this world has ever seen. We proud few stood against that army, and we defeated it.'

Sigmar pointed to the huge orc skull that hung on the wall above his throne, that of the warlord who had led the greenskin horde at Black Fire Pass. Larger than the mightiest stallion's, the skull boasted two enormous tusks that jutted from the lower jaw like those of the mythical beasts of the Southlands. Even in death, the fearsome power of the monster once known as Bloodfang was palpable.

'The world will never see its like again, yet here we are, a year from that day and you squabble with a brother whose warriors stood shoulder to shoulder with you in the battle line. Sword Oaths were sworn in the years before Black Fire Pass and we renewed them by the flames of Marbad's pyre. Or at least I thought we did.'

'My Sword Oath is yours,' said Aloysis immediately. 'My *life* is yours.'

'And mine also, Lord Sigmar,' said Krugar, unwilling to be shown up before his rival. 'I gave my oath to your father and I gave it again to you, freely.'

'Aye, you both swore Sword Oaths with me,' nodded Sigmar. 'And swearing an oath with me is the same as swearing an oath with your brother counts. Aloysis, have you forgotten how you fought alongside Krugar and my father to drive the Norsii from your lands? And Krugar, can you not remember when the charge of the Cherusen Wildmen split apart the greenskin trap that encircled your riders at the Aver?'

'An attack on one of you is an attack on me, remember?' continued Sigmar, waving Eoforth forward. 'Your lands are threatened, so I must ride to your aid. Each of you claims the other attacks you, but upon whom should I make war?'

Neither count answered as Eoforth handed the long roll of parchment to Sigmar. He undid the leather cord binding it, and unrolled a beautifully rendered map on one of the tables that ran the length of the great hall. Aloysis and Krugar gathered close to Sigmar, their enmity forgotten in the face of this incredible piece of cartography.

The forests, rivers and cities of the empire were picked out in coloured inks, each feature drawn with wondrous skill and precision. The territories of each tribal group were clearly marked, and golden lettering named the major settlements, rivers and mountain ranges.

Sigmar stabbed his finger into the centre of the map, where an exquisitely drawn castle in black ink represented Hochergig, the largest city of the Cherusens and seat of Count Aloysis.

'Do I march north and fall upon the Cherusens, smiting them with my wrath for attacking my brother Krugar?'

Without waiting for an answer, Sigmar's finger trailed downwards across the Taalbec River to where a great basin nestled in the eye of the forest. 'Or do I ride to Taalaheim, smash down its gates with my war-machines, and slaughter the Taleutens for daring to attack my friend Aloysis? Tell me, brothers, what should I do?'

One after the other, Sigmar looked each of his counts in the eye, letting them see his deadly earnestness. Indecision warred in their souls, the need to save face against their rival vying with the desire to spare their lands and people from the Emperor's wrath.

Sigmar did not want to march north, especially when his warriors were mustering for war against the Jutones, so he was prepared to offer each man a way out. He traced a line down the course of the Taalbec, which marked the border between the counts' territories.

'On the other hand, perhaps the reavers that plague your lands are simply brigands,' said Sigmar, thoughtfully. 'Mayhap there are several of these rootless sword bands with secret forest camps in both your lands. Instead of my army marching north, perhaps you might hunt them down and destroy those that skulk in your lands. That would resolve your difficulties and see an end to this matter would it not? Tell me your thoughts, my friends.'

Krugar saw the resolve in Sigmar's eyes and nodded slowly.

'I believe you may be right, my Emperor,' he said. 'Now that I look closer, these raids have all the hallmarks of banditry.'

The words were spoken without conviction, but that they were spoken at all was good enough for Sigmar. He looked over to Aloysis.

'Indeed,' agreed Aloysis, quick to seize the opportunity to save face that Sigmar had offered. 'I have skilled trackers who should be able to locate such bands.'

'That is great news, my friends,' said Sigmar. 'Then you will put an end to this dispute, and return to your lands as brothers. This is my command.'

'It shall be as you say, my lord,' said Aloysis with a bow.

'I will return to Taalaheim immediately,' said Krugar.

Aloysis turned to Krugar and the two counts embraced. The gesture was forced and awkward, but it was enough for now. Both men faced Sigmar, and bowed before withdrawing from the great hall. As the door shut behind them, Eoforth rolled up the map, and Alfgeir descended from the dais of the throne. The Grand Knight of the Empire sheathed his sword and sat on the edge of the table as Eoforth tied the leather cords around the map.

'Do you think they will do as you say?' asked Alfgeir. 'Krugar and Aloysis, I mean.'

'They had damn well better,' said Sigmar. 'Or else they will see what it means to incur my displeasure.'

'You don't really believe there are bandits in the forest, do you?'

'There are always brigands,' said Sigmar, 'but not raiding Cherusen or Taleuten lands. Each of them was right, they were being attacked by their neighbour.'

'Why? It makes no sense,' said Alfgeir.

'Human nature,' replied Eoforth. 'Without a common enemy, men will look for foes in the one place they can guarantee finding one: the past. The Cherusens and Taleutens have fought to control the fertile lands around the Taalbec for centuries. They only came together when King Björn forced them to join forces during the Winter of Beasts, you remember?'

'Aye,' said Alfgeir. 'The vermin-beasts from beneath the Barren Hills, I remember it all too well. I had my first taste of battle and blood in the snows around Untergard.'

'Long before I was born,' said Sigmar with a wry smile.

'Not *that* long,' muttered Alfgeir.

'The point is,' continued Eoforth, 'that powerful men with warriors to command will always look for someone to attack, and past grievances, unsettled wergelds and ancestral grudges are a good place to find them.'

'So what are you suggesting?' asked Sigmar.

'That we give our troublesome kings a better target for their warlike tendencies.'


THE SUMMER MUSTER began early, with riders bearing letters, sealed with wax and imprinted with the twin-tailed comet emblem of Sigmar, despatched to the furthest tribal lands of the empire to rouse the counts to war.

The marching season had come, and it was time to call Marius of the Jutones to account.

As the days of spring warmed to summer, hundreds of warriors pitched their tents in the cleared fields around Sigmar's capital, and over the next two moons, sword bands from the furthest corners of the empire arrived to join the Unberogen.

Autumn-hued Asoborns rode in on chariots of lac-quered black and gold, provoking cheers and wolf-whistles from the richly-attired Brigundians who waved their spears and bared their many scars to the fierce warrior women.

Armoured warriors from the Fauschlag Rock marched to Reikdorf bearing news from Pendrag and Myrsa, and Sigmar smiled as he read of his friend's tribulations in attempting to modernise a populace rooted in tradition. As difficult as Pendrag was finding the task, Sigmar could read between the lines well enough to know that he was relishing the challenge, and he was pleased at the optimistic tone of his friend's words.

The southern kings had sent two hundred warriors each: grim-faced Merogens in their distinctive rust-coloured cloaks, and slender Menogoth swordsmen in shimmering greens and golds. Taleuten horse archers rode though the campsite, showing off their skills to any who cared to watch, and competing with the shaven-headed Ostagoth bowmen for bragging rights in the coming march. Galin Veneva led the Ostagoths and he presented Wolfgart with a gilded bottle of *koumiss* and a promise of a drinking challenge at the end of this muster.

In addition to two hundred swordsmen, Count Krugar sent a company of his Red Scythes, armoured horsemen bearing glittering lances and wickedly curved sabres. Krugar did not attend the muster. Nor did the Cherusen count ride south, though the sending of five hundred tattooed warriors in earth-coloured cloaks and tunics was a grand gesture indeed. A hundred of the famed Cherusen Wildmen had also come to Reikdorf, their near-naked bodies crusted with coloured chalk and writhing tattoos.

By spring's end, over nine thousand warriors had assembled beyond Reikdorf's walls. The majority of these were Unberogen, though close to a third were men who called another land home. So great a host required feeding and watering, and since Sigmar had first begun to build the empire, the size of its armies had grown enormously. Consequently, the task of supplying them had grown ever more complex.

To make war so far from home, an army needed huge amounts of wagons, and thus Sigmar sent loggers out to chop down vast swathes of forest to enable carpenters to construct them. The lands around Reikdorf were squeezed of every last grain of corn, and the fletchers, bowyers and smiths of the city worked day and night to fashion thousands of arrows, swords and axes. Ropes, picks, levers, scaling ladders, saws, adzes and shovels were stockpiled alongside the heavy timbers of Sigmar's disassembled catapults. Such was their weight that new yokes had to be designed to enable the oxen to pull them. Mobile forges were hauled onto the backs of reinforced wagons, and hundreds of craftsmen joined the muster in order to maintain its equipment ready for battle.

Tens of thousands of pounds of grain, flour and salt were stacked alongside hundreds of barrels of cured meat and fish, and enough food to feed the army for several months was quickly assembled. Eoforth and a virtual army of scribes and bookkeepers kept track of the supplies coming in from the country, and yet more wagons were set aside for the quartermaster's records, for so large an army could not operate without a thorough understanding of the available resources.

As the sun rose on a glorious summer's morning, Eoforth declared the army ready to march, and the priests of Ulric burned offerings to the god of battles on a great pyre atop Warrior Hill. Led by Alessa, the priestesses of Shallya moved through the host of warriors, blessing their hearts and asking the goddess of mercy and healing to watch over them.

Sigmar, Wolfgart and Redwane rode through Morr's Gate at the head of two hundred White Wolves and took up their position at the front of the column. A great cheer echoed from the hills around Reikdorf as Redwane lifted the crimson banner of Sigmar high, and with the Emperor's banner unfurled, a rippling flurry of tribal colours rose above the assembled host.

The White Wolves led the way along the paved western road as the army set off to war.

* * *

A WEEK LATER, Sigmar's army was joined by five hundred Endal warriors in dark armour at the river crossing of Astofen. A cavalry squadron of Raven Helms led by Count Aldred and Laredus met Sigmar in the centre of the bridge where Trinovantes had died, and Sigmar wished good fortune to the spirit of his old friend.

Swollen with these reinforcements, Sigmar's army now numbered nearly ten thousand swords, with perhaps a thousand camp followers bringing up the rear. As the army halted each night, ostlers, craftsmen, drovers, healers, merchants and night maidens would make their way through the camp to ply their trade and maintain the army's battle readiness.

Spirits were high, and each night Sigmar moved from campfire to campfire, speaking with his warriors and listening to their tales. All the men were looking forward to teaching the upstart Marius the price of cowardice and driving his warriors across the sea. Sigmar would remind them that the Jutones were still men and that it would be better to bring them into the empire than destroy them, though the words sounded hollow, even to him. Marius had deserted them in their hour of need. What manner of ally would such a man make?

The army turned northwards, and Sigmar led the march across the fertile flatlands that made up the northern reaches of the Endal lands, skirting the marshes and swampland around the Reik estuary. Though the vast expanse of marshland was still a treacherous mire of sucking bogs and stagnant pools of black water, the mists no longer clung to the earth, and sunlight bathed the landscape in warmth.

At the Great North Road, which had once marked the boundary between the lands of the Teutogens and Jutones, Sigmar's army encountered a force of Thuringian warriors led by the giant Count Otwin. The berserker king had answered Sigmar's call to arms with four hundred warriors, painted men and women in a riotous mix of plate armour, mail shirts and baked leather breastplates. Otwin's warriors proudly bore the scars earned at Black Fire Pass, and Sigmar saw the berserker woman, Ulfdar, among the Thuringian host.

Otwin presented Sigmar with three prize bulls from his herd, and hundreds of Thuringian beef cows were slaughtered to feed the fighting men before they began the march to Jutonsryk. A grand feast was held on the Jutone border, with offerings made to Ulric, Taal and Shallya.

The following morning, with Otwin and Aldred at his side, Sigmar's army crossed the Great North Road.

The war against the Jutones had begun.

## ◄ SEVEN ►

# The Namathir

THE BOULDER SAILED through the cold morning air, describing a graceful arc before slamming into the damaged walls of Jutonsryk with a distant crack of splintered stone. Heavy wooden thumps and the creak of ropes signalled the release of the other catapults, and two more missiles were hurled towards the walls of the Jutone capital.

Accompanied by a bodyguard of ten White Wolves, Sigmar watched the rocks slam into the walls with a grim nod of satisfaction. The impact cratered the repaired stonework and broke loose a tumbling avalanche of masonry from the promontory.

'You knew your craft,' whispered Sigmar, speaking of whoever had raised these formidable walls, 'but I will break your work down, stone by stone if need be.'

The battlements were finally beginning to crumble, but Sigmar raged that he had allowed Marius so long to prepare his city's defences, for it had taken nearly two years of siege to bring Jutonsryk to the edge of defeat. To have constructed walls this strong must have cost Marius dear, but wealth was clearly one thing that Jutonsryk had in abundance.

Situated in a sheltered, sandy bay of the Reik's coastal estuary, Jutone settlers driven from their lands by the Teutogens had quickly recognised its worth as a natural harbour. They had built their settlement on a raised, leaf-shaped promontory known as the Namathir, and over the last twenty years Jutonsryk had developed into a thriving city of merchants. Traders arrived in Jutonsryk every day, their ships laden with exotic treasures from lands far to the south and, it was rumoured, from the mythical kingdoms beyond the Worlds Edge Mountains.

Dominating the coastline, Jutonsryk was an imposing city of formidable walls and solid towers. Snow shawled its battlements, and the machicolations worked into its towers were hung with icicles that looked like fangs of glass. Beyond the unbroken walls, the red clay roofs of the city huddled close together, and sails billowed from towers and flagpoles, proudly bearing the five-pointed crown of Manann.

Marius's castle sat at the highest point of the Namathir, a citadel of pale stone, slender towers and large windows of coloured glass. The majority of the city was built on the promontory's western slope, spilling haphazardly down to the harbour on the edge of the ocean's dark waters. The city's architecture reflected the maritime culture of the Jutones, and a great many of its buildings were constructed from the hulks of wrecked ships, or were hung with nets, ships wheels and brightly coloured figureheads.

A long wall of dark stone encircled the town, and solid drum towers topped with curving battlements shaped like the hulls of ships studded its length. A dozen warships sailed the wide estuary, blocking any passage down the river towards Marburg or out to sea. In the opening days of the siege, Endal ships had attempted to blockade the city, but the Jutone fleet had sunk them all in a horribly one-sided battle.

A single mast jutting from the icy water was all that remained of the Endal ships, and Count Aldred had sworn vengeance for their drowned crews.

Since then, Sigmar's army had battered itself bloody against the walls of Jutonsryk, and the first attempts to carry the walls by storm had taught them all a valuable lesson in underestimating their foe. Expecting the Jutones to be weak and cowardly, a tribe more suited to trading and commerce than battle, Sigmar's warriors had charged the walls with scaling ladders and grappling hooks.

As the warriors came within bow-shot of the crenellated walls, a long line of warriors with swarthy skin had appeared at the embrasures, carrying strange weapons at their shoulders. Like a thick bow laid upon its side and mounted on a length of wood, the weapons were loosed, and hundreds of men were cut down as volley after volley of short, iron-tipped bolts punched through shields and mail shirts.

The attack faltered, but kept going under continuous hails of bolts. By the time the ladders were thrown against the walls there were too few warriors to pose a serious threat to the defenders. The hardy souls who survived to reach the wall-head were killed without a single warrior gaining the ramparts, and the survivors fell back in disarray. Jutone axemen had sallied out and captured the ladders, and the humiliation of the defeat had stung the pride of every man in Sigmar's army.

Since then, the attack on Jutonsryk had proceeded at a more methodical pace, with retrenchments built on the ground before the main gate, cutting off the northern approaches to the city. Jutone sally parties hampered the work at every turn, and it was a full two months before the trenches and palisades were completed.

Sigmar's catapults were assembled within reach of the walls and the bombardment had begun. The walls of Jutonsryk had been built against the slope of the promontory and were as solid as the rock they stood upon. Hundreds of rocks had been hurled at the walls over the next seven months, but no practicable breach had been made. A number of fresh assaults were launched, warriors moving forward under cover of wetted mantlets and darkness, but blazing bales of straw turned night into day, and the chopping blades of the Jutone fighters kept the battlements clear of attackers.

The campaign, which had started in such high spirits, stalled, and cold and hungry warriors huddling around their campfires began to lose faith that the city would ever fall. The days grew shorter and the temperature dropped, but Sigmar rejected talk of lifting the siege and retreating for the winter. To withdraw would only give the defenders heart and further opportunities to fortify their city. Jutonsryk would fall, and it would fall to this army.

Winter closed in, and freezing storms blew off the sea, whipping past the Namathir and across the flatlands around Jutonsryk like a blade. Food grew scarce, and only convoys of wagons from Marburg and Reikdorf kept the army from starving.

Morale rose with the coming of spring, but any optimism that the battle would soon be over was dashed when fleets of strange ships bearing the flags of unknown kings arrived from the south, their hulls groaning with provisions and mercenary warriors with dark skin and brightly coloured tunics.

Spring turned to summer, with Sigmar's army growing ever more frustrated as the siege dragged on and every attack was repulsed. A section of the eastern wall was brought down at midsummer, and the Thuringians immediately charged towards the breach, screaming bestial war cries and brandishing their axes and swords like madmen. An unbending line of the southern mercenaries held the breach with long pikes, and Count Otwin's warriors were hurled back without ever reaching its summit.

By morning, the breach had been filled with rubble and refortified, but Sigmar's catapults had concentrated their efforts on this weakened portion of the wall. At first, it had seemed like this was the change in fortune the attackers had been waiting for, but that night Jutone raiders had made their way through the circumvallations and set three of the mighty war-machines ablaze before being caught and killed.

Sigmar had the night sentries put to death, and stationed a permanent guard of fifty men from each tribe to protect the remaining catapults, for he could ill-afford to lose any more of his precious war-machines.

Months passed, and still the walls of Jutonsryk stood in defiance of Sigmar as his army faced its second winter on the western coast. His anger towards Marius grew at the thought of spending frozen nights huddled around a brazier, wrapped in a wolfskin cloak and subsisting on meagre rations, while Marius ate heartily in his great hall before a roaring fire.

Sigmar shook his head free of such thoughts, knowing they would only cloud his judgement, and watched as sweating Unberogen warriors hauled fresh cart-loads of rocks from the shoreline far below. Drovers whipped the starved oxen that pulled the catapults' windlass mechanisms, and the process began again. He told himself that the damaged section of wall was ready to collapse. Once it was down, his warriors would storm the breach, and they would not stop fighting until Jutonsryk fell.

Footsteps on the wet ground made Sigmar turn, and he saw Count Otwin climbing the hill towards him. The Berserker King – for he had never shed that name, despite his new title – wore little to insulate himself from the weather except for a furred loincloth and a threadbare cloak of foxfur, yet he seemed not to feel the cold.

'Working such a machine is no task for a warrior,' said Otwin, staring in distaste at the backbreaking labour required by the catapults. 'Blade to blade, that's the way to kill a man.'

'Maybe there is no glory in employing such weapons,' said Sigmar, 'but if the walls of Jutonsryk are ever going to be brought down, then the catapults need to be manned night and day.'

'But where is the honour in such a weapon?' pressed Otwin. 'To kill a man without cleaving your axe through his body or feeling the sensation of his blade cutting your flesh is to deny the joy of battle and the sweetness of life when it hangs in the balance.'

'There will be plenty of opportunities to risk your life soon enough,' said Sigmar. 'The wall is almost breached and we'll be dining in the great hall of Jutonsryk before the first snows.'

'Damn, but I hope you are right,' said Otwin, his fists clenching and unclenching repeatedly. 'I lost a hundred warriors to those devils with the pikes, and their deaths must be avenged.'

Sigmar refrained from pointing out that those warriors had died when the Thuringian King had led a reckless charge against the breach without support. Even as he admired the man's courage, he disapproved of such reckless disregard for the order of battle. Raw courage had its place on the battlefield, but battles were won with discipline and courage alloyed together in the right balance.

Instead, Sigmar pointed to the fleet of mercenary ships beached on the sandy bay below them.

'You may not get a chance, my friend,' he said. 'If that breach breaks open as wide as I hope, then it is likely that those warriors will sail south. Those men are paid to fight, but they will not die for Marius.'

'Only a cur would fight for money,' snarled Otwin, flecks of blood dribbling down his chin as he chewed the inside of his mouth. 'And only a coward would pay others to fight his battles.'

'Marius is no coward, Otwin. He is a canny warrior, who has kept us at bay for nearly two years. We need to harness that and turn it to our advantage. Think how much the empire will flourish if Jutonsryk joins with us.'

'You expect too much, Sigmar,' growled Otwin. 'Marius will never submit to you. Even if I am wrong and he gives you his Sword Oath, the line of Marius will always have a troublesome streak of independence.'

'Perhaps,' allowed Sigmar, 'but that is a problem for another time.'

A WEEK LATER, the wall had still not fallen, though Sigmar's engineers assured him that it was only a matter of days until they formed a practicable breach. The first snows had not yet arrived, but the promise of their coming was on the northern winds.

Sigmar's camp was shrouded in darkness, with only a few fires scattered over the flatlands to keep the thousands of warriors warm through the night. As had become the custom each night, the leaders of the army gathered in Sigmar's tent with skins of wine to tell tales of their homelands and lay plans for the following day.

Goblets were filled, but the talk was muted, for the Jutones had driven yet another escalade from the walls. Six battering rams had been lost, three siege towers toppled and another four burned to ashes. The butcher's bill had been high and the screams of the wounded carried from the surgeons' sheltered camp.

Sigmar studied the faces around the fire, each as familiar to him as his own, for they had spent the better part of two years on campaign together. Otwin was still vast and threatening, but the years of battle had thinned him considerably and his ribs were clearly visible on his chest. Aldred too was thin, his features pinched with grief. The Endals had led today's assault and the majority of the dead were his warriors.

Wolfgart and Redwane had visibly aged since marching from Reikdorf. The young White Wolf had matured, and though his reckless spirit still burned brightly, he had seen too much death on this campaign to ever forget. Sigmar knew Wolfgart ached to return to Reikdorf, for his daughter would be nearing her second year, and he had not seen her in all that time. Sigmar had given Wolfgart leave to return to Reikdorf, but his sword-brother had refused, claiming that he would not be shamed by leaving a fight before it was done.

More wine flowed and as Sigmar outlined his plans for the assault on the Namathir promontory, Wolfgart commented on the oddness of the name, wondering aloud which tribe had chosen it.

'My father believed it was a word in the language of the fey,' Aldred said, not looking up from the fire that smouldered in the brazier.

'A fey word?' asked Wolfgart. 'How did Marbad know their language? They're long dead aren't they?'

'I heard they sailed across the ocean to paradise,' said Redwane.

'No, that's not right. I heard they betrayed their oaths of kinship with the dwarfs and were driven across the sea as a punishment,' put in Otwin, making the sign of the horns over his heart. 'Our wise men say they covet this land and leave changelings in the cribs of unwary mothers.'

'Why do they do that?' asked Wolfgart.

Otwin shrugged, and a thin line of blood leaked from the scars around the spikes he had driven through the muscles of his chest that morning. 'Out of spite, I suppose. This is a land of men, and they hate us for it. Why else do we have so many charms for newborns? You should know that, Wolfgart.'

Wolfgart nodded and said, 'The priestess of Shallya made sure that Ulrike was well protected.'

Sigmar saw the sadness on Wolfgart's face as he spoke.

'You will see Maedbh and Ulrike again soon, my friend,' he said.

'I miss their warmth,' said Wolfgart. 'It feels like a piece of me is missing.'

No words Sigmar could say would comfort his friend, so he simply nodded towards Aldred.

'You were talking about how the promontory got its name,' he said.

'Yes, it was when my father discovered Ulfshard in the depths of the black rock. He loved delving into dark places in search of the past, and it was during one of his many expeditions into the rock beneath the Raven Hall that he found a secret chamber. It was hidden well, but the enchantments concealing it must have faded over the centuries, and my father was able to gain entry. He found Ulfshard unsheathed and stabbed into the rock floor, surrounded by ancient bones that must have once belonged to a dwarf.'

'See!' said Otwin. 'I told you they betrayed their oaths.'

'Well, it certainly looked like whoever had last wielded Ulfshard had killed the dwarf,' said Aldred. 'Though it was clad in strange armour that crumbled to dust as soon as my father pulled the sword from the ground.'

'What else did he find?' asked Sigmar.

'Some golden coins, some clothes and a few books. He couldn't read them, but he spent his every free moment trying to translate them. He didn't get very far, as the language was very complex and seemed to have lots of subtle differences in meaning that relied on pronunciation to make them clear, but he did manage to understand a few words. He deduced that Namathir was part of a larger name that hadn't survived the passage of years.'

'So what does it mean?' asked Wolfgart when Aldred didn't continue.

'My father couldn't say for certain, but he thought that Namathir meant "star gem".'

'Then perhaps there are gems hidden beneath Jutonsryk?' suggested Wolfgart hopefully.

'It's possible,' allowed Aldred. 'Though surely the fey would have carried any such treasures across the ocean with them.'

'They left Ulfshard behind, didn't they?'

'It might be an idea to let that circulate among the men,' said Otwin. 'Could give them an extra incentive to get over the walls if they think there's treasure buried beneath the city.'

'No,' said Sigmar emphatically. 'When we take Jutonsryk there is to be no looting or unnecessary killing. Do you all understand that?'

Silence greeted Sigmar's pronouncement, each man weighing up how best to answer him.

'That might be easier said than done,' said Wolfgart eventually, with sidelong glances at Otwin and Aldred. 'You know what it's like in the heat of battle, especially in a siege. When you've fought as long and as hard as we have, and suffered so much loss, it's an easy thing to lose control when you've battled your way over a wall. Warriors who've seen their sword-brothers killed aren't too choosy about who gets in their way when they're out for vengeance.'

'Wolfgart speaks true,' said Otwin. 'When the red mist descends upon a Thuringian, there's no man can stop him until the killing rage is spent. Well, apart from you, Sigmar. You choked it out of me on the battlefield, but I do not think there will be many men like you beyond Jutonsryk's walls.'

Sigmar stood and lifted Ghal-maraz, holding it out before him. 'Tell your warriors that any man who disobeys me in this will pay with his life.'

'You have to allow the men some reward for taking the city,' said Aldred. 'They have camped out here for nigh on two years, and they'll need something to take back home or they will be reluctant to march out again.'

Sigmar considered Aldred's words and nodded.

'You are right,' he said. Tell the men that when Jutonsryk is ours, I will send a portion of its wealth to each of the counts to distribute among the warriors who fought to capture it for as long as they live. Will that suffice?'

'I think it might,' said Aldred. 'We can work out what that portion is later, but if our warriors know they're going to get some reward if the city is kept safe, then that should help stay their hands.'

'It had better,' warned Sigmar. 'I want to bring the Jutones into the empire, but that won't happen if we burn their city to the ground and murder its inhabitants.'

FLAMES FROM A burning siege tower flickered and danced on the timber walls around Sigmar, and the smell of mingled wood-smoke and seared flesh set his nerves on edge. Reaching up to wipe sweat from his brow, he felt the tension within the upper compartment of the siege tower he travelled inside. Sigmar wore his silver armour and a golden helmet, and bore an iron-rimmed shield with a spiked boss in one hand and Ghal-maraz in the other.

Wolfgart stood next to him, his enormous sword held at his side. The blade was safely in its scabbard, as the Unberogen warriors were too closely packed together within the siege tower to risk unsheathing it until the wooden ramp crashed down on the parapet.

'Ulric preserve me, but I don't like this,' said Wolfgart. 'We could die without even being within striking distance of the Jutones.'

'Don't remind me,' said Sigmar, looking through a gap in the timbers.

Yoked oxen, draped in shields and breastplates, hauled on thick ropes attached to a windlass mechanism set behind a covered position built in a patch of dead ground at the foot of the walls during the night. Each strained pull of the ropes drew the tower closer to Jutonsryk and an end to the siege. This high up, the tower rocked and swayed as it crossed the uneven ground, and Sigmar tried not to think of what would happen should it topple before reaching the walls.

A hundred warriors were packed into the siege tower, divided through the four levels, and a dozen archers crouched behind movable screens on its roof. Sigmar had positioned himself in the uppermost level of the machine aimed at the ramparts, closest to the towers protecting the city gates. The fighting was sure to be heaviest there, and that was where he needed to be.

It had taken the catapults another three days to finally smash down the damaged section of the city walls to the point where an armoured warrior could climb the rubble slope and still fight. A fresh sense of excitement galvanised Sigmar's army as the news of the breach spread. Swords were sharpened and armour polished to shine like new. This was to be the final battle and the gods would be watching, so every warrior desired to look his most heroic.

As Sigmar had predicted, the mercenary warriors who had sailed into Jutonsryk early in the campaign took to their ships soon after the wall collapsed. Though he understood why they were leaving, Sigmar felt nothing but contempt for these men. To fight for freedom, for survival, a noble ideal or to protect the weak were just reasons to go to war, but those who fought for money sullied the warrior ideals upon which Sigmar had founded the empire.

He had ordered every warrior in his army to fight, gambling everything on this assault, for there would be no second chance if it should fail. The camp that had housed

Sigmar's army for the last two years was dismantled, sending a clear signal to the Jutones that the battle was ending one way or another.

Six more siege towers had been constructed and sheathed in soaked animal skins, bringing the total number of towers to twenty-five. Taleuten archers built hundreds of mantlets to shelter behind while showering the ramparts with arrows, and every sword band fashioned dozens of scaling ladders from the detritus of the camp.

The Red Scythes, Raven Helms and White Wolves mounted their horses, ready to repulse any sallies from the city gates, and Cherusen Wildmen howled and screamed alongside Count Otwin and his Thuringian berserkers as they worked themselves up into a battle frenzy. Otwin had requested the task of storming the breach, and Sigmar had agreed, knowing that there were no better shock troops in the army. The Thuringians had failed to carry the breach once, and honour demanded they not fail again.

A series of heavy thuds on the armoured front of the siege tower told Sigmar they were within crossbow range of the walls. The mercenaries who had come to Jutonsryk may have left, but their new weapons had stayed behind. Once this siege was over, Sigmar resolved to have such weapons distributed throughout the empire.

'How long do you think?' asked Wolfgart, and Sigmar was surprised at the fear he heard in his sword-brother's voice.

'Not long,' said Sigmar, hearing a wild roar as the Cherusens and Thuringians charged the breach. The intensity of crossbow impacts on the front of the siege tower grew in volume, and, with every pull of the oxen, Sigmar saw the barbed tips of the bolts punch further and further through the hide and timber coverings draping the tower. Something bright struck the tower, and Sigmar smelled smoke as burning arrows thudded into the wood.

'Ulric save us, we're on fire!' cried Wolfgart.

'No we're not,' snapped Sigmar. 'The Jutones are loosing flaming arrow, but we're safe. The tower was soaked before we moved out.'

His words calmed the warriors around him, but the sheer volume of fire the tower was attracting would soon cause the timbers to catch light, regardless of how much water had been poured over it.

Screams came from above them, and a body fell from the top of the tower. Sigmar could hear the shouted curses of the Jutones and the thud of hooves on cold ground. The clash of iron on armour and the screams of the dying drifted over the battlefield.

'Stand ready!' shouted Sigmar, gripping the haft of Ghal-maraz, and feeling his heart race and his mouth go dry as he picked up his shield. 'Every man on his knees and get your shields ready. When that ramp goes down, get onto the walls as quickly as you can!'

The warriors around him lifted their shields and crouched on the wooden floor of the tower, a feat that was only accomplished with some difficulty given how many warriors were crammed together.

Sigmar felt the yardstick on the front of the tower strike the wall and shouted, 'Ulric grant you strength!'

He smashed the locking pin securing the tower's bridge free with a blow from Ghal-maraz, and daylight flooded the tower as the winch spun and the bridge dropped. It slammed down onto the ramparts, and a flurry of black-shafted arrows slashed into the tower. Many went high, but many more found homes in Unberogen flesh despite their shields and armour. Half a dozen arrows hammered into Sigmar's shield, but it was of dwarf origin and proof against such irritations.

With a fearsome war cry, Sigmar surged to his feet with his shield held out before him. A pair of arrows bounced from his shield, and he grunted in pain as another scored across his bicep. He sprinted across the ramp, and leapt to the ramparts, swinging his warhammer in a murderous arc. A Jutone tribesman with a bronze breastplate and armed with a short stabbing sword ran at him, but Sigmar smashed him from his feet before he could draw back his arm to strike.

Warriors poured from the siege tower, but the Jutones were not about to give up this section of wall without a fight. Unberogen fell with arrows jutting from their chests, and the Jutones dragged them from the walls with hooked pikes. The press of bodies from the tower was forcing the Jutones back and more and more of the Unberogen were gaining the walls.

Sigmar pushed towards the squat tower at the gate, kicking one enemy warrior from the walls and slamming another to his knees with the edge of his shield. His hammer struck left and right, killing with every stroke, and he pushed deeper into the mass of Jutone warriors.

Wolfgart fought with deadly sweeps of his enormous sword, killing handfuls of men with every stroke. The size of his blade ensured that he fought alone, but he was clearing the way for more warriors from the tower.

Smoke billowed from somewhere nearby, but Sigmar could not spare the time to see where. The Jutones had been driven back along the ramparts by his and Wolfgart's wild charges, but were gathering for a counterattack.

'On me!' he yelled. 'Wedge formation!'

Sigmar ran at the Jutones, hammered Ghal-maraz through an enemy skull, and threw his shield up to catch a pair of arrows loosed from the tower. Jutones surrounded him, and a lance stabbed into his side. The blade snapped on Sigmar's dwarf-forged armour, and he backhanded his warhammer into the lancer's face. More enemy warriors pressed him, but he drove them back with a wide sweep of his hammer that shattered armour, crushed ribs and splintered limbs.

The Jutones fled from his fury, jumping to the court-yard below or fleeing towards the great tower protecting Jutonsryk's main gate. More arrows arced downwards, but they flashed past Sigmar and clattered harmlessly from the battlements. A clash of iron and the scream of horses sounded from beyond the walls, and Sigmar looked down to see a mass of his cavalry fighting in the shadow of a burning siege tower. The oxen that had pulled it close to the walls were dead, skewered by heavy spears.

Sigmar realised what had happened in an instant.

Jutone spearmen had charged from a concealed sally port at the base of the tower to kill the oxen dragging two of the siege towers. They had succeeded, which left the warriors within the towers trapped and burning as archers loosed volleys of flaming arrows at their timbers. Before the Jutone raiders could escape, the Raven Helms had caught them and were cutting them to pieces.

Count Aldred, resplendent on a black gelding, plunged Ulfshard's blade into the chest of a Jutone captain armed with an enormous axe, as Laredus drove the rest of the Raven Helms towards the sally port.

'Unberogen!' shouted Sigmar. 'The tower! We need to get on the ground!'

Sigmar ran towards the tower as the last of the Jutones dragged the door shut. It was a thick slab of heavy oak banded with black iron, virtually impenetrable and proof against anything short of a battering ram.

Sigmar hammered Ghal-maraz against the centre of the door, smashing it to splinters with a single blow. The door flew from its frame, and Sigmar vaulted into the tower over its shattered remains. Horrified Jutones filled the room, and Sigmar gave them no chance to recover from the shock. His hammer struck out, and two Jutones died in as many strokes. Unberogen warriors followed Sigmar, slaying their enemies with sword and axe.

Sigmar led the way down the curving tower stairs. Arrows flashed upwards, ricocheting from the walls and off his shield. The level below the ramparts was also filled with Jutone warriors and a volley of gull-feathered shafts and iron crossbow bolts flashed. Sigmar's shield finally broke apart, and he hurled it aside as crossbow bolts hammered into the warriors next to him.

Sigmar charged the Jutones with a terrifying war cry.

Then he was amongst them and Ghal-maraz sang out. The fury of battle was on him, and Sigmar's world shrank to the space around him and the movement of blades and limbs through it. He fought with hammer, elbow and foot, using every weapon available to him to throw the Jutones back. Sigmar swept up a fallen short sword and hamstrung a Jutone archer, before charging for the stairs that led to the ground.

An arrow flashed past his head, and Sigmar pressed himself to the wall as another archer loosed up the spiral stairs. The arrow clattered from the walls and struck his breastplate, but its strength was spent and it fell clear. The spiral stairs were curved so as to impede a right-handed attacker from swinging his weapon. They were designed for swordsmen to defend, not archers. Sigmar charged down the stairs, keeping as close to the centre as possible so that any arrows would skitter around him.

He could hear shouting voices calling for more archers, and the clash of swords and shields. Sigmar glanced over his shoulder, to see grim-faced Unberogen warriors gathered behind him, their swords and faces red with blood.

'Let's take them,' he said, and spun around the last steps of the staircase. A line of archers knelt by the far wall of the tower's lower chamber, and no sooner had Sigmar appeared than they loosed. Sigmar threw himself flat, rolling beneath the slashing volley of shafts. Screams sounded behind him, and a second volley flashed overhead.

An arrow thudded into Sigmar's breastplate, and another bounced from his helmet. His dive had carried him to the archers, and he rolled to his knees, sweeping his hammer in a wide, slashing arc that shattered thighs, crushed kneecaps and scattered his foes like straw men. Another shaft ricocheted from his pauldron and sliced across his neck, drawing blood, but the wound was not deep.

Unberogen warriors poured from the stairs, following Sigmar into the Jutones. The men in the tower were doomed, yet they fought on, and Sigmar was forced to admire their courage even as he killed them. A screaming Jutone lancer tried to skewer him, but Sigmar batted away the barbed tip of his weapon with his forearm before slamming his hammer down on the man's skull.

In seconds it was over, the interior of the tower a charnel house of the dead.

Sigmar took a moment to catch his breath and let the visceral rush of combat drain from his body enough for him to think. Around him, Unberogen warriors roared in triumph, and Sigmar saw the potential for a massacre in every gap-toothed bloody grin. Worse, he saw his own lust for violence reflected in their eyes.

Sigmar felt a savage joy when he fought his enemies, but this was different, this was a war that could have been averted. Looking at the Jutone corpses, he knew that but for one man's ambition, these men would still be alive. He knelt beside the last Jutone warrior he had killed, a man with a family and dreams of his own no doubt, and wondered whose ambition was worse, his own or that of Marius.

Daylight and the clamour of battle sounded from beyond the doorway, and Sigmar took a deep breath. This battle was not yet won, and more would die before this day's bloody work was done.

## ◄ EIGHT ►

# A Darkness of the Heart

OUTSIDE, ALL WAS chaos. Smoke from burning siege towers painted the sky, and the walls were bloody battlegrounds where the difference between life and death could depend on a step in the wrong direction or an accidental sword thrust. The inside of the city reminded Sigmar greatly of Reikdorf, though he had no citadel to match that of Marius.

Rearing up from the Namathir like a collection of stalagmites, the citadel was a fortress within a fortress, with gates of iron, protected by a deep ditch and a barbican of solid, hoarding-covered parapets. Flags bearing Marius's crown and trident symbol flapped from the blue-tiled roofs of the towers, while flights of arrows arced from the highest ramparts.

Behind the citadel, the city of Jutonsryk spread down the flanks of the promontory to the sea, and Sigmar could feel the fear of its inhabitants. He read the pulse of the fighting in a second, and his masterful eye saw that the battle for Jutonsryk rested on a knife-edge. Wolfgart appeared at his side, his enormous blade wet and dripping.

'The walls are still holding,' cursed Sigmar.

'We're too exposed here,' said his sword-brother. 'If the Jutones counterattack from that citadel, we'll be slaughtered.'

'I know,' said Sigmar. 'We need more warriors inside the city.'

'Looks like you'll have some soon!' cried Wolfgart, looking along the length of the wall.

Two hundred yards to Sigmar's left, Count Otwin stood atop the breach, his naked, spike-pierced body red with blood, and his chained axe raised to the heavens in triumph. Thuringian and Cherusen warriors poured over the rubble, hacking down their fleeing opponents. Having fought their way through the bloodiest possible aspect of a siege, the berserkers and wildmen were drunk on slaughter and hungry for death.

Sigmar took Wolfgart's arm.

'Go!' he said. 'Put something between Otwin and the Jutones. He'll drown this city in blood if you don't.'

'Where are you going?'

'I am going to get more warriors inside the city.'

'The gate?' asked Wolfgart

'Aye, the gate, now go!'

Wolfgart nodded and dragged half of Sigmar's warriors towards the screaming Thuringians and Cherusens. Wolfgart wouldn't be able to stop the berserk warriors completely, but Sigmar hoped he could prevent the inevitable fury that followed the carrying of a breach from becoming a wholesale slaughter. He put that thought from his mind, and turned his attention to the task at hand.

He had around thirty warriors with him, hopefully enough for what he had in mind. More would follow when they realised that this gate tower had been taken, but these few were all he could count on for now.

'With me!' he yelled.

Sigmar followed the curve of the tower until he reached the cobbled roadway that ran between it and another gate tower just like it. The mighty gateway of Jutonsryk loomed in the torch-lit darkness between the towers, shuddering under repeated blows from an iron-sheathed battering ram on the other side.

The gate's heavy wooden structure was braced with thick timbers that had once been the keels of ocean-going ships. Giant chains of iron ran from the top of the gate to an enormous winch and wheel mechanism, which was protected by around a hundred Jutones clad in colourful tunics worn over mail shirts.

The gate's defenders carried heavy pikes, and were formed up in three lines facing the gate, ready to repulse any assault. Should the gate be broken down, any attackers would run into a solid wall of sharpened iron, or at least any attackers coming from the front...

A strident trumpet blast sounded from the tallest tower of the citadel, and Sigmar looked over his shoulder to see its iron portal opening. A glittering host of armoured horsemen wearing the blue cloaks of Jutone Lancers emerged, riding out to assemble beneath a vivid turquoise and green banner depicting a crown and trident.

'Marius,' whispered Sigmar.

Part of him wanted to charge out to face the king who had caused them to shed so much blood, but that part was Sigmar the warrior. To win this battle, he had to be Sigmar the Emperor. Marius would wait.

Sigmar turned to his warriors and shouted, 'For the glory of Ulric! The gate must open!'

He charged towards the gate, Ghal-maraz held over his shoulder. His warriors pounded after him, ferocious war shouts driving them onwards. They were feral hunters, warriors with the taste of blood on their lips and the fires of battle in their veins.

The Jutones cried out in alarm at the sight of them, a thunderous wedge of bloodstained warriors that howled like madmen. They tried to turn and face the threat to their rear, but in the confines of the gateway and with long, cumbersome pikes, such a manouevre was doomed from the outset.

Sigmar smashed his hammer through the spine of a Jutone pikeman, plunging his borrowed sword into the chest of another. The man fell, tearing the sword from Sigmar's hand. He shifted his grip on his hammer and swung it two-handed, killing again as he plunged deeper and deeper into their ranks. Unberogen warriors cut through the heart of the Jutone defenders, fighting with the strength of Ulric as they sought to emulate their Emperor.

Polearms were cast down and swords unsheathed as the Jutones realised their pikes were useless, and the battle for the gate devolved into a close scrum of stabbing blades and brutal axe blows. Sigmar's hammer was a blur of dark iron, slashing left and right as he slew the defenders of the gate without mercy. Swords and knives scored his armour, and a stabbing dirk sliced the skin of his arm.

Even with the bloody slaughter of the opening moments of the fight, the Jutones outnumbered the Unberogen three to one, and those numbers were telling. More of Sigmar's warriors were being cut down, and he knew it was only a matter of time before a lucky blow found a gap in his armour.

A screaming warrior in an orange-dyed tunic stabbed his sword at Sigmar, the blade lancing into his thigh. Sigmar grunted in pain and stepped back as he thundered his fist into the man's face. He spun away from a thrusting spear and backhanded his hammer into the Jutone warrior's chest. An axe clanged against his breastplate, and he dropped to one knee as his wounded leg gave out beneath him.

He threw up his hammer to ward off another sword blow, and an iron-shod boot hammered against his helmet. Sigmar rolled and ripped the helm from his head as dizziness swamped him. A pair of Jutone warriors closed on him with their spears aimed at his neck. They stabbed, but before their speartips struck a slashing blur of silver hacked the points from the ends of the polearms. Sigmar looked up to see Wolfgart roaring in anger as his sword swept back and clove through the first Jutone. His reverse stroke all but beheaded the second.

Bestial howls echoed from the gate towers and a host of near-naked warriors with painted and tattooed skin smashed into the Jutones. Wolfgart hooked his arm beneath Sigmar's shoulder and helped him to his feet. All around him, Thuringians and Cherusens were butchering the Jutones, hacking them to pieces with their swords and axes in a frenzy of bloodletting. King Otwin bashed a man's brains out on the cobbles, and a naked warrior with hooks embedded in his arms wrestled a Jutone to bloody ribbons.

Within moments, the Jutone defenders were dead, and the berserkers and wildmen roared their triumph in the torch-lit gateway.

Still groggy from the blow to the head, Sigmar said, 'What...? How did you get here?'

'You said to put something between Otwin and the Jutones,' said Wolfgart. 'I figured this gate would do.'

Sigmar watched as Otwin continued to slam the virtually headless body against the ground, the light of madness in his eyes.

'How?' gasped Sigmar, nauseous from the blow to his head. 'The red mist is upon him.'

'I told him you were in danger,' said Wolfgart, showing Sigmar an enormous dent in his breastplate. 'Though I had to let him hit me a few times before he knew who I was.'

Sigmar nodded, hearing the shrill blast of a Jutone cavalry horn.

'Get those supports down!' he shouted. 'The gate must open or we are lost!'

The Thuringians hurled themselves at the timbers bracing the gate and attacked them with ferocious axe blows. Wood splintered under the assault of blades, and one by one the supports came crashing down.

'Wolfgart,' said Sigmar, 'the winch mechanisms! I will get the one on the left, you take the one on the right.'

'It'll take more than you and I to open this!' cried Wolfgart, but he ran to the winch on the opposite side of the tunnel. Sigmar ran to one of the winches that lifted the gate and shifted the locking bar from the wheel. He dropped Ghal-maraz and began hauling on the spoked wheel, but the gate was designed to be opened by teams of horses yoked to the mechanism.

'It won't move!' shouted Wolfgart from across the gateway.

'Otwin!' shouted Sigmar. 'Gather your warriors and help us!'

The Berserker King looked up from his slaughter and bellowed in answer. Two score men ran to help Sigmar and Wolfgart, bending their backs to haul on the chains and winch. Sigmar's muscles burned with exertion, and he felt the sinews straining as he fought to push the mechanism.

A thin line of daylight appeared as the gate lifted a hand's span, and the Thuringian count bellowed at his warriors to push harder. Not to be outdone, the Cherusens chewed more of their wildroots and dug deep into their madness for strength. The line of daylight grew larger, and as the gate began to move upwards, Unberogen, Taleuten and Endal warriors crawled under and wedged iron bars beneath it. More warriors ran in to help with the winch mechanism, and Sigmar released his hold to allow stronger warriors than him to push.

He swept up Ghal-maraz as a squadron of black-armoured horsemen rode under the gate. Count Aldred and Laredus rode at their head, and the captain of the Raven Helms raised his lance in respect when he saw Sigmar. Two score Taleuten Red Scythes and a half-century of White Wolves were mixed with the Endal horsemen, and Sigmar saw Redwane carrying his crimson banner like a lance.

With the gates raised enough to allow cavalry within, the locking bars were dropped, and warriors streamed through the open gate. More horsemen rode with them, and Sigmar ran to a riderless gelding with bloodstains coating its flanks. He gripped the saddle horn and vaulted into the empty saddle. He looped the reins loosely around his wrist, and the horse reared, its front hooves pawing the air.

'Warriors of the empire!' he shouted. 'This is our moment! This is where we make our land whole. We will defeat our enemies and make them our brothers. Now ride with me!'

SIGMAR THUNDERED FROM the gatehouse at the head of a hundred and fifty horsemen, black-armoured Raven Helms, wild and bearded White Wolves, shaven-headed Taleutens, and Unberogen bowmen. They formed a wedge like a wide-bladed Asoborn spear aimed towards the heart of the Jutone defenders. Warriors on foot followed them in their hundreds, and the misery of two long years of siege was forgotten as they charged into the city of their enemies.

Trumpeting war horns sounded from the walls, and roars of triumph erupted from the attacking warriors as they saw their Emperor ride out with his banner unfurled like a slick of blood on the air. A Jutone flagpole was hacked down from the gatehouse towers, and Sigmar's army surged towards the opened gate.

From the back of his horse, Sigmar saw the Jutone lancers fighting at the breach in the city walls, riding down any warrior who survived the hails of arrows from the citadel's towers. A warrior in golden armour with a silver helm led the Jutone cavalry, riding beneath Marius's banner. Though he could not see the warrior's face, Sigmar instantly recognised the man's majestic bearing.

With the Jutone king beyond his fastness, Sigmar angled his horse towards the lancers, knowing that he could end the battle in one fell swoop. A rising series of notes from a Jutone clarion sounded a warning note, and the blue-cloaked lancers expertly wheeled their horses.

Sigmar expected the lancers to ride for the citadel, but he was surprised and not a little impressed that they turned to face him instead. The lancers formed up in a wedge with the golden warrior at their point, and galloped across the killing ground behind the walls towards them. Sigmar guessed there were around a hundred lancers under Marius's command, heavily armoured horsemen who were clearly skilled warriors. Though Sigmar had more riders alongside him, they were a mix of tribes and most were not as heavily armoured as the Jutones.

Sigmar leaned forwards in his saddle, pressing his heels back hard against the stirrups. He held Ghal-maraz high for all to see and let loose a fearsome war cry. Less than a hundred yards separated the two wedges of horsemen, and Sigmar felt the familiar exultation at riding into battle on the back of a charging steed. The sensation of speed and power was like a wild elixir, and he laughed as he gripped the reins tightly. Truly, the cavalrymen were the kings of the battlefield!

He steered his horse with his thighs, aiming his charge straight towards Marius. The Jutone king unsheathed a curved blade that shimmered with a blue green light. The noise was incredible, the rumbling thunder of so many horses like being in the midst of a storm.

The cavalry met in a deafening clash of iron, bellowing warriors and screaming horses.

Men were punched from their saddles as lances spitted them and splintered under their weight. Swords swung, axes chopped, and the two groups of horsemen were soon tangled together in a heaving mass of struggling warriors. The Jutone Lancers carved a bloody path into Sigmar's warriors, but they did not escape unscathed. The Raven Helms and White Wolves gave as good as they got, unhorsing scores of enemy warriors with their dark lances and heavy cavalry hammers. The Red Scythes lived up to their name, reaping a fearsome tally with their broad-bladed swords.

Sigmar swung Ghal-maraz at Marius, but the Jutone king swayed aside and slashed his sword at Sigmar's back as he passed. The blade clanged from Sigmar's armour, the dwarf-scribed runes flaring as they repelled the enchantments bound within Marius's sword.

Sigmar heeled his horse, the hooves throwing up sparks from the cobbles as it skidded to a halt. Beside him, Redwane slammed his hammer into a lancer's chest, toppling him from the saddle with his ribs shattered. Laredus threw aside his splintered lance and drew his black-bladed sword. Count Aldred circled his kicking horse, Ulfshard rising and falling in ghostly arcs of blue light.

What little sense of order the cavalry clash might once have had vanished in the heaving press of horsemen. This was a fight for warriors protected by iron armour, and the Taleutens had ridden clear, though they galloped around the edges, loosing goose-feathered shafts into the combat when targets presented themselves.

Warriors on foot joined the fight, surrounding the battle against the lancers. Cherusen Wildmen dragged them from their saddles, while Count Otwin leapt upon a loose horse and ran amok through the Jutones.

The silver-helmed warrior pulled his mount around in a tight turn, and Sigmar was impressed by the man's horsemanship. He had expected Marius to be an effete trader, but he had proven himself to be a cunning general. He had also not expected him to be as skilled a rider as he was proving to be. What other surprises might the Jutone king have in store?

Sigmar raked back his spurred stirrups and yelled as he rode at Marius once again. The Jutone king's sword was aimed at his heart, and Sigmar held Ghal-maraz close.

Marius slashed with his sword, and Sigmar brought Ghal-maraz up to block, but the blade flashed down, aimed not at Sigmar, but at his horse. Blood sprayed the cobbles, and the beast's front legs went from under it as its lifeblood fountained from its opened throat. Sigmar kicked his feet from the stirrups and hurled himself clear as the horse collapsed. He hit the ground hard and the breath was driven from him as he rolled.

A Jutone lancer swept his sword down at Sigmar, but he ducked beneath the blow and dragged the man from his horse. He slammed his hammer down on the warrior's chest, and turned to pull himself up into the saddle, but the horse bucked and ran from him before he could mount.

The battle raged around him, and Sigmar desperately hunted for another horse as Marius wheeled his mount and rode back at him. He planted himself before the charging count and sent a prayer for strength to Ulric. The Jutone king's steed was a towering beast of midnight black, its chest wide and powerful. It wore a caparison of blue silk over its long coat of mail, and Sigmar felt a moment's regret at what he was going to have to do.

Sigmar watched Marius as he charged in, and the world seemed to recede as his vision narrowed and time became sluggish. All he could hear was the clattering hoofbeats of the horse, all he saw was the snorting breaths from its flared nostrils and the wind of its speed ruffling its plaited mane. Marius's blue green sword gleamed as it cut the air.

Sigmar's hammer came up, and, in the moment before he struck, he begged Taal's forgiveness for taking such a fine specimen from the world.

Marius swung his horse to Sigmar's right, and the Jutone king's sword lanced out.

Sigmar stepped straight in front of the horse and brought his hammer down in a sweeping arc upon the beast's head. All his strength was behind the blow and the horse's skull split apart as it died. Marius was thrown from his saddle, and the full weight of the charging steed slammed into Sigmar.

The force of the impact was enormous, and Sigmar landed in a sprawled heap on the edge of the cavalry clash. Stars spun before him and he tasted blood. Sigmar groaned and tried to stand, but his body flared with pain. Gritting his teeth, he pushed himself upright, feeling that several ribs had snapped beneath his armour. But for King Kurgan's gift, he would have broken every bone in his body.

His sky-blue tunic torn and bloody, Marius lay close by, supine amid the chaos his unwillingness to join the empire had spawned. Hundreds of men lay dead or dying around the Jutone king, the cobbles slick with warriors' blood, blood that need not have been shed if Marius had only submitted to Sigmar's rule. Sigmar cried out as he pushed himself to his feet, his entire body a mass of bloody wounds and fiery pain.

That pain fanned his fury at Marius into a raging inferno, and he felt the iron chains of his control slipping from him. Sigmar the Emperor diminished, and Sigmar the warrior surged to the fore as he staggered over to his enemy.

Sigmar hauled Marius to his knees, who cried out in pain and fear at the sight of the bloodstained warrior

Emperor. Marius had lost his silver helm in the fall from his horse, and long blond hair spilled from a leather circlet at his temples. Dirt coated his handsome face, and he looked up at Sigmar through a mask of blood and sweat.

There was fear in his eyes, and Sigmar revelled in that fear as a red haze of anger and vengeance swept through him.

'Please!' cried Marius. 'Mercy!'

'For the likes of you?' roared Sigmar. 'Never!'

He lifted his hammer high, ready to dash his foe's brains out over the cobbles.

Marius raised his hands, as if to ward off his imminent death, and Sigmar laughed at the futility of the gesture.

'So perish all who defy me!' cried Sigmar, and brought the hammer down.

Marius screamed, but before the hammer struck, a powerfully muscled hand flashed out and grabbed the weapon's haft, halting it in mid-swing. Sigmar looked up in fury, seeing a giant warrior, covered in blood and tattoos, whose temple was pierced by a crown of golden spikes.

Sigmar knew he recognised the warrior, but his fury was a raging storm that blotted out any thoughts, save those of violence. He thundered his fist into the warrior's face, but the giant lowered his head, and the golden spikes embedded around his skull tore bloody chunks from Sigmar's hand. The pain was excruciating, and he staggered away from the warrior, as Ghal-maraz was torn from his grip.

The giant dropped the hammer and simply said, 'Enough.'

'I'll kill you!' raged Sigmar, snatching up a fallen axe. 'Get out of my way!'

'Don't be a fool, man!' said the giant. 'Killing Marius will be an act of darkness that will taint everything you have achieved.'

'He deserves death,' snarled Sigmar. 'Look at all the men who have died here.'

'Aye, maybe he does, but if you kill him, this will all have been for nothing.'

Sigmar's anger fled in the face of the giant's words and the pulsing waves of rage and hatred melted away. He dropped to his knees, and blinked away tears as the full horror of what he had been about to do flooded through him.

He looked up at the bloodstained giant.

'Otwin? he said. 'Is that you?'

'Aye, Sigmar, it's me,' said the count of the Thuringians. 'Are you calm now?'

Sigmar nodded and took a deep breath, dropping the axe and letting the swelling darkness in his heart diminish. Otwin held out his hand and Sigmar took it, cradling his bloody fist close to his chest. He looked over at Marius, who knelt in the midst of fallen warriors and horses. The Jutone king had climbed unsteadily to his feet, and Sigmar saw that the fighting had ceased. A deathly stillness filled Jutonsryk, as though the world had paused to witness how this drama would play out.

The lancers had thrown down their weapons, but the battle hunger of Sigmar's warriors was poised and ready to devour the defeated Jutones. He could feel the anger in the air, the battle-born hatred that was the father of all massacres and bloodletting. In that moment, Sigmar felt the truth of the Hag Woman's warning.

She had warned him to beware the darkness in his heart, but he had believed that he could control it, that he was its master and could wield it in battle without fear of losing control.

He saw the folly of that belief and, but for Otwin's hand, he would have crossed the line from battle to murder.

Once that line was crossed there was no going back.

Sigmar had allowed his darkness to slip its leash, and it very nearly destroyed everything he had built in one moment of hatred. That it had taken Count Otwin, a warrior who was no stranger to slaughter, to save him from himself was no small irony and a measure of how close Sigmar had come to letting his all too human failings get the better of him.

The future of the empire hung in the balance, and Sigmar knew that this was the most important moment of his life. He nodded to Otwin and reached for Ghal-maraz.

'Give me my hammer,' he said.

'You're not going to do anything foolish are you, lad?' asked Otwin.

'No.'

'You sure? I don't want to have to put you on your arse again.'

'I am sure, my friend,' promised Sigmar. 'And thank you.'

Otwin shrugged and handed him Ghal-maraz. The hammer felt natural in Sigmar's grip, a symbol of his rule more than a weapon, a tool for the uniting of men, not their destruction. Sigmar moved past Otwin, and stood before Marius. The Jutone king took a step back, looking warily at Sigmar's bloody hammer.

'King Marius,' said Sigmar. 'We are divided, and in division we are weak. It is my desire that we be united. One land, one people.'

Marius licked his lips and ran a hand through his hair. He straightened his tunic and stood proudly before Sigmar, every inch a king of men.

'You offered me that before,' said Marius. 'What makes you think I will accept now?'

'Look around you. Your walls are carried and your warriors defeated. If I order it, your city will burn and all your people will die.'

'Threats are no way to win me to your cause.'

'That was not a threat, it was a statement of fact.'

'Hair-splitting, nothing more.'

'No,' said Sigmar. 'I came here with anger in my heart and it almost cost me my soul. I think I hated you, and that hatred blinded me to what it was doing to me. I wish for nothing more than you and your people to be part of the empire. It is all I have ever wanted, and if you could see all that we have achieved, I know you would wish to be part of it.'

'All I wanted was for my people to be left in peace,' said Marius. 'It is you who have brought war and bloodshed.'

Sigmar nodded and said, 'I know what I have done and I will bear the burden of that for the rest of my days, but put aside notions of blame for the moment. Think of what you might gain as part of the empire: the protection of every warrior in the empire and the brotherhood of fellow kings and your emperor. Jutonsryk grows fat on trade, but with the whole of the empire opened up to you, how much richer might it become? In time, your city will become the jewel of the empire, a gateway to the world beyond our shores!'

'I will be no man's vassal,' said Marius, but Sigmar saw that his appeal to Marius's greed and vanity had struck home. 'You may have taken my walls, but I'll not swear allegiance to any man who demands it at the end of a bloody weapon.'

'Nor should you,' agreed Sigmar, dropping to one knee and holding Ghal-maraz out to the king of the Jutones. 'I offer you the hammer of Kurgan Ironbeard and place my life in your hands as a symbol of the honest brotherhood I offer. Bear the symbol of my power and judge my heart. If you judge it pure, join with me. If not, then strike me down, and I swear that no man here will ever violate your lands again.'

Sigmar felt a wave of sudden fear sweep through his men as Marius lifted Ghal-maraz. The ancient hammer seemed to pulse with the power of days past, and a tremor worked its way up Marius's arms. His expression, which had been belligerent and defiant, eased, and his eyes widened at the awesome power bound within the dwarf weapon.

Sigmar saw Marius's desire to strike him down with the hammer at war with the truth Ghal-maraz represented, and the knowledge of what might be forged with it as a beacon to all men. The Jutone king let out a shuddering breath and reversed the hammer, holding it out to Sigmar in both hands.

'We have been fools,' said Marius. 'Pride and anger have divided us, and look at what it has wrought – death and misery.'

'We are but men,' said Sigmar. 'It is our curse to allow pride and anger to lead to hatred and fear. From them are spawned the wars that feed the cycle of hatred. Join me so we might put an end to the darkness that sees men divided.'

Sigmar reached out and placed his hands next to those of Marius, so that they held Ghal-maraz together, bound as brothers by that ancient weapon of power.

'One land, one people?' said Marius.

'Always,' agreed Sigmar.

And it was done.

# BOOK TWO

## Empire of Blood

*Thus did Sigmar call to account*
*Those who turned their backs.*
*And great was the war waged*
*On a king that lived by the blood of heroes.*
*Mighty was Sigmar's wrath,*
*Yet guarded not was his weary heart,*
*And evil of ancient times*
*Found root in the present.*

## ◄ NINE ►

# Northern Fire

OF ALL THE Udose settlements Cyfael had seen, Haugrvik was amongst the most pleasant. Most villages on the empire's northern coastline were battered by the cold winds raging southwards from the ice-bound lands beyond, but a high ridge to the north of Haugrvik sheltered it from the worst of the coastal weather. Built on a crescent bay of shingled shores, the low dwellings had a rustic charm not seen in the townships and settlements south of the Middle Mountains.

Cyfael made his way from the house the village chief, Macarven, had assigned him, a single storey structure of wattle and daub with timber struts and a rough coating of harling to the exterior. As he stretched in the early morning sunshine, he massaged his head and reflected that rustic charm was all well and good so long as you didn't have to wake up every morning with a raging thirst and monstrous hangover.

The women and youngsters of the village were already at the shoreline, folding the nets, and packing barrels with meat and bread for the fishermen. Six longboats were pulled up onto the shore, ready to be sent out into the Sea of Claws to bring back the day's catch. The village elders joined the women in their work, for the majority of the village's men were marching south to the Fauschlag Rock to answer a sword muster called by Count Pendrag.

Since arriving in Count Wolfila's castle of Salzenhús from Middenheim a month ago, Cyfael had ridden the length of the northern coastline with his fiercest clansmen to bring word of that summons to the villages of the Udose.

They were welcomed in the main, for Emperor Sigmar's armies had saved the Udose from destruction at the hands of the Norsii many years ago, and highland memories were long. Honouring the blood debt to the Unberogen and the Emperor was a matter of pride, and none of the many Udose clans would bear the shame of not living up to that obligation.

So far, Cyfael had mustered three hundred men, more than enough for this stretch of coastline, for it would not do to strip it completely of its warriors. The northern coasts of the empire were dangerous, and though Norsii raids were few and far between this far east, no one forgot the terror of the mighty Norsemen.

That fact was made clear by the presence of the timber hill fort atop a low mound on the northern curve of the bay. Surrounded by a palisade wall of sharpened logs and a wide, water-filled ditch, Macarven's fort was one of the largest Cyfael had seen in Udose lands. A tall watchtower rose from the walls, and, though the stronghold wasn't a patch on the grand fortress of Middenheim, there was a barbarous splendour to its construction.

The size of his hill fort was an indication that Macarven was a clan chief of some importance in the area, commanding respect from at least six other clans. The chieftain had been a generous host and had demanded

Cyfael stay on for a few more days to sample Udose hospitality, which mainly involved flagon after flagon of strong drink and endless feasts of beef and fish.

Cyfael pulled his cloak tighter about himself as a bitter squall whipped up from the sea, and a shiver of unease travelled the length of his spine. He made his way down the stony path to the shore, enjoying the wildness of the country around him. He called the Fauschlag Rock home and from its towering heights a man could see to the edges of the world. The view across the endless forests of the empire was something to be treasured, but here... Here a man could *live* in that landscape.

The land of the Udose spread out before him like a great tapestry, rugged and harsh, but possessed of a haunting beauty that would never leave his soul. The ocean was an impossibly vast expanse of shimmering blue that stretched to the horizon and promised far off lands as yet unexplored. At least it would be, were it not for the thin morning mist that clung like fallen clouds to the surface of the water.

Donaghal, one of Count Wolfila's Hearth-Swords, waved at him from the shore, his near-naked body wrapped in a plaid cloak. The man was soaked from an early morning swim, and Cyfael saw the pale lines of scars criss-crossing his chest and arms. A long, basket-hilted claymore sat propped up against one of the longboats next to him. Donaghal was a fine warrior, a man whom other men looked up to.

'How's the water, Donaghal?' shouted Cyfael.

'Bracing. You should get yourself in and find out.'

Cyfael shook his head and grinned.

'I don't think so, my friend,' he said. 'Us southern types don't like the cold. I do not wish a fever before I return to Middenheim.

'Cold? Ach, whisht, man, this isn't cold, it's like swimming in a hot spring.'

'To you perhaps,' said Cyfael. 'You Udose have ice in your veins.'

Donaghal started to reply, but his mouth snapped shut as a ringing bell echoed from above. Cyfael turned at the sound, shielding his eyes as he looked up towards the hill fort. A clansman at the top of the watchtower was ringing the warning bell and pointing to the ocean. Cyfael couldn't make out what he was saying, but Donaghal clarified the nature of the threat with a single shouted word that was part warning, part curse.

'Norsii!'

Cyfael looked out to sea, and a trio of dark ships slid from the mist like phantoms. Tapered hulls angled upwards with wolf-headed prows arced towards the shore, driven by banks of oars that swept up and back in perfect unison.

'Ulric save us...' hissed Cyfael, wishing he'd thought to buckle his sword-belt on this morning. The Wolfships arced over the water, each vessel carrying at least thirty warriors in dark armour and horned helms, their swords and shields gleaming in the sun.

'Go!' shouted Donaghal. 'Get the women and children to the stockade!'

'I can help you,' said Cyfael.

'Don't be daft, you have no weapon and this is my shore. Now go!'

Though it tore at his heart to leave the clansman, Cyfael knew he would be little use without his sword.

'Ulric bless you, my friend,' he said. 'Take as many of the bastards with you as you can!'

Donaghal grinned, and said, 'No bother.'

Cyfael ran back to his lodgings, and quickly ducked inside to retrieve his sword, a fine Asoborn weapon with a leaf-shaped blade. Buckling on his sword-belt as he ran, he glanced back to the shoreline, and a cold lump of fear settled in his belly as he saw the three Wolfships driven up the shingle and Norsii warriors leaping over the side.

Donaghal charged to meet them with an Udose war cry on his lips, and his sword smashed through the armour of the first warrior to land on the beach. He killed a second Norsii with a devastating overhead sweep, and another with a disembowelling cut that tore up through the Norseman's mail shirt. His defiance couldn't last, and Cyfael watched in horror as a giant warrior in midnight-black armour leapt to the shingle with a red-bladed axe that seemed to burn with an evil flame.

Donaghal attacked the warrior, but his sword was batted aside with ease, and the burning blade swept back to cleave the clansman from neck to groin. The brave clansman fell to the bloody water, and Cyfael ran as Donaghal's killer turned his baleful gaze towards the settlement.

Cyfael sprinted through the village, passing homes that he had visited many times, and which would probably be burned to the ground before the day was out. In his short time here he had come to love this place, and the thought of its destruction at the hands of the Norsii filled him with a towering rage.

Women carrying children were fleeing along the roadway of hard-packed earth that led to the stockade on the hill. Cyfael ran after them, but his pace faltered as he saw something amazing.

Streaming from the forests around Haugrvik were at least two hundred warriors in patterned cloaks of red and green with heads shaven except for long braids at their ears. Each man was armoured in a mail vest and bore a small wooden buckler and a wide-bladed sword.

Roppsmenn!

The women of Haugrvik cried out in relief at the sight of the Roppsmenn, tribal warriors from the east who, while not sworn allies of the empire, were certainly more welcome than the Norsii.

A swordsman in form-fitting silver armour, who bore twin blades of slender beauty, led the Roppsmenn, and Cyfael recognised a deadly killer in his every move. A dark suspicion formed in his mind as the warriors took up positions in the heart of the village on the road that led to the stockade.

Cyfael shouted a warning, but it was already too late.

The Roppsmenn fell upon the women with swords, and the screaming tore at Cyfael's heart. He dragged his own weapon from its sheath and ran at the nearest of the Roppsmenn, plunging the blade into the man's side. Even as he died, he lashed out at Cyfael, who leapt back to avoid a killing blow from the dying man's weapon.

A Roppsmenn warrior lunged at him, and Cyfael swept the man's blade aside and spun around him, slashing his sword across the back of his foe's knees. Hamstrung, the man collapsed with a foul scream, and Cyfael tore the man's buckler from his arm. The Roppsmenn circled him, and Cyfael knew that he couldn't hope to survive the fight.

'Right, you bastards!' he yelled. 'Who's next?'

A shaven-headed Roppsmann with a scarred face raised his sword, but the silver-armoured swordsman shook his head.

'No,' he said, 'this one's mine.'

The warrior circled Cyfael, and his courage fled as he recognised the lithe footwork of an expert swordsman in the man's every move. Cyfael had once been privileged to witness a display of Ostagoth *Droyaska*, blademasters who elevated sword combat to an art-form. Next to this man's fluid movement, they seemed like crippled simpletons.

'You should be honoured,' said the warrior. 'You will be my first.'

'First what?'

'The first empire man I will kill.'

'You are arrogant,' said Cyfael, mustering the last shreds of his warrior spirit. 'Perhaps I will kill you.'

The man laughed and shook his head.

'No,' he said. 'Already, fear is turning your bowels to water and you know you do not have the skill to defeat me.'

'A fight is about more than just skill. There is luck and fate. You might slip, your sword might break or I could surprise you.'

'No. You won't.'

The man removed his helm, and Cyfael's jaw dropped at the sight of the wondrously handsome man before him. Lustrous dark hair was bound in a long scalp-lock, but it was the man's face, sensuous and perfectly symmetrical that snared Cyfael's attention.

Handsome to the point of obscenity, the man's features were clearly not those of the Norsii tribes. His curving cheekbones, full lips and softer jaw spoke of southern tribal ancestry. Cyfael was a lover of women, and had no interest in men beyond their comradeship, but he felt an undeniable attraction to this beautiful man.

'Who are you?' whispered Cyfael, his sword lowering.

The swordsman's blade lanced out in a gleaming blur, and a rush of blood poured onto Cyfael's chest. He looked down, and saw that his throat had been opened, the blade that killed him so sharp he hadn't even felt it cut his flesh.

He dropped to his knees as his life poured out of him. The swordsman stood over him, and Cyfael was glad that his death had come at the hands of this perfect warrior and not some stinking, traitorous Roppsmann.

'I am Azazel,' said the swordsman, 'but before that I was called Gerreon.'

Cyfael tried to form a reply, but his mouth filled with blood and the words wouldn't come.

'I once called this land home,' said Azazel, kneeling beside Cyfael and unsheathing a dagger. 'But I was betrayed and driven out by a man who called me sword-brother. His name is Sigmar, and I have come home to kill him.'

Azazel gripped Cyfael's neck and held the glittering blade of his dagger a hair's-breadth from his eye. As the last of his strength faded, Cyfael saw the swordsman's face twist in anger, and what he had once thought beautiful was now hideous and terrifying.

'I am going to put out your eyes and cut out your tongue,' hissed Azazel with obvious relish. 'You will walk blind and without voice in the void for all eternity. Your torment will be exquisite.'

The dagger stabbed home, and Cyfael knew no more.

HAUGRVIK BURNED. THE stockade on the hill had fallen within the hour and its chieftain was nailed to its splintered gates. His wife and children were thrown, still living, onto the pyre of the dead. The elders and warriors were impaled on sharpened logs that had once encircled the hill fort, and the women too old to bear children were given to the blooded warriors for sport or taken by Azazel for torture.

The young women were whipped and chained before being taken aboard the Wolfships as spoils of war. The settlement's children were offered to Kharnath, the dark god of blood, and their skulls woven into trophy chains to be hung from the banner of Cormac Blood-axe.

Kar Odacen watched as the settlement burned, pleased at the victory and at the sense of ancient plans in motion that he felt all around him. The wizened, stoop-shouldered shaman sat on a fallen log, as Cormac stalked through the blazing village, his powerful form clad in blood-coloured armour taken from the lost tomb of Varag Skulltaker the previous year. The warrior's axe, a dread blade into which Kar Odacen had bound a creature from the pit, was dark and lifeless, its hunger for slaughter sated for now.

With eyes that saw the world beyond that of mortals, Kar Odacen perceived the red haze of anger that enveloped Cormac, and smiled. That anger had been a potent force in rebuilding the Norsii tribes, an anger that Kar Odacen had carefully fanned and built, ever since Cormac's father had been killed and the Norsii driven from their homes by Sigmar Heldenhammer.

Forever on the fringes of the southern lands, the Norsii had honoured the ancient gods of the world, and for this they had been hated and feared. The soft-bellied southern tribes knew nothing of the power of the northern gods, and so were prey to the Norsii. Then the hated Sigmar had united the tribes beneath his banner and made war on the chosen of the gods.

Against such a powerful enemy, the Norsii had had no choice but to flee to the icy wastelands across the sea. Here they scraped a pitiful existence from the bleak landscape, dreaming of the day when they would sing the songs of war and sail the Wolfships south to bring death to their enemies.

Alone of all the Norsii, Kar Odacen embraced his new home, for he had travelled these forsaken lands before in ages past. Centuries before Cormac's birth, Kar Odacen had dared venture into the northern reaches of the world, where the very air seethed with power, and the land writhed with the breath of the gods. Unimaginable energies had poured into his body, the gods blessing him with extended life and the power to change the world. The elements bent to his will, daemons of the pit were his to command, and the myriad patterns of the future came to him in dreams and visions.

Upon his return to the world of men, he walked amongst the Norsii for many lifetimes, shaping their destiny and ever working to bring about the End Times, the days of blood when the Dark Gods would finally claim this world as their own. Kar Odacen had held to the old ways, and with Cormac's anger binding the Norsii together, they had rebuilt the tribes, gathering the survivors of Sigmar's wrath and filling their hearts with hatred.

With the coming of Azazel, that time was closer than ever before.

Kar Odacen looked over the burning hill fort as the young warrior walked from its ruins. He stopped beside Cormac, and the two warriors made their way towards him. As they drew close, Kar Odacen studied them both.

Cormac Bloodaxe was the greatest of the Norsii warlords, a warrior who had brought many of the disparate tribes of the north together under one banner and promised them revenge. A core of molten rage burned in his heart, and that anger would burn the empire to ashes.

Azazel's silver armour was drenched in blood, and lines of red streaked his cruelly handsome face. The man revelled in torture, and the burning fort was filled with the mutilated bodies of his victims. The swordsman had come a long way in the ten years since his arrival on their shores in a stolen boat, delirious and near death. The womenfolk nursed him back to health, and as soon as he had regained his strength, Kar Odacen took the warrior into the northern wastelands. Deep in the abode of the gods, Azazel fought creatures of nightmare and felt the blessings of the gods flow in his veins. The warrior had been reborn there and, like Cormac, Azazel had good reason to hate the empire.

His thirst for vengeance was a sword aimed at the heart of its ruler.

It had been hard for Cormac to accept the southlander as an equal, but in the years of battle since he had first come to their lands, Azazel had proved himself a warrior of superlative skill and ruthlessness. His cruelty and beauty were feared and beloved in equal measure, and he had willingly turned from the weak gods of the southern tribes to worship the hungry gods of the dark.

'A grand day's slaughter,' said Kar Odacen as the two warriors reached him.

'This?' spat Cormac, removing his helm. 'This was nothing.'

Cormac Bloodaxe had the face of a fist fighter, his nose a flattened nub of gristle that had been broken many times, and his eyes were hooded and malicious. His hair was the colour of copper, and his skin was windblown from a life lived in the tundra of the northern realms.

Cormac bore numerous tally scars on his cheeks, each one representing a great mound of skulls offered to his patron god. He looked over at the line of impaled Udose prisoners. 'There was barely a fighter among them, save the clansman I killed at the shore,' he said. 'The chieftain opened his gates after we slew the first of his women. A man like that does not deserve to be a leader.'

'The men of the empire are sentimental,' said Azazel. 'It will be their undoing.'

'Exactly,' agreed Kar Odacen. 'They do not live a life of battle and blood like the Norsii. Comfort and peace makes women of their warriors.'

'You were once one of them,' pointed out Cormac, never passing up an opportunity to remind Azazel of his southern heritage. 'I have yet to see your sentimental side.'

Kar Odacen expected anger from Azazel, but the man simply shrugged.

'I cast off such weakness when I killed my sister,' he said. 'I am no longer one of them. I am Norsii.'

'Aye,' said Kar Odacen, 'that you are. Tell me, Cormac, did the Roppsmenn fight well?'

Cormac shrugged.

'Well enough,' he said. 'They know what will happen to their womenfolk should they falter.'

Kar Odacen smiled. With the breaking of the ice around the Norscan coastline, Cormac and Azazel had sailed the Wolfships across the ocean and plundered the towns and settlements of the Roppsmenn. They had taken the Roppsmenn's women and tribal leaders hostage, and demanded a season's servitude from the eastern tribe's warriors in return for their safety.

It was a bargain Kar Odacen had no intention of living up to. He sensed Azazel's dark eyes boring into him.

'The Roppsmenn must know you will not return their hostages,' said Azazel. 'You will burn them upon a great pyre to ensure the success of next year's campaigning.'

As always, Azazel's beguiling allure gave Kar Odacen pause, but he forced himself to see past the haunting beauty the dark prince had bestowed upon the swordsman.

'You see much that is hidden, Azazel,' said Kar Odacen. 'You have the sight?'

Azazel shook his head and smiled.

'I don't need sorcerous powers to know that you will kill them,' he said. 'It's what I would do. Slowly.'

Kar Odacen smiled. Truly the man Gerreon was no more. Only Azazel, disciple of Shornaal, remained.

'It matters not,' said Kar Odacen. 'There is nothing they can do to prevent it. But time is passing, and we should leave this place. The smoke will bring Udose warriors from other settlements.'

'Let them come,' snarled Cormac. 'I grow weary of killing women and old men, shaman.'

'Yet you take such relish in the task.'

'Kharnath cares not from where the blood flows,' spat Cormac, 'but we gain nothing by killing such wretches. My blade hungers for worthy foes to slay.'

'You must be patient, Cormac, this is not a time for war; it is a time for terror.'

'Terror? Terror does not reap skulls for Kharnath. Terror does not win us back land that is rightfully ours!'

Kar Odacen held up a placatory hand.

'Terror is a potent ally, Cormac,' he said. 'It moves through the land faster than any army, and saps the courage of every man it touches. Your name is known in the south already, for it is carried on every panicked scream and cry of loss. The terror of what you have done here will spread like a plague, and tales of your slaughters will reach the furthest corners of the empire. With every retelling, they will grow in magnitude until terror gnaws at the hearts of Sigmar's warriors like rats in the darkness.'

'Then it is time to march south?' asked Cormac.

'No,' said Kar Odacen. 'Not yet. There is work to be done before the empire burns.'

'Damn you, shaman, you say that every time I ask. What is left to be done?' asked Cormac.

'Patience, young Cormac, you have nursed your hatred for ten years. What matters one more turning of the seasons?'

'Tell me, shaman, or I shall feed your soul to my axe!'

'Very well,' said Kar Odacen, feigning submission, though he knew his death would not be at the hands of a mortal like Cormac Bloodaxe. 'There is an enemy that dwells in the south who draws power from the pulse of the earth.'

'A sorcerer like you?'

'No,' hissed Kar Odacen, 'not like me. There are no others like me, but this one… This one has real power, and the gods have spoken words of death that cannot be denied.'

'Then kill this mystic and be done with it.'

'I shall,' promised Kar Odacen. 'I must travel deep into the lands of the south, but I shall not be going alone.

Azazel must accompany me, for he knows the ways of its people. He shall be my guide and my protector.'

'And then we take the fire south?' demanded Cormac.

'Then we take the fire south,' promised Kar Odacen.

THANKS TO THE paved roads leading from Reikdorf, it took Sigmar and his warriors less than two weeks to travel north to Count Otwin's castle in the Dragonback Hills. Here they rested for three nights, enjoying the rough and ready hospitality of the Thuringian count before pressing on towards the Fauschlag Rock.

So far the journey had been uneventful, with each town and settlement greeting the Emperor and his warriors with open arms and generous hospitality. The settlements were protected by tall palisade walls and armed men equipped with mail shirts and sturdy iron swords. As secure as they were, the arrival of three hundred White Wolves was most welcome.

The settlement of Beckhafel marked the most northerly extent of the road to Middenheim, and Sigmar was pleased to see hundreds of men hard at work in the forests beyond the village. Robed map-makers and scribes consulted with foresters to plot the route of the road, and logging gangs felled trees from its path as well as cutting undergrowth back from the road to allow armed warriors on horseback to protect the working men.

Burly men with iron-bladed augers broke the ground for the diggers to form the wide trench that would be filled and levelled with sand before the stonecutters laid flattened slabs on a bed of lime mortar. Scores of tents and wagons lined the road, filled with sand, stone and tools. The scope and scale of the work filled Sigmar with pride as he and Redwane rode alongside the ever-lengthening road.

Workmen waved as they passed, and Sigmar held Ghal-maraz out for his subjects to see, holding the weapon aloft until they rode out of sight of the work-gangs and into the wild reaches of the forest. The regular sound of axes biting into timber was soon swallowed by the thick woodland, and Sigmar shivered as the trees seemed to crowd in that little bit closer.

He looked into the forest on either side of him, unable to see further than ten or fifteen feet.

Anything could be lurking in the darkness, and Sigmar's hand slipped back onto the haft of Ghal-maraz. A palpable tension descended on Sigmar's warriors as they appreciated how isolated they were. The sensation was not entirely unwelcome and as their guide, a huntsman named Tomas, led them deeper into the shadowy reaches of the forest, Sigmar had a potent sense of venturing into the unknown.

As though picking up on his thoughts, Redwane leaned over and said, 'Are you sure this man knows where he's going? It doesn't look like anyone's come this way in years.'

Sigmar had to agree with the young White Wolf. Their route was overgrown, and tangled with plants and gently waving ferns. He could barely see the faint trail of hard-packed earth that wound its way between the trees.

Without looking back, Tomas said, 'You're welcome to try and find your own way, boy.'

Their guide was a tall and rangy Thuringian, clad in leather and buckskin that blended with the neutral tones of the forest. A long-hafted axe was sheathed on his back and, unusually for one of Count Otwin's subjects, he carried a compact recurved bow, Taleuten by the craft of it.

'Redwane meant no disrespect, friend Tomas,' said Sigmar. 'Though the trail *does* look abandoned.'

'It's not,' said Tomas. 'Few use this path now, only foresters and hunters. And good ones don't leave signs of their passing.'

'What about the bad ones?' quipped Redwane.

'They end up dead. The forest doesn't forgive mistakes.'

'You travel this way regularly?' asked Sigmar as Redwane made a face of mock terror at the huntsman's back.

Tomas nodded.

'Aye,' he said. 'End of each hunting season I'll take my furs north to the Fauschlag Rock. Wolf, deer and fox mainly, but sometimes I get a bear. Trade them for supplies to last out the winter.'

'A hard life,' said Sigmar.

The huntsman shrugged, as though he hadn't given the matter any thought. 'No harder than most, I suppose. I don't like towns. I like the peace of the forest.'

'How long till we reach Middenheim?' asked Redwane.

Tomas looked up. 'A week. Maybe less if the weather holds.'

The huntsman pushed deeper into the forest ahead and, careful to keep his voice low, Redwane said, 'A dazzling conversationalist, eh? Makes Alfgeir look like a blabbermouth.'

'He is a man who spends a lot of time on his own,' said Sigmar, 'and someone who can bring a bear down on his own is clearly not a man to antagonise.'

Redwane nodded, glancing over at Tomas and the well-used axe on his back.

'I take your point,' he said.

'Still,' continued Sigmar, 'I like the idea that we are treading paths few others have followed. It feels as though we are discovering somewhere new, for the empire is becoming a smaller place.'

Seeing Redwane's confusion, Sigmar said, 'The roads I am building are bringing lands once thought unreachable within our grasp. As traders from Jutonsryk and beyond the southern mountains forge new trade routes throughout the land, it sometimes feels as though the unknown places of the world are becoming fewer and farther between.'

'That's a good thing, surely?'

'Yes,' agreed Sigmar. 'While my intellect rejoices at the idea of unlocking the land for my people, allowing trade and travel to flourish, my heart mourns the passing of its mysteries. Soon there will be no secret places left in the world, and the light of civilisation will usher in a new age.'

'Sounds grand,' said Redwane, though Sigmar knew the young warrior did not grasp the implications of a land made small by the expansion of man. As much as the world needed illumination, it needed the promise of realms unexplored to drive the imagination.

Sigmar remembered journeying south to Siggurdheim and the sense of boundless space he had felt while alone in a landscape free from the stamp of civilisation. Travelling through the northern forests had awakened that wanderlust in Sigmar, and he felt the excitement of an explorer daring to brave new horizons.

He wondered how much longer this would last, for loggers were clearing forests all across the empire. New towns and farms and grazing land were emerging every day, and his people were carving out their homes in areas that had once been beast-haunted wilderness. It seemed as though the forest and lands of the empire were limitless, but Sigmar knew they were not.

What would happen when the land grew too small for his people?

## ━◄ TEN ►━

# Curse of the Dead

MIDDENHEIM, CITY OF the White Wolf. The sheer pinnacle of rock looming from the forest canopy never failed to amaze Sigmar. More than a thousand feet high, the mighty Fauschlag Rock dominated the landscape for miles around, inescapable and impossible.

Stark against the evening sky, Middenheim towered over the land of mortals like the home of the gods, an impregnable bastion whose summit glittered with light. Sigmar followed the road towards the granite-hewn gate fortress at the base of the rock, feeling a strange unease settle upon him as he glanced towards the towering Middle Mountains beyond the city.

Spreading into the north-east, they were a bleak and inhospitable range of jagged peaks and soaring cliffs, perpetually wreathed in snow and flensed by icy winds from the far north. Inhuman monsters made their lairs deep within the mountains, and many an expedition to purge them from its haunted valleys and shadowed gorges had ended in disaster.

Cresting the last rise before the city, Sigmar saw the forests around the city had been cleared for almost a mile in every direction, and a vast expanse of canvas tents surrounded the base of the rock like a besieging army. Looking closer, he saw that the tent city was instead home to carpenters, builders, stonemasons and labourers.

If Sigmar had thought that the work on the road linking Middenheim with Reikdorf was impressive, it was nothing compared to the scale of industry that surrounded the Fauschlag Rock. Thousands of craftsmen toiled in makeshift quarries and carpentry shops to service the construction of the giant structure rearing from a wide clearing in the forest floor.

Like an ever-ascending bridge of stone aimed at the summit of the Fauschlag Rock, a giant viaduct rose from the ground at the southern compass point of the city. The viaduct climbed to around a hundred feet before coming to an abrupt end, a forest of scaffolding clinging to its sides like vines on some ancient ruin. Workmen swarmed around its upper reaches on rope pulleys and harnesses, and the sound of hammers, chisels and saws reminded Sigmar of the clash of iron in a battle.

'Great Ulric's beard,' hissed Redwane as the full scope of the work was laid out before them. 'How in the world did they ever...'

'Pendrag is a clever man, and he had some help from the dwarfs,' said Sigmar, pointing to a number of short, stocky figures in iron shirts and pot helmets at the top of the viaduct. 'This is only the first of four of such structures Pendrag plans to build.'

'Four!'

'If Middenheim is going to be one of the great cities of the empire, it is going to have to be easier to get to than it is now,' said Sigmar. 'Until the viaduct is complete, we have to travel to the summit on one of the chain lifts.'

Redwane shielded his eyes from the setting sun as he followed the swaying progress of one of the chain lifts as it made its juddering way from the ground to the timber structure that leaned out from the top of the rock. Sigmar smiled as he saw the young warrior's face pale.

'Of course, if you really want to prove your courage, you could climb the rock like I did.'

'You climbed that?' asked Redwane. 'From the ground up?'

'I did,' said Sigmar, still amazed that he had dared attempt so dangerous a climb. 'So did Alfgeir. But then we were young and foolish. Or at least I was.'

'And you killed Artur once you got to the top?'

Sigmar nodded, remembering the desperate fight with the Teutogen king, and the soul-chilling fall he had taken through the Flame of Ulric that burned eternally at the heart of the peak's summit. In that glacial moment, he had felt the briefest touch of a power greater than any mortal mind could hope to perceive. As he had felt its touch, it too had sensed his presence. The cold, pitiless echo of that moment had never left him.

'I regretted killing Artur,' said Sigmar. 'He was once a good man, but he had grown arrogant atop his fortress, and thought himself above all men.'

'But not you, eh?'

'No,' said Sigmar sadly. 'Not me.'

Their Thuringian guide had left them yesterday, when the towering spire of Middenheim had come into sight. The taciturn huntsman had merely taken his coin and vanished into the forest without any word of goodbye. Sigmar had been sorry to see Tomas go, for he had liked the man's self-reliance and independence.

They rode towards the gate fortress along temporary roads of rough-laid stone, passing workshops of carvers and stonemasons, assembly shops of carpenters and scaffold makers, hospitals, cook tents and the hundred other trades required for so colossal an undertaking. Numerous guild flags were planted throughout the campsite, and Sigmar recognised many of them as having worked on the buildings of Reikdorf.

In the years that Sigmar had spent campaigning in the west, Reikdorf had grown and prospered, with the great library taking shape in its heart and many new temples erected within its walls. Though it broke his heart to leave so soon after the successful conclusion to the war against the Jutones, a request for aid from his oldest friend could not be ignored.

As he led his warriors through the enormous camp, Sigmar felt a strange unease settle upon him, like a cold wind blowing with the breath of despair. He looked to the eastern mountains, and felt ancient eyes of incalculable evil watching him. For the briefest second, a profound sense of hopelessness swept over him, as though his very existence were meaningless in the face of death's inevitability.

Sigmar shook off the feeling, but as he watched the sullen faces of the camp's inhabitants, he saw he was not alone in this feeling. An unspoken fear hung over the camp, men and women moving with leaden steps and expressions of hopelessness. On the journey northwards, the people he had seen had welcomed them and smiled with each new dawn, but around Middenheim it was as if the sun were setting on the last day, and no one believed it would ever rise again.

'What in the name of all that is good is wrong here?' asked Redwane, riding alongside Sigmar. 'It's like everyone's mother suddenly dropped down dead.'

'I do not know,' said Sigmar as the wide drawbridge of the gate fortress lowered. 'Pendrag will tell us more when we reach the summit.'

Redwane looked up as a series of chain lifts rattled and clattered their way down the sheer cliff face of the

Fauschlag Rock, and he swallowed nervously at the thought of ascending the rock in such a contraption.

'Couldn't we wait until the viaduct's finished?' asked the White Wolf.

PENDRAG AND MYRSA were waiting when Sigmar stepped from the chain lift and onto the roofed platform built out from the rock on a series of mighty cantilevers. His sword-brother had changed in the five years since he had last seen him, but Sigmar hid his surprise. Pendrag's waist had thickened and the cares of the world, which he had always carried in his eyes, seemed magnified by the dread that seeped from the mountains. His flame-red hair was no less wild, and his joy at seeing Sigmar was like the first rays of sunlight after a winter of darkness.

Pendrag swept Sigmar into a crushing embrace, and the two men laughed at the sight of one another. Sigmar held his brother's shoulders as they relished this long overdue meeting.

'Damn me, Sigmar, but it's good to see you,' said Pendrag when he finally released him.

'You are a sight for sore eyes, Pendrag,' replied Sigmar. 'Wolfgart sends you his best.'

'The rogue isn't with you?' asked Pendrag, his disappointment clear.

'He wanted to come, but I told him that he needed to spend time with his family,' said Sigmar. 'Ulrike is nearly four now. Even if I hadn't forbidden him to come north, Maedbh would have cut off his manhood had he tried to ride out with me.'

'Aye, she's a fierce one, right enough,' said Sigmar turned to Myrsa and took his wrist in the warriors' grip.

Where Pendrag had changed, Myrsa was as solid and untouched by the passing of the years as his mountain home. His white armour was polished and pristine, his grip as firm as ever and his eyes like chips of ice.

'My lord,' said the Warrior Eternal. 'Welcome to Middenheim.'

Myrsa was pleased to see him, but where Pendrag greeted Sigmar like the old friend he was, the Warrior Eternal welcomed him as an Emperor. As he released Myrsa's wrist, Sigmar was reminded of the Hag Woman's warning not to let the Warrior Eternal die before his time. It had seemed like a ridiculous request then, and seemed doubly so now. How could any man promise such a thing?

'It is good to be here,' said Sigmar as his White Wolves formed up behind him. Ten warriors had accompanied Sigmar in the chain lift, and they looked anxiously at the creaking wooden floor, conscious that there was nothing beneath it but fresh air and the ground hundreds of feet below. 'I have left it too long to come north, but there has been much to do in the west.'

'So I hear,' smiled Pendrag. 'Two years... Jutonsryk must have been a tough nut to crack.'

'It was,' admitted Sigmar. 'I could have used some of your dwarfs to help break it open.'

Pendrag led Sigmar and his bodyguards from the platform and onto the streets of Middenheim, as the lifts descended to bring more White Wolves to the summit.

Despite his outward calm, Sigmar was grateful to feel solid rock beneath his feet, and he was once again struck by the distinctive architecture of this northern city. It was as if the close-packed buildings had been carved out of the rock, dour and low-roofed, with little in the way of ornamentation. They were crowded together, as Sigmar would expect of a city with a finite amount of land on which to build. Few were higher than two storeys, for unforgiving winds whipped across the Fauschlag Rock and quickly toppled any structure that dared to test its power. Many of the buildings bore the hallmarks of dwarf craftsmanship,

but even these solid structures clung close to the surface of the rock.

The people of the north were hardy and pragmatic, and
their dwellings were a reflection of that grim tempera-
ment. Most of the city's inhabitants were dark-haired and
broad-shouldered, as firm and unbending as their city.
Though Sigmar sensed the same unnatural gloom that
possessed the camp below, he saw an impressive determination to resist it.

The busy streets were narrow and filled with people, far
more than Sigmar remembered from his last visit to Middenheim, and Myrsa's plate-armoured warriors were
forced to clear a path with shouted oaths and blows from
their scabbarded greatswords.

'So many people,' commented Redwane.

'Aye,' said Pendrag guardedly. 'The city is almost full.'

Sigmar sensed a deeper meaning in Pendrag's words,
but saved his questions for later as they forged a path
through the crowds.

'I doubt I could have spared you any of the mountain folk,'
said Pendrag answering Sigmar's earlier comment. 'Without
them we wouldn't have managed to get the viaduct so high
in so short a time. In any case, you took Jutonsryk in the end,
though I'm still amazed that Marius swore his Sword Oath
with you. I thought he would die first.'

Sigmar shook his head.

'Marius is no fool,' he said, 'and if a Sword Oath was
the price of his life and his city's fortune, then he was
more than willing to give it.'

'The man is an opportunist,' spat Pendrag, turning
down a wider avenue that led to the stone circle where
Sigmar had fought Artur. A tall building of white stone
was in the process of being built around the menhirs
encircling the Flame of Ulric, and Sigmar felt a tremor of
bone-deep chill as he caught a glimpse of its flickering
light, like a speartip of dancing ice.

He shook off the memory of the flame's chill and said, 'True, but great wealth is pouring into the empire from the west. Without that, there would not be the gold to pay for Middenheim's viaducts. That is after a twentieth of Jutonsryk's yearly income is tithed for distribution amongst the warriors who fought so hard to take it.'

'I'll bet Marius hated that,' laughed Pendrag, passing the construction site and leading the way down a deserted street that was even narrower than the others they had traversed.

'That he did, but even with the tithe, his city's coffers are swollen with gold from all the trade that has opened up for him,' said Sigmar. 'If Marius had realised how lucrative swearing a Sword Oath would be, I think he would have done it long ago.'

'And you trust him to live up to his oath? He failed to stand by us once before.'

Sigmar smiled and put his arm around his friend's shoulders. 'I left a thousand warriors in Jutonsryk to make sure of it.'

'Unberogen?'

'A mixed force of warriors from all the tribes,' said Sigmar. 'Each of the counts sent fresh troops from their homelands.'

'Hoping to pick Jutonsryk clean, no doubt.'

'No doubt,' agreed Sigmar, 'but I did not want warriors who had lost friends garrisoning a city they had shed blood to take. The time had come to send the army home.'

Pendrag nodded and said, 'Two years is a long time for a man to be away from his family.'

'It is,' agreed Sigmar, hearing the wistful longing for home in Pendrag's voice, 'but enough reminiscing, my friend, are you going to tell me why you have brought me here?'

'That is why we are here,' said Pendrag, indicating a simple structure of polished granite at the end of the street. The building had a heavy wooden door guarded by two Ulrican templars and its few windows were shuttered. A White Wolf with painted red eyes set in a sunken reliquary above the door provided the only colour on a building that was grim even in a city of dourly constructed buildings.

'A temple of Ulric?' asked Sigmar.

'The building belongs to the Ulricans,' said Pendrag, sharing an uneasy glance with Myrsa, 'but it is not a temple. It is a prison.'

'A prison for whom?'

'Something evil,' said Pendrag. 'Something dead.'

THE BUILDING'S INTERIOR was smothered in gloom, the only illumination provided by a series of tallow candles set into niches shaped like the gaping maws of snarling wolves. Sigmar felt the hairs on his arms and the back of his neck stand erect, and his breath feathered the air before him. The walls were dressed ashlar, unmarked by a single devotional image or carving. A sullen sense of despair clung to the stonework, as though it carried the weight of the city's sorrows.

Four priests in dark wolfskin cloaks awaited them, each carrying a candle that gave off a cloying, sickly aroma. Pendrag closed the door behind Sigmar, shutting out the last of the evening light, and he felt a crushing sense of soul-deep unease settle in his bones.

Something was very wrong here, something that violated the very essence of human existence. This place reeked of abandonment and decay, as though the ravages of centuries had taken their toll in an instant. More than that, a palpable sense of fear lingered in every passing moment.

'What happened here?' whispered Sigmar, feeling the full toll of all his thirty-six years. He felt the pain of long-healed scars, the ache of tired muscles and the unending, ever-increasing weight of his rule upon his shoulders.

'I'll show you,' said Pendrag, following the priests as they turned and made their way down the shadowy corridor. Moisture pooled on the floor, and Sigmar noticed that droplets hanging from the ceiling were forming icicles.

Myrsa matched step with Sigmar as the priests led them deeper into the cold and echoing building.

'While you made war against the Jutones, the Norsii have been raiding all along the coast, destroying dozens of settlements,' he said. 'Entire villages have been massacred: men, women and children impaled on sharpened stakes. Even the livestock is butchered and left to rot.'

'You have seen this yourself?' asked Sigmar, knowing how such tales could grow in the telling until they bore little resemblance to the truth.

'Aye,' nodded Myrsa, 'I have,' and Sigmar did not doubt him.

'Many of the people in Middenheim are from those few settlements that have not yet been attacked,' continued Pendrag. 'The northern marches have been virtually abandoned.'

'Abandoned?' asked Sigmar. 'The Norsii have always raided the coastline. What more is there that drives people from their homes? There is something you are not telling me.'

'That is why I sent word to you, my friend,' said Pendrag. 'As you drew closer to Middenheim you must have felt the nameless fear emanating from the mountains?'

'We felt it,' confirmed Sigmar, stepping into an echoing chamber filled with lecterns of dark wood, 'a black dread that tears at the heart with talons of despair.'

No scribes sat at the lecterns, though open books and pots of coloured ink awaited their careful hands. The chamber smelled of copper, vinegar and oak apples, though Sigmar had the sense that no one had sat here in many years.

'What causes it?' asked Redwane. 'An enemy we can fight?'

'Perhaps,' said Myrsa, leading the way from the lettering chamber along a bare stone corridor towards a thick timber door secured with heavy iron bolts top and bottom. 'There is one beyond who may know something of what afflicts us.'

Another two priests flanked this door, each carrying a spiked man-catcher, a long polearm with a vicious collar on the end and sharpened spikes on its inner surfaces that would rip a prisoner's throat out if he struggled.

'The dead thing you spoke of?' said Sigmar, and Redwane made the sign of the horn.

'The same,' replied Pendrag, drawing the bolts and opening the door. Sigmar saw a set of curving steps that spiralled deep into the rock. Pendrag set off down the stairs and Sigmar followed him. The temperature dropped with every downward step. Hoarfrost formed on the walls, and each intake of breath was like a spike of cold ice to the lungs.

'The priests of Morr came to me two months ago,' said Pendrag, as the stairs wound deeper and deeper into the rock. 'They spoke of dreams coming to their gifted ones, dreams of a long dead evil stirring in the Middle Mountains. The high priest claimed that Morr himself appeared in a dream to warn them that a terror from the ancient days had awoken from its slumber and sought dominion over the lands of men.'

'Did the high priest say what this terror was?'

Pendrag shook his head, and said, 'No, only that it would spread like a plague, bringing misery and death to the race of man. Less than a week later, we heard the first tales from the villages in the foothills of the mountains.'

'Tales? What manner of tales?' asked Redwane.

'Of the dead walking,' said Pendrag. 'Entire villages destroyed in the night, every living person vanished and every grave emptied. Soon this began spreading ever further from the mountains, and more and more people fled to Middenheim as the shadow crept ever onwards.'

'You suspect a necromancer?' asked Sigmar as the cramped stairwell grew steadily brighter.

'Or worse,' said Myrsa. 'I sent warriors into the mountains – Knights of Morr and Ulrican Templars – but none ever returned.'

'Until now,' added Pendrag, as the stairs opened up into a wide chamber hacked from the rock with picks and bare hands. A swaying lantern hanging from the ceiling on a long chain and a host of torches set in iron sconces illuminated the chamber. A rough-hewn tunnel in the far wall led into darkness.

The candle-bearing priests took up positions on either side of it, chanting soft prayers to their god as those armed with the spiked collar weapons stood before it with their weapons held at the ready.

As Sigmar stared into the darkness of the tunnel, he felt as though the last breath was sucked from his body and icy hands had taken his heart in a cold, clammy grip. Though he had faced death many times, he felt unreasoning terror seize his limbs at the sight of the darkened passageway.

He gripped Ghal-maraz tightly, the warm, reassuring presence of the ancient warhammer steadying his nerves and easing his terror. The runes worked into its haft and head shone with a warm light, and, gradually, the paralysing fear holding him immobile began to diminish.

'What lies at the end of that tunnel?' asked Sigmar, fighting to hold his voice steady.

'It's better if I show you,' said Pendrag, taking a torch from the wall.

With the priests of Ulric leading the way, Pendrag, Myrsa, Sigmar and Redwane entered the darkened passageway. The darkness seemed to swallow the light from the torches, pressing in on them like a smothering blanket. Only the light of Ghal-maraz shone steadily, and never was Sigmar more thankful for King Kurgan's gift.

As a warrior, he had known fear, for he had faced many terrible foes, but this was not the fear of defeat, this was something else. This evil wormed its way into his soul with the fear of rotting flesh, of decomposing organs, his soul enslaved to an eternity of damnation.

The tunnel began to widen, though the light of the torches barely illuminated the walls. Sigmar saw they were scrawled with feverish lettering, as though someone had copied vast tracts of text onto the bare rock of the walls. He eased closer and saw that the words were charms of protection and warding, and entreaties to the god of the dead. The very walls of the prison were enchanted to keep whatever lay ahead bound to this place.

The journey along the passageway seemed endless, though it could only have been a hundred yards or so. Sigmar looked over his shoulder to see the dim rectangle of light from the antechamber shrinking away from him, as though an impossible distance away. Swallowing hard, he kept his attention fixed on Myrsa's glittering white armour.

At last the passageway opened out onto a wide ledge in an echoing cavern. A deep chasm plunged into the infinite darkness, and a raised drawbridge swayed gently in the cold gusts from below. Fresh torches burned with the same sickly aroma as the priests' candles, and Sigmar finally recognised it as wightbane, a plant cultivated by the priests of Morr to ward against the walking dead.

Across the chasm was a solitary individual, chained to the rocks with fetters of silver and cold iron. Clad in bloodstained white vestments and rusted armour, the man raged against his bindings, hissing and spitting with animal fury. His flesh was grey, and thin strands of white hair hung from his mottled skull.

Sigmar gasped as he saw the wolf symbol of Ulric on the man's chest, but when the prisoner's head came up, he saw the true horror of his condition. The knight was a man no longer, but a thing of corruption and decay. What little flesh remained on his body writhed with maggots and carrion beasts of the earth, and his breath was ripe with the stink of the grave. Glistening innards hung from his ruptured belly, and snapped ribs jutted from his chest where an axe blow had split him open. A fell radiance waxed and waned in the skull's empty eye sockets, and Sigmar saw the promise of extinction in that light.

'Ulric preserve us!' hissed Sigmar, taking an instinctive step back from this monstrous thing. 'What is it?'

'It is – or *was* – Lukas Hauke, a warrior priest of Ulric,' said Myrsa. 'He led the expedition into the mountains to defeat this evil. He left Middenheim in the spring and returned alone two months ago, barely alive. I knew Hauke well, my lord, and he was a full five years younger than I, but when he rode into the eastern gate-fortress he appeared older than any man I have ever seen. The priestesses of Shallya treated Lukas with their most potent remedies, but he was ageing a year for every day that passed.'

The horror of such a dreadful ailment struck at the core of Sigmar's humanity, and he felt his mouth go dry and his stomach knot in fear.

'Eventually, he appeared to die,' continued Pendrag, 'but when the priests of Morr came to remove his body, Hauke rose from his deathbed and attacked them with his bare hands. He killed three men and eleven priestesses before they were able to bind him with blessed chains and bring him here.'

Sigmar lifted Ghal-maraz from his belt and Lukas Hauke, or what he had become, turned his creaking skull towards him.

The evil light in Hauke's eyes glittered with unholy power, and he spat a wad of black phlegm.

'That toy of the stunted ones will not save you, manthing,' he said. 'Its power is a flickering ember before the might of the crown! If you knew the power of my master, you would end the pitiful, meaningless parade you call life and offer yourselves to Morath!'

Sigmar's skin crawled at Hauke's loathsome voice, a monstrously rasping, gurgling sound that conjured images of diseased lungs frothing with corruption.

He held Ghal-maraz out before him, and despite the dead thing's earlier words, it recoiled from the pure light that shone from the warhammer's head.

'Who is this Morath?' asked Sigmar. 'Speak now or be destroyed!'

Hauke spat and shook his chains as the light of Ghal-maraz touched him, but the evil in his eyes remained undimmed as he said, 'He is your new master and the living are his playthings.'

'I call no man master,' roared Sigmar, advancing to the edge of the chasm, feeling his courage growing with every step he took towards the unnatural monster. 'You will tell me of Morath, his plans and his strength. Do this and I will free your soul to travel to Ulric's hall.'

Hauke writhed in pain as the hammer's light grew brighter. The silver of its chains burned hot as its essence unravelled in the face of such ancient power. The creature's jaw gnashed in fury, but the dread force animating the brave knight's corpse could not resist the power that compelled it to answer. Its back arched and an awful crack of splitting bone echoed as it fought to keep its secrets. Bones ground and wasted muscles tore.

At last, Hauke's body sagged against the chains as the monster revealed itself.

'Morath is the Lord of the Brass Keep that holds dominion over Glacier Lake, and he is the doom of you all!' said the dead thing, the words dragged from its unwilling throat by the power of Sigmar's hammer. Each word was hissed through rotted stumps of teeth and spoken as a curse. 'He alone survived the doom of Mourkain and bore the crown of his master to this land in an age forgotten by the living.'

Much of what the creature said made no sense to Sigmar. He had no knowledge of Mourkain, whether it was a place or a person, but the mention of a crown piqued his interest. In its defiance, the creature had claimed its power was greater even than that of Ghal-maraz.

Lukas Hauke flailed and tore at the bindings, the silver chains glowing with the heat of their forging. Dust fell from where the iron bolts were driven into the rock, and the creature's limbs writhed with unnatural strength.

'You shall die!' screamed Hauke. 'The flesh will slide from your bones yet you will serve my master until endless night covers the land in darkness!'

With a final surge, the dead creature tore its chains from the wall and leapt across the chasm, its claws outstretched to tear Sigmar's throat. Its eyes burned with killing light, but Sigmar was ready for it.

He swung Ghal-maraz in a swift upward stroke, smashing the monster's skull from its shoulders. The deathly animation within the fallen knight's body was snuffed out by the power of the dwarf hammer, and a howling shriek of oblivion echoed from the walls of the cavern as the body tumbled into the chasm, disintegrating with every yard it fell. Within moments, all that remained was a drifting cloud of grave dust, and even that was soon lost to sight. Sigmar heard a gentle sigh of release, and knew that the soul of Lukas Hauke was freed.

'Gods of Earth and Sky!' said Redwane. 'Is it… dead?'

'It is,' said Sigmar, stepping back from the edge of the chasm. 'But this was just a messenger. This Morath wanted us to hear what it had to say.'

'Why?'

'Because he seeks to draw us into his lair.'

Redwane wiped his brow and risked a glance into the chasm, and said, 'And we're going?'

'We are,' said Pendrag, seeing the iron determination in Sigmar's eyes. 'That creature was a challenge to us, and we must answer it.'

Sigmar turned to Myrsa and said, 'Gather your bravest warriors and raise the Dragon Banner from the highest tower.'

'It will be done, my lord.'

'We shall find this Brass Keep and bring it down stone by stone,' promised Sigmar.

# ~◄ ELEVEN ►~

# The Mountains of Fear

THE ARMY OF the north set off as the sun passed its zenith the following day, six hundred warriors of courage and iron. Only the bravest had rallied to the Dragon Banner, for to march out under that blood-red standard was a declaration that no quarter was to be given to the enemy and none expected in return. It was a banner of death from the ancient days of the Unberogen and had not been raised since before the time of Redmane Dregor.

Cold winds blew off the snow-capped peaks, and Sigmar could feel the black amusement of the hidden necromancer in every warmth-sapping gust. He marched at the head of the column of warriors as they made their way from the eastern gate fortress and followed the road that skirted the rippling haunches of the towering mountains. The army moved on foot, for no horse would be able to negotiate the treacherous paths of the towering mountains.

Redwane marched with the White Wolves, his body swathed in a thick bearskin cloak, and he clutched Sigmar's banner close to his body. The youngster's face was pale and he was quieter than Sigmar could ever remember. Myrsa and Pendrag accompanied the warriors of the Count's Guard, giant men encased in glittering suits of plate armour who carried enormous greatswords across their shoulders. These proud northern warriors towered over the White Wolves, and already Sigmar could see proud rivalry developing between the stalwart fighting men. It was a rivalry born from confidence won in battle and the knowledge of mortality, and Sigmar knew that it would help the men conquer the fear he heard in the forced banter hurled between the different orders.

Pendrag carried the Dragon Banner, and his silver hand reflected wan, lifeless sunlight that did nothing to lift the army's spirits. Cheers followed them as they marched through the camps at the base of the Fauschlag Rock, but they were flat and without the infectious enthusiasm that had sent the Emperor's army to Jutonsryk.

These people did not expect them to return alive.

THE ARMY MARCHED into the mountains beneath a sky the colour of bone. The ground rose, the weather deteriorated with every mile, and the gently sloping hills and wide valleys around Middenheim quickly gave way to craggy gullies and a broken landscape like crumpled leather.

Rain fell in unending sheets and purple lightning smote the heavens from black clouds at the centre of the mountains. The sky was screaming at some unnatural violation and it was towards this that Sigmar led his army. The whispered mutterings of his warriors grew more fearful with every passing day, and Sigmar could not shake the feeling that he was leading his men to their doom.

Wolves howled in the night, but these were no welcome heralds of Ulric. They were black wolves of the
mountains, beasts that had turned from the god of winter in ancient days and now roamed wild and masterless.
Their howls plucked at the nerves of every fighting man,
and wolf-tail talismans and protective amulets were held
tightly as each night closed in like a fist.

On the morning of the third day's march, Sigmar saw a
burial party at a crossroads upon the last valley of the
foothills, and was reminded of the sad sight of the
corpse-carts leaving Marburg.

A crookbacked priest of Morr stood beside an open
grave marked only with a simple fencepost. A man in the
tribal garb of a Middenlander and a gaggle of weeping
children knelt beside the grave. Sigmar ordered the army
banners dipped. Lying next to the grave was the body of
a woman wrapped in a white burial shawl that left her
head exposed to the elements. The man gently stroked
her head, her blonde hair stark against the black ground
of the hills.

The priest nodded towards what Sigmar had assumed
was the haft of a shovel stuck in the earth, but which he
now saw was a wide-bladed felling axe. The man took up
the axe as the priest spoke again and the children rolled
their mother onto her front. The axe swept up and then
down, and the woman's head rolled clear. Weeping, the
man dropped the axe, before helping the priest lower her
face down body into the grave.

The tribesman lifted his wife's head and placed it in a
canvas bag as the priest intoned the blessing of Morr, and
the children began scooping earth with their bare hands.
Sigmar raised his hand to the priest, who bowed and
helped the grieving family to fill the grave.

The army continued on its way, marching higher into
the soaring peaks, winding a treacherous course through
icy valleys and mist-shrouded gorges as they climbed

high above the snowline. Sigmar chose their course without truly understanding what guided him, for this region of the north was little mapped, and few had travelled this way and lived to tell of it.

It felt as though the coldest wind in the world blew from the heart of the mountains, and Sigmar was merely following it, like an explorer tracing the course of a river back to its source. At each fork in the landscape, Sigmar would strike out without hesitation, leading his army deeper and deeper into the unknown. Scouts reported signs of greenskins and other dangerous monsters dogging their course, but none dared attack so numerous a body of warriors.

As the army camped in a rocky gully and darkness fell upon the camp like an unwelcome guest, Redwane said, 'I've been thinking.'

'That bodes ill,' said Pendrag with a forced smile. Sigmar chuckled and threw a handful of twigs on the fire. Myrsa held his hands out to the flames as the dead wood caught light.

'Thinking about what?' asked Sigmar.

'That burial we saw yesterday. I mean, what was that all about with the axe? Did that man hate his wife?'

'Far from it,' said Myrsa. 'He must have loved her dearly.'

'So that's what passes for love in the north, chopping your dead wife's head off. Nice.'

'He was making sure she wouldn't return from the dead,' replied Pendrag. 'Her husband will take the head away and burn it out of sight of the grave so that if an evil spirit possesses the body it will spend eternity searching for something it can never find.'

'Don't they have gardens of Morr in these parts? We're miles from the nearest village. It must have taken them hours to get here.'

'I think they buried her here *because* it is far from their home,' said Sigmar. 'Putting her face down in the ground at a crossroads means she will not know which way to go to wreak havoc among the living. And if some evil spirit lingers in her flesh and wakes, it will dig its way downwards, never to return to the world above.'

Redwane shook his head and pulled his cloak tighter around his body. 'Damn, but whatever happened to dying and just going on to Ulric's hall? It's not right having to do all this stuff to a body to make sure you get to the next world.'

'Better that than coming back as one of the walking dead,' pointed out Sigmar. 'Better that than having to destroy a dead thing that wears the face of a loved one. If this necromancer is as powerful as Hauke claimed, then there are men in this army who may well have to face their sword-brothers in battle. The warriors Myrsa sent into these mountains may well be waiting for us.'

'There's a happy thought,' grumbled Redwane. 'A man ought to die with a sword in his hand and be carried by the battle maidens to Ulric's hall. I don't want to die in these mountains and come back as one of the walking dead. You hear me? I want you to promise me you'll make sure of that.'

Pendrag reached out and shook Redwane by the shoulder.

'If it comes to it, I'll cut your head off myself and burn your body to ash,' he said.

'You'd do that for me?'

'Just say the word,' promised Pendrag. 'What manner of sword-brother would do less?'

Sigmar hid a smile and idly drew shapes in the dust around the fire. It felt good to sit around the fire with his friends, yet he could not shake the feeling that the words spoken in jest carried fears that ran deeper than any of them cared to admit.

'But to do that to your woman? Or to have her do that to me?' said Redwane. 'I don't know if I could do that to a woman I loved.'

Pendrag snorted. '*Have* you ever loved a woman? I thought you bedded one and then moved on to the next conquest.'

'Guilty as charged,' agreed Redwane. 'But that was in my younger, wilder days.'

'So are you saying you're in your older, more settled days now?' asked Myrsa.

'Not exactly, but you know what I mean. If I was ever to find a woman I wanted to fasten hands with over the Oathstone, then I don't know if I could ever do that to her.'

'If you ever wanted to fasten hands with a woman, we'd know the End Times were upon us,' said Pendrag.

'I'm serious,' snapped Redwane, and Sigmar saw that the undercurrent of fear that gnawed at the nerves of every man was preying especially hard on the young White Wolf. It was easy to forget that, for all his skill in battle, Redwane was still only twenty-five; old enough to be considered a veteran, yet still young enough to feel the immortality of youth.

Close to home in the warm lands of the south, it was easy to put thoughts of mortality from the mind, but here in the mountains, with each breath of cold wind promising death, such thoughts were harder to ignore.

Like Sigmar, Redwane had risked his life many times, but the fear that wormed its way into the mind was not of falling in battle but the slow, lingering death that came at the end of years of pain and suffering, indignity and madness.

To a warrior, death was something to be faced and defeated in battle, not something that came with talons of age and infirmity. With the cold dread of mortality hanging on every icy breath, the stark fact that they would one day die seemed achingly, horribly close.

Redwane shook his head and stared deep into the fire.

'I've loved a lot of women,' he said, 'but I never found one I wanted to spend the rest of my life with. Or, if I'm honest, one I thought would want to spend her life with me.' He looked deeper into the mountains and pulled his cloak tighter. 'But here? Here I'm getting to think that carousing is not what I want anymore. It might be time to find a good woman and sire strong sons. Don't you feel that?'

Sigmar studied the faces of his friends and knew that Redwane's words had cut through the armour protecting their souls. None of them had ever expected Redwane to speak such words, and they had been caught unawares and unguarded.

'I've felt that,' said Pendrag bitterly, 'but I do not believe in love. It is for fools and poets.'

Sigmar felt the pain behind his sword-brother's words, and wanted tell him that a life lived without knowing love was a bland and tasteless thing, but the memory of Ravenna appeared in his mind, and the black mood of the mountains crushed the words in his heart.

Myrsa nodded in understanding, looking at each man in turn. 'The role of Warrior Eternal denies me the chance of a wife and sons, but I have made my peace with a life lived alone.'

Redwane looked over at Sigmar, but before Pendrag could silence the question that he saw was coming, the White Wolf said, 'What about you, Sigmar? Have you never thought of finding a wife? An Emperor needs heirs after all.'

A heavy silence greeted Redwane's words, but Sigmar nodded.

'Yes, Redwane, I have,' he said. 'Once, I loved a woman. She was called Ravenna.'

'What happened to her?'

'Ulric's bones, Redwane!' stormed Pendrag. 'You are a prize fool and no mistake. Can you not leave well alone?'

Sigmar raised a calming hand. 'Don't blame the lad, Pendrag. He would only have been a boy when it happened, and no one dares speak of it now.'

Sigmar looked across the fire and said, 'Ravenna was a beauty of the Unberogen, and I loved her from the first moment I saw her. She loved me for all my faults and knew me better than I knew myself.'

'Did you marry her?'

'I was going to,' said Sigmar. 'I promised her that when I was king I would marry her, but she died before I could. Her brother Gerreon had a twin named Trinovantes, and when he died at Astofen Bridge, Gerreon blamed me. I thought he had accepted what happened to his twin, had accepted the truth of it, but he nursed his hatred in a secret place in his heart and almost killed me as I swam with his sister. He failed to slay me, but he murdered Ravenna.'

'No!' cried Redwane. 'Gods, man, I'm sorry, I didn't mean to…'

'From that moment, I vowed I would love this land and no other,' said Sigmar. 'I have devoted my life to the empire and it will be my bride, my one abiding love. I swore this on Unberogen soil before the tomb of my father, and I shall live and die by that oath. I know that there is talk of my taking a wife, for people think I must sire an heir for the empire. They lament a future without me, but they do not know the strength that lies within this land and its people. They do not see that what I am building is greater than any one man. After all, I did not found the empire for it to become the possession of a single dynasty.'

Sigmar stood and looked at each of his friends in turn, and none doubted the sincerity of his words. 'The empire is an idea that lives in the hearts of all men and women who dwell within it, and when I am dead and gone, the empire will live on in them. For they are all Sigmar's heirs.'

\* \* \*

THE WELCOME LIGHT of morning crept over the hills, only reluctantly pushing back the darkness and spreading down the icy valleys and jagged gorges of the mountains. Fires that had burned through the night were doused, and the army swiftly broke camp after a meal of warm oats. Sigmar's banner was raised, and his warriors followed him as he marched purposefully into a snow-shawled valley that loomed like a vast, columned gateway.

Six days had passed since the army had left Middenheim, and the friendly rivalry that passed back and forth between the warriors was forgotten as each man fought against unbidden thoughts of crows pecking at his eyes and worms gnawing at his decaying flesh.

The valley was deathly silent, the walls glistening with spears of ice and swallowing the sound of marching feet and the clatter of armour. The sun did not reach to the base of the valley and the army climbed in shadow, what little relief had been provided by daybreak crushed by the deadening gloom. Clouds of dark-pinioned birds circled overhead, ravens and other scavengers of the battlefield. Their raucous cries echoed in the narrow valley and scraped like blades down each man's nerves.

Pendrag came alongside Sigmar. His sword-brother had lost weight since the march had begun, and Sigmar nodded as Pendrag slapped a hand on his pauldron.

'That's fine armour,' Pendrag said. 'You could work a whole lifetime and never have enough coin to buy such a gift.'

'Alaric is a master of his craft,' said Sigmar.

'That he is,' agreed Pendrag. 'Do you know the runes worked into the metal?'

'Kurgan told me they were runes of protection crafted centuries ago by a Runesmith called Blackhammer. He said they would do me more good on their own than the finest suit of armour crafted by man.'

Pendrag patted his mail shirt. 'The dwarfs do not have a high opinion of our metalworking skills, do they? You remember that breastplate I crafted for Wolfgart's hand fastening ceremony, the one with the gold embossing and fluted rims?'

'Of course, it is a masterful piece.'

'Alaric told me it was "serviceable", perhaps the equal of an apprentice's work in his forge.'

'High praise indeed,' noted Sigmar.

'That's what I thought,' said Pendrag wistfully. 'It has been too long since he has visited Reikdorf.'

'I think he has his hands full making the swords King Kurgan promised. And you know Alaric – he will not rush their creation.'

'He won't, no. Perhaps we might arrange to visit Karaz-a-Karak?' ventured Pendrag.

Sigmar shrugged. 'I do not think the mountain folk encourage visitors, my friend. Except maybe other dwarfs, and even then there are all manner of formalities before they are granted permission to journey to a hold. Why are you so keen to see Master Alaric?'

'No reason,' said Pendrag. 'He is my friend and I miss him, that's all.'

They lapsed into silence for a while, the trudging monotony of the climb and the constant twilight wearing at their spirits like a millstone. Sigmar found his hatred towards this necromancer growing with every mile that passed.

'Why would anyone desire this?' asked Sigmar, looking around at the bleak, inescapable hostility of the landscape.

'Desire what?'

'This,' replied Sigmar, sweeping his arms out to encompass the sepulchral valley. 'I understand the lust for power, but surely if a man can cast spells and use magic, he would live somewhere less dismal. I mean, why would any man choose a life that sees him banished to a place like this?'

'The path of the necromancer necessitates a solitary existence,' said Pendrag. 'To violate the dead breaks one of our most sacred taboos. You do not do such things where people can find out about it, so you live where no one else wants to.'

'I suppose,' agreed Sigmar, 'but that leads to another question.'

'Which is?'

'Why be a necromancer at all?'

'To live forever?' suggested Pendrag. 'To cheat death?'

'If living like this is cheating death, I would sooner not bother. Even if you *were* to cheat death, is what you would have really life? Living like this, shunned by your fellow man and surrounded by corpses? No, if that is what living forever entails, then I want no part of it.'

'They say that some men are drawn to necromancy in the hope of bringing back a loved one,' said Pendrag, 'that they do not begin as evil men.'

'Maybe that is true, but to delve into such darkness can only drive a man to madness. I loved Ravenna and I lost her, but I would not dream of using the dark arts to bring her back.'

'Not all men are like you, Sigmar,' said Pendrag, casting an uneasy glance towards the tombstone sky. 'To fear death is not unusual.'

'Trust me, Pendrag, I am in no rush to find death, but I do not fear it. Death is natural, it is part of what makes us human. That is why we must strive to make every moment special, because it might be our last. Some men live in fear their whole lives. They fear to fail, so they do nothing. You can hide from danger all your life, but you will still die. What matters is how we make use of the gift of life, bettering ourselves and helping our fellow man wherever we can. That is why this Morath is so dangerous: he lives only for himself and contributes nothing of value to the world. In the realm of the necromancer, nothing grows, nothing lives and nothing dies. And stagnation is death.'

'So is *starvation*,' said Pendrag, looking over his shoulder at the six hundred men who marched through the valley behind them. 'Between what the pack ponies and the men are carrying, we only have food enough for another two days march into the mountains. If we're going to find this Brass Keep, we'd better do it soon.'

'We will,' said Sigmar, feeling the deathly chill of the cold wind blowing from the centre of the mountains grow stronger, reaching into his chest and caressing his heart with icy talons. 'We are close, I know we are.'

'I hope you are right,' said Pendrag. 'I don't know how much more of this I can take.'

The shadows moved across the valley sides, the only visible indication that time was moving on at all. After a mid-afternoon stop for food and water, Sigmar's warriors continued on through the valley as the ground became even more broken and uneven.

Jagged rocks tore at tunics and flesh as the day lengthened and the slopes of the mountain grew steeper. The unnatural silence of the mountains loomed over everyone, broken only by the pebbles that skittered from ledges high above. Pallid shapes darted between narrow clefts carved in the mountainside by scouring winds, and arrows loosed at the shapes clattered harmlessly on the rocks before Myrsa ordered his men to stop wasting their shafts.

The valley began to widen ahead of a sharp northward turn around a black spur of knife-sharp rock, perhaps a mile distant. A gust of cold air, like the last laugh of a suicide, swept the landscape, and Sigmar knew that he had reached its source.

'Raise the banners,' said Sigmar. 'Assume battle march formation.'

'Battle formation?' queried Redwane, looking up to the sky. 'But it's nearly dark.'

'Do it,' said Sigmar. 'We are here.'

The White Wolf nodded, and the word was passed along the line. No sooner was the order given than the warriors moved smoothly into formation. Swords were bared, and a fresh sense of purpose infused every warrior. Sigmar loosed Ghal-maraz from his belt and a squadron of White Wolves formed up around him.

With Pendrag at their head, the Count's Guard took up position on the right, while Myrsa led the warriors of Middenheim on Sigmar's left. Moving at a swift yet economical pace, the army marched towards the black spur, shields locked and swords held at the ready.

As Myrsa's warriors reached the turn, he slowed their pace as the Count's Guard wheeled around it, the entire shallow wedge of the army swinging around like a closing gate with the spur as the hinge.

Beyond the spur, the landscape fell away in rippling slopes of icy rock towards a wide crater gouged in the heart of the mountains, thousands of yards in diameter. The ground shone like a mirror, a vast and stagnant lake that had frozen in an instant during some forgotten age. Broken spires and strange collections of jumbled stone jutted from the frozen lake, like stalagmites in a cave. Towering over this grim and frozen tableau was a mighty edifice that could only be Morath's lair.

'Ulric preserve us,' breathed Redwane at the sight of the gleaming fortress.

The name Lukas Hauke had given it was apt, for it shone in the last light of day as though sheathed in brass. Its towers were tall and slender, and its walls were smooth and fashioned with great cunning. A great iron portal wreathed in sharpened spikes barred entry, and spectral light shone from every shuttered tower and lofty turret of the gatehouse. At the heart of the dreadful castle, a single tower of pearlescent stone rose above all others, and from it shone a pulsing dead light, a glow that drained life from the landscape instead of illuminating it. Sigmar felt a powerful attraction to the tower, as though this were the source of the cold wind that had led him to this place.

He had expected to find the creatures of Morath waiting for them, but the crater was empty, unnaturally so, for even the carrion birds that had followed them from the foothills kept their counsel. Thousands of black-feathered ravens observed his army from perches high on glittering spires of icy rock, and Sigmar sensed their dreadful appetite.

These birds had gathered in anticipation of a feast.

'Move out,' ordered Sigmar, and the army advanced down the icy slopes towards the dreadful Brass Keep. The ground underfoot was slippery and treacherous, and many warriors lost their footing as they made their way down to the icy plain.

Darkness gathered over the fortress, bruised clouds heavy with rain and lightning. A fell wind issued from the far reaches of the valley, and Sigmar tasted the foulness of dead things at the back of his throat. As the army marched out onto the frozen surface of the lake, Sigmar gasped in astonishment as he saw a sunken city lying far beneath its glassy surface.

As though he looked through the clearest glass instead of ice, Sigmar saw an ancient metropolis, grander and more massive than Reikdorf, with towers and structures taller even than the Fauschlag Rock. Cries of astonishment and fear spread along the battle line as his warriors saw the same thing.

Sigmar had never seen its like in all the realms of man, though it was clearly a city designed and raised by the artifice of his race. The towering buildings were colossal and defied understanding, such was their magnificence. Enormous temples, sprawling palaces and rearing statues filled the city, and its grandeur stole Sigmar's breath. Yet for all its glory, it was a dead place, a mockery of a city where lives were lived and dramas, both vital and banal, were played out on a daily basis. As he formed this last thought, the image wavered for a second, as though the city was no more substantial than morning mist.

'What is this place?' asked Redwane, still keeping pace with the battle line as he stared in horror as the sunken city. Collapsed portions of the city's tallest towers jutted through the ice, lying in crumbled piles of fallen masonry, sad remnants of something wondrous that had passed into ruin and decay.

'I do not know,' answered Sigmar. 'Perhaps this is Mourkain? When Lukas Hauke said its name, I did not know whether it was a place or a person. Now I know.'

'Mourkain? Never heard of it,' said Redwane, shaking his head as though to deny the city's existence. 'Surely if there was a city here, we'd know about it?'

'Perhaps,' said Sigmar, tearing his eyes from the ghostly city's wreckage as a shimmering mist formed around the battlements of the gleaming castle. 'I think maybe that we are seeing an echo of something that has long since vanished from the face of the world. Hauke said that Morath survived the doom of Mourkain, so maybe this is his way of remembering it.'

'What happened to it?'

'I will be sure to ask him,' said Sigmar dryly.

'Point taken,' said Redwane, grinning and hefting his hammer. The White Wolf's earlier fears had receded in the face of imminent battle, and looking along the line of determined faces of his warriors, his heart soared to see such strength. The fear that had dogged the army's every step into the mountains fled in the face of their courage.

Sigmar felt a cold gaze fasten upon him, and looked towards the dread tower at the heart of the castle as Ghal-maraz grew hotter in his grip.

Atop the bone-white tower stood a figure wreathed in black, a slit of darkness against the sky that seemed to swallow the light around it. Robes of night billowed in ethereal winds, and even from this distance, Sigmar saw the pale, ravaged features of a thing more dead than alive. The necromancer carried an ebony staff, and upon his skull-like brow he wore a glittering golden crown that seemed to pulse in time with Sigmar's heartbeat.

'Morath,' hissed Sigmar as the dark sorcerer raised his staff. A withering light pulsed from the ice, the rocks and the very air, as though some ancient rite were nearing completion.

'Stand firm!' shouted Sigmar, his voice echoing from the valley sides to bolster his warriors' resolve. Shouts of alarm came from both flanks, and Sigmar saw scores of shambling horrors climbing from the ruins of the towers that jutted through the ice. Loathsome cadavers in tattered robes and rotted flesh lurched and stumbled from the ruins in their dozens, and then in their scores.

Their armour was rusted from the long centuries that had passed since their deaths, yet their swords and spears were still deadly. Skeletal fists punched through the ice, and armoured warriors of bone hauled their fleshless bodies upwards, before turning grinning skulls upon their warm-bodied foes with dreadful malevolence. As though commanded by a living general, they marched in hideous lockstep, forming sword-bands like those facing them.

Sigmar's army halted at so terrifying a sight, for these abominations were an affront to the living, a dreadful violation of the natural order of things. The fear that had been quashed by courage returned to tear at each warrior's heart, and they could not take so much as a single step towards the dead things.

But that was not the worst of it.

The iron gateway of Morath's keep swung open like the maw of hell, and an unliving host of armoured warriors marched out in dreadful unison. A pall of fear went before them, and a low moan of anguish swept through Sigmar's army as the dead warriors in silver armour and bloody robes drew relentlessly closer.

Sigmar's flesh crawled and his bladder tightened at the sight of the hideous warriors, for they wore the heraldry of Ulric and of Morr. The flesh decayed and rotted on their bones, but they were not so long dead that that their faces were unrecognisable. Brothers and sons marched at the command of the hateful necromancer, and every man in Sigmar's host felt piteous horror at the sight of their fallen comrades.

'Men of the Empire!' shouted Sigmar, his voice carrying across the field of ice, and striking home into the hearts of his men like arrows of truth. 'You are the bravest warriors in a land where bravery runs in every man's blood! You have climbed into these mountains in the face of fear, and you have reached this place of death by the iron in your souls and the fire in your hearts! Though they may wear the bodies of our friends, these monsters are not your sword-brothers. Their souls are bound to the will of an evil man, and only you can free them to travel onwards to Ulric's hall. We march beneath the Dragon Banner, so let not your blade hesitate from destroying these dread foes, for theirs shall seek to bring you down!'

A ragged cheer greeted Sigmar's words, desultory and half-hearted, but he had broken the paralysing terror that held his men rooted to the spot. The fear of this dead host still cast a dark pall over his warriors, but swelling embers of courage were steadily pushing it back.

Sigmar looked up at the necromancer's tower as the hosts of the living and the dead marched into battle. The golden crown at Morath's brow shone like a beacon of unimaginable power.

'The cowardly sorcerer skulks atop his tower,' shouted Sigmar. 'I shall tear the crown from his brow and take if for my own!'

# ◄ TWELVE ►

# The Battle of Brass Keep

THE DEAD WERE silent, no battle cries or bellows to a watching god for strength of arm or divine protection. Somehow that was worse. When man fought man there was hatred and anger, emotions that both clouded the mind and granted strength, but these abominations fought with none of that. They came towards the army of men with singular determination, their rotten meat faces and skeletal grins terrible, giving each warrior a glimpse of the fate that awaited them should they fall.

Sigmar knew of no other way to lead his warriors save by example, and he lifted Ghal-maraz high as he charged towards the living dead.

'For Ulric and the wolves of the north!' he proclaimed.

The White Wolves followed him, howling like their namesakes, their hammers swinging. Pendrag's Count's Guard charged the enemy with their greatswords held high, shouting oaths that would make a Jutonsryk docker blush. The Middenland warriors on the left each shouted their own battle cry and then slammed into the decaying creatures spilling from the tumbled ruins of the towers.

A skeletal warrior stabbed a spear at Sigmar, but the thrust was slow, and he smashed his hammer down on the fleshless skull. The creature dropped, its bones falling apart as the power holding it together was undone. Another came at him, but he spun away from its attack and smashed its ribcage to splinters with an overhand sweep. The White Wolves fought all around him, their hammers breaking bones and skulls with every blow.

The dead were no match for these brave warriors, but there seemed no end to them. As each creature fell, two or more pushed forward to take its place. Shambling creatures with pallid skin sloughing from their bones crawled from the wreckage of the city, and Sigmar saw hundreds more climbing the ruins beneath the ice towards the surface.

A rusted lance hooked around his pauldron and hauled him off balance. He swung Ghal-maraz and crushed the pelvis of the lance wielder, but his feet slipped on the ice. Sigmar landed heavily, and no sooner was he down than the dead were upon him. Axes and swords chopped downwards with mechanical precision, and he rolled and blocked to keep them from him.

He kicked out, breaking legs and kneecaps, but still they came on. A spear jabbed downwards and skidded from his breastplate as a bony foot stamped down on his face. He twisted aside and swung his hammer in a wide arc, splintering thighs and creating some space around himself.

'Here!' shouted Redwane, holding his hand out. The White Wolf had slung his hammer, but still held Sigmar's banner aloft. Sigmar gripped Redwane's wrist and hauled himself upright, careful not to spill them both to the ice.

'My thanks,' said Sigmar. 'Lost my balance.'

'So I saw. Lots of them, eh?'

'Too many for you?' asked Sigmar.

'Never,' grinned Redwane, unhooking his hammer and plunging back into the fray.

Pale light, evil and suffused with emerald, bathed the fighting in a lambent glow. A flickering radiance seemed to dance around the blades of each warrior, both living and dead. The dread moon had risen, its rough surface leering down at the carnage beneath it, and a shiver of fear passed down Sigmar's spine as he saw that it was as full as it had been when they had fought in the swamps around Marburg.

White Wolves stood sentinel over him, and Sigmar nodded to them as he set off after Redwane. The fighting wedge of the army, with the wolves at the centre, was a spear thrust at the gateway to Morath's fortress, with the flanks keeping the tip from becoming bogged down. Sigmar looked for his standards, quickly finding them in the morass of fighting warriors.

Beneath the Dragon Banner, the Count's Guard fought with killing sweeps of their enormous blades, cleaving great paths through the dead. Each warrior fought his own battle: for the reach of such swords ensured that no warrior dared fight nearby for fear of being struck. To fight in such a manner was courageous and heroic, but to wield a greatsword was heavy work and rapidly sapped a warrior's strength. How much longer would Pendrag's warriors be able to keep pushing on?

To his left, Sigmar saw Myrsa battling a host of black wolves, their mouldering fur and decaying flesh hanging in tatters from rotten bones. The wolves fought with savage strength and speed, and only Myrsa's superlative skill with his enormous hammer kept them at bay. Fangs flashed and bloody jaws snapped as Myrsa's men were torn down and devoured.

The blue and white banner of the Fauschlag Rock still flew proudly over the fighting, but Sigmar saw that the men of the north were in danger of being overrun. The ferocity of the frenzied wolves was slaughtering them, but they refused to break. With the Dragon Banner raised, every man understood that against such a dreadful foe there could be no retreat.

It was fight or die.

Myrsa fought in the centre of a circle of snarling, snapping wolves and the Hag Woman's warning returned to him at the thought of the Warrior Eternal being brought down.

'Emperor's Guard, with me!' shouted Sigmar, pushing through the host of fighting men towards Myrsa. Armoured warriors of bone fought to reach Sigmar, but deadly strikes from Ghal-maraz and the weapons of his guards smashed them down.

Sigmar battered a path towards Myrsa through the dead warriors as the clouds above the Brass Keep vomited up arcing bolts of lightning that slammed down and exploded in purple sheets of fire. Men were hurled skyward as bolt after bolt struck the ice with shattering force. He risked a glance towards the keep, and saw Morath with his hands raised to the heavens, laughing insanely as his staff crackled with the same purple lightning that smote his warriors.

Wolves leapt and bit as they pushed into the ranks of Myrsa's warriors, tearing with diseased claws and ripping flesh from bones with jagged fangs. The Middenheim banner bearer had no time to scream as a wolf's jaws fastened on his head and crushed his skull with a single bite. The snarling wolf swallowed its morsel, and a great wail went up from the northern warriors as their standard fell towards the ice.

Sigmar leapt forward and swept up the banner before its silken fabric touched the ground. He raised it high before hammering its sharpened base into the ice.

'The banner still stands,' he shouted. 'And so shall you!'

A pair of wolves launched themselves at him, but Sigmar leapt to meet them. Ghal-maraz smashed the spine of the first and clove through its dead heart. The second beast's enormous jaws snapped at him, but he dived beneath them, rolling to his feet and gathering up the fallen banner bearer's sword. As the beast turned to face him, Sigmar thrust the blade between its jaws. The wolf howled and dropped to the ice, its flesh crumbling and decaying as it fell.

Given fresh heart by his courage, Myrsa's warriors fought back against the wolves, driving them onto the spears of their brothers with flaming torches and wild charges.

Myrsa came alongside him, his white armour streaked with blood and torn with deep gouges. Yellowed claws and gore-flecked fangs were buried in the metal of his breastplate. The Warrior Eternal's hair had come unbound, and he looked every inch the northern barbarian warrior from which his tribe descended.

'Tough fight,' said Myrsa.

'It's not done yet,' replied Sigmar, nodding towards the tower from which Morath brought down yet more bolts of lightning. 'You with me?'

Myrsa nodded and swung his hammer up to his shoulder.

'Always, my lord,' he said.

'Then let us finish this!'

PENDRAG'S AXE CHOPPED through the face of a decaying corpse, the stagnant ooze that remained in its veins spattering his armour. He spat flecks of rotten meat as he pushed onwards through the shambling horde of the dead. They fell easily to the hacking blows of the Count's Guard, but they staggered from the ruins of fallen towers without end.

His arm ached from hewing through the wet bodies of men and women who had once depended on him for protection, and though every creature slain was a soul freed, each one was a rusty nail in his heart. They pressed in on him and the Count's Guard with grasping fingers and teeth as their only weapons, and such a contest of arms would have been ludicrous but for the fact that there was no give in them.

Any normal foe would have long since broken and run from the deadly blades of his warriors, but with no thoughts of their own, enslaved to the will of Morath, they would never retreat. Only when their dead bodies were destroyed would they stop fighting.

More of the dead things fell to his axe, and he looked to his left to ensure that the speed of his warriors' advance was keeping pace with the White Wolves. He couldn't see Sigmar, but knew he would be in the thick of the battle where the fighting was heaviest. Across the valley, the banner of the Fauschlag Rock still flew, and Pendrag felt a moment's guilt that he was not fighting beneath it.

Sigmar had asked him to carry the Dragon Banner, and Pendrag could not refuse that honour, for only warriors of unbreakable courage were offered such a duty. He looked up at the banner, its once white fabric dyed red with the blood of the men who fought with it as their declaration of courage. The dragon was stitched in gold thread, and it flickered in the light of the moon and the flashing bolts of lighting that battered Sigmar's army.

A chill wind swept over Pendrag, and his body was suddenly gripped in a deathly cold embrace, as though he were drowning in the icy lake beneath him. The disgusting, cadaverous monsters moved aside, and a band of armoured warriors with mighty two-handed swords that shimmered with eerie light marched towards the Count's Guard. Clad in rusted armour of bronze and dark iron, these grim sentinels of death advanced beneath a banner of deepest black that rippled with dark winds and heart-stopping cold.

Spectral blades flashed as the dead warriors smashed into the Count's Guard. Where the corpse-things fought with mindless hunger, these creatures were skilled, and fought with all the deadly fury they had possessed while alive. Enormous blades flashed in the moonlight, and warriors, alive and dead, were cut down by brutal sweeps of long, heavy blades. Against the weight of the Count's Guards' greatswords, the rusted armour of the dead was no protection, and every blow smashed a skeletal warrior to shards.

Yet the blades of the dead were no less lethal and the dead warriors struck with a power that belied their rotten frames. Darkly-glowing swords cut into the northlanders, and each man that fell died with his head hacked from his shoulders. The swords of the dead warriors flashed with a speed that would have been impossible for a mortal man, each blow precisely weighted and aimed to kill with a single stroke.

A towering warrior in corroded bronze armour coated in verdigris fought at their centre, the flesh withered to his bones and a light from beyond the grave flickering in the pools of his eye sockets. Armoured in the fashion of hundreds of years ago, Pendrag knew that he faced one of the ancient warrior kings of old, a great leader interred within a hidden barrow beneath the earth, only to be torn from his eternal rest by the magic of the necromancer. The undead king's sword glimmered with frost, and Pendrag could feel it hunger for his neck.

Pendrag slammed the Dragon Banner into the ice and hefted his axe in both hands.

'You are mine!' Pendrag bellowed, holding the double-bladed axe towards the dead king.

The mighty king heard the challenge and could no more ignore it than could a living warrior. He dragged his shimmering blade from the chest of his latest victim, and charged Pendrag with a cold fire burning in the sockets of his skull. The sword swept up, a blur of rusted bronze, and Pendrag barely had time to block it, twisting his axe to sweep the blade aside. Pendrag spun around the king and swung his axe at his back, but the blade was blocked as the warrior impossibly brought his sword around to parry the blow.

The leathery flesh of the ancient king creaked as he smiled in triumph. The jaw gaped and rancid breath, like gases expelled from the depths of a bog, enveloped Pendrag. He stumbled, retching, blinded by the rankness of the grave king's exhalation. He threw himself back and brought up his axe, knowing that an attack was coming. The king's sword slammed into his breastplate and smashed him from his feet. Pendrag lost his grip on his axe and skidded across the ice.

His silver fingers gouged the frozen lake as he hit something jammed in the ice that halted his slide. The ancient king of the dead walked towards him with measured paces, his sword raised to finish him off. Something red flapped above Pendrag's head, and he looked up to see the Dragon Banner, its bloody fabric shimmering in the light of the dread moon.

The dead king brought his sword up to take his head, as Pendrag wrenched the banner from the ice, rolling to his knees as the sword swept towards his neck. Pendrag launched himself forward with the bladed finial of the banner pole aimed at the heart of his deathly foe.

Both weapons struck at the same instant, the silver point of the banner pole plunging through the rusted mail of the ancient king's chest, and the dread blade slamming into Pendrag's neck. Bright light exploded before Pendrag's eyes as the dead king's sword struck the torque ring that Master Alaric of the dwarfs had given him many years ago. He screamed as the torque seared his skin, fighting to resist the dreadful power of the dead king's blade.

The silver point of the banner pole tore from the dead king's back, swiftly followed by the bloody banner as his weight dragged him deeper onto it. The balefire in his eyes guttered and died, the blood of heroes driving the fell animation from his long dead frame. With no trace of that power remaining, the king's body fell to pieces, the skeleton and armour clattering to the ice in a rain of bone and rusted bronze.

Pendrag let out an agonised breath, still holding the banner aloft, and reaching up to drag the deformed torque from his neck. Forged from the star-iron of the dwarfs and shaped with runic hammers, the metal was blisteringly hot. He dropped it to the ice, and it sank into the frozen surface of the lake in a cloud of boiling steam.

No sooner had the ancient king's body disintegrated than his skeletal guards began to fall apart. Bound to the service of their liege lord in death as in life, their souls fled the decaying shells in which they were trapped. Pendrag breathed a relieved sigh as the deadly warriors collapsed into piles of bone and iron. His warriors stood amid a billowing dust cloud, surrounded by the headless bodies of their comrades. Every blow the dead had struck had killed one of his warriors.

Pendrag planted the Dragon Banner, and used the pole to haul himself to his feet.

On the far left of the battlefield, Myrsa's warriors pushed onwards, hacking a gruesome path through a host of snapping wolves of rotten flesh and mangy fur. The warriors Myrsa led were rough and ready, yet their courage had seen them willingly follow their Emperor into the jaws of battle.

In the centre of the battlefield, the White Wolves battered their way onwards, yet Pendrag could still not see Sigmar in their midst.

The Count's Guard formed up around the banner he clutched tightly in his silver hand. He saw their expectant faces and, lifting the crimson banner high, he aimed it towards the gleaming walls of the necromancer's keep.

'Onwards!' he cried. 'For Sigmar and the empire!'

FIGHTING SIDE-BY-SIDE, Sigmar and Myrsa bludgeoned a path through the walking dead. The warriors of Middenheim followed their Emperor, wheeling around and pushing hard towards the gateway of the brass fortress. Before the great iron portal, dead warriors clad in the livery of Ulric and Morr awaited them.

Myrsa smashed another of the dead from its feet and took a moment to recover his breath. These monsters were without skill, but the horror of their very existence drained a man's spirit and will to fight. It took every ounce of his courage to stand firm in the face of these abominations.

Beside him, Sigmar fought with a fury and strength that put Myrsa in mind of the greatest heroes of ancient times: legendary warriors such as Ostag the Fell, Udose Ironskull or Crom Firefist. Ghal-maraz swung around the Emperor's body in a blur, and wherever it struck, a dead thing was destroyed. Its bones would fly apart, shattered into fragments, and the horrid animation in its eyes would be snuffed out.

Myrsa's skill with a warhammer was great indeed, but as hard as he fought, he could not match Sigmar's strength. The speed and precision with which Sigmar wielded Ghal-maraz was truly breathtaking, as though the weapon was a part of him, or had always *been* a part of him. Myrsa had heard the story of how the Emperor came to bear the hammer of the mountain king, but no dwarf had borne this hammer to such deadly effect. Myrsa knew with utter certainty that whoever had forged Ghal-maraz had done so in the knowledge that Sigmar would be the warrior to bear it.

Myrsa drove the head of his own hammer through the face of a rotten death mask of a creature wielding a butcher's cleaver as another came at him with a grain-cutter's sickle. These were not warriors, these were ordinary men and women enslaved to the will of the necromancer. Each blow he struck fanned the flames of Myrsa's rage, for these were *his* people, Middenlanders all, and they deserved a better end than this.

Myrsa swung his hammer up in readiness to face the next foe, but all that remained standing between them and the keep's black gateway was a shield wall of warriors in all too familiar tunics. Myrsa let out a low moan as he saw dozens of familiar faces before him, men he had despatched to seek out the source of the evil in the mountains.

Sigmar stood before the Ulrican templars and Knights of Morr, the dead-faced warriors as unbending and firm in the face of the enemy as they had always been. Myrsa's soul rebelled to see these fine, honourable warriors so debased.

He looked over at Sigmar, seeing the same revulsion that men who had fought against such evil were now forced to serve it. His fury overcame the dread he felt at seeing the dead walking, and Myrsa charged the shield-wall with his hammer swinging in wide, crushing sweeps.

The warriors of Middenland followed him, and he heard their wild yells as they pounded across the ice. He felt Sigmar charging alongside him, and the sheer presence of the Emperor steadied Myrsa's nerves. The shield wall loomed before them, the dead warriors bracing their shields and lifting their swords over the tops.

Living and dead clashed in a surging mass of armour and flesh. Myrsa blocked a sword thrust with the haft of his hammer and swung the head into the shield before him. Sigmar punched a huge hole in their ranks of the dead, and hurled himself into the gap, battering his way into the shield wall with a blend of skill and brute strength.

'With me!' he shouted. 'Break it open!'

Warriors poured after him, cutting their way into the formation. A normal shield wall would fly apart now, but the dead warriors remained where they were, cutting and stabbing and blocking as though nothing had happened.

A sword clanged on Myrsa's armour, slashing up to his helmet and tearing off his cheek guard. Blood sprayed from his chin as the blade caught him, and he spat a tooth.

He lost sight of Sigmar as the dead warriors closed ranks, pushing back with their shields and stabbing down with their blades. Though they were dead, their armour was still bright and their swords were still sharp. The ice was sticky with blood and entrails, fresh and rotten, and screams of pain echoed from the sides of the crater as men were killed by warriors who had once sworn to stand beside them.

Myrsa blocked a clumsy sword thrust and swung his hammer in an upward arc, tearing the shield – and the arm that bore it – from the dead warrior who carried it. He lifted his hammer high to finish the job, but his jaw dropped open and the blow never landed as he saw the face before him.

'Kristof?' he said, seeing the face of his sword-brother from before he had sworn the oath of the Warrior Eternal. Together they had fought greenskins in the Middle Mountains and Norsii raiders on the coast, and they had cleared whole swathes of the forest of hideous beast creatures. Kristof had saved his life on dozens of occasions, and Myrsa had repaid that debt many times. He had known there was a chance he would have to face his sword-brother on this march, but he had held out hope that Kristof would not have been among the risen dead.

He lowered his hammer.

'My sword-brother… What have they done to you?' he said.

Kristof's sword lanced out in answer, a blade that Myrsa himself had presented to him. He tried to dodge aside, but memories of his lost friend cost him dearly. The blade hammered home just below the breastplate, and mail links snapped as the north-forged iron plunged into his stomach. Myrsa cried out, feeling cold fire spread out from the wound, such that he felt as though he had been stabbed with a shard of winter.

He dropped to his knees, and cried out as the sword was torn from the wound. He looked up at the man with whom he had sworn eternal brotherhood, seeing that the sunken orbs of Kristof's eyes held no memory of him.

The pain of his wound faded, and Myrsa watched as the blade swept up and then down, moving as though in a dream. Metal flashed, and he heard a thunderous ring of metal on metal as a hammer of magnificent workmanship intercepted Kristof's blade. The hammer twisted the sword aside, and its wielder smashed the end of the haft into his former sword-brother's face. Decaying skull matter broke apart, and the hammer's reverse stroke shattered Kristof's ribcage to cleave his body in two.

Myrsa felt strong hands dragging him back, and saw Sigmar looking down at him with fearful eyes. The pain of his wound returned with a savage vengeance, and he cried out as he saw that his lap was soaked in warm blood.

'Take him!' ordered Sigmar, lying him down on the ice and shouting at some people that Myrsa could not see. Warriors of Middenheim knelt beside him, pulling open his armour and pressing their hands against his wound. The pain was indescribable, but was fading with each passing moment.

The clouds were dark and purple, split by crackling lightning, and Myrsa thought that it would be a shame to die with such an ugly sky looking down. Sigmar loomed above him, his face creased with lines of terrible fear.

The Emperor tore something from around his neck and pressed it into his hands. Myrsa craned his neck and saw that it was a bronze pendant, carved in the image of a gateway.

'Hold to this, Myrsa,' said Sigmar.

'Morr's gateway,' he whispered. 'Then it's my time? I'm dying?'

'No,' promised Sigmar, though he flinched at Myrsa's words. 'You will live. My father gave it to me when death hovered near and it kept me safe. It will do the same for you.'

Sigmar nodded to the men behind him. 'Do not let him die, no matter what occurs!'

Myrsa lifted the bronze pendant to his heart as Sigmar turned back to the battle.

SIGMAR RAN FOR the gateway of Brass Keep. Ragged bands of warriors followed him, all semblance of order gone in the desperate fighting to break the shield-wall. The necromancer's citadel was breached, but not without cost. Hundreds of Sigmar's men were wounded, and even if he could defeat Morath, many would not survive to reach Middenheim.

This thought spurred Sigmar to greater speed, and he emerged from the darkened gateway into a cobbled plaza in the midst of the ancient keep. Within the walls, he saw that Brass Keep was no more real than the manufactured city beneath the ice. Like that drowned city, the keep was little more than a shimmering artifice created by Morath, a fiction to recall past glories and ancient triumphs.

The walls were simply walls, bereft of ramparts or stairs, and the towers were simply columns of stone without any means of accessing them. What buildings there were in the courtyard were simply ruined shells, little more than rubble and decay. Perhaps there had once been a mountain fortress here, but it had long since been forgotten by the race of men.

The only structure of any reality within the fortress was the tower fashioned from glistening, pearlescent stone. The pinnacle of the tower was haloed with dark lightning, the withering light from the necromancer's staff bathing the underside of the clouds with a demented, sickly aura. A spectral mist oozed from a skull-wreathed archway at the base of the tower, and hideous shapes writhed in its depths, howling souls bound to Morath's evil.

Sigmar ran towards the tower, and the warriors of the Fauschlag Rock came with him, their swords bright and their hearts hungry for vengeance on the hated necromancer. The mist twitched and danced as the spirits felt the lash of their master's will, and they streaked across the ice towards Sigmar's warriors like glittering comets.

Streamers of light surrounded them, and Sigmar saw they were the spirits of ghostly women, flying through the air as though moving underwater. They were beautiful, and he lowered his hammer, loath to strike out at a woman, even a ghostly one.

Then their jaws opened wide and they screamed.

Their dreadful wailing tore into Sigmar's soul with talons of fire. He dropped to his knees and Ghal-maraz fell as his hands flew to his ears to block the agonising sound. One of the she-creatures hovered in the air before him, robed in grave shrouds that swirled around its emaciated body with a life of their own. Its beauty sloughed from its remarkable face to reveal a fleshless skull with eyes that blazed with bitter hatred. A long mane of spine-like hair billowed behind it, and Sigmar instantly knew that these were not victims of Morath at all, but creatures of evil.

They shrieked around the men of the empire, wailing in torment, seeking to wreak a measure of their eternal suffering upon the living. Ghostly claws ripped open armour, and shrieking laments cut deeper than any blade. Some men went mad with fear and fled back through the gateway, while others dropped down dead, their faces twisted into rictus masks of terror by nightmares only they could see.

Sigmar's mind filled with visions of lying beneath the earth with worms feeding on the diseased meat of his body. He cried out as he saw Ravenna, her once beautiful features ravaged by the creatures of the earth, her flesh bloated and rotten, blue and waxy as the world reclaimed her.

Tears streamed down his face and his heart thudded against his chest in terror. The pain in his head was beyond measure and he could feel his soul being prised from his mortal flesh with every shrieking wail.

Then he heard something else, a sound that spoke to his spirit and cut through the unnatural fear of these monstrous women. It was a sound of the wild, a sound that represented the core of who he was and everything for which he stood. It was the sound of the empire and its patron.

It was the sound of wolves.

Sigmar twisted his head towards the sound to see a host of warriors pouring through the gateway: a mass of Pendrag's Count's Guard and Redwane's White Wolves. Armoured in silver and red, their wolfskin pelts and the Dragon Banner billowed as though they marched through a winter storm. Their wild hair was unbound, and each man howled with all the ferocity he could muster. Their wolf howls were like the pack of Ulric, and Sigmar saw his friends leading these brave men with a hammer and sword, hewing the dead with every stroke.

Freed from the awful, soul-shredding agony of the witches' shrieks, Sigmar bellowed in rage. The women howled again, but they had no power over the men of the empire, for faith in Ulric had armoured their souls.

Pendrag ran towards him.

'Are you hurt?' he asked.

'No,' said Sigmar, pushing himself upright and forcing the visions of death from his mind.

'Here,' said Redwane, holding out Ghal-maraz. 'You dropped this.'

Sigmar took the warhammer, feeling a strange, jealous stab of power surge up his arm as he turned his gaze upon Morath's tower. The spirit-haunted mist was dispersing, as though blown by a strong wind, and the skull-wreathed archway yawned like the deepest cave in the rock of the earth. Only death awaited in such a place, and Sigmar felt his innards clench at the thought of venturing within.

Monstrous laughter boomed from above, and Sigmar's resolve hardened like dwarf-forged iron. He turned to his warriors and saw that same resolve in every face.

'Men of the empire, today a necromancer dies,' he snarled.

## ⊰ THIRTEEN ⊱

# A Warning Unheeded

Darkness swallowed Sigmar as he led his warriors into the tower, and icy winds swirled around him as though he had stepped into an ice cave far beneath the earth. The tower was hollow, a soaring cylinder that rose dizzyingly to a pale, deathly light. An unnatural, echoing silence filled the tower, the noise of the furious battle raging beyond its walls extinguished the instant he crossed the threshold.

Fallen headstones and crumbling tombs filled the tower's interior, a sprawling necropolis impossibly filled with thousands of graves. The earth on each was freshly turned, as though the dead had only recently been lowered beneath the ground, though some unknown instinct told Sigmar that whoever was buried here had been dead for centuries or more.

'I don't like the looks of this,' said Redwane, nodding towards the mass of graves.

'There are thousands of them,' added Pendrag.

Sigmar didn't answer, seeing a series of mossy, tread-worn steps cut from the inner circumference of the tower.

The cold wind that had led him to this hidden valley gusted from above. It seemed to beckon him, as though daring him, or perhaps *needing* him to climb the steps. Sigmar sensed a power greater than any man could master in that sickly summons, but it was a summons he had come too far to ignore.

'This way,' he said. 'We cannot stop now, we have to push on!'

He ran towards the stairs with Redwane and Pendrag at his side. The White Wolf kept one eye on the gloomy necropolis, a faint green glow from the dread moon bathing the city in its hateful illumination.

'I suppose it's too much to hope that the dead things we fought outside were in these graves?' asked Redwane.

'I wouldn't count on it,' replied Pendrag as a hideous moaning filled the tower.

It sounded as though it came from somewhere deep underground, as if the earth itself were howling in its depths. Seconds later, the dirt upon the graves trembled, and the slabs sealing each tomb crashed to the ground with the grinding of stone on stone.

'Ulric's bones, doesn't this ever end?' hissed Redwane as grasping, skeletal hands clawed their way from beneath the ground and over the lips of dusty sepulchres. A fresh host of the living dead rose from their slumbers, warriors armed with short curving swords and clad in rusted plate of a style that Sigmar had never seen. Elaborately crafted with sweeping curves and horned spikes, it seemed that they were designed for intimidation as much as protection. These warriors had last made war thousands of years ago.

'There's too many of them,' said Redwane. 'We can't fight our way through them all.'

Sigmar looked up the curving spiral of the stairs towards the nimbus of light that gathered at the top of the tower.

'Maybe we will not have to,' he said.

'What do you mean?' asked Pendrag as the ancient warriors shuffled and dragged their rotten carcasses towards the waiting men of the empire.

'Morath is up there, and with him, the source of his power,' said Sigmar. 'The priests of Morr told me that without the will of the necromancer binding them, these wretched souls will return to the realm of the dead where they belong.'

Redwane nodded, as though that were the most natural thing in the world. He shifted his grip on his hammer and nodded again, taking a deep breath.

'Then go,' said the White Wolf, hauling warriors into position to form a rough battle line at the bottom of the stairs. 'We will hold these dead things back. Get to the necromancer and bury your hammer in his skull!'

SIGMAR AND PENDRAG took the stairs two at a time, pushing upwards without pause for breath or any words. Already tired from the march through the mountains and the battle on the ice, Sigmar's thighs burned with exertion, yet he did not dare stop. The sound of clashing blades and screams drifted up from below.

Pendrag had refused to let Sigmar face Morath alone, and his sword-brother puffed and panted as he followed behind. He still clutched the Dragon Banner, and Sigmar was reassured by his brother's unwillingness to be parted from it. To fight the necromancer with such a potent symbol at their side would send a clear message that Sigmar was in no mood for mercy.

The fear that held sway over the battlefield was concentrated and distilled within the tower, a black dread that sank down from above like blood in water. Shadows howled and spun in the gloom, faceless phantoms that swirled like flocks of crows. Each time the hungry shadows swooped towards the two climbers, Pendrag held the

Dragon Banner high, and they screeched and spun away from its power.

Sigmar did not know what that power was, but was grateful to whatever enchantments had been woven into the banner... or to whatever it had acquired in the course of the battle.

He glanced over his shoulder, feeling his armour and hammer weigh heavily upon him. Every step he took towards the top of the tower, the heavier they became. His limbs ached and he fought the urge to give up. He was exhausted, his body and mind pushed beyond the limits of human endurance. A sibilant, voiceless imperative urged him to rest, to lay down his burdens and accept that there was no more he could do. He fought it with every scrap of his will.

Sigmar gritted his teeth and put his head down. When he had climbed the mountain to face the Dragon Ogre Skaranorak, he had concentrated on simply putting one foot in front of the other, and that single-mindedness served him as well now as it had then. Even so, his steps were leaden, each one a small victory.

He heard Pendrag's laboured breath and knew that his sword-brother was suffering as he was. The tower darkened until all Sigmar could see was the faint glow from the rune-carved haft of Ghal-maraz. The climb was sapping Sigmar's strength, draining his vitality and feeding every dark thought that lurked in his mind, telling him he was too weak, too stupid and too *mortal* to ever succeed. Only by embracing the power of dark magic could any man hope to cheat death and see his labours truly bear fruit, for what ambition of any worth could be satisfied in the span of a single life?

Sigmar shut out that voice, that damnable voice of doubt that lodged like a parasite in every man's heart and chipped away at his resolve. *Don't bother trying anything, for all your dreams are dust*, it said. *It is pointless to struggle, for in a hundred years no one will remember you.*

'No,' hissed Sigmar. '*I* will be remembered.'

Mocking laughter rang from the walls, and Sigmar fought against the arrogant superiority that he heard in the echoes. *You will fail and be forgotten,* said the laughter. *Give in now.*

'If failure is so certain, why do you work so hard to make me believe it?' he cried.

Behind him, Pendrag let out a soft moan, and Sigmar felt warmth at his brow where the crown fashioned by Alaric slotted neatly over his helmet.

'I may fail and, in time I *will* die, but I am not afraid of that!' Sigmar shouted at the oppressive, smothering blackness. 'I am not afraid to fail. I only fear not to try!'

With every word, the gloom lifted, until he could once again see the steps beneath his feet and the glowing light at the top of the tower. Barely a dozen steps lay between him and a square-cut opening. The sickly light and cold wind that had guided him here shone like a hopeless beacon at the end of the world.

Sigmar looked down to see Pendrag at his back, blinking and letting out short, hiking breaths, as though awaking from a dreadful nightmare.

'Whatever he's telling you, don't believe it,' said Sigmar.

Pendrag looked up at him through tear-filled eyes. 'He told me of my death.'

Sigmar saw the terror in Pendrag's eyes and shook his head.

'All men die, Pendrag, it takes no sorcery to know that,' he said. 'If that is the best this necromancer can conjure, then we have nothing to fear.'

Pendrag looked past him at the square of light at the top of the stairs. His face crumpled in self-loathing.

'I can't.' he said. 'I'm afraid.'

Sigmar came down the stairs to Pendrag and gripped his shoulder.

'It is Morath who should fear us,' he said. 'He knows the strength of mortals and he fears it. He seeks to break our spirits before we can destroy him.'

Reaching up to the Dragon Banner, Sigmar took hold of the stiff, crimson fabric and held it before his friend.

'You carry a banner of heroes, Pendrag,' he said. 'The blood of brave men stains this cloth, and we dishonour them if we falter. You are a warrior of great courage, and I need you at my side.'

Pendrag took a great gulp of air, and Sigmar saw that he had overcome the dark enchantments that were working against them. The fear was still there, but the warrior spirit that made Pendrag so formidable remained firm.

'I will always be by your side, my friend,' Pendrag said.

Sigmar nodded, and together they climbed into the lair of the necromancer.

THE MOUNTAINS STRETCHED out for hundreds of miles around them, and the view was so spectacular that Sigmar almost forgot that they stood upon a tower raised by dark magic. Giant, snow-capped peaks marched off into the distance, jagged and impossible, immense structures of rock that were surely sculpted by the hands of the gods.

In the distance, bands of pink clouds clung to their summits like feathers, but here they were ugly, sooty smears, the black smoke of a flaming midden, greasy and reeking of rotten meat. Lightning arced in broken spears around the circumference of the tower, and more of the shrieking skull-faced witches spun around it like trapped hurricanes.

The necromancer was waiting for them, and the sight of him took Sigmar's breath away.

Like a sliver of the deepest darkness imaginable, Morath stood at the edge of the tower, a monstrous creature of evil who sucked the life from the world. Tattered robes of black flapped and blew around the necromancer, though no wind disturbed Sigmar's cloak or the cloth of the Dragon Banner.

The necromancer had his back to them and gave no sign that he was even aware of their presence. For a reckless moment, Sigmar thought of rushing forward and pushing the sorcerer from his pearl tower, and wanted to laugh at the ridiculousness of such a foolish plan.

Morath turned his head, and his ghastly visage struck a deep wound in Sigmar's heart, for here was the very face of death. The necromancer's face was not a skull, yet the skin was drawn so tight across his jutting, angular bones it might as well have been. Morath's hood was drawn up over his gleaming head, and his features were bathed in the glow of the pellucid lightning and his staff's dreadful illumination.

That human eyes could stare out from so hideous a face was a horror neither he nor Pendrag had been prepared for. In his hatred, Sigmar had assumed that Morath would be an inhuman monster, a creature of darkness and evil with whom they could share no commonality.

But in the haunted orbs of Morath he saw rage and bitterness fuelled by emotions that were all too human: an age of fear, regret, loss and thwarted ambition that had driven him to madness and acts of such depravity and horror that nothing, not even the gods, could redeem his damned soul. Such a man had good reason to fear judgement beyond death.

'By all the gods,' breathed Pendrag. 'What are you?'

Morath grinned, exposing a glistening and blackened tongue that licked the yellowed stumps of his teeth. Any lingering trace of humanity was dispelled by that grin and Sigmar forced himself to take a step forward, gripping Ghal-maraz tightly, focusing all his courage into that one act.

He locked his gaze with Morath as the necromancer lifted a withered hand and swept the hood from his head. Sigmar's steps faltered as ancient light shimmered on the golden crown that sat upon the necromancer's brow. It was a beguiling thing, crafted in an age long dead, a wondrous artefact imbued with all the power of its maker.

Morath hissed, and turned to fully face Sigmar and Pendrag. Shadows swirled around him, as though the darkness of the deepest night enshrouded his form. Now that he looked closer, Sigmar saw that Morath was hunched and emaciated, his physical form withered and decayed. Skeletal ribs were visible through the tattered fabric of his robes, but Sigmar knew not to judge the necromancer's power by his frail appearance.

'You have come a long way to die,' said Morath, his voice silken and seductive, at odds with his dreadful appearance.

'As have you,' said Sigmar. 'Mourkain is a long way from here.'

Morath laughed, the sound rich and full, as though they had shared a private jest.

'You speak of a place you do not know,' said the necromancer, 'of an empire that fell before your degenerate tribe even came to this land.'

Sigmar flinched at Morath's words, as though each was a dart tipped with poison.

'But you could not let it die, could you?' asked Sigmar.

'Would you allow yours to be ended by the foolishness of one man, Sigmar the Heldenhammer?' asked Morath, taking a step towards him.

'All things have their time, and all things must die in time.'

'Not all things,' promised Morath. 'I came to this land near death, but I slept away the centuries beneath the world and far from the sight of men. Now I am risen, and already your empire is dying. Can you not feel it? The cold touch of the death I bring is carried on every breath of wind and all that you love will soon be gone.'

'Not if I kill you first,' said Sigmar. 'This land is strong and it will survive your magic.'

'It will not,' promised Morath, 'but I am done talking with you. It is time for you to die, but fear not, I will bring your soul back and you will stand at my side as we carve a new empire from the bones of your doomed race.'

'I am here to make sure that never happens,' said Sigmar, forcing himself to close with the terrible, wretched form of the necromancer. If he could only get close enough to strike a single blow, he knew he could end this.

Morath chuckled, and a chill entered Sigmar's heart.

'You think you are here by your own design? Foolish, arrogant man,' said Morath. 'Even entombed beneath the world I sensed your power, and I knew I would need to draw you to me. One such as you will make a fine general for my army of the dead when I rebuild the glory of Mourkain.'

Morath raised his hand, and Sigmar's step faltered as the chains of duty that bound him to his people crushed him within their grip. To rule a united empire of man had been his dream since he had wandered the tombs of his ancestors on Warrior's Hill as a young man, but he had not been prepared for the reality of the task.

Smothered beneath the hideous weight of his undertaking, Sigmar's arms fell to his sides. He knew this was Morath's sorcery, but he was powerless to resist.

Sigmar dropped to his knees.

'I can't do this,' he whispered.

Pendrag stood tall at his side, his chest heaving with effort as he clutched the Dragon Banner tightly to his breast.

'What are you doing?' he asked.

'It's too much,' said Sigmar.

Pendrag caught his breath and looked over at Morath.

'Fight him! Your warriors are buying us time to kill Morath with their lives!'

'I don't care,' said Sigmar tearing off his helmet and hurling it away. Pendrag watched helplessly as the magnificently crafted helm fell through the opening in the floor, hearing it clatter down the steps as it fell to the bottom of the tower.

'Stand and fight!' demanded Pendrag, hauling on his arm.

'Don't you understand?' shouted Sigmar. 'It's too much for any one man. The empire... We will never be safe. Never. There will always be someone or something trying to destroy us, whether it's greenskins from the mountains, Norsii or worse from across the seas, twisted forest beasts or necromancers. We can't fight them all. We fight and we fight, but they keep coming. Eventually, one of them will drag us down, and drown this land in our blood. It's inevitable, so why bother fighting to keep the flame alive when it's eventually going to be extinguished?'

Morath's triumphant laughter swirled around him, and Sigmar saw the black form of the necromancer swell and billow, his robes spreading like the wings of a huge bat.

Pendrag roared and hurled himself at the necromancer, but a flick of Morath's shrivelled hand sent him sprawling, the banner torn from his silver grip. The standard skidded across the smooth stone before coming to rest at the edge of the tower, its bloody cloth flapping in the shrieking winds that circled the tower.

Morath slid through the air to hover above Pendrag, his leering features twisted in ghoulish relish, his head cocked to one side, like a carrion bird deciding which eye of a freshly dead corpse to devour first.

'I spoke words of your death, yet still you came,' hissed the necromancer. 'You will make a fine lieutenant for my new general.'

A pale light built within Morath's outstretched hand, and Pendrag cried out in pain, his face twisted in agony. His sword-brother's skin grew pallid and leathery, the colour bleaching from his hair until it was utterly white.

The life was being sucked out of him, yet Sigmar could no more lift himself from his knees than he could sprout wings and fly. One of his oldest and dearest friends was dying before his eyes, and he could do nothing to prevent it. Nothing.

He closed his eyes as his dreams collapsed. His vision of a strong and united land fractured and died within him. Morath was right. No empire of mortals could ever really last, for such was the fate of all works of man. Empires grew and prospered, and then became fat and complacent. Before long, one of their many enemies would rise up and destroy them.

It was as inevitable as nightfall.

In Sigmar's mind's eye he saw a ruined city by a river, a once magnificent capital built around the mighty tomb of some ancient king. It had once covered a vast area and been home to thousands, but now only greenskins dwelled there. Its gilded plazas served as arenas for battling warlords, its sunken marble bathhouses as pens for wolves, boars and foul, cave-dwelling beasts that skulked in the shadows. Tomes and scrolls that had been gathered over thousands of years burned on campfires, and works of art that had stirred the hearts and minds of those who studied them were smashed for sport.

Morath's honeyed words sounded in his mind. *This is the doom of your empire.*

Sigmar wept to see so fine a city despoiled, realising with a jolt that this was the same city he had seen recreated beneath the ice. Was this Mourkain? This was the city mourned by the necromancer, the dream he sought to rebuild from the ashes of Sigmar's empire.

The ruin of Mourkain faded from sight, and Sigmar was glad to see it go, for it spoke of ancient loss and the inevitable doom of dreams. Yet the achievements of its builders were no less impressive for its having fallen. They had built a great city and carved out a mighty empire, and that was something to be proud of. That it had eventually been brought to ruin did not lessen the wonder of that achievement.

Yes, empires fell and men died, but that was the way of the world. To defy that was to go against the will of the gods, and no man dared stand before those awesome powers with such arrogance. His father had once told him of how the ageing leader of a wolf pack would leave and roam the mountains alone when his strength was fading and stronger wolves were ready to lead. For a thing to endure beyond its time was a sad and terrible thing, and to see what was once glorious and noble reduced to something wretched and pathetic was heartbreaking.

Sigmar's empire would one day fall, and when that time came, men would mourn its passing. Other empires would arise to take its place, but this was the time of *his* empire, and no necromancer was going to take it away from him!

Sigmar lifted his head, and stared at Morath as he sucked the life from Pendrag.

His heart hardened and growing strength filled his limbs. He forced himself to his feet, crying out as the chill touch of the necromancer fled his body in the face of his acceptance of the future's inevitability. With every second that passed, the despair and hopelessness shrouding him diminished in the face of his determination to resist Morath's dark power.

'Empires rise and fall,' snarled Sigmar as he stood tall, 'but that matters not. All that matters is that they rose, and in their time men walked with honour and fought for what they believed. What matters is what we do with the time we have.'

Morath turned at the sound of his voice, and the necromancer's sunken eyes widened in surprise. His hands stretched out towards Sigmar, and streaming bolts of cold fire leapt from the necromancer's fingers. Dancing sheets of icy flame erupted from the air around Sigmar, but he smiled as the runic script worked into his armour blazed in reply.

Sigmar walked untouched through the inferno, Ghalmaraz ablaze with the white fire that Morath hurled.

'You have no power over me,' said Sigmar. 'Your despair means nothing to me, for I have no fear for the future. That I shall die and all my achievements turn to dust does not make them pointless. Living forever and creating nothing of worth... *that* is pointless. You have no place in this world, necromancer. You should have died a long time ago, and I am here to send your soul into the next world and whatever torments await you.'

Morath raised his arms, and Pendrag sagged to the stones of the tower. With every step Sigmar took, Morath took one away from him. Once more he stabbed his hands towards Sigmar, and the shrieking ghosts that swirled around the top of the tower gathered in a mass of howling spirits. Morath hurled them towards Sigmar, and they came at him in a mad, swirling pack of screaming skulls.

They howled around him, snapping with fleshless claws and ethereal fangs. Sigmar ignored them, his towering self-belief carrying him through their hate unharmed. His heart was iron, his soul a stone, and the depraved spirits could not turn him from his path.

'What manner of man are you?' demanded Morath as Sigmar came closer. 'No mortal can resist such power!'

The necromancer's staff blazed with dark light, but Sigmar raised Ghal-maraz, and the staff shattered into a thousand fragments, each one blowing away like ash in a storm. Morath fell to his knees, his hunched form now pitiful and contemptible. He reached out with reed-thin fingers, but Sigmar batted them away. The necromancer seemed to shrink within his robes, as though his form was diminishing, whatever power that had sustained him over the centuries withdrawing from his flesh.

'No…' hissed Morath, holding his withered hands up before his face. 'You promised…'

The roiling stormclouds above the tower began to break up as the dark energies that bound them dissipated. A fresh wind blew over the tower, carrying the scent of highland forests and fast-flowing rivers of cool water.

Morath crumpled, his bony frame folding into itself with every second. His flesh was wasting away, and the golden crown he had worn with such arrogant pride fell from his brow. It landed with the heavy metallic ring of pure gold, and rolled across the tower before coming to rest at Sigmar's feet.

Sigmar wrapped his hand around Morath's throat, feeling the frailty of his bones, and he knew that he could snap his neck with ease. There was no weight to him, and Sigmar looked upon the icy battlefield to see that the dead warriors no longer fought. Their bones crumbled to dust, and the city beneath the ice began to fade like a distant memory as he watched.

His warriors cheered as they saw him atop the tower with the necromancer as his prisoner. They bayed for Morath's death, and they were not the only ones. Half-heard moans of anger were carried on the wind, the freed spirits of the dead demanding vengeance.

'I think there will be many souls awaiting your arrival in the next world,' said Sigmar.

Morath's gnarled and ancient face stretched in fear, and he gibbered nonsensical pleas for mercy as he clawed at

Sigmar's arm. His struggles were feeble, and Sigmar quashed the flickering ember of pity that threatened to stay his hand.

'You have existed for too long,' said Sigmar, lifting Morath over the edge. 'It is time for you to die.'

He hurled Morath from the tower, and watched as his thin body tumbled downwards, spinning end over end until he smashed into the ice. Sigmar let out a long, exhausted exhalation and felt a wave of gratitude wash over him. Thousands of faces and names flashed through Sigmar's mind, each one a soul freed from eternal damnation, and tears of joy spilled down his face as they passed on.

Sigmar turned from the edge of the tower and felt something at his feet: the crown Morath had worn and which had granted him such power. He reached down and turned it around in his hands. The workmanship was incredible, easily the equal of any dwarf-forged metal, yet its design was unfamiliar. Worked in gold and set with jewels, it was a thing of beauty, and he felt the vast power bound to it, an ancient power beyond the ken of even the mountain folk to craft.

For a fleeting moment, he beheld an ancient city of the desert, and a host of bejewelled armies marching across the scorched sands beneath great banners of blue and gold. Then it was gone and the incredible vista of the Middle Mountains returned to him. He saw Pendrag lying on his side at the edge of the tower, crawling towards the fallen Dragon Banner.

Sigmar rushed towards his friend, his vision of the desert armies forgotten as he knelt at his side and turned him over. He tried to hide his shock, but Pendrag saw the horror in his eyes.

'It's that bad is it?' whispered Pendrag, his voice little more than a parched croak.

'No... It's—' began Sigmar, though he could not bring himself to lie.

Pendrag's face was sunken and hollow, the very image of Lukas Hauke, the creature that had been imprisoned beneath the Faushlag Rock. His eyes were rheumy with cataracts and his skin wrinkled like ancient parchment. What Morath had taken was Pendrag's youth, for Sigmar cradled a man hundreds of years old.

He wished he could save Pendrag. He wished he had not succumbed to Morath's dark magic, that he could have broken the spell of his despair sooner. Tears fell from his eyes and landed on Pendrag's face at the thought of his death, and Sigmar knew that all the power in the world was meaningless in the face of such loss.

'Sigmar!' cried Pendrag, and Sigmar opened his eyes as the crown grew hot in his hands.

Golden heat flowed from the crown and into Sigmar. It filled him with light, and the weight of his burdens lifted in an instant. But the crown had not yet finished its work. Amber light flowed from Sigmar and passed into Pendrag, filling his body with light and undoing the necromancer's hateful magic.

Pendrag cried out as his hair thickened and the red that had drained from it returned more lustrous than ever. His flesh filled with life and the colour returned to his eyes. Old scars on his arms faded, and his chest rose and fell with powerful, deep breaths.

Both men looked in astonishment at the golden crown. The light faded from the jewels, yet Sigmar could sense that its power was far from spent.

'I don't believe it!' cried Pendrag, climbing to his feet and examining every inch of his body as though afraid to believe in the miracle of his renewal. He threw his head back and laughed, the sound filled with renewed life and hope: the laughter of one who has faced death and come back stronger than ever.

'The crown…' said Sigmar. 'I have never seen anything like this… It healed you. This is powerful magic indeed.'

'Aye,' agreed Pendrag, staring in joyous wonder at the magnificent artefact. 'Magic used for evil by a necro-mancer.'

Sigmar turned the crown in his hands, knowing that he held the key to making the empire stronger than ever before. With such power, he could defend his land and people, ruling with justice and strength. Morath had twisted the power of the crown, but Sigmar would use it to heal, not to kill. To govern with wisdom and compassion, not to enslave.

He looked at Pendrag, and his sword-brother answered his unasked question with a nod.

'Yes. It is yours now,' said Pendrag.

Sigmar lifted the golden crown and slipped it over his head. Though Morath's skull had been thin and hairless, the crown was a perfect fit. He felt its power, and he took Pendrag's hand in the warrior's grip.

He heard the sound of footsteps behind him and a group of battle-weary warriors poured onto the top of the tower. Redwane was at the forefront, his face streaked with blood and his armour hanging from him in torn links of mail and battered plate. In his hands he held Sigmar's helmet, the metal dented and scraped from its fall down the length of the tower. Alaric's crown still sat upon it, and a flicker of unease passed through Sigmar.

Redwane held the helmet with an amused grin.

'Must I always be picking up after you?' he asked.

Sigmar laughed. 'Keep it,' he said, sweeping past the White Wolf. 'I have a new crown.'

UNWILLING TO REMAIN a moment longer within the valley of the necromancer, Sigmar's warriors gathered their dead and wounded and marched through the darkness. The Dragon Banner was lowered and, as the moon traversed the clear night sky, Sigmar spoke to each man in his army, praising his courage and honouring the sacrifice of the dead.

The wounded were carried on makeshift litters, and, as Sigmar took their hands, it seemed their suffering lessened. He sought out Myrsa, and was relieved beyond words to find that he still lived. No sooner had he laid his hand upon the Warrior Eternal's brow, than the colour returned to the wounded man's face and his breathing deepened.

Forgetting his promise to bring Brass Keep down, stone by stone, Sigmar led his warriors from the mountains, taking a more direct westerly route through thickly forested valleys that would bring them out on the western flanks of the mountains.

Four days later, the weary men of the empire emerged from the foothills of the Middle Mountains, following a curving path towards the forest road that led south to Middenheim. On the morning of the fifth day, scouts reported a large column of people and wagons coming from the north, and Sigmar went out to meet them with his new crown glittering at his brow. Redwane and three White Wolves marched with him, and the invigorated Pendrag carried the Emperor's crimson banner aloft.

The first groups of people to emerge from the tree line marched in a long, weary column, and Sigmar swore softly under his breath at their wretched, sorry state. As more and more came into view, he saw that they came on foot, on rattling carts or on overflowing wagons. He had expected travelling merchants or a labourers heading to Middenheim to find work. What he had not expected was hundreds of refugees, for there could be no mistaking that these were people fleeing from some terror behind them.

'Udose by the look of them,' said Pendrag.

'Aye,' agreed Redwane. 'I see plaid, and some of the men have claymores.'

'What in the name of Ulric happened to them?' asked Sigmar, approaching a wagon with a ragged scrap of an

Udose flag bearing the patchwork colours of Count Wolfila flapping on a makeshift banner pole. A pair of weary pack ponies pulled the wagon, and a one-armed man with wide shoulders and the face of a pugilist sat on the buckboard. A young woman with three children sat behind him, their faces pinched and fearful.

'Ho there, fellow,' said Sigmar, walking alongside the wagon. 'What do they call you?'

'Rolf,' said the man. 'Though most call me Oakfist on account of my left hook.'

'I can see why,' said Sigmar, seeing the meaty scale of the man's remaining fist. 'Where have you come from?'

'Salzenhús,' said Rolf. 'Or what's left of it.'

Sigmar felt a knot in his stomach at mention of Count Wolfila's castle and said, 'What do you mean? What has happened?'

The old man glared at him and spat a single word, 'Norsii.'

'The Norsii? They did this?'

'Aye,' said the old man. 'Them and their traitorous allies.'

'Allies? Who?'

'Bastard Roppsmenn,' said Rolf. 'Wolfships been raiding up and down the coast all season, but there's been sword bands of Roppsmenn riding with 'em this year, killing and burning and driving people south.'

'Are you sure they were Roppsmenn?' asked Sigmar, feeling a throbbing pulse of fury at his temple as the full weight of what he had been told sank in. 'They hated the Norsii as much as any tribe ever did.'

'Damn right I'm sure,' snarled Rolf, rage and sadness choking his voice. 'I seen them with my own eyes. Shaven heads and curved swords they had. Burned Wolfila's castle to the ground and cut him into pieces for dogs to eat. Killed his family too. Wife and child butchered and crucified on the only tower left standing.'

Sigmar felt the knot in his stomach unravel with a dreadful sickness at this news, and the fiery pulse at his temple grew stronger. He remembered Wolfila at his coronation, the garrulous northern count introducing his wife to Sigmar during the feasting days. Her name was Petra, and she had been pregnant with their first child. Sigmar had sent a silver drinking chalice to Salzenhús upon the birth of the child, a boy they had named Theodulf. The boy would have been around six or seven years old, but if what Rolf was saying was true, the line of the Udose chieftains had ended.

'Wolfila killed?' Sigmar said, still unable to believe that one of his counts was dead.

'Aye,' said Rolf, 'and all the men able to hold a sword. Boys and old men. Bastards only left me alive since I ain't got no sword arm. I'd have fought though, but they laughed at me, and I had my daughter and her young 'uns to look after. I thought they'd take 'em, but they let us go, like we weren't worth bothering with.'

Sigmar heard the shame in Rolf's voice, knowing the man would have died with his chieftain but for the need to protect his family. Such things were at the heart of what made a man proud, and to have that taken away by an enemy was a bitter blow indeed.

Sigmar stepped away as Rolf shucked the reins and the wagon moved on. His fists clenched and he turned his furious gaze northwards, as though he could see his enemies through the forest.

When he had driven the Norsii from the empire, the Roppsmenn had claimed their territory, largely because no one else had wanted it. Barren and said to be haunted by the ghosts of those their shamans had burned on sacrificial pyres, the land of the Norsii was bleak and lashed by freezing winds from the north.

In his quest to unite the tribes of men, Sigmar had not sought the Sword Oaths of the Roppsmenn chieftains, because they lived so far to the east that they were for all intents and purposes a tribe of a different land. It had been an arrangement of convenience, for he had been reluctant to wage war or pursue diplomacy so far from Reikdorf.

'Damn me,' said Redwane, shaking his head as yet more frightened people passed. 'Roppsmenn? Who'd have thought it? They've never raided south into the empire. Why would they do such a thing, and why now?'

'It does not matter,' said Sigmar, his fists bunched at his side. 'They have allied with the Norsii and that makes them my enemy.'

Sigmar turned to his friends, his face scarred with hostility.

'Pendrag, raise the Dragon Banner,' he said. 'I have need of it again.'

'The Dragon Banner?' asked Pendrag in alarm. 'Why?'

Sigmar squared his shoulders before his sword-brother, as though daring him to gainsay his words.

'Because I am going to gather an army and march east,' he said, his voice all fury and hurt. 'I am going to avenge the death of my friend. The Roppsmenn are going to learn the fate of those who make war on my people.'

'What does that mean?' asked Pendrag.

'It means their lands will burn!' roared Sigmar.

# ✦ FOURTEEN ✦

# Sigmar's Justice

NORMALLY THE BRACKENWALSCH Marsh was a gloomy place of mist and shadow, but this day was glorious, the sun shining upon the waters like glittering shards of crystal. A cool breeze kept the temperature pleasant, and the aroma of late-blooming flowers and fragrant reeds perfumed the air with myriad pleasing scents.

The Hag Woman sat upon a fallen tree trunk, its mouldy bark alive with insects and thick with moss. Where others would recoil at such things or find them repulsive, she enjoyed the rich cycle of death and rebirth. As one thing died, it became a home to some creatures, a hatchery for others and food for yet more.

'All things have their time,' she said to no one in particular, watching as a raven settled on the low branch of a nearby tree. The bird cawed, the sound echoing over the deep pools and hidden pathways of the marshes.

'What do you have to say this fine morning, bird of prophecy?' she asked with a smile.

The bird regarded her with its onyx eyes, and hopped from foot to foot as it cawed again.

'What am I to make of that?' she asked. 'I can no longer see the future, so I hoped you might spare me a shred of your knowledge.'

The bird cawed once more before taking flight. The Hag Woman watched it until she could no longer pick its form out in the sky. She shrugged and pushed herself upright with the help of her rowan staff. Her joints were stiff, and popped with the sound of snapping twigs. She winced, knowing that her forced levity masked the fear that had been gnawing at her ever since her powers had begun to fade.

The awakening of the necromancer in the Middle Mountains had heralded the decline of her power. She had fled from a terrible nightmare of a towering, monstrous evil arising from the desert, and had felt the spread of dark magic in the north like a growing cancer.

The malice of the dread sorcerer seeped into the earth like a poison, tainting the energies that flowed along its rivers and saturated the very air. Ever since that night, it took longer and longer for her spirit to unchain itself from her flesh, and soar on the winds of magic that drifted like oracle smoke from the earth. In her youth, she merely had to lie back and close her eyes, but now her spirit could not fly at all, no matter how hard she tried.

Without that freedom, she felt the ravages of time upon her physical form more than ever.

Worse was to come, for no sooner was her spirit confined to her body than the brimming vistas of possible futures that crowded her thoughts drifted away like guests from a feast, until she was utterly alone. Despite living a solitary existence in the Brackenwalsch, she had witnessed the great dramas of the world and had helped to shape their course.

Until now, that had been enough.

Before her powers vanished, she had followed the progress of young Sigmar as his empire grew and flourished.

She saw his rescue of Princess Marika, and smiled at the naivety of men. Despite what they called the swamp creatures they fought, she knew well that they were not daemons; the immortal servants of the Dark Gods were far more terrifying.

She watched the siege of Jutonsryk, and her heart despaired as she saw Sigmar raise his hammer to kill the rebellious King Marius. But for the intervention of the Berserker King, the lord of the Jutones would have died, and the doom of the empire would have begun.

Though she could not see it, she felt the death of the necromancer. Yet a dark miasma of ancient evil still polluted the healing energies of the world, as if his power still lingered. It cast a pall over the world and the promise of her ending hung over every day. That was why she cherished this day, a beautiful time of gold, blue and vivid green.

Bereft of her powers and unable to perceive the world beyond what her failing eyes could see, the Hag Woman felt lonely for the first time in her life. Out here, with nothing but the birds and marsh creatures for company, she felt divorced from the race of man, as though she were no longer part of it.

The Hag-Mother had confessed similar feelings in the days leading up to her death at the hands of the greenskins. Was this then her time to leave this world? Was this day a last gift to her before she completed her journey through life? She had lived many years, and death held no terror for her, but it was not death that quickened her steps as she made her way back to her cave along paths only she knew.

She skirted a rippling pool of clear water, seeing a tall plant growing at its edge, its stems dotted with white flowers in flat-topped clusters. A sickly smell wafted from the plant, and she frowned at the sight of the water hemlock. She had not seen such a plant for many years, and the sight of it stirred uncomfortable memories.

The Hag Woman's steps faltered. She looked up as a shadow crossed her eyes, and she felt a shiver of dread. The sky was clear and bright and empty. The sun hung low and fat above the horizon, and a black-feathered bird circled above her. She hurried her steps, not yet ready to be a meal for a hopeful carrion bird.

That age should undo her rather than the wiles of her enemies was no bad way to end a life that had been lived for the good of others. Her steps had taken her along some dark roads, and she had done much that she was not proud of, but the race of man endured, and she would not second-guess the choices she had made for the greater good.

The image of a young woman with dark hair leapt to her mind, but she quashed the thought before it could fully form. That had been a necessary sacrifice, a death required to set Sigmar on the path to the birth of the empire. Had Ravenna lived, the greenskins would now rule this land of men, and all that she had fought to save would have come to ruin.

*Is that how you sleep at night?*

The thought took her by surprise, for she had long since come to terms with Ravenna's death. More and more, she found her thoughts skipping randomly around her mind, revisiting memories and past regrets thought long buried.

*She was an innocent, and you killed her.*

No, thought the Hag Woman, as she turned from the path towards a ragged black rock that jutted from the marshland like a sunken mountain that left only its topmost peak visible. The ground leading towards a black cleft in the rock was soggy underfoot, and a wrong step in any direction would see her sucked beneath the bog.

She reached the mouth of her cave and paused, taking a last look at this magnificent day.

This world was harsh and unforgiving, yet it was also beautiful and miraculous. If you knew where to look, wonders could be found in every corner and she would miss it when she was gone.

The Hag Woman ducked her head and entered the cave, her eyes taking a moment to adjust to the shadowy interior. She moved deeper into the cave, allowing sense memory to guide her in the dim light. The smell of herbs and heat came to her, reassuring in their familiarity, and following hot on their heels was the smell of cold iron and the sweat and dust of travel.

The Hag Woman halted, realising she was not alone. Orange light flared in the darkness, and a crackling fire appeared in the circle of stones that served as her hearth. A wizened old man sat cross-legged before the fire, his head bowed and his hands steepled before him as though in prayer. She narrowed her eyes, needing no wych-sight to tell that this man was more than he seemed. The breath of the Dark Gods filled this one, and his power was palpable.

'Who are you?' she asked.

'A traveller who walks a similar path to you, Gráinne,' said the old man.

The Hag Woman started at his use of her given name. 'No one has called me that in many years. How is it you know it?'

'The Dark Gods know your name and they have spoken the words of your death,' said the old man, raising his head and looking at her with cold eyes that had seen the passage of centuries and the slaying of thousands.

She swallowed and reached deep into herself for any last shreds of power that remained to her, knowing that she would only have one chance to fight him. She felt a movement behind her, but before she could move, strong hands seized her and held her fast.

'Remember me?' said a silky, seductive voice at her shoulder.

The Hag Woman twisted in her captor's grip, but her struggles lessened as she saw the face of the man holding her. He was wondrously handsome, with a beautifully cruel grin that was beguiling and yet curiously repellent.

Though the light was poor, there was no mistaking the young man who had come to her cave many years ago in search of vengeance. Lost innocence hid behind his killer's eyes, but beyond that, a hidden face shone with unspeakable desires and monstrous arrogance. With a sinking heart, she knew it was his true self, and she marvelled that she had not seen it before.

These were not the eyes of a man; they were the eyes of a daemon.

She turned away and the old man laughed, saying, 'She remembers you, Azazel.'

'That is not your name, Gerreon,' she whispered, knowing it would do no good.

'It is now,' hissed Azazel, drawing his knife and holding it to her throat, 'and it will be the last name you hear as you die.'

WOLFGART SAT BEFORE his fire and watched Ulrike fight sleep, curled on Maedbh's lap, smiling at the sight of his family and wondering at his luck to be blessed with two such fine women in his life. Maedbh smiled at him and stroked her daughter's golden hair, so like her own. Ulrike was five and a half years old, as beautiful as her mother, and already Wolfgart could see that he would be hurling suitors from his door in the years to come. He remembered his own wild youth, carousing and trying to bed as many of the village girls as possible. The thought of Ulrike encountering someone like him when he had been that age was more terrifying than any enemy he had faced in battle. He pushed the thought aside. That was a problem for another day, and he had a few years yet before he would be replaced in his daughter's affections by some young buck eager to take her maidenhead.

The room was warm and lit with golden light from the fire. The surround was carved from Asoborn wildwood and had been a gift from Queen Freya upon her last visit to Reikdorf. The workmanship was exquisite, depicting a host of entwined trees with a multitude of roots that plunged deep into the earth before coming together. Maedbh said it depicted the Asoborn belief that all living things were connected. Wolfgart just thought it looked pretty.

The stone-built house kept the heat, and chopped logs stacked against the north wall kept the wind from sapping its warmth. It was a fine building, one Wolfgart had commissioned from Ornath the Stonemason, a man whose prices were outrageous but whose genius with a hammer and chisel was such that it was rumoured the dwarfs had trained him in their mountain halls. Wolfgart knew that wasn't true, but the man's skill was prodigious nonetheless.

Less than a generation ago, a man would have built his own home, but in the two years since the siege of Jutonsryk had ended, gold had flowed in an unending river from the west, and the empire had flourished like never before. Traders from lands so far distant as to be almost mythical travelled the roads linking the cities, bringing exotic goods and swelling the coffers of Sigmar's counts.

With trade bringing peace and prosperity to their lands, tribal chieftains who had once fought bloody wars with one another were now the best of friends. The common enemy of the greenskins had brought them together, but wealth was the glue that held them. Well, with the exception of the Taleutens and Cherusens who, in defiance of Sigmar's threats, still insisted on raiding one another's lands and feuding over some ancient grievance.

Wolfgart received a portion of Jutonsryk's wealth for his part in its capture, and also earned a generous monthly coin as Sigmar's Captain of Arms in Reikdorf. Taken together with his horse breeding farms and the merchants in which Maedbh had persuaded him to invest, Wolfgart was one of the wealthiest men in Reikdorf, and his home was as luxuriously appointed as any of the empire's counts. Thick rugs of bear fur from the Grey Mountains were spread throughout the downstairs rooms, and finely crafted tables and chairs of oak and ash were set with plates of delicate ceramics that had come from a land far to the east.

Endal tapestries hung from the walls, though pride of place was given to a silver breastplate with gold embossing in the shape of a snarling wolf and fluted rims of bronze. Pendrag had forged the breastplate as a gift to him, and it had served him well in the campaigns he had fought in Sigmar's name. His eyes drifted to the mighty sword hung on the wall above the fireplace, its blade six feet long and still razor-sharp.

It had been several years since Wolfgart had swung his sword in anger. He remembered the last blow he had struck, an upward sweep that smashed through the shield of a Jutone lancer before he buried the blade in his chest. With Alfgeir appointed regent of Reikdorf while Sigmar fought the Roppsmenn in the north, Wolfgart had taken over the training of the Unberogen youth in the arts of war. It was worthy work, but not the same as a real fight.

'Do you miss it?' asked Ulrike, startling him from his reverie.

'What's that, my dear?'

The young girl pointed above the fireplace.

'Fighting,' she said. 'You keep looking at your sword.'

He shook his head.

'No, beautiful girl, my days of war are over,' he said. 'The kings have all sworn fealty to Sigmar, and the empire is at peace. Well, mostly.'

'Are you sure?' asked Maedbh with a sly look. 'I think Ulrike might be on to something.'

'Ganging up on me now, eh?' grinned Wolfgart. 'Gods preserve me from two women in the house.'

'That is our right as women, husband of mine,' said Maedbh. 'You are outnumbered, so you might as well surrender and answer your daughter's question.'

Wolfgart stood and he lifted Ulrike from his wife's lap. He walked a slow circle around the room, pausing by each of the fine things that filled their home. 'Trade is how a man makes his name now,' he said, 'not how well he can swing a sword.'

'That's not an answer,' pressed Ulrike.

Wolfgart was about to give another flippant response, but he saw real fear in his daughter's eyes. She was clever, and she knew that not all men who went to war came back.

'Honestly? Yes, I do miss it,' he said. 'I wish I didn't, but I do.'

'That's silly,' said Ulrike. 'Why would anyone *want* to fight? You could get hurt or… or killed. War is stupid.'

'I can't argue with you there, girl, but sometimes we need to go to war.'

'Why?'

Wolfgart looked over at Maedbh for help, but his wife shook her head with a wry grin.

He was on his own for this one.

'The empire is safer than it's ever been, but there are still enemies to be fought.'

'Who? You said all the kings were our friends now.'

'Aye, that they are, but there are other enemies we have to fight. Like greenskins or the forest monsters. They aren't our friends and they never will be.'

'Why not?' asked Ulrike.

'Because, well, because they hate us,' said Wolfgart.

'Why? What did we do to them?'

'It's not anything we did to them,' said Wolfgart, exhausted by his daughter's never-ending questions. 'They're monsters, and they only want to kill and destroy. They don't want to live in peace, because it's not in their nature. They can't do anything else except fight.'

'But you want to fight,' said Ulrike. 'Does that make you like them?'

'No, my sweet girl, it doesn't. Because I only fight to protect you and your mother, and our friends. I fight when our enemies want to take what is ours from us. I am a warrior, and yes, I can't deny that the call of an Unberogen war horn sets the blood pounding in my veins. But I don't make war on others unless they make war on me first.'

'Is that why Uncle Sigmar is fighting the Ropps-menn?'

Wolfgart felt a knot of tension in his gut, and shared an uneasy glance with Maedbh. He was spared from thinking of an answer by a knock at the heavy wooden door of his home. He walked back to Maedbh and handed Ulrike to her.

'Take her to bed,' said Wolfgart. 'She needs to sleep.'

'I'm not tired,' said Ulrike, even as she drowsily slipped her arms around her mother.

Maedbh took their daughter upstairs, and Wolfgart opened the door.

Alfgeir and Eoforth stood at his threshold, clad in long, hooded cloaks.

'You're late,' said Wolfgart.

THEY SAT AROUND an oaken table carved by an Endal craftsman as Wolfgart poured rich red wine into silver goblets. Alfgeir took a long swallow, while Eoforth sipped his more delicately. He poured himself a drink and took his place at the head of the table as Maedbh came downstairs and sat next to Eoforth.

'Tilean,' said Eoforth as he took another sip. 'Very nice.'

'Pendrag persuaded me to try some, and I got the taste for it in Marburg,' said Wolfgart, 'but we're not here to discuss my well-stocked wine-cellar.'

'No,' agreed Eoforth, 'we are not.'

'Have you had word from Pendrag or Myrsa?' asked Alfgeir.

'I have,' said Wolfgart, 'and it makes for evil reading.'

Wolfgart rose and pulled an iron box from beneath a loose stone in the floor beside the fireplace. He returned to the table and opened the box, lifting out several folded parchments.

'It's getting worse,' he said. 'Sigmar's army numbers over eight thousand warriors, mainly Ostagoths and Udose, but there are some Asoborns with him too.'

Alfgeir glanced at Maedbh and asked, 'Asoborns?'

'The forests thin out in the east,' she said. 'Good killing ground for chariots.'

Wolfgart ran a hand through his hair, still dark, though strands of grey were beginning to appear at his temples and in his beard.

'The news from the north is bloody,' he began. 'Myrsa sends word that the Norsii are raiding up and down the coast in greater numbers than ever before. He thinks they are testing our readiness to repel an invasion.'

'An invasion?' hissed Alfgeir. 'Damn, but we need Sigmar back.'

'Don't hold your breath expecting that any time soon,' said Wolfgart. 'I don't think Sigmar will stop until he's wiped the Roppsmenn from the empire. He's fought three major battles under the Dragon Banner.'

'Sweet Shallya's mercy!' cried Eoforth. 'The Dragon Banner was raised every time?'

'Aye,' said Wolfgart grimly. 'Pendrag reckons around ten thousand Roppsmenn dead so far. Their towns and villages are burning and their people are fleeing into the east. Pendrag says that any who do not move fast enough are caught and killed.'

'Surely no Unberogen warrior of honour would take part in such slaughter?' asked Alfgeir.

'They are warriors fighting beneath the Dragon Banner,' said Maedbh. 'It makes no distinction between warriors and ordinary people. Unberogen warriors know that too.'

'Thankfully there are few Unberogen in Sigmar's army,' said Wolfgart. 'The worst excesses are being perpetrated by the Udose. After all, it was their lands that were ravaged and their own count was murdered in his castle.'

'These deeds bring dishonour upon us,' said Eoforth, shaking his head as though unable to believe what he was hearing. 'To think that Sigmar is responsible for such slaughter.'

'The Roppsmenn brought this on themselves,' snapped Wolfgart. 'They attacked the empire and killed Count Wolfila and his family. What else did they expect?'

'Retribution, yes,' said Eoforth. 'But such slaughter? No one could have expected this.'

'Word is already spreading,' put in Alfgeir. 'I have had letters from Otwin, Aldred and Siggurd all demanding to know what is happening in the north. They are talking of "Sigmar's Justice" and what it really means.'

'They fear for their lands and people should they ever voice a contrary opinion,' said Eoforth. 'They fear they will suffer the same fate.'

'That will not happen,' said Maedbh. 'The Roppsmenn suffer because they betrayed Sigmar and killed his friend. They deserve this.'

'You're a harsh woman, Maedbh,' said Eoforth. 'You are right that they deserve to feel Sigmar's wrath, but this goes too far. Villages burned to the ground, prisoners executed and entire families butchered? It is too much, and it shames me that our Emperor allows this.'

'The question is, what do we do about it?' asked Wolfgart.

'What *can* we do?' asked Alfgeir. 'He is the Emperor.'

'He is our friend,' stated Eoforth, 'first and foremost. The loss of Wolfila must have unhinged him, and he vents his anger and grief on the Roppsmenn.'

'Does that excuse such slaughter?' asked Alfgeir.

'Of course not, but knowing why a thing occurs makes it easier to understand,' said Eoforth. 'When Sigmar leads his warriors back home, we will speak with him on this matter. Knowing what drove him to such excess will help us to soothe the fears of the other counts.'

'Where was Sigmar when last you heard from Pendrag?' asked Alfgeir.

'Last I heard, what's left of the Roppsmenn were falling back towards the great dividing river,' said Wolfgart. 'It's the last line on the map before you head into the unknown.'

'Does anyone even know what lies beyond that river?' asked Alfgeir.

'Ulric alone knows what's on the other side,' said Wolfgart with a weary shrug. 'But we know what's certain on *this* side.'

'What's that?'

'Sigmar and death.'

IT WAS DARK by the time the old man decided they had come far enough. Though her hands were bound, Gerreon – she could not think of him as Azazel – held her fast the entire way, whispering the terrible things the old man was going to do to her. The Hag Woman had thought that death would hold no fear for her, but that had been foolish on her part.

She did not want to die like this.

The night sky was cloudless, the stars bright pinpricks in the velvet darkness, and she saw that they had travelled almost to the very edge of the marsh. Somehow the old man had known the secret routes through the deadly swamps. The moon's reflection shimmered on the surface of the water, and its uncaring face bathed the silent landscape in a pale, dead glow.

'How did you find your way through the marshes?' she asked. 'The paths are unknown to most men.'

'I am not "most men", Gráinne,' said the old man. 'Your powers may be gone, but you can still tell that, can't you?'

'You follow the Dark Gods,' she said.

'I follow the *true* gods,' he replied, 'the gods that rule in the realm beyond this ashen existence and whose breath fills me with life. They are the real power in this world, not the feeble avatars dreamed up by the minds of men. They existed before this world and they will exist long after it is dust in the void.'

'If you are going to kill me, then tell me your name,' she said. 'At least tell me that.'

'Very well,' shrugged the old man. 'I am Kar Odacen of the Iron Wolves, shaman to Cormac Bloodaxe of the Norsii.'

'You are a long way from home, Kar Odacen of the Iron Wolves. What makes you think you will live long enough to return? You are deep in Unberogen lands and Sigmar's hunters are very skilled.'

'As am I, woman,' hissed Gerreon. 'I knew this land well enough to escape those hunters once before, and I will do it again. No man can match my skills and cunning.'

She laughed and twisted in his grip. She saw the raging desire to kill her in his eyes.

And the chance to escape the fate Kar Odacen had planned for her.

'You think you evaded them?' she asked. 'Sigmar sent no one after you. He let you go to honour Ravenna's memory.'

'You lie,' said Gerreon, and the Hag Woman relished the flinch she saw at the mention of his sister's name: the sister he had killed. The sister she had sacrificed to tem-per Sigmar's ambition with determination.

The Hag Woman sagged in his grip.

'I feel sorry for you, Gerreon,' she said. 'You lost Trino-vantes and then Ravenna. That must have been hard. You were a pawn in a grander plan, but I did not foresee what those losses would drive you towards. Nor did I see that I would pay for your fall with my death.'

'I do not want your pity, woman,' he hissed, pushing her to her knees. 'And call me Gerreon again and I will gut you right now.'

The Hag Woman spat in Gerreon's face.

'I should have strangled you with your mother's cord when you were born,' she said. 'I told her that one of her sons would grow to know the greatest pleasure and great-est pain. If she had known you would murder her only daughter, she would have begged me to kill you while you slept in her belly.'

Gerreon slammed his fist into her face, and bright lights exploded before her eyes. Her nose and cheekbone broke, and tears streamed down her face. She fell to her side, feeling the dank wetness of the marshy ground on her skin.

She coughed up a wad of blood and marshwater as Gerreon hauled her upright.

'Your sister knew your soul was sick, but she still tried to help you,' the Hag Woman said through the pain. 'You repaid her goodness by sticking a sword in her belly and ending her life before its time. She would have borne strong children and been a mother of kindness and strength.'

Gerreon drew his knife, and the blade hovered an inch from her eyeball.

'Do not mention her name again!' he screamed.

'Why? Because you cannot face the horror of what you did?'

'My sister was a slut!' yelled Gerreon, the killing lust of the daemon behind his eyes flaring with rage. 'She opened her legs for Sigmar and deserved to die for that. I was the greater man, she should have loved me! I loved her with all my heart and she spurned me.'

'She knew your true face, Gerreon,' said the Hag Woman. 'That is why she rejected you.'

'No!' hissed Gerreon, his shoulders shaking with the effort of control. 'She loved me, and I know what you are trying to do. It will not work.'

Gerreon looked up, and Kar Odacen dragged her to the edge of the marsh, his strength surprising for so wizened a man.

'There is no escape for you,' said the shaman. 'The Dark Prince has claimed the one you knew as Gerreon. I know you see this, and it pleases me for you to know that you gave birth to this. How does it feel to know that every soul Azazel has sent screaming into the next world, and every soul he will kill during his immortal life, is thanks to you? You created Azazel, and for that I thank you.'

The Hag Woman wanted to spit defiance at Kar Odacen, but she knew he was right. Her designs had shaped Gerreon into a vessel, into which the shaman of the Iron Wolves had poured venomous evil and corruption, making him easy prey for a creature from beyond the veil. She had done this, and now she would pay the price for all eternity.

'Do it,' she said.

'No last words for hate's sake?' smiled Kar Odacen.

'What would be the point?'

'A chance to feed the self-righteousness that moves you to meddle in affairs that do not concern you,' suggested Kar Odacen.

'You are no different from me, shaman,' said the Hag Woman. 'You meddle with the fate of the world and will come to no better end than I.'

'I already know how I will die,' said Kar Odacen. 'It holds no fear for me.'

Defeated, the Hag Woman sagged in Gerreon's grip.

'I did the best I could to guide mankind,' she said. 'I did what I thought best at the time, and I would do the same again.'

'So arrogant,' said Kar Odacen. 'So like you to excuse your actions.'

'No,' said the Hag Woman. 'I make no excuses.'

'Very well,' said Kar Odacen, bending to pick up a fist-sized rock. 'Then let it be done.'

She saw a flash of iron in the moonlight, and her eyes widened as hot blood poured down her front. Gerreon held her upright as her body began to convulse. Even as she felt the pain of the cut, Kar Odacen smashed the rock against her temple. Bone cracked and was driven into her brain. Fresh blood streamed down her face.

Her mouth worked soundlessly as the life drained from her body, but before either of her wounds could send her down into death, Gerreon turned her around and pushed her body down into the Brackenwalsch.

Black water rushed into her mouth even as her lifeblood poured out to mix with the marsh water. The pain in her head was incredible and she bucked and heaved against her killer's grip. It was dark beneath the water, but she could see the wavering image of stars and the moon through the churning water.

They were laughing as the thrice death claimed her.

## ⊸ FIFTEEN ≻⊸

# The Price of Betrayal

PENDRAG SAT TALL in the saddle on a snow-covered crest overlooking the banks of a bloody river. He supposed that it had a local name, but on his map it was simply known as the great dividing river. Behind him were the lands of the empire, but the far bank was undiscovered country, a bleak and inhospitable landscape of windswept tundra and open steppe. Freezing winds swept down from the north, and Pendrag watched as the last remnants of a destroyed people fled across the cracking ice of the river.

Perhaps a thousand people huddled in terror on the muddy banks, a ragged mixture of survivors: warriors, cavalry and ordinary men and women. It seemed absurd and monstrous that this was all that was left of an entire tribal race, yet the advance of Sigmar's army had been merciless and thorough. No settlement had gone unmolested, and nothing of value had been left intact in its wake. Every day, pyres of the dead sent reeking plumes of black smoke into the sky, and what had once been fertile eastern grassland was now a charred, ashen wasteland.

A hundred Roppsmenn warriors in iron hauberks and bronze helms tried to impose some order on their people's flight across the river, but it was a hopeless task. The horror of their tribe's destruction overcame any thought other than escape, and braving the still-forming ice was preferable to annihilation at Sigmar's hands.

Pendrag heard a dull cracking sound, and a portion of the ice gave way. Dozens of people were plunged into the sluggish black water. Weighed down with all their worldly possessions, they did not return to the surface. Pendrag closed his eyes as shame threatened to overwhelm him.

'Shallya's tears,' said Redwane as weeping women pulled children away from the hole in the ice, unable to help those who had fallen through. 'What are we doing, Pendrag?'

'I don't know any more,' he said honestly, rubbing the heel of his palm against his temple, and regarding the White Wolf through eyes that carried a lifetime of sorrow acquired in the passage of a season. Redwane had aged in the six months since he had left Reikdorf, his demeanour sullen and his youthful eyes no longer sparkling with roguish charm.

Pendrag knew that he looked no better. The healing energies that had undone the necromancer's dark magic had restored the physique of his youth, yet he was bone-tired and wanted nothing more than to fall into a dreamless sleep. The softness of his former life as Count of Middenheim had vanished from his spare frame, but there was little left of the young man who had set out with Sigmar on the grand journey of empire.

Both he and Redwane had seen too much horror on this campaign to ever be young again.

'Surely this will see an end to the slaughter?' asked Redwane, waving a hand at the terrified people below. 'The Roppsmenn are destroyed. Surely Sigmar will halt the killing?'

Pendrag did not answer, and watched as Sigmar and Count Adelhard surveyed what was left of the Roppsmenn tribe. Beside them, an Udose clansman held the Dragon Banner, for Pendrag had refused to carry it after the Battle of Roskova. Nearly three thousand Roppsmenn warriors had been killed on that blasted heath, and there had been no quarter for the wounded. Once the Dragon Banner was raised, it could not be lowered until every enemy warrior was dead.

Twice more they had brought the scattered Roppsmenn warrior bands to battle, and each time Sigmar ordered the bloodthirsty banner raised. The slaughter had been terrible, and the screams of the dying and images of burning villages haunted Pendrag's dreams each night.

'I don't know how much more of this I can take,' said Redwane, numbly picking at the wolfskin cloak he wore. 'This isn't war anymore. It hasn't been for some time.'

Pendrag nodded as a fresh dusting of snow began to fall from the slate-coloured sky. To either side of him, thousands of fur-cloaked warriors gathered in sword-bands under the colours of their tribes, ready to be unleashed on the fleeing Roppsmenn. Chequered Ostagoth banners of black and white billowed in the winter wind next to the gold and red flags of the Asoborns, but they were far outnumbered by the patch-work banners of the Udose.

The clansmen had taken bloodthirsty relish in the war, killing all before them with hearts hungry to avenge the death of Count Wolfila. The stories of his death had been told and retold so often that the truth was lost and the horror of what the Roppsmenn were said to have done grew to ridiculous levels.

'All the better to justify what we do here,' he had told Redwane one night as they gathered around the campfire and the White Wolf had told him the latest gruesome embellishment.

Sigmar and Adelhard marched up the iron-hard ground towards the army, and Pendrag felt a chill at the sight of the Emperor that had nothing to do with the plummeting temperature. Though snow swirled in the air and his breath misted before him, Sigmar was clad in only a thin tunic of red with a silver wolf stitched upon his chest. The warriors of the army were wrapped in thick furs, but Sigmar appeared not to feel the intense chill that stabbed like knives from the north.

Since leaving the Middle Mountains, Sigmar's face had hardened, and the death of Wolfila hung like a noose around his neck. His hair was lank and thin, and the flesh seemed somehow tighter on his body, as though his bones were pushing out a little harder than before. His eyes were haunted by the loss of his friend, but glittered with a light that seemed to come from a dark place deep inside him. He still wore the golden crown he had taken from Morath, and instead of Ghal-maraz, the long, basket-hilted claymore that had once belonged to Count Wolfila was scabbarded at the Emperor's hip.

King Kurgan's hammer was wrapped in an oiled cloth in Pendrag's pack, nestled beside the crown crafted by Alaric the Mad for Sigmar's coronation. It sat ill with Pendrag that he carried such legendary items, but Sigmar had insisted that the Roppsmenn be fought with the blade of the man they had so brutally killed.

Sigmar drew Wolfila's weapon and held it out before him. The sword was heavy and fashioned from thick, dark iron. It was not the weapon of a swordsman, it was the weapon of a butcher.

'I want those warriors dead,' said Sigmar aiming the sword towards the Roppsmenn by the river. 'Redwane, take your White Wolves and ride them down.'

'Very good,' said Adelhard. 'I order Ostagoth horse archers to hem them in and you will drive them into the river.'

'My lord?' asked Redwane, looking at Pendrag for support.

'Is something about my order unclear?' asked Sigmar.

'No, my lord,' said Redwane, 'but is it really necessary to attack?'

'Necessary?' hissed Sigmar. 'These treacherous curs killed a count of the empire. Of course it is necessary! Now follow my orders.'

Redwane shook his head.

'No, my lord, I won't,' he said.

Sigmar planted the claymore in the ground before him, his face twisted in fury.

'You dare to defy me, boy?' he asked. 'I am your Emperor and you will obey my orders or I will see you dead.'

'I'm sorry, my lord, but I won't lead the White Wolves to murder those men.'

'You will do as you are ordered!'

'No,' said Redwane, and Pendrag's heart soared with pride. 'I will not.'

Sigmar stepped towards Redwane, and Pendrag dropped from his horse to put himself between the two warriors.

'There is no need for this,' he said. 'The Roppsmenn are defeated. They are a broken people, and you have avenged Wolfila's death.'

Sigmar turned on Pendrag, and the well of hate he saw in the Emperor's face sent a jolt of fear down his spine. For the briefest moment, it seemed as though someone far older looked out from behind Sigmar's eyes, but it vanished so quickly, Pendrag wasn't sure he had really seen it.

'Always the peacemaker, Pendrag.' hissed Sigmar. 'It was your counsel that stayed my hand when I could have destroyed the Norsii. Look at what that mercy has brought us. Wolfila dead and fleets of Norse raiders attacking our coast every day. No, I will not make the mistake of leaving any of these vermin alive to return with vengeance in their hearts.'

'You speak of the Norsii,' said Pendrag, fighting to keep his voice even. 'Then why are we not readying ourselves to fight them? You must know they will come at us soon. Our people live in terror of their warlords and, with every day that passes, that fear grows more powerful and saps their courage.'

'The people of the empire will stand firm against the Norsii,' promised Sigmar.

'No,' said Pendrag. 'The north is wide open. All we have done here is weaken our land. We need to return to Reik-dorf and gather the forces of the counts to strengthen the north.'

'Spoken like a true coward,' snapped Sigmar. 'I remem-ber you telling me you were not fit to rule Middenheim, that there were others more suited to the task. It seems I should have listened to you.'

'Listen to *yourself*, Sigmar,' begged Pendrag. 'This blood-shed is madness. It sullies everything we have achieved over the years. Is this how you want to be remembered, as a butcher of men? A tyrant king? A killer of women and children, no better than a greenskin?'

Sigmar's face darkened with anger, but Pendrag felt a weight lift from his shoulders with every word he spoke. 'I am soul-sick of this killing. Every man here has blood on his hands, and our honour is stained by what we have done here.'

He reached out and put his hand on Sigmar's shoulder, and said, 'It is time to go home, my friend.'

Sigmar's hand closed on the hilt of the claymore and drew it from the earth. He stared at the butcher's blade, and for a dreadful moment, Pendrag thought that his friend was about to run him through.

Though imperceptible to the eye, Pendrag could feel that Sigmar's entire body was trembling. The muscles at his jawline were as tight as a drum, clenching and releasing as though he sought to quell a dreadful killing rage.

At last his head came up, and Pendrag's heart broke to see the pain in his friend's eyes, swimming to the surface as if from a great depth.

Sigmar looked back at the desperate scramble of people fighting to cross the river to escape his wrath, and his shoulders sagged.

'You are right,' said Sigmar, letting out a shuddering breath. 'It *is* time to go home.'

NEARLY FOUR HUNDRED Wolfships filled the sheltered bay, their clinker-built hulls crafted from the scarce wood of the tundra and timbers carried from the ruins of plundered Udose settlements across the sea. Cormac Bloodaxe felt a potent sense of purpose as he stood on the cliff above the shoreline and admired the host of warships bobbing in the heavy swells. It had taken an entire year to build them, and no warlord in the history of the Norsii had ever assembled so mighty a fleet.

Behind him, what had once been a ramshackle collection of crude dwellings constructed from the cannibalised remnants of Wolfships was now a settlement to match any from their old lands. As well as the rebuilt tribe of the Iron Wolves, the nameless settlement was now home to thousands of tribesmen who had come from far and wide to make war on the southern lands.

It had begun as the first rays of weak summer sun had thawed the iron ground. The season of night had come to an end, and the power of the gods had swept the lands of the north, summoning their followers to battle. Warriors with golden skin and almond-shaped eyes, who called themselves the Wei-Tu, had come out of the east and sworn their lives to Cormac. Two days later, warbands of tattooed fighters called the Hung had emerged from the swirling lights of the far north on towering steeds of darkness.

That was just the beginning.

Over the course of the season of sun, warriors from tribes with names like the Gharhars, Tahmaks, Avags, Kul, Vargs and Yusak had crossed the northern sea and pledged their swords to his banner. Every day brought fresh champions and fighters to the coast, drawn by the thrumming pressure in their veins that demanded war. Over ten thousand Northmen were camped within a day's ride, and the totems of a dozen warlords were planted in the earth. The rivalry between them was fierce, and only Cormac's vision of destruction and the growing sense of history unfolding was keeping the violence in check. It would not last forever, and, as soon as the pack-ice around the coastline melted, Cormac would lead his fleet of Wolfships across the sea.

He turned from the cliffs and made his way back down to his longhouse, passing the camps of warriors from the Khazags and Mung. The latter tribe of flat-faced warriors were short and stocky, and fought with enormous axes that were almost comically oversized. Cormac had seen one of them split a column of seasoned timber with a single blow, and any doubts as to how lethal they would be in battle were forgotten.

As he passed yet more totems rammed into the hard ground, Cormac thought back to Kar Odacen and Azazel. Kar Odacen had predicted that there would be a gathering of might, and he had been proven right. As much as he detested the vile shaman, Cormac was not so blinded by his devotion to the Dark Gods that he did not value the man's insight.

He had not seen or heard from Kar Odacen in months, and had no way of knowing whether his mission into the south had been successful. Whether the shaman and Azazel still lived was a matter of supreme indifference to Cormac. The subjugation of Sigmar's people would begin at the next turning of the world, with or without them.

The year of raiding and slaughter had spread terror through the lands of the empire.

There would never be a better time to attack.

'Now it is time to take the fire south,' he said.

THE AFTERMATH OF the destruction of the Roppsmenn was a sombre time for Sigmar's army. It was not called a war, for the empire's wars were fought for noble reasons, and no one could think of a noble reason for this slaughter. Wolfila's death had been avenged, but vengeance was not so noble a reason for the virtual annihilation of an entire tribe.

No sooner was the campaign declared over, and the army withdrawn from the great dividing river, than the Asoborns turned their chariots south and rode away from the army with their banners lowered. They said no fond farewells nor made oaths of brotherhood, for the warriors of Queen Freya wished to forget their part in this killing.

Count Adelhard led his Ostagoths eastward the following morning, exchanging words with Sigmar that no one could hear. Sigmar never spoke of what Adelhard said to him, but his face was murderous as he turned away from the eastern count and mounted his horse.

Only the Udose warriors felt no remorse at the bloodshed, and they marched with the Unberogen as far as the tip of the Middle Mountains before turning north to their homelands. They had a land to rebuild and a new leader to find. Months of skirmishing and political infighting was sure to follow as the powerful clan lords manoeuvred for supremacy and sought to position themselves or their heirs as the new count of the Udose.

Sigmar led his warriors around the snow-wreathed peaks of the mountains towards the Fauschlag Rock. Winter was at its zenith and the land was deathly quiet, as though afraid to intrude upon the Emperor's sombre isolation. The army trudged through the snow, each man lost in his thoughts and wrapped in misery as they skirted the rocky haunches of the mountains. The Emperor kept a distance from his friends, unwilling to be drawn into conversation beyond what was necessary for the upkeep and course of the army.

Redwane and Pendrag said little to Sigmar on the journey home, for the brutality of the campaign still played out in their nightmares, and neither man wished to relive their part in it. Pendrag still carried Sigmar's crown and hammer, for the Emperor had not relinquished Count Wolfila's claymore, and the golden crown of Morath still glittered upon his brow.

The days were long, the nights bitter and hard. The Unberogen huddled close to the fires, wrapped tightly in their wolfskin cloaks to survive the darkness until the sun crested the Worlds Edge Mountains.

Each night, Redwane walked the camp, unable to close his eyes without seeing the faces of the dead that seemed to hang over them like a curse. Passing the Emperor's tent, he would hear Sigmar crying out in his sleep, as though in the grip of a never-ending nightmare. He spoke of this with Pendrag, who confessed that he had often seen Sigmar whispering under his breath, as though conversing with unseen spirits.

Sigmar dismissed their concerns with the same sullen expression with which he made every pronouncement, and the march through the snow continued.

At last, the soaring rock of Middenheim came into view, and the spirits of the army lifted as thoughts turned to homes and wives unseen for more than half a year. Even Sigmar seemed buoyed by the sight of the incredible city when it became apparent that the first of the great viaducts had been completed. The camps around the city were deserted, the labourers and craftsmen having returned to their villages for the winter, but work had already begun on clearing the forest at the site of the second viaduct.

Myrsa marched down from the city to greet them, surrounded by a bodyguard of plate-armoured warriors. The Warrior Eternal had made a full recovery from the wound he had taken at the fortress of the necromancer, yet his joy at seeing his friends return was tempered by the tales of slaughter from the east, and the hollow-eyed appearance of the Emperor.

The Middenlanders climbed to their city with Myrsa at their head, and Pendrag bade Sigmar farewell with stiff formality. Something precious had been lost between them and, though they would always be sword-brothers, it seemed their friendship had died along with the Roppsmenn. The journey into the north ended as it had begun, with Sigmar and Redwane riding at the head of the White Wolves.

A month and a half later, with the promise of spring prising loose winter's claws, the ruler of the empire rode through the gates of Reikdorf.

FROM HIGH UPON the walls of his city, Sigmar watched the Red Scythes as they crossed the Ostreik Bridge. The sun was setting, and the last of winter's light gleamed on the iron hauberks worn by the forty men in vivid red cloaks surrounding Count Krugar. The leader of the Taleutens was dressed in a fine tunic of crimson and gold over his heavy suit of armour, and a banner of the same colours flew in the brisk wind.

Sigmar felt a thrill of anticipation at what was to come, and gripped the hilt of Wolfila's sword tightly. The eastern gate of the city was open and, as the riders made their way towards it, Sigmar turned and descended the steps to the hard-packed earth of the gateway.

Six White Wolves followed him, men who had marched into the north, whose loyalty he could trust absolutely. Since he had returned from the land of the Roppsmenn, he had felt the eyes of his people on him constantly. Men and women he had called friends for years now cast side-long glances at him when they thought he wasn't looking. He felt their suspicious looks, and knew that they spoke ill of him when his back was turned.

Men who claimed to care for him spoke in hushed whispers when he was near, no doubt plotting against him, imagining a day when his back would make a good home for a traitor's dagger. They questioned him constantly, and though the war against the Roppsmenn was months old, Eoforth and Wolfgart would not let it rest, endlessly asking why he had led his army with such brutality.

Brutality they called it, yet without such brutality the empire could not be maintained. They did not understand that betrayal had to be punished in a manner that would send a clear message to those who thought their oaths of loyalty could bend as they saw fit. Loyalty to Sigmar's empire was inflexible, and the war against the Roppsmenn had been a bloody reminder to his counts of the price of disloyalty.

It would not be the only one.

Sigmar reached the roadway as the Taleuten warriors rode through the gate, moving to the sides of the esplanade as Krugar's horse approached him. He felt the White Wolves around him tense in readiness.

'Count Krugar,' said Sigmar. 'Welcome to Reikdorf.'

The Taleuten count smoothly dismounted and removed his helm. His hair was matted with sweat, and his beard was plaited in three long strands. The man was weary and Sigmar saw suspicion in his eyes, for the summons that had brought Krugar to Reikdorf had been direct and without any hint of a reason.

Sigmar's eyes were drawn to the curved leather scabbard at Krugar's hip, in which was sheathed Utensjarl, the sword of the Taleuten kings. When he had seen it first, it had seemed little more than a well-crafted blade, but now he saw that it was a weapon of power. Dangerous.

'Emperor,' said Krugar, his voice strong and resonant. He took Sigmar's hand in the warrior's grip, and said, 'It is good to see you. My congratulations on your victories in the north of the empire.'

Sigmar nodded and released Krugar's sweaty hand as though it were a poisonous snake.

'Yes, a usurper destroyed, and the Roppsmenn will trouble me no longer. All in all, a fitting end to a season of campaigning.'

'You have a new crown,' said Krugar. 'What happened to the old one?'

Sigmar reached up to touch the golden circlet at his brow, feeling the reassuring warmth of its power coursing through him.

'It was destroyed,' said Sigmar. 'The dwarf magic was not so strong after all.'

'Destroyed?' said Krugar. 'Damn me, but I didn't think I'd see the day when something forged by dwarf-craft could be undone.'

'It matters not. As you say, I have a new crown,' said Sigmar, eager to change the subject. 'I trust you encountered no trouble on the road?'

'Nothing we couldn't drive off with a few charges,' said Krugar proudly. 'My Red Scythes are nothing if not fearsome.'

'They are that,' agreed Sigmar, 'but they must be weary. To have reached Reikdorf so soon, you must have ridden like the *Scrianii* themselves were at your heels.'

'We made good time,' said Krugar, handing his helmet to one of his warriors and running his hands through his hair. 'We skirted the forest to the edge of the Asoborn lands, and then followed the river here.'

'Your men will be fed and watered, and their horses given the best of care in Wolfgart's stables,' promised Sigmar, waving his men forward.

'My thanks,' said Krugar with a curt bow. 'Before I forget, Queen Freya sends you her best greetings.'

'You saw the Asoborn queen?' asked Sigmar with a frown.

'Aye, we did. An impressive woman to be sure,' said Krugar with a lecherous grin that made Sigmar sick to his stomach. 'Came out to greet us in a chariot made of gold and brass, I swear it! Changed days, eh? Time was she'd have been riding out to kill us and mount our heads on her banner pole! Had her two boys with her, Fridleifr and Sigulf. Fine lads they are, strong and tall. A few years and they'll be riding out to their first battle!'

'I have no doubt they will,' said Sigmar with a toothy grin. He guided the Taleuten count from the gateway as stable lads and White Wolves led the lathered horses of the Red Scythes towards the ostler yards. The Taleuten cavalrymen went with them, leaving four stout warriors to accompany their count.

'Have to say that she seemed more than a little put out not to have been summoned to Reikdorf also,' said Krugar. 'I was surprised, because your letter talked of a gathering of counts.'

'It will be a select gathering,' said Sigmar.

'Oh? Who else is coming?'

'All will become clear soon enough, my friend,' said Sigmar. 'But come, I have something to show you.'

Sigmar and Krugar made their way into Reikdorf, along quiet streets, towards the heart of the city with a dozen White Wolves following them. Darkness was closing in on the world, and Sigmar felt himself growing calmer as the light faded and the shadows deepened.

He could sense Krugar's unease and said, 'Tell me what else Freya had to say for herself.'

'She talked about the Norsii mainly,' said Krugar. 'You'll have heard the tales of the warlords, Bloodaxe and Azazel? Well, the north is wide open now that the Roppsmenn are... gone... and the clan lords of the Udose are fighting among themselves. It seems clear that the Norsii are going to come south as soon as the ice melts in the northern oceans, and we need to be ready to face them when they do.'

'I will be,' promised Sigmar, 'I assure you. By the time any Norsii arrive, there will be an army the likes of which has not been seen in over a thousand years.'

Krugar gave him a confused look, but followed him through a heavy wooden gate set in a high wall and into a cobbled courtyard. At the centre of the courtyard stood a large building of dark stone with narrow windows sealed with iron bars. Eight warriors with heavy hammers stood guard around a wooden door of banded iron, and they moved aside as Sigmar approached.

'What in the name of Ulric is going on?' asked Krugar. 'Is this a prison?'

'Yes,' said Sigmar. 'But only you and I can enter. Our warriors will need to wait outside.'

'What? Why?'

'Trust me, all will become clear in a moment.'

'It had better do. I don't mind telling you that I don't like this.'

The Unberogen guards opened the door, and Sigmar indicated that Krugar should enter. He followed the Taleuten count into an empty vestibule lit by oil lanterns. The sound of shouting could be heard from deeper in the building, but the thick walls muffled the sense of them. Sigmar lifted a lantern, and set off down a corridor to his left. He led Krugar along a series of narrow passageways towards an iron door secured with a heavy padlock.

He unlocked the door, and they descended square-cut steps that led to another narrow corridor, this one lined with empty cells.

'Almost there,' said Sigmar, making his way towards a cell at the end of the corridor.

He hung the lantern on a hook outside this cell, and watched as Krugar tried to make sense of what he was seeing. A lone figure stirred at the sound of their footsteps and the warm glow of the lantern.

Chained to the wall and dressed in rich clothes that were tattered and filthy, Count Aloysis of the Cherusens shielded his eyes from the light.

'What is the meaning of this?' demanded Krugar, reaching for his sword.

Sigmar was faster.

With one hand, he snatched Krugar's blade from its sheath, and with the other took the man by the throat and slammed him against the bars of the cell. The point of Utensjarl hovered an inch from Krugar's throat.

'I commanded you to put an end to your dispute!' roared Sigmar. 'I told you to go back to your lands as brothers! Now I return from the north to find you have betrayed me.'

'Betrayed?' gasped Krugar, clawing at Sigmar's wrist. 'What?'

'In defiance of everything I said to you both, you continue to fight one another. You plunder one another's lands, raiding and killing in spite of my command. I gave you a way to save face and return home in peace, but no, that was not good enough for you, was it?'

'Sigmar, I–' began Krugar.

'Sigmar, please,' said Aloysis from his cell. 'There is no need for this!'

'Enough!' shouted Sigmar. 'The Roppsmenn paid the price for attacking me. Now you will both see what it means to betray me. At dawn tomorrow you will be taken to the marshes of the Brackenwalsch and put to death.'

## ◄ SIXTEEN ►

# The Temptation of Sigmar

GREY SKIES GREETED the day of the executions. Sigmar rode through the streets of Reikdorf at the head of twenty White Wolves, moving quietly and without conversation. Counts Krugar and Aloysis were borne upon a hay wagon, their heads swathed in hessian hoods and their hands bound with iron fetters. A bell tolled from the steeple of the temple of Ulric, and a light rain began to fall.

It was still early, and the few people abroad at this hour stopped to stare in surprise and fear at the sight of him leading so strange a procession. Beneath their hoods, both prisoners were gagged, and all signs of their former station had been removed. To all appearances, the prisoners were no more than base criminals, yet Sigmar was not fool enough to think that their identities were not already common knowledge.

The thought did not trouble him, for the warriors who had ridden with Krugar and Aloysis were even now under guard in a number of warehouses on the southern bank of the river. The city gates had been closed to prevent word from spreading beyond the walls, but Sigmar could not stop tavern talk, and news of Aloysis and Krugar's arrests had swept through the city like marsh pox.

Aloysis had arrived in Reikdorf only two nights previously, and the Cherusen count had been similarly outraged at his harsh treatment. Sigmar ignored his protests and left him chained to the dungeon wall until he had brought Krugar down to join him. As he held the blade to Krugar's throat, the killing urge that had been with him since Morath's defeat threatened to overwhelm him. It had taken all his self-control not to cut Krugar's throat there and then.

Such urges were anathema to him, but the desire to kill Krugar and Aloysis was like a craving to which he dared not surrender.

These men were his friends.

*No, they were his enemies, defying him and breaking their oaths of loyalty.*

They were men who made foolish errors of judgement, letting ancient hatreds whose origins had long been forgotten blind them to their ties of brotherhood.

*No, they were fools who deserved to die!*

Sigmar's head ached with conflicting thoughts and emotions. As much as he knew that what he was doing was very wrong, the rage that fed his urge to kill pulsed like fiery waves in his skull, blotting out any thoughts of compassion. So vile and bitter was this rage that he did not even recognise it as his own. Sigmar had known anger in his life, but this rage had been nursed for thousands of years, a hatred that had grown to such immense proportions that Sigmar's mind recoiled from such darkness.

Even as he understood that this hatred was alien, calming warmth spread through him, seeping down from his temple and into his chest. It spread along his limbs, easing his fears and soothing his troubled mind. All remembrances of this morning's evil fled from his thoughts.

The Ostgate loomed in the pre-dawn light, and the armoured warriors stationed there pulled the locking bar from its runners. The gate was opened, and Sigmar rode between the high towers flanking it. None of the gate guards dared meet his eyes, and he sensed great fear in their lowered gazes and submissive postures.

Even as he relished that fear, anger swelled as he saw that they pitied the prisoners.

These men had betrayed him, and his own warriors dared look at them with pity?

Keeping his hands tight on the reins, Sigmar rode from his city, keeping the pace steady as they travelled through the morning along the eastern road that skirted the edges of the Brackenwalsch. Weak sunlight warmed the earth, yet wisps of fog still oozed from the bleak fens to the north. The muddy greyness of the day lingered, and when the road bent towards Siggurdheim, Sigmar stopped his horse and dismounted.

'Bring them,' he said, his voice cold and laden with ancient relish.

The White Wolves manhandled the two captives from the wagon, and Sigmar marched over to them. He pulled off their hoods, and both counts blinked in the sudden brightness. Sigmar looked into their eyes, pleased at the fear he saw behind their bravado. Men always feared to die, no matter what they claimed.

'This is the day of your deaths,' he said, pointing into the fog-shrouded marsh. 'Some years ago I watched the Endals execute a traitor named Idris Gwylt in the marshes around Marburg. They called it the thrice death, and it was a bad death. The priests of Morr tried to stop it. They said that for a man to die like that would deny him his journey onwards to the next world. I say it is the only death appropriate for traitors.'

He smiled as they blanched at the mention of the thrice death. Word of Idris Gwylt's fate had spread throughout the empire, and the horror of his death was writ large in their eyes.

Sigmar led his warriors from the road and into the marsh, leaving a handful of White Wolves to guard their horses. The air tasted of life, and Sigmar felt his bile rise at the rancid stench of growth and fecundity. This was a liminal place, where worlds overlapped, and where the walls that separated them grew thin. He could sense power seeping up through the ground, the essence of life and creation, and his flesh crawled at its nearness.

No paths existed through the marshes, yet Sigmar led the way through the fog as though following a well-remembered route. He had never travelled these marshes, but he knew with utter certainty that he would not be sucked beneath the dark waters. Behind him, his warriors splashed and cursed as they dragged the reluctant prisoners through the sodden ground.

The marshes were alive with sound, and Sigmar shut out the cries of birds, the buzz of insects and the croaks of swamp creatures. His flesh grew clammy and warm with the life energy pouring from the waters. His warriors were oblivious to it, yet he could see it as a translucent green mist that rippled from the water and fens like noxious swamp gas.

When he decided they had come far enough, he raised a hand and turned to face his victims. He stood at the edge of a dark pool, the waters brackish and dead. It was perfect.

'This is far enough,' he said. 'Bring them.'

Krugar and Aloysis were dragged forward and pushed to their knees at the edge of the pool. Their eyes bulged with fear, wordlessly pleading with Sigmar not to do this. He drew Krugar's sword, carrying Utensjarl now instead of Count Wolfila's blade. The hilt felt warm in his hand, the power within it cowed by something greater.

He held the gleaming blade before Krugar, and said, 'To be killed by a weapon bound to your lineage will send a message that will be heard throughout the empire.'

Krugar struggled against his bonds, but the White Wolves held him firm.

'This gives me no pleasure,' said Sigmar, 'but betrayal can have only one punishment.'

'And what of murder?' asked a familiar voice.

Sigmar turned as Wolfgart emerged from the mist, his sword-brother leading a lathered horse that picked its way fearfully over the sodden ground.

'What are you doing here, Wolfgart?' asked Sigmar. 'This does not concern you.'

'Oh, this concerns me, Sigmar,' replied Wolfgart. 'This concerns me a great deal.'

'These men defied my command. What message does it send if my counts can pick and choose which of my commands they obey and which they do not?'

'I don't deny that action must be taken, but this?'

'This is a legitimate execution,' said Sigmar.

'It is murder,' replied Wolfgart.

Sigmar shook his head, aiming Utensjarl at Wolfgart.

'Of all the people I thought would betray me,' he said, 'I never once thought you would be one of them.'

Wolfgart took a step towards Sigmar, his hands held out in supplication.

'I'm not betraying you, my friend. I'm trying to save you,' he said.

'From what?'

'From yourself,' said Wolfgart, moving closer. 'Something happened to you in the north. I don't know what, but something changed you, made you more ruthless, more… I don't know… heartless.'

'Nothing happened in the north, Wolfgart,' said Sigmar, 'save my eyes being opened to the true nature of man. He is an animal, and it is in his nature to betray. All the race of men understand is blood and vengeance.'

'Vengeance is pointless, Sigmar. Continuing the feuds that divide us will only lead to further hatred. You taught me that.'

'I was young and foolish then,' said Sigmar. 'I was blind to the reality of the world.'

Wolfgart was right in front of him, and Sigmar felt a nauseous spike of pain in his gut, as though his sword-brother's very nearness was somehow its cause. Wolfgart reached out, placing a hand on his shoulder, and he flinched.

'What do you think will happen to the empire if you kill Krugar and Aloysis?' Wolfgart asked. 'The Cherusens and Taleutens won't stand for it. They'll rebel, and you'll have a civil war on your hands. Some of the counts might support you, but others won't, and what will you do then? March on their lands and burn them like you did the Roppsmenn?'

'If need be,' said Sigmar, shrugging off Wolfgart's hand.

'I won't let you do this,' said Wolfgart.

'You cannot stop me,' laughed Sigmar. 'I am the Emperor!'

Sigmar turned his back on Wolfgart.

'I am done explaining myself to you. It is time to deliver my judgement upon these traitors,' he said.

'Sigmar, don't,' pleaded Wolfgart.

'Begone,' he said. 'I will deal with you when I return to Reikdorf.'

Sigmar lifted Utensjarl, but before he could strike Wolfgart hurled himself forward, sending them both tumbling to the ground. The sword landed point down in the mud.

Sigmar roared in anger as Wolfgart fought to hold him down. His fist cannoned into Wolfgart's face, and he heard a crack of bone. Wolfgart slammed a right cross into Sigmar's jaw, but he rode the punch and slammed his forehead into the middle of Wolfgart's face.

Blood burst from Wolfgart's broken nose, and Sigmar brought his knee up into his groin. His sword-brother grunted in pain, but did not release his hold.

'This is murder,' hissed Wolfgart through a mask of blood.

Hands gripped Wolfgart, hauling him from Sigmar.

'No!' roared Sigmar. 'Leave him!'

They rolled in the mud and sopping pools of the marsh, punching, kicking and clawing at one another like wild animals. All thoughts of honour and nobility were forgotten in the brawl. Sigmar spat out a mouthful of stagnant water, and drove his elbow into Wolfgart's neck.

Wolfgart clutched at his throat, crawling away as he gasped for air.

Sigmar reached out as he saw a gleam of silver, his hand closing on Utensjarl's hilt. He dragged the sword from the mud. A ring of warriors surrounded him, but he cared nothing for their expressions of shock and confusion. All that mattered was that his enemy died.

He half-crawled, half-scrambled on his knees through the mud towards his sword-brother. Wolfgart lay at the edge of water, and Sigmar turned him onto his back. The water bubbled and churned around them, as though their struggles had stirred something beneath them. Rank swamp gas frothed to the surface.

Wolfgart's face was bloodied, and he fought for breath. Sigmar took Utensjarl in a two-handed grip, the blade aimed at Wolfgart's chest.

'Brother!' cried Wolfgart, and Sigmar's killing fire faltered as he saw not fear, but sadness in his sword-brother's face. The water around them heaved again, and Sigmar heard a wet, sucking sound, like a boot pulled from the mud.

A body broke the surface of the water, a corpse once held in the stygian darkness below, but now returned to the world above. The body rolled upright, and Sigmar gagged on the stench of the marsh's depths as he found himself staring at a pallid, dead face.

It was the Hag Woman. Though dark water slicked from her face and marsh fronds garlanded her hair, there was no mistaking the Brackenwalsch seer.

Her throat had been cut and her skull was caved in at the temple.

Her eyes were open, and they stared directly at Sigmar.

And in them, he saw his soul shining back at him.

SIGMAR CRIED OUT as he saw himself reflected in the Hag Woman's eyes, sitting astride his oldest and dearest friend with murder in his heart. As though looking up through her cold, lifeless orbs, he saw the horror in the faces of those around him, and the berserk rage on his own. For the briefest instant, he did not recognise himself, the drawn, parchment-skinned monster that revelled in bloodshed and the pain of the living.

The moment stretched, as though frozen in time, and Sigmar felt a feather-light brush of a power greater than anything he had ever known, including the Flame of Ulric. It was elemental and vast beyond understanding, a power that had existed since the dawn of the world, and which would endure beyond the span of men or gods.

It was old this power, old and strong, and with that one, almost inconsequential touch, Sigmar recognised it as a power he had long ago sworn to serve in a moment of grief. The Hag Woman had promised he would see her again, and he understood the meaning of her last words to him in one sudden, awful burst of clarity.

He looked beyond the ring of White Wolves, seeing that which was invisible to the sight of mortals. Was this a last gift of the Hag Woman, an echo of her powers granted to him that he might understand what he had become?

Sigmar saw the tautness of his body, as though his flesh and soul had been stretched and twisted like a fraying rope on the verge of snapping. A black miasma surrounded him, a cloying shroud that smothered the very things that made him the man he was and poisoned everything within him that was good and noble. Within this miasma, a towering shadow hung over him, a monstrous outline of something long dead, yet which endured impossibly down the thousands of years since its doom.

A clawed hand of glittering gold and silver seemed to reach from the miasma with fingers of black smoke that pressed upon his skull like the blessing of a priest. Yet this was no blessing, this was a curse, for, even as he watched, the essence of the shadowy creature was slowly, moment by moment, passing into Sigmar.

'No!' he cried, but he was not a player in this scene, merely a passive observer.

In an instant, he relived the war against the Roppsmenn, the hideous massacres, the burning villages, the blood-thirsty rampages of the Udose which he had not only allowed but encouraged. The slaughter of an entire people. Tears welled in his eyes as he knew that he had passed the darkness of his heart to every man who fought with him in the north.

The souls of all who took part in the destruction of the Roppsmenn would be forever tainted by that unjust war, and Sigmar knew he could never atone for it. Looking around him, he saw the same shadow that enveloped him as a haze around the warriors he had brought from Reik-dorf. Through him evil had touched them, bringing the hidden darkness within them to the surface.

Looking closer, Sigmar saw that the dark shadow seeping into his soul was slithering around the golden crown at his brow. The soothing warmth that quietened his fears and quashed any rebellious thoughts had silenced the shriek-ing voice of his heart that knew what he was doing was wrong. Every day since the defeat of Morath crowded his thoughts, and he wept to see the passage of days, knowing they were his yet experiencing them as a stranger might hear the tale of a long-lost brother.

'This is not me!' he screamed, watching as the shadow that loomed over his body swelled in anticipation of this murder.

Images flashed before him, and his soul fought against the dark spirit invading him.

Ravenna by the river.

*A city swallowed by the sand…*

His father in the Grey Vaults.

*A murderous enemy with a fell sword…*

The kings of men swearing sword oaths with him.

*The forging of a mighty crown of sorcery…*

The soaring nobility of the race of man coming together as one.

Utensjarl fell from Sigmar's hands, and the world snapped back into focus as he looked, once again, through his own eyes. The black miasma surrounding him vanished, and Sigmar looked down at Wolfgart, heartsick with grief and horror. He sobbed, and the sound clawed from his throat as though from a great distance.

'Sigmar?' cried Wolfgart. 'Is that you?'

He blinked, tears of shame and fear spilling down his cheeks as he felt the awesome rage of something older and more terrible than anything he had ever known turn upon him.

'Gods, brother,' he whispered. 'What has become of me?'

Sigmar grasped the golden crown at his brow, but no sooner had his fingers touched the metal than fiery agony exploded inside his head. He screamed as shooting spikes of pain ripped into him, like a choke-chain violently pulled at the neck of a disobedient hound.

He surged to his feet, screaming as his humanity warred with this invasive force that poisoned him with its evil. Wolfgart scrambled to his knees, reaching out to him, but his sword-brother could not help him now.

He had to fight this battle alone.

With a cry of anguish, Sigmar turned and fled into the depths of the marsh.

\* \* \*

THE MIST CLOSED around him as he ran blindly through the depths of the Brackenwalsch. He heard alarmed cries following him, but they were soon swallowed by the deadening fog and eerie silence of the marsh. Sigmar ran without care for where he stepped, knowing that at any moment he might wander from the path, stumble into a sucking bog and be lost forever.

He welcomed the thought, but with every stumbling step he plunged deeper and deeper into the haunted fens, driven by the imperative to flee from any he might corrupt with the evil power growing within him.

How could this have happened? The blood of an entire tribe was on his hands. He wept as he ran, his entire body wracked with heaving sobs for the lives he had ended and the souls blackened by his actions.

The mist thickened until he could see no farther than his next step. He ran faster than he had ever run in his life, yet the blackness that hung over him followed him wherever he went. He splashed through shallow streams, blundered into tearing bracken and gorse, tripped over buried rocks and breathed in great lungfuls of swampy air. He ran until he could run no more, and dropped to his knees before a deep pool of peaty water, the surface like a black mirror.

Ripples spread from the edge of the pool, and eyeless things disappeared beneath the surface as they sensed his presence. Fat flies with iridescent wings droned over the surface of the water and loathsome plants with white, sticky fronds brushed him with hideous caresses as he fell forward.

His arms sank to his elbows, and segmented worms blindly wriggled around his flesh. He pulled his arms from the mud and held his hands out before him. Black water ran from them like blood, and the horror of the last few months surged to the forefront of his mind.

How could he have done this?

That was not him. Sigmar Heldenhammer was a better man than that.

*Are you so sure?*

Sigmar's head lifted at the question. Had he spoken aloud? Was this the voice of his conscience? Or was there someone else in the marsh?

Something black moved in the mist, like an enormous figure swathed in robes of utter darkness, but when Sigmar snapped his head around to look, he saw nothing but the undulant banks of yellowish-white fog drifting at the edge of the pool.

'Show yourself!' he demanded.

*I am not here,* the voice said. *You know where I am, and you know what I can give you.*

'I want nothing from you!' screamed Sigmar. 'Whatever you are, you are a monster. A creature of evil!'

*True, but I could not have reached out to you had there not already been a darkness within you. The door was open. All I needed to do was step through.*

'No! I am a good man!' wailed Sigmar

*You are a man, and man is born with darkness in his heart,* hissed the voice and Sigmar saw the phantom shadow at the edge of his vision once more. It circled him, though part of him knew it was but a fragment of some far greater power.

'I will not listen to you,' said Sigmar, reaching up to tear the crown from his head. Once again spikes of pain stabbed through his eyes, and he fell to the ground, clawing at his head.

*You will listen, for you are to be my herald. You shall usher in an age of death to the world. You will craft a realm of bone for me to rule. Such has been your destiny since before your insignificant ember of life was spat into existence.*

Sigmar picked himself up as yet more memories of his slaughter of the Roppsmenn flooded his thoughts.

*You see? This is what you are. This is who you are. Embrace it and the pain will end. Cease your resistance and give me your flesh to wear. You cannot keep my spirit out forever, and when you are mine, I shall give you power beyond your wildest imaginings. This petty empire of man that you have built is nothing to what we might achieve together. There are lands far beyond these shores to be conquered, worlds beyond this paltry rock to be enslaved! Stand at my side and this entire world will be yours!*

Sigmar saw it all, the warring states of the eastern dragon kings, the mysterious island of the fey in the west, the endless jungles of the south where lizards that walked like men built towering cities, and the seething lands of chaos and madness in the north.

All of it could be his, and he saw himself at the head of an invincible army of warriors that stretched from horizon to horizon. Wherever these warriors marched, the land blackened and shrivelled, dying with every footstep taken in dreadful unison. This was an army of the dead, an unstoppable force that defied the living and left nothing but ashes in its wake. This was an army that would never die, led by a warrior whose name would live forever.

*That name could be yours.*

He saw himself atop the world with all the power such a position could grant. He saw worlds beyond his own, worlds of unimaginable wealth. It was all just waiting to be brought low. This could be his, and world upon world would know and fear Sigmar's name.

The allure of such eternal power spoke to the ambition that had driven Sigmar to build the empire, promising the fulfilment of every desire, the satisfaction of every dream and the power to achieve the impossible. His ambition revelled in such potential, yet the flickering candle that was Sigmar's humanity rebelled at this perversion of his vision of a united land.

'No,' he whispered. 'This is not what I want. This is a domain of the dead.'

*It will live forever. As will you.*

'No,' repeated Sigmar, the very act of denial giving him strength. 'I will not!'

*Then if not for you, perhaps for another.*

The mist before Sigmar parted and a tormented moan issued from deep within him. Across the water, he saw Ravenna, as beautiful as the last time he had seen her by the river. Her dark tresses spilled around the sculpted arc of her pale shoulders, and the light in her eyes was like the dawn of the brightest day. Nearly two decades had passed since her death, yet Sigmar remembered every curve of her body, every subtle aroma of her flesh, and this vision was just as he pictured her in his dreams.

'My love,' whispered Sigmar.

She smiled at him, and his heart broke anew.

*Join me and she can live again. Death is meaningless in the face of the power I can give you. Surrender to me and she will be yours forever.*

Sigmar pushed himself to his feet, knowing that the vision across the water was not Ravenna. Nevertheless, he stepped into the pool, sinking to his knees as he went to her. He took another step, the black water rising to his waist. Another step and the water was at his chest.

*Yes, let the water claim you.*

Sigmar heard the glee in the shadow's voice, but didn't care. All he wanted was to cross the pool to get to Ravenna. With her in his arms, the world could go away. He would have reclaimed his lost love.

The water rose to his neck, and he felt the clammy embrace of underwater fronds like grasping hands on his body. Water splashed his eyes, and the image of Ravenna shimmered like a ghostly mist before him. Thoughts of life and death vanished from his mind as the water closed over his head, and Ravenna disappeared.

Then he was alone in the darkness, and all he could hear was booming laughter echoing across the gulf of time.

* * *

WHEN HE OPENED his eyes, he was lying beside a river, its fast-flowing waters like shards of dancing ice and the scent of the surrounding woodlands intoxicating with its vitality. He watched as children played in the river, two boys and a girl. Their laughter was like musical rain, sweet, joyous, and unburdened by the passage of years.

He felt a presence beside him, and smiled to see his wife lying next to him. Her hair was grey, and though she was close to seventy years old, she was as beautiful as ever. He stroked her hair, seeing that his own flesh was gnarled and lined with age. The thought pleased him.

'Is this real?' he asked.

Ravenna turned to face him and smiled.

'No, my love. It is but a dream,' she said, 'a last, sweet memory of a future that never came to pass.'

'Ours?'

'Perhaps,' said Ravenna, watching the children playing in the river. 'Though I doubt it.'

'Why?' asked Sigmar, hurt by her honesty.

'Is this what you wanted?' she asked him. 'Really?'

'A future where I have lived a full life, with many children and now grandchildren? What man could ask for more?'

'You are no normal man, Sigmar,' said Ravenna. 'You were always destined for things beyond the reach of mortal men. As much as I would have wished you to live out the span of our days together, it could never be. I know that now.'

'Then it is really you, Ravenna?' asked Sigmar. 'This is not some evil fantasy?'

'It is me, my love,' she said, and the sound of her voice was like a soothing balm upon his soul. 'I have watched with pride as you achieved everything you set out to do.'

'I did it all for you,' he said.

'I know you did, but you are being corrupted from within. A dread power has come to this land and threatens everything you and all who came before you have built. Even now it seeks to drag you down into death.'

Sigmar sat up as a cloud passed across the face of the sun and the surrounding forest, which had seemed so benign beforehand, was now haunted by shadows. The laughter of the children faltered, and his heart beat a little faster as unbidden images of dead Roppsmenn flickered behind his eyes. A hot wind blew through the trees, dusty and dry, and laden with the powdered bones of a long-dead civilisation.

'Tell me what I must do!' he cried. 'I cannot fight it alone. I… I have done terrible things, and I am losing more and more of myself with every day. I can feel it, but I cannot stop it. The evil that poisons me grows stronger as I grow weaker.'

'You are Sigmar Heldenhammer,' said Ravenna, taking his head in her hands as the winds grew stronger. 'You are the greatest man I know, and you will not give in to this.'

'It is too strong for me,' he gasped, hearing the children's laughter turn to cries of fear as the darkness closed in. Trees bent with the force of the howling winds of the desert, though Ravenna's face remained unwavering before him. Grit carried on the wind scoured his flesh, peeling back his solidity as if seeking to erase him from this dream. The forest faded, and he held on to Ravenna's words even as the wind fought to obscure them.

'You are the Chosen of Ulric,' said Ravenna, her voice fading as he was torn away from her by the wind. 'The wolf of winter runs in your blood and the power of the northern winds gives you life. You can stand tall against this reborn evil, though it poisons you through that sorcerous crown. The land must be united as one, for its maker will soon come to claim it, and you must be ready to face him!'

'I don't know how!' he cried with the last of his breath.

'You will,' promised Ravenna as the winds plucked him away and sent him spinning off into the darkness.

* * *

Sigmar's eyes snapped open, and he saw nothing. Absolute darkness filled his vision. No, that wasn't right. Bright spots of light danced before his eyes, and his head pounded with searing pain. He tried to scream, but achingly cold water poured down his throat, and he gagged as the rank, stagnant taste of it filled his lungs.

He coughed, and his whole body spasmed as he realised that he was beneath the water of the Brackenwalsch. Half-remembered fragments of dreams and memories came to him, but through all of it he saw Ravenna's face. Her bright eyes willed him to live, and he struggled against the deathly grip of the water. He kicked upwards as he fought to reach the surface, but no matter how hard he fought, a leaden weight kept him from rising.

The pain in his head intensified, as though a red-hot band of iron was slowly tightening upon his temple, burning its way through his skull to his brain. Swirling in the water around him, the phantom darkness spun him grand illusions of wealth, power, women and immortality, but without Ravenna, they were hollow, worthless promises.

*If not for her, then for your land*, hissed the voice, undaunted by his resistance.

Sigmar's vision blurred, and he saw barren, windswept tundra, a northern realm haunted by daemons and ancient gods of blood. His mind's eye swooped and dived like a bird, and he flew over this bitter, hateful landscape in the blink of an eye, seeing signs that thousands of people had, until recently, called this place home.

His immaterial form swept out over the grey waters of the Sea of Claws, following a course southwards through riotous tempests, until he came upon a vast fleet of ships sailing over the crests of surging waves: Wolfships.

These were the Norsii ships of war, and there were hundreds of them bound for the northern coasts of the empire. An army of conquest or an army of destruction, it made no difference. They would invade the north and ravage his land unless he could defeat them.

*I can help you. With the power I offer, the Norsii will be food for crows. Your land will be safe and one day we will cross the water to wipe their race from the face of the world!*

Sigmar ignored the voice and shook off the vision, pushing hard for the world above. Each passing moment increased the pressure and pain in his lungs. He could not last much longer. Then the pounding in his head eased, and he felt his struggles grow weaker as the weight at his head dragged him deeper into the water.

Yet more images flashed before his eyes: Blacktusk the Boar, Trinovantes as his body was carried into his tomb on Warrior's Hill, the towering peak of the Fauschlag Rock, and a hundred other moments from his life. It was a life lived for the good of others: a life lived with honour, courage and sacrifice.

*A wasted life*, sneered the voice.

Then he heard another voice, one with a deep and resonant timbre that instantly transported him to his youth, when he had sat with the veteran warriors of the tribe and thrilled to their tales of heroic sagas, of kings long since taken to the Halls of Ulric.

'I want no other son,' said this voice. 'I have you. I know you will be a great man, and people will speak the name Sigmar with respect and awe for years! Now *fight!*'

The new voice echoed in his head with absolute authority, and he could no more disobey its command than he could breathe underwater. Sigmar cast off the last of the crown's blandishments, knowing that he had a *duty* to live. He had to return to the world of light and life to protect his people.

All else was folly, and he grieved at how easily his heart had been turned from its course.

Sigmar took hold of the golden crown.

It burned with dark magic, and he saw that its golden light was hideous and filled with malice. It fought him, filling his thoughts with ever more outrageous promises of power. His weary soul had been blinded to the crown's malevolence, but now he knew what a terrible trap it had been.

With a soundless scream, Sigmar tore the ancient metal from his brow.

His entire body was a searing mass of pain, but not even the touch of Shallya could compare to the joy that filled him as the crown's terrible hold was broken. Sigmar pushed up from the bottom of the pool with the last of his strength, feeling a wordless scream of frustration echo from somewhere far, far away.

Slicks of light whirled above him, strange stars and unknown worlds, but he kept his gaze fixed upon the water's rippling surface. At one and the same time it seemed unbearably close, yet impossibly distant. His strength was gone, and he knew he could not reach the surface.

A questing hand splashed down into the water, and Sigmar reached out for it, feeling an iron grip take hold of his wrist and pull.

Sigmar burst from the pool, his chest heaving and expelling a torrent of scum-frothed water. He clawed his way up the muddy banks, revelling in the sweetness of the air and the myriad scents that filled the swamp. A strong pair of hands hauled him the rest of the way and he rolled onto his back, sucking great gulps of air into his tortured lungs.

A hulking form sat on a nearby rock, a warrior covered from head to foot in black mud, whose face was bruised and bloody. Sigmar wiped his face and gathered breath to thank his rescuer, but the words died in his throat.

'Thought I'd lost you there,' said Wolfgart.

WHEN HE HAD strength enough to stand, Sigmar embraced his sword-brother, shamed and honoured by his devotion.

The cool air of the marsh felt wondrously sharp against his skin, and Sigmar revelled in the sensation. He breathed as though it were the sweetest nectar. His entire body shook with cold and pain, but he welcomed it, for it was a reminder that he was alive.

At last they parted, and Sigmar looked down at the crown he held in one hand. He dropped it as though it were red-hot and stepped away from it. Wolfgart bent to examine the crown, but Sigmar kicked it away.

'Do not touch it!' he cried. 'It is a thing of evil!'

'I know,' said Wolfgart, 'and you should have known too. What kind of fool trusts a treasure taken from a necromancer?'

Sigmar knew that Wolfgart was right, but would anything be gained in trying to explain the glamour with which the ancient crown had ensnared him? That it had preyed upon his ambition and exploited the warlike heart that made him so formidable a warrior? Anything he said now would sound like an excuse, an attempt to abrogate responsibility for his actions.

And that was something that Sigmar would never do.

'The Roppsmenn,' he said, burying his head in his hands. 'Oh gods, what have I done?'

That the crown had saved Pendrag's life did not matter, for there were no excuses that could atone for what he had done in the months since Morath's defeat.

'Aye, you'll carry that one for the rest of your life,' said Wolfgart, 'and you'll have a job earning back the trust of the counts.'

'What about you?' asked Sigmar haltingly. 'I almost killed you.'

'But you didn't,' said Wolfgart, offering him his hand. 'That's what's important. It was the crown, it made you do those terrible things. But that's done with now.'

'The crown is evil,' agreed Sigmar, 'but it could have done nothing to me unless it had found some darkness within me to latch onto. The Hag Woman tried to warn me about replacing Alaric's gift, but I did not listen.'

'Ah, speaking of the mountain folk,' said Wolfgart, reaching down to lift a canvas bag from the edge of the pool, 'I brought some things for you. I had hoped to give them to you earlier, but… Well, things got a bit out of hand.'

Wolfgart reached into the bag, and Sigmar almost wept at the sight of what he pulled out.

Ghal-maraz glittered in the light, and Sigmar felt his hand curl with the urge to grip the ancient warhammer.

'How?' he asked.

'Pendrag gave it to Redwane when you parted company at Middenheim, and he carried it south to Reikdorf,' said Wolfgart. 'Go on, take it.'

Hesitantly, Sigmar reached out, and slowly wrapped his fingers around the rune-encrusted haft of Ghal-maraz, flinching as the last of the golden crown's influence was purged from him by the dwarf rune-magic. He smiled as the weapon settled in his grip, just as a well-made cloak which had weathered the harshest winter would feel after being warmed by the fire.

Wolfgart reached into the bag again, and pulled out another gift

The crown fashioned by Alaric the Mad.

Sigmar took a step back.

He shook his head.

'No, I do not deserve to wear it,' he said.

'Of course you do,' said Wolfgart. 'You're the only man who can. This has been a dark period, but it's time for you to be our Emperor once again. A fresh start. What do you say?'

Sigmar looked into his friend's eyes, seeing devotion and forgiveness he did not deserve.

Through everything, Wolfgart still believed in him.

'I do not deserve a friend like you,' he said.

'I know, but you're stuck with me,' said Wolfgart. 'Now take your crown.'

'No,' said Sigmar, dropping to his knees before Wolfgart. 'If this is to be a fresh start, then I want you to crown me anew.'

'I'm no Ar-Ulric, but I think I can manage that.'

Sigmar bowed, and Wolfgart placed the crown upon his head. Like Ghal-maraz, Alaric's crown welcomed him without reservation or rancour, and the wisdom and love that had gone into its craft filled him with strength he had not realised had drained from him.

He stood and looked out over the marshes. The sun was breaking through the clouds and clearing the mists away. Sigmar felt the sunlight on his skin and smiled. It felt good to be alive, but even as he relished this rebirth he knew there was much yet to be done.

'We must get back, my friend' said Sigmar at last. 'The empire is in great danger.'

'Isn't it always?' asked Wolfgart.

'There are two counts of the empire I need to set free,' said Sigmar. 'I have behaved shamefully towards them, and I only hope they can forgive me.'

'Ach, they'll be fine,' said Wolfgart. 'Krugar and Aloysis know they did wrong, and one thing's for sure; they'll not be sending raiders into each other's lands again any time soon. But that's not what you meant, is it?'

'No,' said Sigmar. 'The Norsii return to reclaim the lands I took from them. Hundreds of Wolfships are already crossing the Sea of Claws, and the north is virtually undefended.'

Wolfgart shrugged.

'It was only a matter of time until they came at us again,' he said. 'At least I'll get to put that sword above the fire to good use, though you'll be the one explaining to my little girl why her father is going to war again!'

# BOOK THREE

## Empire of War

*Twelve swords, one for each chief,*
*And holy Sigmar bade each to wield it*
*In justice for his people,*
*And pledge to fight for one another*
*In undying unity,*
*Thus did every chief's hall*
*Become a stronghold in the realm of men.*

## ─◄ SEVENTEEN ►─

# Wolves of the North

THEY HAD LOST.

Dawn was minutes old, and the army had been on the march for eight hours already. Thousands of warriors in ragged bands of bloodied survivors marched south in the shadow of the Middle Mountains. Sigmar watched each man as he passed, seeing the same sullen disbelief in every face.

*They had lost.*

The armies of the empire never lost a battle.

It hadn't quite sunk in.

No one could believe it, least of all Sigmar.

It had been a bright spring afternoon, the perfect day for a battle. Sigmar had felt powerful and invincible as he sat atop his horse and watched the Norsii of Cormac Bloodaxe march out to give battle. Eight thousand warriors of the empire – Udose, Unberogen, Thuringians and Jutones – stood in disciplined ranks on a forested ridge some fifty miles from the northern coast. Each of the tribal contingents was led by its count, and Sigmar had relished the chance to march alongside Otwin and Marius.

The counts had gathered the previous evening to plan the coming battle, and Sigmar found himself missing Wolfila's garrulous company more than ever, for the Udose chieftain who attended the war council was a dour, humourless man named Conn Carsten. Since last spring, the Udose lands had been riven with skirmishes as the clan lords fought one another to claim the title of count, but the Norsii invasion had put an end to the feuding long enough for them to name Conn Carsten as their war-chieftain.

Hard to like, Carsten was nevertheless a canny soldier who knew the land well. Under his command, the northern clans had slowed the Norsii advance, and given Sigmar time to gather a sword host. But for Carsten, the north would have already fallen.

With plans drawn and the courage of their warriors bolstered by the presence of the Emperor, the army had marched out to victory. Every warrior could taste the sweetness of triumph, the honour and glory that would be theirs. The tales of blood and courage they would tell upon their return home were already taking shape in each man's head.

But they had lost.

No sooner had the counts taken the field beneath a wild panoply of colourful banners than malformed storm-clouds swelled in the clear sky. They crackled with gleeful lightning, fat with the promise of rain. Howling storm winds blew, and a sour, battering downpour began, like the legendary floods said to have drowned the world in ages past.

Arcing bolts of lightning slammed into the earth as the storm broke, and tremors of fear rippled along the empire line at such unnatural phenomena. Worse was to come.

Sigmar rode with the White Wolves in the centre of his army, and each warrior sought to restore their honour after the war against the Roppsmenn.

The thunder of their hooves was the sound of victory.

Then a shrieking bolt of azure lightning had struck the bearer of the White Wolves banner.

The warrior fell from his horse, his flesh blackened, and the symbol of the Emperor's Guard afire. The banner fell to the ground, its crimson fabric utterly consumed by blue flames that were apparently impervious to the endless rain. Horrified cries rang from the forested ridge, but it was too late to quell that fear. Torrential rain turned the ground to a quagmire, and the advance became a trudging hell of sucking mud and blinding lightning strikes.

As Sigmar's warriors floundered, the Norsii attacked with a savage bray of war horns. The host of Norsemen marched out beneath the skull-banner of Cormac Bloodaxe and fought with discipline, courage and, worst of all, a plan. Instead of the usual mass of charging warriors, the Norsii gave battle in imitation of Sigmar's army. Norsii fighters marched in tightly-packed ranks, moving in formation with a hitherto unheard of cohesion.

Whooping tribesmen with dark skin and short-bows rode horses of black and gold to encircle Count Otwin's Thuringians and hammer them with deadly accurate blows. Otwin's advance faltered, and a host of Norsii warriors, mounted upon dark steeds taller than any grain-fed beasts of the empire charged the scattered Thuringians. Led by a mighty warlord in bloody armour, a warrior who must surely have been Cormac Bloodaxe, the Norsii hacked the Thuringians down without mercy.

Jutone lancers drove back the marauding warriors, but not before Otwin had taken a lance to the chest. Marius led the countercharge, and carried the wounded Otwin from the fighting slung across his saddle. Even now, the camp surgeons fought to save the Thuringian count's life.

Sigmar's stratagems were met and countered at every turn, his warriors hurled back time and time again. As afternoon waned into evening, he realised the sick feeling in his gut was despair. The battle could not be won, and Sigmar had ordered the army's clarions to sound the retreat. Only here, at battle's end, did the discipline of the Norsii finally break down, the tribal champions leading their men in an orgy of slaughter amongst the wounded.

As terrible as it was to leave the wounded to their fate, the vile appetites of the Norsii ensured there was no pursuit, and Sigmar was able to lead his men from the field of battle unmolested. The night march had been cold and cheerless, with the wounded treated on the move or during one of the infrequent breaks from the retreat.

Wolfgart rode alongside him, the flanks of his horse lathered in bloody sweat. Sigmar's sword-brother had come through the battle unscathed, save for a long slash along his jerkin that had missed cutting his gut open by a hair's breadth.

'Long night, eh?' said Wolfgart.

'It won't be the last,' replied Sigmar, 'not now.'

'Aye, you have the truth of it, but we'll get them next time.'

'I hope you are right.'

'Do you even doubt it?' asked Wolfgart. 'Come on, man. They're barbarians, and looking at how many totems I counted, there's a lot of war leaders there.'

'Is that supposed to be a good thing?'

'Of course,' said Wolfgart. 'You put that many barbarian chiefs together, and they'll fall to fighting each other soon enough.'

'I am not sure, my friend,' said Sigmar, recalling the deadly precision he had seen in the Norsii, in particular a warrior in glittering silver armour, who fought with twin swords. 'I swear it was as if they knew our every tactic. We will lose the empire one battle at a time if we think of the Norsii simply as barbarians.'

'You're giving them too much credit,' said Wolfgart. 'I can teach an animal to do tricks, but that doesn't mean it's clever.'

'No, but the way they fought… It was as if they had a warrior schooled in the empire leading them, someone who knew how we fight. All through the night, I have gone over the battle, picturing every clash of arms and each manoeuvre, hoping to find some clue as to how the Norsii beat us.'

'And what have you come up with?'

'Time and time again, I come back to the same answer,' said Sigmar. 'I underestimated them, and my warriors paid for that mistake with their lives.'

'Then we'll not do that again,' stated Wolfgart, and Sigmar was forced to admire his sword-brother's relentless optimism. He had faith in Sigmar, even in defeat.

Wolfgart rubbed a hand over his face, and Sigmar saw how tired he was.

Since Sigmar's attempted execution of Krugar and Aloysis, Wolfgart had spent virtually every waking minute with the Emperor. The two counts had been freed, and Sigmar begged their forgiveness on bended knee. It took the combined skills of Eoforth and Alfgeir to avert what could have been a devastating civil war but, in the end, both Krugar and Aloysis accepted that Sigmar had been under the dread influence of the necromancer's crown.

Their slighted honour demanded recompense, however, and both counts returned to their castles laden with gold, land and titles. Sigmar could only promise that what had happened would never happen again, for the hateful crown was buried deep in the heart of Reikdorf.

Wolfgart had wanted to hurl it deep into the marsh and be done with it, but Sigmar knew he could not so casually dispose of such a dangerous and powerful artefact. Lifting the crown with a branch broken from a rowan tree, he carried it straight to High Priestess Alessa at the temple of Shallya. With solemn ceremony, the crown was sealed in the deepest vault and warded with every charm of protection known to all the priests of Reikdorf.

Never again would the crown see the light of day, and if its maker ever dared come to claim it, he would find it defended by every warrior in the empire.

\* \* \*

A CONTINGENT OF painted Thuringian warriors marched past Sigmar and Wolfgart, each with a twin-bladed axe slung across his shoulders. They were bloodied and angry, having lost many comrades on the battlefield, men and women both. They wore little armour, for these were the King's Blades, the fiercest and most deadly of all the Thuringian berserkers. They escorted a covered wagon pulled by horses more usually employed to carry Jutone lancers, but which Count Marius had offered to serve the wounded Berserker King.

Sigmar saw a familiar face among the Blades, and nodded to Wolfgart. Together, they rode alongside the tattooed warriors. A berserker woman with long hair pulled in tight braids, naked but for a mail corslet and bracers, looked up at them with eyes haunted by defeat.

'How is he?' asked Sigmar.

'Ask him yourself,' said Ulfdar, the berserker warrior Sigmar had defeated when he had fought the Thuringians to secure their king's sword oath. Her mail was torn and links fell to the muddy road with every step.

'I saw you fight,' said Sigmar. 'I lost count of how many you killed.'

'I don't keep count,' replied Ulfdar. 'I remember little of battles. When the red mist is upon me, it's hard enough to tell friend from foe.'

Sigmar lifted his voice for all the Thuringians to hear.

'Yesterday you fought like heroes,' he said, 'every one of you. I watched as the enemy bore down on you, and not one of you took a backwards step. That is iron courage that cannot ever be broken. The Norsii proved a stronger foe than we remembered, but we are better than them. They are far from home and we are defending our homelands. No force in the world can compare to the warrior defending their hearth and home and loved ones.'

The Thuringians marched past without acknowledging him, and Sigmar could not tell whether his words had any effect on them. The wagon bearing Count Otwin approached, and he waited for it to reach him. The Blades parted before him, and a hatchet-faced Cradoc pulled the canvas flaps at the rear of the wagon aside.

'Don't tire him out,' warned the surgeon. 'The lance broke three of his ribs and nicked his right lung. He's lucky to be alive, though to hear him you'd think he'd just cut himself shaving.'

'Damn it, man,' said Otwin from behind Cradoc. 'I've been hurt worse after a night on the beer. Come morning, I'll be back on my feet.'

'It *is* morning,' snapped Cradoc. 'And if you try to stand you'll die.'

Cradoc lowered himself from the wagon, looked up at Sigmar, and said, 'I have others to treat today, so keep an eye on him. And don't let him up from his bed. If he dies, I'll blame you.'

'I understand. You have my word he will not leave this wagon.'

The irascible healer nodded, and wearily made his way towards more of the walking wounded. Sigmar walked his horse behind the wagon and looked in at his wounded friend.

Count Otwin reclined on a cot bed, his upper body completely wrapped in linen bandages. The Berserker King's skin was waxy and pale, his chest rising and falling with shallow hiked breaths. He smiled weakly, and Sigmar saw how close to death he had come.

'I hope you listened to what Cradoc told you,' said Sigmar.

'Ach, surgeons, what do they know about being wounded in battle?'

'Plenty, you old rogue,' said Wolfgart. 'Cradoc's stitched my wounds more than once, and back in his day he swung a sword as well as a wielding a needle and herb bag.'

'Fair enough,' conceded Otwin, 'and I heard what you said to the Blades. Good speech, but they're not big on fancy words.'

'So I saw,' said Sigmar. 'But it needed to be said.'

Otwin nodded. 'Aye, it did. The damn Norsii handed us a beating and no mistake, Sigmar, so I hope you're giving that same speech to everyone. The men need to hear how those bastards got lucky and that we'll drive them back the next time we face them.'

'That's what I told him,' put in Wolfgart.

'So how many did we lose?' asked Otwin.

'We've still to tally the final butcher's bill, but it looks like we lost close to a thousand men,' said Wolfgart.

'Shallya's tears, that's a lot,' cursed Otwin. 'And the Norsii?'

'Hard to judge,' said Wolfgart, 'but I'd wager no more than three hundred.'

'Aye, a beating,' repeated Otwin, shaking his head. 'It would have been more if not for Marius. His lancers and crossbows really pulled our arse out of the fire.'

'That they did,' agreed Sigmar.

The Jutone count had surprised them all with his courage and steadfast resolve in the face of defeat. Mercenary crossbowmen with pockets lined with empire gold hammered the rampaging Norsemen with merciless volleys of iron-tipped bolts, covering the retreat and preventing it from becoming a rout.

'Who'd have thought it, eh?' asked Otwin with an amused grin. 'Bloody Marius. I'll bet you're glad I didn't let you kill him at Jutonsryk, aren't you?'

'More than you know,' said Sigmar.

Otwin took a drink from a wineskin, grimacing as his stitches pulled tight. He slumped back on his bed, his brow sheened in perspiration, though the day was still chill.

'So what now?' asked Otwin when he had recovered enough to speak. 'I trust you have a plan to send these bastards back across the water?'

'I think so,' said Sigmar. 'This Cormac Bloodaxe is a clever general, but the very savagery that makes his warriors so fierce was our salvation. Had they been disciplined enough to mount a pursuit, they would have destroyed us. Cormac will not make that mistake again.'

'What about the other counts?' asked Otwin. 'Is there any word? We need their strength.'

'I know, but it will take time for them to gather their armies and march to our aid.'

Otwin hesitated before saying, 'And you're sure they'll come? I mean, after what happened with the Roppsmenn and that... unpleasantness with Aloysis and Krugar.'

'They will come,' said Sigmar, with more conviction than he felt. 'If for no other reason than the Norsii will surely turn their axes on them if we fail.'

'There's truth in that,' agreed Otwin. 'So how will you buy the time they need to march?'

'I underestimated the Norsii,' said Sigmar, 'but I will not do that again. We need to draw them to us and destroy them as a surgeon lances a plague sore.'

'And how do you plan to do that?' asked Wolfgart. 'They outnumber us by several thousand now.'

'We will retreat to Middenheim,' said Sigmar. 'It is the greatest fastness in the empire and it has never fallen.'

'It has never been attacked,' pointed out Wolfgart. 'A city on a mountain? You'd have to be mad to attack it. Why would they not just ignore us and push on to Reikdorf? Or any other city that won't be as impossible to take.'

'Their leaders are thinking like us, and they will know they cannot simply ignore Middenheim,' said Sigmar. 'To push further into the empire while leaving an army at their backs would be madness. They will have no choice but to come at us.'

'Then let us hope you are right about the other counts,' said Otwin. 'If they do not heed your summons then Middenheim will be our grave.'

PYRES BURNED, PYRAMIDS of skulls were built long into the night, and Cormac watched the bloody torture of the prisoners. Their screams were prayers to the Dark Gods, and the forests echoed to the chants and prayers of the Norsii. Drunk on slaughter and victory, thousands of men filled the shallow valley where they had faced the might of Sigmar and prevailed.

Cormac could still hardly believe they had won.

Watching the army of Sigmar upon the hillside, his mouth had been dry and his guts twisted in apprehension. The Emperor had never been defeated, and the men of the empire fully expected to crush the invaders in one great battle.

Though he hated to admit it, Kar Odacen's plans and the training regime of Azazel, who had spent the last two seasons teaching the Norsii the empire way of war, had borne fruit. Cormac relished the sense of panic that seized their foes when they had seen the Norsii fighting as a disciplined whole. Kar Odacen's host of shamans had worked their sorceries to bring the heavens down upon the enemy, and their doom was assured.

The slaughter had been mighty, and he had given an equal share of the living plunder to each of his vassal warlords. The Kul had ritually disembowelled their captives, and hunchbacked shamans with gibbering shadows at their shoulders had eaten the entrails. Groups of Wei-Tu riders attached ropes to the limbs of prisoners and rode off in different directions to tear them apart, while Khazag strongmen pummelled their prisoners to death with their fists.

Cormac had fought and killed two dozen warriors in a hastily-dug battle pit ringed with swords. With bare hands and naked ferocity, he had beaten each prisoner down, and drunk their blood as it gushed from necks torn open with his teeth.

The Hung had violated their captives in every way imaginable, and then given their broken, abused bodies to the slaves as playthings. Of all the fates suffered by the prisoners of the empire, this was the one that had offended Cormac the most. Every warrior, even an enemy, was entitled to a death of blood, his skull offered to the brass throne of Kharnath.

Kar Odacen placated him by speaking of the myriad aspects of the Dark Gods and how each was honoured differently. Were not the reeking plague pits of Onogal a means to serve the gods of the north? Though they took no skulls in battle, the shamans who ventured into the madness of the far north and returned twisted and insane with power were just as devoted to the old gods. The pleasure cults of the Hung were no less honourable, elaborated Kar Odacen, though they seemed so to Cormac's eyes.

Besides, as Azazel had pointed out, Cormac could ill-afford to invite dissent into his army by keeping the Hung from their sport. Its unity was a fragile thing at best, and to single out the worshippers of Shornaal would start a rot that would see the army break up within days.

Cormac threaded his way through the camp, pausing every now and then to watch a particularly amusing or grotesque sacrifice at a makeshift altar. His skin was hot and red from the pyres, for there was plenty of wood to burn. In time, the empire would be one gigantic pyre, with the skull of its Emperor mounted on a great pyramid of bone and ash.

As he reached the head of the valley, he saw Kar Odacen and Azazel. His mood soured, for he could not look upon them without thinking that they plotted behind his back. A shaman and a traitor to his own kind. Such lieutenants he had!

A brutalised corpse lay at the shaman's feet, and from the hideous mutilations wrought upon its flesh, Cormac knew that Azazel had indulged his lust for torture. The corpse's belly was opened, and Kar Odacen's hands were buried in its intestines. With a wet, sucking sound, Kar Odacen removed a glistening liver and turned it over in his red hands.

'What do the entrails say?' asked Cormac, and Azazel only reluctantly tore his eyes from the ruptured corpse. Cormac was about to ask again when Kar Odacen held up a hand.

'Be silent,' said the shaman. 'The art of the haruspex requires concentration.'

Cormac fought the urge to take his axe and bury it in the shaman's head for such disrespect, releasing the iron grip on his weapon. He hadn't been aware he was holding it.

'It was a good victory,' said Azazel, gazing rapturously at his own image in the gleaming metal of his sword blade. 'Hard fought and well won.'

Cormac nodded, unsure whether Azazel was talking to him or the reflection. He forced himself to answer without anger.

'Aye, it was that,' he said. 'Many skulls taken and fresh trophy rings for every champion.'

'It is a shame you did not capitalise on it,' said Kar Odacen without looking up from his reading of the dead man's meat. 'Discipline broke down at the end and our enemies escaped us. Now we will need to fight those men again.'

'Then we will fight them again,' hissed Cormac, 'and we will defeat them again.'

'I wouldn't be too sure about that,' said Azazel. 'We beat Sigmar's men because they were not ready for us to fight like them, but they will learn from that mistake.'

Cormac tried not to look at Azazel, and waited for the shaman to speak.

'Did you hear me?' asked Azazel.

'I heard you,' snapped Cormac, finally meeting the swordsman's gaze. As much as he detested the rites of Shornaal, the dark prince's powers must surely have shaped Azazel's features. To raise his voice in anger to such a specimen of perfection seemed abhorrent.

He forced himself to look past Azazel's glamours to the corruption beneath.

'I thought your training made us their equals in battle?' he said.

Azazel laughed, and such was its beguiling quality that Cormac felt his anger melting in the face of such a wondrous sound.

'Hardly,' said Azazel, flashing him a smile. 'We have trained for little more than two seasons. Sigmar's men have trained and fought together for years.'

'Your army outnumbers Sigmar's,' said Kar Odacen, 'and the power of the Dark Gods makes us invincible.'

'No, it makes us vulnerable,' said Cormac.

'That makes no sense,' hissed Kar Odacen. 'My power has never been greater.'

'It is a mistake to think yourself invincible, shaman. Over-confidence will see us defeated. Think like that and we will make mistakes, leave openings for the enemy to exploit. We must assume nothing, and expect that our enemies will come back from this defeat stronger and more prepared. The master of the empire is no fool and will surely learn from his humbling.'

'Then what do you think Sigmar will do next?' asked Azazel.

'He will fall back to Middenheim,' said Cormac. 'It is his only option.'

Azazel nodded and said, 'I will climb to the heavens and tear him from his lofty perch.'

'No, you won't,' said Cormac. 'At least, not yet.'

Azazel's expression hardened and his eyes grew cold.

'What?' he said. 'Our enemy is within reach, why do we not strike for his throat?'

'Because that is what he will expect us to do,' explained Cormac. 'Sigmar must win time for his forces to gather. He will do so by drawing us onto the walls of an impregnable city.'

'Then what do you suggest?' hissed Azazel. 'My blades ache for Sigmar's body.'

'That we do not dance to his tune. We ignore Middenheim and push eastwards. Burn the forests and villages of the empire, and seek out the forces answering Sigmar's call for aid. Destroy them one by one, and soon tales of our victories will draw more of our kin across the sea. Within a season, we will see the empire in flames.'

'No,' said Kar Odacen, rising from the corpse and holding the liver out for them to see. Its hard, fibrous interior was yellow with sickness. 'You are mistaken. That will not happen.'

'What do you mean?' demanded Cormac.

Kar Odacen stroked the liver, stringy ropes of rancid pus dripping from his fingers.

'We follow Sigmar to Middenheim,' said the shaman.

'That is a mistake,' said Cormac. 'We can destroy the empire without facing the Emperor in battle until we have taken everything from him.'

'You think this is about the empire?' snapped Kar Odacen, his bitter gaze sweeping over Cormac and Azazel. 'It is not. It is about Sigmar. You think you fight for lost lands, for revenge? No, this war is the first of many, and all others will hang upon it.'

'Though I dislike the thought of leaving Sigmar in his mountain city, Cormac's plan has merit,' said Azazel, and Cormac was surprised at the swordsman's support.

'Cormac's plan?' hissed Kar Odacen. 'Since when do the tribes of the north heed the word of a mortal man? He is warlord and champion of this host by the will of the gods, and when they speak he must obey!'

'Then what is the will of the gods?' asked Cormac, fighting down his killing urge.

The shaman's eyes took on a glazed, faraway look, and his voice seemed to echo from a place or time far distant.

'The Flame of Ulric must be extinguished and Sigmar must die,' he said. 'I have seen ages beyond this time of legends to a place where darkness closes in on the world, and the forces of the old gods stand poised to bring ruin upon the world. The final triumph of Chaos is at hand, but one name holds back the darkness, one name of power that gives hope to men and bolsters the courage of all who hear it. That name is Sigmar, and if we do not destroy him here and now, then his name will echo down the centuries as a symbol for our enemies to rally behind.'

Cormac felt a shiver of dark premonition travel the length of his spine as the forests around his army trembled with motion. His first thought was that Sigmar's army had returned in the night to fall upon them as they gave thanks for their victory, but that thought died as he saw what emerged from the tree line.

Thousands of beasts that walked, crawled and flew stood illuminated in the firelight, completely encircling the northern army. Blessed by the warping power of the Dark Gods, no two were alike, a glorious meld of man and animal. Armed with crude axes, rusted swords or studded clubs, they had come at the shaman's call, a host of monsters with the snarling heads of wolves, bears, bulls and a myriad other forms that defied easy identification.

As one, they split the night with their howls, brays and shrieks, and Cormac's sense of might and power as master of this army retreated in the face of such atavistic devotion to the old gods. Primal and devoid of any urges save to destroy and revenge themselves on a race that hated and feared them, the beasts were ready to tear the throat from the empire.

'These are days of great power,' said Kar Odacen. 'The tribes of the north, the beasts of the forest, and a great prince of Kharnath will fall upon Middenheim, and we will baptise this world in blood!'

NIGHT WAS FALLING, but still they kept coming.

Like a living sea of fur, flesh and iron, the host of the north swirled and flowed around the base of the Fauschlag

Rock without end. Sigmar stood at the edge of the city with the wind billowing his wolfskin cloak behind him, while his fellow warriors stood a more prudent distance from the sheer drop.

The last time so many of them had been gathered together was at Sigmar's coronation, nine years ago. So much had happened since then that Sigmar barely remembered the promise and hope of that day.

Some of those hopes had been fulfilled, some had been dashed.

Friendships had been forged and strengthened. Others had been soured.

The coming war would test which would endure.

Conn Carsten of the Udose stood with his hands resting on the pommel of a wide-bladed broadsword, while Marius of the Jutones simply watched the gathering enemy impassively. Against all advice, Otwin had joined them, held upright by Ulfdar and a Thuringian warrior whom Sigmar didn't know. The Berserker King's vast axe was freshly chained to his wrist and would only be parted from him in victory or death.

Myrsa and Pendrag were on his left, with Redwane and Wolfgart at his right. His greatest friends and allies stood with him, and their continued faith and friendship was humbling. Despite everything he had put them through over the years, they remained steadfastly loyal.

'They came,' said Wolfgart. 'Just like you said.'

'Aye,' agreed Redwane. 'Lucky us, eh?'

'I didn't think they would,' said Pendrag. 'They must know they cannot take this city.'

'I do not think they would have come if they did not expect to defeat us,' said Sigmar.

'They won't get up the chain lifts, so the only other way in is the viaduct,' said Wolfgart. 'With the warriors we have, we can hold that until the end of days.'

Sigmar read their faces. High on this rock, they believed themselves secure and invincible. They would learn soon enough the folly of that belief.

'If the viaduct was the only way into the city I might agree with you,' said Sigmar, 'but it is not. Is it, Myrsa?'

The Warrior Eternal shook his head, looking as though he were being forced to reveal an uncomfortable secret.

'No,' he said. 'It is not. How did you know?'

'I am the Emperor, it is my duty to know such things,' he said. He smiled, and then tapped the rune-inscribed circlet of gold and ivory at his brow. 'Alaric told me how his miners and engineers helped Artur reach the summit of the Fauschlag Rock. He told me that the rock beneath us is honeycombed with tunnels and caves. Some carved by the dwarfs, others made by hands that are a mystery to even the mountain folk.'

'It's true,' said Myrsa. 'We have a few maps, but they are mostly incomplete and, truth be told, I don't think anyone really knows exactly what's beneath us.'

'There is another way in to my city and I do not know of it?' asked Pendrag. 'You should have told me of this, Myrsa.'

'The city's defence is my domain,' said Myrsa. 'Long ago it was decided that the fewer people knew of the tunnels the better. In any case, our enemies cannot know of them.'

'They will,' said Sigmar. 'They will find them and we must defend them.'

They watched the assembling forces of the Norsii in silence for a while, each trying to guess how many enemies they faced, for Cormac Bloodaxe's force was far larger than before. Inhuman beasts had swelled its ranks, and the sight of so vast a gathering of monsters was horrifying.

'The forests have emptied,' said Otwin. 'I never dreamed there were so many beasts.'

'There will be fewer by the end of this,' snarled Conn Carsten.

Though Sigmar could claim no fondness for the Udose clan-chief, he silently thanked him for his defiant words as he saw resolve imparted to his fellow warriors. He returned his gaze to the enemy army, his keen eyes picking out the banner of Cormac Bloodaxe.

Beneath the banner, a towering warrior in black armour and horned helm looked up at the mountain city. Though great distance separated him from his foe, Sigmar felt as though Cormac was right in front of him. If he whispered, his enemy would hear what he had to say.

'You will not take my empire from me,' he said.

Two figures attended the Norsii warlord, a hunched form that reeked of sorcery, and the lithe warrior in silver armour who bore twin swords. The swordsman's hair was dark, his skin pale, and as he drew one of his blades Sigmar felt a tremor of recognition.

It was impossible. The distance was too great, and though the warrior's face was little more than a tiny white dot amid a sea of warlike faces, Sigmar was certain he knew him.

'The swordsman,' he said, 'next to Cormac Bloodaxe.'

Wolfgart squinted in the crepuscular gloom. 'Aye, the skinny looking runt. What of him?'

'I know him,' he said.

'What?' hissed Wolfgart. 'How can you know him? Who is he?'

'It is Gerreon,' said Sigmar.

Wolfgart sighed.

'This just gets better and better,' he said.

## ──◀ EIGHTEEN ▶──

# The Empire at Bay

THE ARMY OF Cormac Bloodaxe began the assault on Middenheim at dawn the following day, after a night of braying howls, echoing war-horns, sacrificial pyres and blood offerings. Their chants and songs of war drifted up to the defenders, promising death and rich with the primal urges of the gathered Norsii tribes.

Where the men of the empire craved peace and the warmth of hearth and home, the Norsii craved battle and conquest. Where progress and development were the watchwords of the empire, slaughter and the lust for domination drove the northern tribes. The gods of the south watched over their people in return for worship, but the baleful gods of Chaos demanded worship, and offered only battle and death to those that venerated them.

Eight thousand empire warriors stood ready to defend the city, around half the number opposing them. More than just men were poised to attack: bull-headed monsters, winged bat-creatures, and twisted abominations so far removed from any known beast that their origins could never be known. They bellowed alongside packs of slavering, black-furred wolves, and towering troll-creatures lumbered through the host with clubs that were simply trees ripped from the earth.

Sigmar had long since planned the defence of Middenheim, knowing the Flame of Ulric would draw the followers of the Dark Gods like moths to a lantern. The bulk of the enemy would surely come at them up the viaduct, and despite the best efforts of Middenheim's engineers, the stonework connecting it with the city could not be dislodged. The skill of its dwarfen builders was such that not a single stone could be removed. To compound this problem, the citadel and towers designed to defend the top of the viaduct had yet to be completed. The barbican walls were barely the height of a tall man, and the towers were hollow and without ramparts. Blocks of stone intended to raise the wall to a height of fifty feet were even now being used to plug the unfinished gateway or hauled into position to form a fighting step for the men behind it.

This was where Sigmar would make his stand, and he would do it with a thousand warriors drawn from every tribe gathered in Middenheim. Thuringian berserkers stood shoulder to shoulder with Udose clansmen, Jutone spearmen, Unberogen swordsmen and the city's greatswords. Though the White Wolves fought elsewhere, Redwane had refused to leave Sigmar's side, claiming that Alfgeir would have his hide nailed to the longhouse's wall if anything were to happen to the Emperor.

Pendrag and Myrsa commanded a thousand Middenlanders on the city's northern flank, its count and Warrior Eternal facing their foes' homeland as tradition demanded. The White Wolves stood with the Count of Middenheim and his champion, given the duty of their protection by Sigmar. Though unhappy not to be fighting at their Emperor's side, each warrior had sworn himself to this duty before the Flame of Ulric. The eastern districts were held by Conn Carsten's Udose, while the west was the domain of Marius and the Jutones.

Every able-bodied man and boy in the city carried a weapon, though the very oldest and youngest were spared fighting on the front lines. To them was entrusted the defence of the streets and crossroads leading towards the temple being built at the centre of the city.

Middenheim groaned at the seams with people from the surrounding settlements and refugees fleeing the Norsemen's brutal invasion. The city's wells were covered with iron grates and what food remained was under armed guard. At a conservative estimate, Pendrag's quartermasters calculated there was enough to last a month.

Sigmar stood behind the unfinished wall at the top of the viaduct, and watched as the Norsii gathered behind a smoking construct of brass and bone. Beside him, five hundred warriors of the empire stood with spears and bows and swords, ready to fight alongside their emperor. Behind him, five hundred more awaited his order to advance.

A rhythmic booming echoed from far below, the northern tribesmen banging axes and swords against shields as they marched up the viaduct. Monotonous chanting droned in counterpoint to the clash of iron, and the howls of monstrous beasts completed the dreadful, courage-sapping noise. It was a sound that spoke of destruction for destruction's sake, the urge to kill and maim for no reason other than the suffering it would cause.

No courage or faith a man might possess could fail to be shaken by such a noise, for it had been the primordial sound of mankind's doom since the beginning of the world.

Sigmar felt the fear take root in the hearts of his warriors, and vaulted to the top of the wall, resplendent in the glittering armour of his coronation. Each plate shone like silver, each wondrously-crafted engraving dazzling the eye and capturing the heart with its glory. The visor of his winged helm was raised and all who looked upon him saw his determination to resist this attack. He raised Ghal-maraz in defiance of the Norsii and his golden shield, a gift from Pendrag to replace the one destroyed at Black Fire Pass, captured the sunlight.

'Men of the empire!' he shouted, his voice easily carrying to the farthest extent of the defences. 'The warriors before you have been forged in the harshest lands of the north, yet they have not your strength. Their gods are bloody avatars of battle, yet they have not your faith. They live for war, yet they have not your heart! Because they live only for themselves, they are weak. Because they place no value on the lives of their fellow men, they have no brotherhood. Look around you! Look at the face of the warrior beside you. He may be from a land far distant to your home; he may speak a different language, but know one thing: he is your brother. He will stand beside you, and as you will fight and die for him, he will fight and die for you!'

Sigmar turned to face the Norsii, standing tall and proud and mighty.

'Together we are strong,' he shouted. 'Together we will send these whoresons back across the sea and make them wish their mothers had never birthed them!'

PENDRAG HEFTED HIS axe, and watched in disbelief as the beasts began climbing the Fauschlag Rock. They swarmed its sides, clawing their way up the impossible face of the sheer rock. Sigmar had climbed this rock once and it had almost killed him, but these monsters ascended with no more trouble than a man might climb a ladder.

The sky was the colour of ashes, dripping with clouds, and Pendrag felt a queasy sense of vertigo as he looked beyond the northern horizon. No one knew what lay beyond the eternally snowbound landscape, but the legends of every tribe described it as a land of gods and monsters, where the very air carried madness and the power of creation.

He took a deep breath as he altered his grip on the haft of his axe. His silver hand tingled with the memory of fingers and the scar at his neck, from where the long dead warrior-king had struck him, itched abominably. All his old wounds were retuning to haunt him, and he tried not to think what kind of omen that might be.

Beside him, Myrsa stood in perfect stillness. Pendrag had fought countless foes and stood with heroes in the greatest battle in the history of the race of men, yet still his heart hammered at his chest and his mouth was dry.

Six hundred warriors of Middenheim stood at the defensive wall encircling the city, a chest-high barrier built where the ground sloped down to the vertical face of the Fauschlag Rock. Three hundred warriors occupied perches on roofs and towers further back, armed with hunting bows and slings. Their faces were dour and stoic, a cliché of the grim northern tribesman. In the years since he had come to Middenheim, Pendrag had come to see that stoicism as simple practicality and a recognition of the futility of wasted emotion.

No glorious war cries roused the warriors of Middenheim, and bitter experience had taught Pendrag that grand speeches would be wasted on such men. All that mattered to them was the courage in a man's heart and the strength of his sword-arm. Pendrag had proved himself to them, and thus they stood with him to defend their city. Their presence was symbol enough of his acceptance.

What more could any man ask?

The city's blue and white banner flew above him, and Pendrag was honoured to fight in its shadow. He had fought the dead creatures of the necromancer beneath the Dragon Banner, and it felt good to face an enemy beneath a battle flag of honour, not one of murder.

Among the Middenlanders were a hundred White Wolves, their red armour and white wolfskin cloaks marking them out among the city's defenders. Though they should have fought with Sigmar, Pendrag was glad of their strength.

A group of men clad in the neutrally coloured tunics of foresters scrambled from the very edge of the rock towards the defensive wall. They climbed towards Pendrag, and a host of hands helped them across it.

'They're close,' said one of the foresters. 'A hundred feet or so and climbing fast.'

'Good work,' said Pendrag. 'Join the rest of the archers.'

'Be wary,' said the forester as he pushed through the tightly packed defenders. 'There are flying beasts as well as climbing ones.'

Instinctively, Pendrag looked up, but the sky was empty save for circling carrion birds gathered in anticipation of a feast of flesh.

He turned to Myrsa.

'Fight well, Warrior Eternal,' he said.

'And you, Count of Middenheim,' replied Myrsa.

SIGMAR AND HIS warriors threw the Norsii charge back three times before the strange construction of brass and bone reached them. The morning was only a few hours old and Morr had come to claim the souls of the fallen time and time again. The enemy dead were thrown from the viaduct, and the screams of the wounded warred with the battle-chants of the Norsemen.

Each charge was a furious scramble of blades and blood, screams and courage, with Sigmar killing dozens of frenzied Norsii champions seeking his head.

This latest attack promised to be something different.

'What in Ulric's name is that?' asked Redwane, voicing the question on every man's lips.

'I do not know,' said Sigmar. 'But it can be nothing good.'

It towered over the Norsii, a mighty altar of blood and blades pulled by two mighty steeds with curling ram's horns and smouldering coals for eyes. More nightmares made flesh than animals, the beasts' skins smoked with furnace heat and their flanks ran with steaming blood. Skulls tumbled from the monstrous construction, and endless rivulets of boiling blood poured from the altar, staining the flagstones with hissing red streams. Black smoke twisted and billowed in defiance of the wind, and Sigmar blinked as he thought he saw screaming skulls in its depths.

The Norsii gathered around it, howling a single name that sent spasms of nausea stabbing through his body. It was a name of death, yet Sigmar felt his warrior's heart stirred by the damnable syllables. A towering warrior in blood-soaked armour marched to the fore, bearing a black banner that seethed with the power of a storm, its surface alive with chained arcs of black lightning.

With one last screamed exhortation of their dread god's name, the Norsii charged, a foaming mass of tattooed warriors. A volley of iron-tipped crossbow bolts from mercenaries hired with Jutone gold hammered the Norsii, splintering shields and punching through armour. The front rank fell, only to be trampled by the warriors behind them. Another volley and another hit home, each one reaping a fearsome tally.

Archers loosed shafts, but without the power of the crossbows, many thudded home into heavy shields without effect. Sigmar offered a silent thanks to whichever of the gods had sent Otwin to prevent him killing Marius. Without these crossbows, the Norsii might already have broken through.

Then it was too late for arrows and crossbows.

The Norsii hurled themselves at the wall, and the bloodshed began again.

Sigmar blocked a slashing axe, and smashed his hammer into the face of a screaming warrior. The man fell back, his skull caved in, but another clambered over his body, and thrust his blade at Sigmar's neck. He swayed aside and slammed his shield into the warrior's chest.

Screaming Norsemen used their dead to gain height, and the mound of corpses at the wall was crushed beneath their armoured weight. Sigmar stood firm in the face of the enemy, striking out with killing sweeps of Ghal-maraz and, where he fought, the Norsii were hurled back. The warrior with the black banner raised it high, and Sigmar heard a dreadful hissing as smoke from the diabolical altar was drawn towards it.

A howling bellow seemed to come from the bloody altar, and the monstrous beasts pulling it reared and slashed the air with iron-shod hooves. Sigmar felt the ancient power bound within the terrible altar as a stocky tribesman with one eye and hair spiked with chalk and resin hurled himself forward.

He turned to meet the man's attack, but no sooner had he raised his shield than a flickering black light erupted from the dread banner and a terrific impact tore at him. His shield flared and crumbled to ash, its edges hot and golden like parchment in a fire.

'Ulric's teeth!' he yelled, hurling the last remnants of the grip away. The one-eyed tribesman slammed into Sigmar, and he fell from the ramparts. They landed hard, and Sigmar lost his grip on Ghal-maraz. He rammed his helmet into the tribesman's face, but the man seemed impervious to pain. He bit and spat at Sigmar as iron talons erupted from his fingertips. He clawed at Sigmar with bestial ferocity.

Along the length of the wall, the Norsii threw themselves at the men of the empire with renewed fury, the ancient power of their northern gods searing their veins and filling them with rage. It was a destructive power that would consume them without care, but not one of the Norsii feared such an end.

Sigmar rolled, feeling the man's skin ripple and bulge beneath him, as though a mass of snakes writhed in his chest. The tribesman's lengthening fangs snapped at his neck, and only the silver gorget saved Sigmar from having his throat ripped out.

He punched the man in the face. Bone broke and fangs snapped, but the man's flesh was like iron. His skin was darkening, and a pair of bony horns erupted from his forehead in a frothing shower of pink flesh. A spear plunged into the tribesman's side, and he reared up to tear the belly from the spearman. Sigmar scrambled clear, and swept up Ghal-maraz as the tribesman, now more beast than man, sprang at him once again.

He loosened his grip on his warhammer, letting it slide until he held it just beneath the head. Sigmar stepped to meet the monster and punched Ghal-maraz straight at his enemy's face with all his strength behind the blow.

The creature's head burst apart and its grey-fleshed body dropped to the cobbled esplanade. The body jerked and kicked, as though the change wracking its body was not yet done and fresh horns, limbs and bony protuberances erupted from its flesh.

Sigmar leapt back to the makeshift fighting step, seeing that the entire mass of the Norsii were fighting like beasts, their bodies infused with dark magic and warping to render them less than human. Transformation ran amok through the Norsemen, and Sigmar saw a group of warriors whose skin had become scaled and reptilian. Some sprouted horns like those of a mighty bull, while the bodies of others writhed with blazing green flames. A few hurled themselves from the viaduct, their minds unhinged by the dreadful power coruscating through their ranks.

Redwane fought with a tribesman whose body had swollen to gargantuan proportions, his muscles corded with veins like ropes, whose armour had ruptured into fragments. Crossbow bolts peppered the giant's body, but they were little more than irritants to the berserk warrior. Redwane held the beast at bay long enough for Jutone spearmen to drive the maddened creature back to the wall, where Unberogen swordsmen finally hacked it down.

In the centre of the Norsii charge, the ghastly altar of skulls and brass pulsed with unholy light, a foul beacon of dark sorcery. Its dreadful power surged through the Norsii. Beside the altar, the warrior in bloody armour laughed with the sound of thunder.

It had to be destroyed or this battle was as good as over.

A mass of screaming, maddened tribesmen stood between him and the altar.

Only one group of warriors had a chance of reaching it.

'King's Blades!' shouted Sigmar, vaulting the wall to land in the midst of the Norsii. 'With me!'

THE ROCKS SWARMED with beasts, and Pendrag fought to keep his feet as snarling monsters with the heads of black wolves and lean, sinewy bodies snapped and bit. Blood fell like rain from the top of the Fauschlag Rock, and the ground underfoot was slippery with the stuff. A screeching beast with a cat-like face hissed and pounced towards him, and he buried his axe in its chest. He kicked the body from his blade as an arrow clattered from his breastplate, and he glanced up long enough to see a winged creature with a face like a bat swooping through the air above him. The skies swarmed with such beasts, showering the men below with crudely-made arrows tipped with sharpened flint. Most such missiles either missed or bounced from helmets, but every now and then a warrior would fall as an arrow found a gap in his armour. The archers placed in the buildings behind the defenders at the wall tried to bring them down, but the beasts were fast-moving and difficult to hit. Pendrag had ordered them to ignore the flying creatures and save their arrows for the climbing beasts.

A black-shafted arrow slashed out from his archers behind him, taking the monster in the chest. It squealed in pain and vanished from sight. Pendrag smiled as he watched it die, glad that one archer had thought to disobey his order.

He returned his attention to the battle around him as the beasts roared and howled, clawing their way up the craggy slopes to the low wall at the city's edge. White Wolves and Middenlanders fought side by side, battling furiously to deny the beasts a foothold in the city. Bodies fell from the rock, pierced by arrows or cloven by axes and swords. The creatures fought with fangs and talons, for it was next to impossible to climb with a weapon, and they had come close to gaining the city on four separate occasions.

Myrsa killed with a clinical efficiency, his mighty hammer sweeping out with killing strikes that smashed skulls from shoulders. Where the Warrior Eternal fought without emotion, Pendrag's blows were struck with the knowledge of all that would be lost should they falter.

Along the circumference of the wall, the White Wolves sang songs of battle as they fought, while the men of Middenheim hacked at the beasts in grim silence. These men fought without cries of fear or anger, simply attending to the business of battle with as much emotion as they might butcher cattle. Their foe attacked without strategy or intelligence, simply using their hatred and hunger. Pendrag's axe hewed furred limbs from bodies and split snarling jaws, his arm moving like a mechanical piston on one of Master Alaric's steam bellows.

An enormous, bull-headed beast with a spiked collar reared up and both he and Myrsa leapt to meet it. The Warrior Eternal ducked a savage sweep of its clawed hand and swung for its belly. Pendrag slammed his axe into its side. The blade bit barely a handspan before thudding into hard bone.

The creature reared up, tearing the axe from Pendrag's hands, and slashed its horns towards him. Pendrag leapt back, but not fast enough. The razor edge of the horn caught the leather strap securing his breastplate. He was wrenched from his feet and lifted high into the air as the tip of the horn gouged into his side. Mail links parted and the sharpened horn of bone gored his side. Blood streamed from the wound as the horn sawed through the leather strap of his armour.

Pendrag felt himself falling and landed with bone-jarring force. He rolled, seeing sky and rock swirling above him as he tumbled downhill. He scrabbled for purchase as he slid, his limbs battered bloody by the rocks. Suddenly, there was nothing beneath him and the world dropped away.

He thrust his silver hand out, the metal gouging rock and sending sparks flying. The dwarf-forged metal bit, and Pendrag's shoulder wrenched in fiery agony as he jerked to a halt. Breath hissed from behind clenched teeth as he swung helplessly from the edge of the rock, suspended thousands of feet in the air. His vision swam and his stomach lurched at the vertiginous drop.

Far below, swarms of beasts climbed the Fauschlag Rock, and yet more winged creatures took to the air. Larger than the bat-creatures with their short-bows, these beasts carried others in their claws, though the distance was too great to make out who they were. He heard sounds of battle, and bodies fell past him, both man and beast. A monstrous creature, part-hound and part-bear almost dislodged him, but as his grip began to loosen, a hand grabbed his and hauled him back over the lip of the rock.

Pendrag swung his other hand around, and clawed his way to safety, laughing hysterically at his survival. Hugging the rock, he looked up at his rescuer, a man he didn't recognise, but who wore a blue and white ribbon of cloth around his upper arm.

'I've got you, count,' he said, hauling him upwards.

'The beasts?' gasped Pendrag.

'Driven off. For now. Now come on, don't let's be hanging about down here, eh?'

Pendrag nodded, scrambling up the slope through sticky patches of blood and broken fangs. His legs were shaking by the time he reached the wall. With infinite care, he hauled himself upright, and the warriors of Middenheim cheered to see him alive.

He lost sight of his rescuer as the man returned to his position on the defences. Myrsa pushed his way through the press of fighting men, and his face broke apart in a wide grin.

'Gods, man! I thought we'd lost you!' said the Warrior Eternal.

Pendrag bent double, still in shock at the nearness of his death. He held out his battered silver hand, and said, 'I have the craft of Master Alaric to thank for my survival.'

Myrsa looked at the battered limb and said, 'Then I owe him my thanks too.'

Pendrag lifted a fallen axe.

'If we live through this, we'll travel to King Kurgan's halls together and thank him,' he said. 'But there are more beasts on the way.'

'Stand to!' shouted Myrsa, and the warriors around them braced themselves at the edge of the wall, spears and bows aimed down the slopes. There was no panic in these men, no undue haste and no fear, simply duty and courage. Pendrag had never been prouder to be their leader.

'Men of Middenheim, this is your hour!' he shouted, and no sooner had the words left his mouth than a hundred or more beasts with wide wings and broad shoulders flew up past the edge of the rock. Most carried strangely twisted warriors that thrashed and howled, while others bore robed figures that crackled with sorcerous light.

'Bring them down!' cried Pendrag.

Flocks of arrows slashed upwards.

HUNDREDS OF FEET below, in a lightless cavern beneath the city, Wolfgart listened to the dark. He had presumed it would be quiet down here, but he could not have been more wrong. Metal scraped on stone and the tumble of pebbles and dust echoed from far off caves and distant passageways.

His breathing sounded impossibly loud, and he could feel his heart thudding painfully and fearfully in his chest. Behind him, the heavy breath and muffled curses of a hundred men armed with long-bladed daggers, picks and heavy maces filled the lamplit darkness.

'What was I thinking?' he whispered as Sargall stooped at the mouth of a rough-cut tunnel in the rock. The miner stopped to examine a cut mark on the wall, listening at a hollow in the rock before grunting and moving to another tunnel. The man seemed to know his way, but how anyone could navigate this labyrinth of hewn passageways, high caves and rocky galleries was a mystery to Wolfgart. Moisture glinted on the walls, reflecting the lamplight, and Wolfgart wiped sweat from his brow.

'Is it hot or is it just me?' he asked.

'It's just you,' said Steiner, little more than a silhouette beside him.

Steiner was a siege engineer, a thin, nervous man more at home with calculations, measuring rods and diagrams of castle walls than a weapon, but he had been pressed into service to aid the warriors who volunteered to fight below the city. Like Wolfgart, he was uncomfortable below ground, but where Wolfgart was a warrior, Steiner was an academic.

Nearly five hundred warriors had gone into the secret tunnels beneath Middenheim, split into five groups to better cover the known passages and watch for intruders. Voices and shouts from the disparate groups echoed weirdly through the rock, but it was impossible to tell how much distance separated them.

'How far down do you think we are?' asked Wolfgart.

Steiner shrugged. 'Perhaps a few hundred feet?'

'Don't you know?'

'I can't see anything, and we've twisted up and down through these rocks more times than I can count. How am I supposed to know for sure?' snapped Steiner.

'Quiet, both of you,' hissed Sargall, appearing next to them from the darkness. 'Listen.'

Conversation ceased, and Wolfgart swallowed hard, trying not to imagine all the horrible things that might be lurking somewhere in the dark: oozing black insects, slimy creatures of the night that hated sunlight and feasted on the decaying bodies of those lost in the tunnels…

He shut out such thoughts and tried to concentrate.

'You hear that?' whispered Sargall.

'Aye,' said Steiner, bringing the lamp closer to the wall. Wolfgart couldn't hear anything and pressed his ear to the rock. He still couldn't hear anything, and opened his mouth to say so when he heard it: a tiny *tink*, *tink*, *tink* sound. It was like a long fingernail gently rapping on an iron breastplate.

'What is it?' he asked.

'Sounds like a drill of some sort,' said Steiner. 'Nearby. Parallel to this gallery I think.'

'Close?' asked Sargall.

'Close enough,' agreed Steiner. 'Too close.'

'So what do you think it is?' asked Wolfgart. 'Invaders?'

'Who else would be stupid enough to be down here?' asked Sargall.

The noise was getting louder and faster. Wolfgart drew his dagger and unhooked the iron-headed mace from his belt. Though it had grieved him to leave his sword in the city above, it simply wasn't a practical weapon for tunnel fighting.

Steiner placed his head to the rock once more, his face creased in puzzlement.

'I don't understand,' he said. 'It's like a drill, but it sounds much closer now. No drill can go through that much rock that quickly. It must be an echo from somewhere, perhaps a bell chamber that's magnifying the sound.'

'Then we need to find it,' said Wolfgart, 'quickly.'

A sharp crack of splitting stone shot through the tunnel, and cries of fear echoed from the walls as everyone hunched down and looked at the ceiling. Rock dust drifted down and a groan of cracking stone rumbled from somewhere close by.

'What in the name of Ranald's staff was that?' demanded Wolfgart, hearing what sounded like a distant rock-fall. Screams sounded close by, and he brought his dagger up as he heard a metallic scraping sound, like a groundbreaking auger.

'The wall!' he cried. 'Get away from the wall!'

But it was too late. The deep crack of stone split the wall next to Steiner and a roaring, whirling cone of metal speared from the rock. It slammed into the engineer, and the tunnel was suddenly filled with screams and blood. A spinning drill punched into his back and exploded from his ribs. Gouts of red sprayed from the man's convulsing body. Rocks crashed from the wall, and a strange green light filled the tunnel as dust and smoke billowed outwards.

Lamps fell and shattered. Men screamed, and a chittering mass of rats boiled from the hole in the wall. Wolfgart cared nothing for vermin; it was the enormous creature standing in the newly-opened cave mouth, its arm ending in a bloody, spinning auger that captured his attention.

Taller than the mightiest warrior, it was a monstrously swollen, patchwork beast of furry flesh and metal piercings. Though it stood upright, it was no man, for its head was that of a gargantuan rat. Filthy bandages matted in blood wrapped its arms and head, and brass circlets with thin golden wires trailing from them were sewn into its shaven scalp.

Scars and welts covered its body, and it roared with a deafening screech. Shapes moved behind it. Scores of hunched forms in rusted armour bearing jagged swords, pushed past the great beast and into the tunnel.

'Into them!' shouted Wolfgart.

## ─◄ NINETEEN ►─

# Heroes of the Hour

TATTOOED THURINGIANS DROPPED from the wall at the head of the viaduct, and followed Sigmar as he charged the mass of screaming Norsii. The first warrior Sigmar reached was a bearded giant with dark skin and eyes that smoked with shimmering fire. A great skull was branded on his chest, and he came at Sigmar with thoughtless hate.

Sigmar ducked a decapitating axe blow, and swung his hammer for the warrior's legs. Ghal-maraz smashed into his kneecaps and tore his left leg off below the thigh. The warrior screamed and fell, but still swung his sword as Sigmar ran past him. Ulfdar the Berserker led her King's Blades from the wall, a wedge of painted warriors like savages from the ancient days of the empire. They cut into the Norsii, and Sigmar was struck by the notion that whatever sorcery empowered their foe might also speak to some part of his own warriors.

Though their enemies were engorged with dark magic, Ulfdar and the Thuringians gave no heed to it, for the red

mist was upon them and they thirsted only to slay. The
warrior with the black banner drew a sword of darkness,
its blade etched with runes that mocked those hammered
upon Ghal-maraz. Sigmar felt his ancient weapon's
hunger to destroy them.

Thousands of Norsii pushed up from below, but the
tight confines of the viaduct denied them the advantage
of their superior numbers. Warriors swirled around Sigmar, hideous aberrations of flesh twisted by this shrine to
the Dark Gods. Flesh melted, burned and ran beneath its
power, yet those afflicted by such change howled in
ecstasy to be so touched by the power of the gods. To
either side of him, the Thuringian berserkers cut a bloody
path towards the debased shrine. They fought without
heed for their lives, always attacking, and the Norsii fell
back in dismay before these warriors who killed and
killed and never retreated.

Sigmar fought through a mob of warriors whose skin
had erupted with thorny growths, smashing them aside
with deadly sweeps of Ghal-maraz. They split apart as
they died, their bodies disintegrating to mulch as Sigmar
pushed onwards.

The warrior with the banner stepped towards him, and
the Norsii cleared a path for their champion. A full head
and shoulders above his fellow tribesmen, the warrior
planted the banner beside him, its substance seemingly
woven from a thousand rippling black snakes. Waves of
malice poured from the banner, and Sigmar recognised
the touch of purest evil in its creation.

'You die, mortal!' yelled the warrior, leaping to attack
with his sword raised.

Sigmar turned aside the blow, and spun away from the
reverse stroke. The blade came at him again, faster than
he would have believed possible, but once again he was
able to parry the warrior's attack. Each time the black
sword and Ghal-maraz met, sparks flashed with colours

that Sigmar could not name. He felt the unholy strength of the warrior, but knew that it was not his own, it was a gift from the gods he called master. Sigmar's strength was *his*, earned upon countless battlefields and by right of victory.

The sword lanced out, and Sigmar swayed aside, slamming his hammer into the warrior's helm. The strength of the blow drove the warrior to his knees, and Sigmar kicked him in the face, toppling him over onto his back. Before his foe could rise, Sigmar swung Ghal-maraz in a mighty overhead blow, as though hammering a stake into the ground, and smashed the warrior's skull all over the viaduct.

A great wail of anguish went up from the Norsii at the champion's death, and the Thuringians answered with a howl of triumph. Ulfdar cut down the writhing banner with her axe, and lines of smoke unravelled from its disintegrating substance as it fell, its fate entwined with the champion that bore it.

The battleground before the walls was littered with twisted corpses, and nothing now stood between Sigmar and the damned altar. Howling with manic fury, the Thuringians charged the terrible construction of bone and bloody brass, but the daemon-steeds reared and crushed any who dared come near. Their breath was like furnaces searing the air, and anything that came near them died.

Ulfdar staggered over to him, her naked flesh bruised and streaked with blood. She had been wounded several times, yet appeared not to notice. Her eyes had a glazed, faraway look, and purple liquid dribbled from the corners of her mouth as she pointed at the deathly altar.

'How do we destroy it?' she asked, her words slurred from the enraging narcotics.

'Like this,' he said, turning to face the half-built towers at the top of the viaduct. He lifted Ghal-maraz high and swept it down. A hundred bolts slashed out and hammered into the smoking shrine. The daemon steeds yoked to it screamed as they were cut down, collapsing into mouldering heaps of arrow-shot flesh. The heat from their bones died, and their dark hearts were stilled as the spell that breathed life into their forms was broken.

'Now we kill it,' said Sigmar, hooking Ghal-maraz to his belt and running towards the torn-up shrine. The surviving Thuringians ran with him and skulls tumbled from the monstrous shrine as they took hold of it. Closer now, Sigmar saw that the horrific construction also housed a grotesque reliquary of bones, and a swirling cauldron of blood.

This was why Sigmar had driven the Norsii from the empire. Any last notions of regret at what he had done to that tribe were swept away in the face of this dreadful altar. With the help of the Thuringians, Sigmar pushed the sopping altar to the edge of the viaduct.

'Come on!' he shouted. 'Put your backs into it before they return!'

The altar tipped onto its side, and with a final push, toppled over the edge. It tumbled end over end, spilling skulls and blood as it fell.

Sigmar didn't wait to see it hit the ground.

The Norsii were massing for another attack.

MIDDENHEIM WAS ABLAZE. Pillars of smoke painted the sky, and the smell of burning timber carried to the men on the walls. Smaller, bat-like beasts flew over Pendrag's fighting men, soaring over the city to drop flaming torches, while their more powerful cousins swooped over the defensive walls. The tinder-dry wood of the city was ripe for burning, and high winds fanned the flames.

Laden with warriors, dozens of the larger beasts were brought down with deadly accurate arrows, but this mattered little, for their purpose was not to fight, simply to deliver their armed burdens. Thrashing monstrosities that were not wholly human, but something far more terrible and violent, fell amid the ranks of defenders, and the carnage was terrible.

Pendrag watched as one of the howling creatures landed less than ten feet away. It had once been a man, but its body had twisted and mutated beyond all reason, and it lashed out with a clawed arm that was bulbous and sheathed in bony blades. Its eyes were filled with madness and fury, and it hurled itself at the horrified defenders with a bestial roar of hunger.

'What are they?' asked Myrsa.

'Something forsaken by all the gods of mercy,' replied Pendrag.

More were dropping every second, screaming maniacs whose flesh was twisted by their devotion to the Dark Gods, and whose minds were raging maelstroms of unreasoning hatred. They fought without weapons, their limbs and strength requiring no sharpened iron to do their killing. Unnatural limbs and vestigial body parts pressed out through shattered plates of armour, and the black eyes of the monsters burned with maddening pain.

Desperate fights broke out randomly along the defensive wall as the frenzied warriors clawed their way through the men of Middenheim. Many were brought down by disciplined spear-thrusts and lucky arrow strikes, but they were tearing a bloody wound in the heart of the defenders. Terrified warriors fell back from the walls, and a gap opened in the defences.

'Ulric's name!' cried Myrsa. 'We're wide open!'

Pendrag was torn between the urge to fight the maniacal warriors, and the need to defend the slopes, but the sight of the beasts climbing to the walls in the wake of these attacks made the decision for him. He gripped Myrsa's arm.

'Go! Kill them!' he said. 'More beasts will be at the walls soon, and we must be ready for them.'

Myrsa nodded.

'It will be done,' he said, and set off towards the nearest monsters.

Pendrag watched him go as a body flew through the air, almost severed at the waist, and a sheet of blood arced upwards. Roaring, snapping and screaming spread from the attack, and he looked up as a shadow passed over him.

A flying beast with an arrow lodged in its chest dropped from the sky, a hulking brute of an enemy warrior clutched in its claws.

'Look out!' shouted Pendrag as the dying creature spiralled downwards. It slammed into the ground behind the wall, its fragile body crushed beneath the monstrous form of the thing that it had carried from the ground. Clad in scraps of armour, the warrior's flesh seethed with invention, vestigial forms oozing beneath its skin and its distended face like a wax effigy left too close to a fire.

One of the White Wolves rushed in to kill it before it could rise, but hands like pincers smashed him from his feet and pulled him towards its gaping maw. Bloody fangs crunched the warrior's skull to splinters. Spears punctured its back, but it gave no heed to its wounds as Pendrag rushed to kill it.

Perhaps some part of what was left of its mind recognised a fellow warrior, for it dropped the body it was disembowelling and charged towards Pendrag. Someone shouted a warning, but the Count of Middenheim stood firm in its path. The warped creature reared up, fangs bared and claws extended to tear him apart.

Pendrag's axe swept down and hacked the creature's arm from its body, cleaving into its chest and exiting in a spray of ichor from its belly. The beast fell before him, and the men of Middenheim cheered such a mighty blow.

'They can die!' shouted Pendrag. 'They are touched by sorcery, but they can die. Now kill them all!'

As though ashamed of their brief moment of panic, the warriors of Middenheim fell upon the screaming once-men, cutting them down without mercy and forcing them back to the edge of the city. The White Wolves killed a warrior-beast with a nest of claws for hands and curling horns sprouting from its shoulders and back. It tore at them as it died, its madness driving it to acts of carnage even as its lifeblood pooled beneath it.

Another beast, with budding heads oozing through the flesh of its chest, hurled broken men aside with lashing, blade-tipped tentacles instead of arms.

It had to be hacked into a dozen pieces before it would die.

WOLFGART TRIED TO make sense of the confused mêlée raging through the tunnels, but it was impossible. Flames danced on the floor, and pools of oil burned where lamps had been dropped in death or panic. Shadows leapt across the walls. The caves below Middenheim were lonely battlegrounds, where men fought in the claustrophobic passageways, stabbing at shadows and dying alone in the dark.

Scores of the hooded invaders poured from the cave-in, and his warriors fought to hold them from getting past. It was a losing battle, for tides of bloated rats swarmed the tunnel, biting and dragging men down with their furry bodies. The reek of the sewers came with them, and Wolfgart had already stabbed dozens from his legs. His tunic was in tatters where he had cut himself in his desperation.

As loathsome as these vermin were, it was the hideous, rat-faced beasts that walked upright in imitation of man that struck the greatest terror into Wolfgart's men. So human and yet so bestial, their flame-lit faces were malicious and cunning, a mockery of man's intelligence.

The giant auger-carrier battered its way into the tunnels, and the rat-beasts followed in the wake of its bludgeoning attacks. Elongated fangs bit through flesh and armour, and the power of its enormous arms broke men in two if they came too close.

Wolfgart heard shouts of alarm from far off tunnels. Clearly this was not the only breakthrough into the warrens beneath Middenheim.

The monstrous rat-beast charged him, its spine hunched over in the cramped tunnel, and he ducked a crushing sweep of its deadly auger. The conical blades still spun, sending chunks of rock flying as it bit into the wall. Wolfgart slammed his mace into the monster's side, the flesh stitched and raw-looking. Bones broke and flesh caved in beneath the blow, but the monster gave no sign that it was even aware he had struck it.

Its auger stabbed down, and Wolfgart leapt back, slashing his dagger across its twitching snout. Blood burst from its mouth, and he stumbled away from the monster. A rusted sword scraped across his chest, skidding over the mail links and slashing his cheek. Wolfgart lashed out with instinct rather than skill, and was rewarded by a squeal of pain.

A creature that was a smaller version of the giant fell broken, but before he could even register its death, the huge monster threw itself at him once again. Its claws caught his mail shirt and slammed him against a wall. Stars exploded before him as the force of the impact drove the breath from his lungs. Through the haze of pain, Wolfgart saw its arm draw back for a thunderous punch.

He ducked, and its fist pulverised a section of wall behind him. Wolfgart reached up and slashed his dagger at the monster's throat as it bellowed in pain. Fur and sinew parted beneath the desperate slash, and Wolfgart was sprayed in a hosing squirt of blood. The creature's iron grip relaxed and it dropped to its knees, as though mystified as to why its strength was failing.

He spat blood from his mouth and wiped his eyes clean with his sleeve.

It was impossible to read the flow of the battle, for so much of it was fought in darkness. Weapons clashed, but who, if anyone, was winning was a mystery. Wolfgart leapt over the giant rat-thing and plunged into the tunnels, stabbing and crushing any invaders he came across. His warriors fought in blind terror, a host of panicked men wildly swinging swords at their chittering attackers.

The hot confines of the tunnels were hellish to fight in, and every blow was fuelled by his fear of this dark, terrible place. A sword lunged at him from the shadows, and he batted it aside with his mace. Flickering firelight illuminated the frightened face of the miner, Sargall.

'Watch it, damn you!' shouted Wolfgart, his voice carrying to all the men who still fought in the tunnels. 'Strike the enemy, not your friends!'

'Sorry!' cried Sargall, and Wolfgart saw the man was in tears. 'I thought you were one of them! Ulric save us, we're all going to die down here, they're going to kill us all.'

'Not if I have anything to do with it,' barked Wolfgart. 'Now shut up.'

He heard a scrape of metal on stone, and turned with his weapons raised as a pack of hunched forms emerged from the darkness.

'Come on then, you bastards!' he yelled. 'Here I am! Come and get me!'

They were clad in black armour, and vile segmented tails whipped at their backs. Spears jabbed at him, and no sooner had he turned the first aside than a host of rats swarmed from the walls, leaping from ledges and nubs of rock to attack him.

He hurled himself against the wall, crushing half a dozen and dislodging yet more. A spear slashed for his neck, and he blocked it with the haft of his mace. Sargall screamed as a rat-thing stabbed him in the belly and the rats swarmed over him. Two of the spear-carriers ran at Wolfgart, and he roared as he ran at them.

The first died as Wolfgart jammed his dagger through the rusted plates of armour protecting its chest, and twisted the blade up under its ribs. It squealed in agony as it died, and he hurled it back as the second came at him. He slammed his mace into its toothy jaw, and it dropped dead at his feet. Screams and the sounds of battle rang deafeningly from the walls of the tunnels, the echoes magnified and distorted by the close confines.

He heard a crash of stone, and choking dust billowed along the length of the tunnel.

Gods, more of the damn things!

A spear pierced his side, and he grunted in pain. Rats climbed his trews and bit his legs. Teeth snapped on his hamstrings, and the pain sent a bolt of white fire zipping up his spine. Wolfgart cried out, and dropped to one knee as more rats swarmed him. He dropped to the floor of the tunnel and thrashed like a madman, crushing rats as he rolled in pain and desperation. Blades stabbed at him, some drawing his blood, some that of the rats. His attackers seemed not to care which.

He lashed out with his mace, trying to clear some space, but it was hopeless, and he filled the air with curses at the thought of dying like this, far from the world of men and without his sword in his hand. Wolfgart tried to regain his feet, but the weight of rats was too heavy, and he could not rise.

'Ulrike!' he shouted, as a vision of his daughter filled his mind. Sadness filled him as he thought of all the years he would miss of her life.

A hooded figure in armour reared over him with a long, serrated dagger, and its furry snout twitched in anticipation of killing him. Wolfgart could taste the rankness of its hissing breath and smell the reek of foulness on its twisted body. The dagger swept up, but before it could plunge down, the creature's head flew off, and the tunnel was filled with light.

The rats pinning Wolfgart to the ground fled, scurrying off into the darkness, and he scrambled onto his backside, reaching for his dagger and mace.

Wolfgart shielded his eyes from the source of the blinding light, seeing a number of short, armoured figures in gleaming plates of silver, bronze and gold advancing towards him.

'Back, you devils!' he roared, blinking furiously as his eyes adjusted to the illumination.

One of the armoured figures shouldered a bloody axe and knelt before him. The warrior raised the visor of its helmet, revealing a bearded face and a stern, but not unkind expression of recognition.

Wolfgart laughed and let out a shuddering breath.

'Once again the dwarfs come to the aid of you manlings,' said Master Alaric with a wicked grin. 'It's getting to be a habit.'

THE VIADUCT AND northern flank of the Fauschlag Rock were assaulted with the greatest ferocity, but the eastern and western flanks also came under heavy attack. Conn Carsten's Udose fought with great courage, keeping the swarms of beasts from the makeshift ramparts with powerful sweeps of their wide-bladed broadswords. Their battles were fought to the tunes of gloriously heartbreaking laments played by pipers who marched through the thick of the fighting, heedless of the danger.

Skirling tunes of lost loves and ancient wrongs provided a stirring backdrop for the clansmen, an emotional reminder of that for which they fought. Time and time again the beasts were hurled back, and each time the ingenious insults of the clansmen chased the bloody survivors away. Wineskins of grain liquor were passed around during each lull in the fighting, and though scores of fighters were dead and crippled, the mood was light, for the Udose were never happier than when they were in battle.

Carsten's warriors came from dozens of different clans, men and women who had been killing each other only weeks before in bitter internecine power struggles, but who now fought like lifelong sword-brothers. When the fighting was over they would go back to their feuding, and none would have it any other way.

As Sigmar was casting the dread altar from the viaduct, and Pendrag brought down the last of the forsaken oncemen, another ravening pack of beasts climbed the eastern cliffs. Once again, Conn Carsten called his warriors to battle in his grim and humourless manner, and every clansman readied his sword.

But this attack was to be something different.

Borne up the rock face by a monstrous bear-creature, a robed beast-shaman with the shaggy look of a bullish goat and the twisting antlers of a stag climbed onto the upper slopes of Middenheim. Arrows hammered the forest beasts as soon as they appeared, but the shaman uttered guttural words of power in a dark tongue, and they burst into flame.

Instead of charging the defensive wall, the beasts gathered below the Udose, snarling and roaring as the beast-shaman chanted a filthy incantation. A creature with a body that was a meld of man and fox with sable fur threw itself to its knees before the beast-shaman, its head thrown back and its throat bared. A slash of the beast-shaman's claws and its black blood arced up to spatter the grotesque sorcerer. Bathed in sacrificial blood, the beast-shaman let loose an ecstatic cry, its clawed hands twisting and tearing at the air.

At first it seemed as though nothing was happening, but within moments it was clear that something was horribly wrong. It began among the clan warriors of the Gallis. Their hurled insults changed, losing the form of speech and becoming honking brays, bellowed roars and bestial growls.

Horrified cries rippled outwards as the men and women of the Gallis began convulsing and the full terror of the beast-shaman's sorcery took hold. Proud Udose warriors fell on all fours as their bones cracked and reshaped into new and hideous forms. Flesh slithered and swelled, bristling fur erupted from pink flesh, and screams of terror became animal barks.

Men fought to get away from these abominable transformations, and as the beast within each man took hold, the newly-birthed monsters threw themselves at their former comrades-in-arms. Within moments, the Udose were in disarray as the horribly altered warriors of the Gallis went on a bloody rampage, fangs tearing out throats and claws ripping flesh from bones. The pipes fell silent and the songs died, as what had begun as a gloriously raucous fight became a desperate battle for survival.

As the Udose formation collapsed, the beasts below attacked.

And there was no one to stop them.

A VERY DIFFERENT battle was fought on the western flank of Middenheim, where the forces of Count Marius manned the defences. The Jutones had come to the City of the White Wolf with a host of mercenaries, men with olive skin who hailed from a sun-baked land far to the south. They spoke strangely, yet their skill in the art of killing needed no translation.

Marius watched with disdain as the mutant abominations gathered on the slopes. Creatures with the powerfully muscled bodies of bears and wolves roared and stalked the cliffs of the Fauschlag Rock, wary of the deadly weapons of the men that could kill from afar.

'Why do they bother?' he wondered aloud.

'My lord?' asked his aide-de-camp, a handsome youth named Bastiaan.

Marius waved a manicured hand at the slavering beasts.

'What can such aberrations know of civilisation and commerce?' he asked. 'The Norsii seek to conquer the lands of the south, but what will they do with such a prize? Become merchants? Learn to farm the land? Hardly.'

'I do not know, my lord,' said Bastiaan, ever the sycophant. The boy was efficient and attended to his needs with alacrity. Sometimes he even said things of interest. 'Perhaps vengeance drives them. You yourself have led hunts into the forest to cull such creatures.'

'True, but war is a means of extending one's will across the world,' said Marius. 'War for the sake of vengeance is ultimately pointless. There is no profit in it.'

'Not all wars are fought for profit, my lord.'

'Nonsense, Bastiaan, analyse any conflict closely enough and you will find a lust for gold at its heart.'

'The Norsii and these beasts do not fight for gold.'

'Which is why disciplined volleys of crossbow bolts have hurled every attack from the rock,' Marius said. 'Not a single beast has survived to reach the wall.' He drew his sword, the eastern-styled cavalry blade shimmering with a hazy light in the evening sun. 'You see? This is the first time I have drawn my sword today. It has yet to be blooded.'

Bastiaan nodded towards the rapt faces of the Jutone warriors.

'Maybe so,' he said, 'but I believe your warriors desire to meet their foes blade to blade.'

'I am sure they will, but not yet,' said Marius. 'It will be better for the mercenaries to bear the brunt of the beasts' attack.'

'You doubt the courage of your warriors?'

'Not at all, but dead mercenaries do not require payment,' explained Marius.

'Of course, my lord,' said Bastiaan. 'I shall alter our account ledgers.'

Marius smiled at the thought, picturing the secret treasure vaults hidden in the depths of the Namathir. Even with Sigmar's ludicrously unfair levies and tithes after the battle of Jutonsryk, Marius still had more gold than any man could hope to spend in a dozen lifetimes. A young courtier had once remarked that his love of gold was akin to that of a dwarf, and though the remark was astute, Marius had the boy whipped to death.

More of the beasts were gathering, and they were getting dangerously close. Marius frowned as he realised the mercenary crossbowmen were allowing them to climb unmolested towards the defensive wall. He felt tingling warmth in his hand as a strange, bitter taste of metal fizzed in the air.

'What in the name of Manann are those fools doing?' demanded Marius. 'Why are they not loosing their bolts?' The taste of metal grew stronger and the hairs on the back of his neck stood erect in a primal warning of danger.

'I… I don't know, my lord,' said Bastiaan, his voice sounding dreamlike. 'Perhaps they don't want to hit all the chests of gold.'

Marius gave the boy a sidelong glance.

'What foolishness are you talking about?' he asked. 'What gold?'

'There,' whispered Bastiaan, moving towards the wall. 'So much gold!'

Marius watched in horror as the mercenaries climbed over the defensive wall, fighting one another as they made their way towards the beasts without fear. A muttered ripple of heated conversation came from the ranks of Jutone warriors behind him. He turned to rebuke them for breaking silence, but his harsh words trailed off as he saw the glassy avarice in their eyes, each man lost in a dream of something wonderful.

The warmth in his hand became heat, and he looked down to see the etched lettering running the length of his sword blade shimmering as though bathed in twilight. The golden-skinned king who had presented it to him had claimed it could turn aside evil spells, though Marius hadn't believed him at the time. A whispering evil urged him to sheath the blade, but Marius knew that his sword's power was all that was protecting him from whatever fell sorcery affected his warriors.

Bastiaan had reached the wall, but Marius ran forward and took hold of his arm.

'Get back here, boy,' snapped Marius. No sooner had he touched his aide-de-camp than the boy shuddered and blinked in surprise. He looked from Marius to the beasts and back again.

'What did you do with it?' he cried, tears spilling down his cheeks.

'With what?' demanded Marius. 'Have you lost your mind?'

'The gold!' shouted Bastiaan. 'It was there… All the gold in the world. It was mine!'

'There is no gold there, you fool!' said Marius. 'Snap out of it, you are ensorcelled.'

Bastiaan shook off Marius's grip.

'Of course you'd say that!' he protested. 'You want to keep it all for yourself! You don't want anyone else to have any of your precious gold!'

Marius slapped Bastiaan, tired of the boy's theatrics. He brushed past the youth and leaned over the wall. The olive-skinned mercenaries were almost at the bottom of the slope. None of them had their weapons drawn, and their movements were like those of sleepwalkers.

Marius saw the dreadful hunger in the eyes of the monsters. Saliva drooled from their jaws and he knew that he had only seconds to act.

He turned to shout at his Jutone warriors, but before he could open his mouth, searing pain exploded in his side. Marius looked down and saw the golden hilt of an exquisitely fashioned knife pressed against his leather and silk doublet. Blood welled around the blade, and he watched, uncomprehending, as it spilled onto the stone flags.

Bastiaan twisted the knife, and Marius cried out in pain, clutching his aide-de-camp's shoulder as the strength in his legs gave out.

'I won't let you take the gold!' hissed Bastiaan. 'It's mine. All mine. You can't have it!'

'There is no gold,' whispered Marius, sagging to the ground, and leaning against the wall as his vision greyed. He heard the screams of the mercenaries as the beasts tore them apart, and the slaughter began.

We failed, thought Marius, and this city will fall.

## ━◄ TWENTY ►━

# The Last Days

THE CITY DID not fall.

On the eastern flank, the Udose were torn apart by the twin assaults from the beasts and their transformed comrades. Horrified warriors fled into the city, leaving the eastern approaches to the city wide open.

The west fared little better, with the enraptured Jutones walking blindly towards non-existent treasures and illusory visions of their deepest desires. Most were torn apart by the beasts, but many more fell to their deaths as they chased phantoms of riches, women and lost loved ones over the edge of the cliff.

Sigmar's forces at the viaduct and Pendrag's warriors to the north were cut off from one another as beasts and fires raged through the heart of the city. As Middenheim burned, its people prayed to Ulric and their prayers were answered as a frozen wind blew from the north, preventing the fires from spreading and saving their city from destruction.

The flames were doused, but hungry beasts tore into the city's inhabitants, killing and feeding in an orgy of slaughter. Blood ran in rivers through the streets of Middenheim, but its people were hardy northerners, and were not about to go down without a fight. Just as it seemed the city was doomed, aid came from two unlikely sources.

The warriors that Sigmar had deemed too young or too old to stand on the front lines rose to the defence of their city, and an aged veteran named Magnus Anders rallied the warriors of the eastern districts to him. Already in his fiftieth year at the time of Black Fire Pass, the veteran Anders led his warriors in a series of brilliantly orchestrated guerrilla attacks that blunted the charge of the beasts, and led them into blind alleys where they could be butchered. Civilians and refugees followed his example and fell upon the beasts with axes, cleavers, clubs and pitchforks, driving the last of them into killing grounds of archers who had fallen back in the wake of the slaughter of Conn Carsten's men.

As the Jutone defence of the west was broken, rampaging packs of beasts flooded into the mercantile quarter of the city. The streets here were narrow, and the squat stone buildings bore the hallmarks of dwarf craftsmen. As the monsters surged into the city, the doors of these buildings burst open, and armoured wedges of stocky warriors in gleaming plates of burnished gromril smashed into the forest beasts.

The Ironbreakers of Karaz-a-Karak cut a bloody path through the monsters, hammers and axes hewing warped flesh with grim, merciless skill. Alaric the Mad fought with an axe that shimmered with golden light, and his warriors were like a dam of iron before the tide of monsters. Blinking in the sunlight, Wolfgart fought at Alaric's side, bloody and filthy, but unbroken and elated to be alive.

The beasts broke upon the iron fortitude of the dwarf line again and again, until Alaric deemed the the time was right and a double horn blast sounded the advance. The dwarfs marched through the streets of Middenheim, each separate host of warriors linking and forming an unstoppable wall of iron and blades. Roars of hunger and triumph turned to howls of fear as the beasts fell back before the inhuman killing power of the dwarfs.

The beasts were pushed back to the western edge of Middenheim and driven from the cliffs without mercy. Here, Wolfgart found Marius of the Jutones among the fallen, still gripping his curved cavalry sabre. His rich tunic was soaked with blood, and though Wolfgart feared the worst, the stubborn Count of Jutonsryk still clung to life.

At last, the sun sank below the horizon, and night fell.

The first day of battle was over, and the city had not fallen.

NIGHT BROUGHT A much-needed respite from the battle, for both sides had exhausted themselves in the furious struggle. Warriors rested, having spent the day fighting, but Sigmar, Pendrag and Myrsa made a circuit of the defences, taking time to praise each sword band's courage and assure them of victory. It was draining work, and the strain was telling by the time Sigmar gathered his counts in the Hall of Winter.

The mighty longhouse at the heart of Middenheim had once been Artur's great hall, but now it belonged to Pendrag. It had been a cold place of isolation and power, but Pendrag had transformed it into a place where all men were equal and free to speak their minds.

A great fire burned in the hearth and the walls were hung with the pelts of legendary wolves that had hunted the Forest of Shadows. This was a place of warriors, and Sigmar had summoned his friends and allies to him as they faced a second day's fighting. Normally, vast platters of roasted boar and flagons of northern ale would fuel such a gathering, but with no end in sight for the siege, the leaders of the empire ate sparingly, though they drank as fulsomely as ever.

Alaric's warriors had brought several casks of dwarf ale with them, for no force of Grungni's chosen went into battle without the taste of beer in his beard.

A single day had passed, yet Sigmar felt as weary as he had after a year of fighting at the siege of Jutonsryk. His limbs ached and his head thumped with the same dull pain that had been his constant companion since his destruction of the Norsii's bloody altar. He was bone tired, but proud of all that his warriors had achieved.

Though Sigmar was the Emperor, Pendrag sat at the head of the longhouse, as was only right and proper in his own city. Myrsa stood behind the count of Middenheim, and Alaric sat at Pendrag's side, contentedly smoking a long ashwood pipe. The two warriors spoke with real pleasure at this unexpected meeting of old friends. Wolfgart and Redwane sat on the steps before Pendrag's throne, resting their elbows on a flagon of ale from which they regularly refilled their tankards.

Count Otwin sat by the fire, his body thick with bandages and his chained axe resting next to him. Similarly swathed, Count Marius lay on a padded couch next to the Thuringian count. His skin was an unhealthy grey, but he was lucky to be alive. Though Marius had been deeply wounded, the blade had not pierced his vital organs. The bewitched youth who stabbed him had been torn apart by the beasts, which was just as well, for Marius would have been sure to wreak a terrible vengeance.

Conn Carsten sat staring into the fire, lost in thought, and Sigmar's heart went out to the bluff clansman. In the face of disaster, Carsten had rallied enough of his warriors to fight his way clear of the beasts' attack, and return to the fight alongside the aged warriors of Magnus Anders, but that did not change the fact that clansmen had run from a fight. The honour of the Udose had been slighted, and shame burned in every man's heart.

The atmosphere in the hall was subdued, for the day's fighting had been hard, and the morrow promised to be harder still. Sigmar lifted his tankard of dwarf ale from the table and stood before Pendrag, bowing to the master of the hall before turning to face those gathered around him.

'Ulric bless you, my friends,' he said. 'This has been a day of blood that will never be forgotten. Our foes pressed us hard, but we are still rulers of Middenheim.'

'Aye, but for how long?' asked Conn Carsten. 'I lost two hundred men today. We won't survive another attack like that.'

'We can and we will,' promised Sigmar. 'I swear this to you now. The first day of any siege is always the hardest. It is when enemies test one another and gain the measure of their foe. The attacker hopes to sweep the defenders away in one mighty storm, and those within hope to break the will of the besiegers with the strength of their resistance. Tomorrow will be hard, but it will be easier than today.'

'You can't know that,' said Carsten. 'Pretty words might fool some men, but I have seen my share of battles and I know that's just hot air. You know as well as I do that another attack like today will break us!'

Sigmar moved around the fire to stand before Conn Carsten, and the clansman got to his feet, as though expecting the emperor to attack him. He probably does, thought Sigmar, recognising the bellicose quality common to Udose tribesmen.

'It will not,' said Sigmar, 'and I will tell you why. We only need hold the Norsii here until our sword-brothers reach us. Cormac Bloodaxe has made a mistake coming to Middenheim, for even now armies are closing on him, and he knows he must finish us before they arrive. He surprised us with his skill before, but now he has no time for subtlety and must throw everything he has at the city.'

'I'm no defeatist,' said Wolfgart, taking a long draught of ale, 'but it strikes me that might be enough. We lost close to a thousand fighting men today, and the same again are too badly hurt to fight tomorrow. Like I said, we can hold the viaduct, but Middenheim's a big place.'

'Aye, it is,' agreed Sigmar, circling the fire and meeting the gaze of every one of his friends. 'and we will defend every inch of it.'

'How?' demanded Conn Carsten. 'Where will you get the warriors to man the wall?'

'Pull what strength you have in the tunnels back to the surface, manling,' said Alaric from the end of the hall. 'My Ironbreakers will hold the secret ways into the city. We know them better than any of you.'

'You see?' said Sigmar. 'At every turn we are blessed by the gods. Fire took hold of the city and the people prayed for salvation. The wind and rain of Ulric answered those prayers and the city was saved.'

'It rains every day in the north,' said Marius from his padded couch. 'That is hardly a miracle, for the climate here is quite revolting. Must be bad for the lungs.'

'If you don't like the weather in the north, just wait an hour and it'll change,' said Myrsa.

Sigmar smiled, pleased to hear a note of levity from his commanders.

'When it looked as though we would be overrun, the people drove back the invaders, and our allies from the mountains drove the beasts from the city,' he said. 'The gods help those who help themselves, and Alaric brings some of the greatest fighters from his hold to fight along-side us. How many warriors make up your throng, Alaric?'

'Five hundred stout fighters from honourable clans,' said the dwarf runesmith. 'Warriors from the Grimlok goldsmiths, the Skrundok runesmiths of Morgrim, the Gnollengroms and the Grimargul veterans. But best of all, I bring Hammerers from King Kurgan's personal guard and a hundred Ironbreakers to defend the tunnels.'

'A hundred?' asked Carsten. 'We had five times that number in the tunnels and they very nearly couldn't hold back the vermin-beasts!'

'Aye, and for every battle you have fought, manling, they have fought a dozen more. They've been fighting grobi and trolls and worse in the dark for longer than any of you have been alive.'

Alaric leaned forward, blowing a puff of aromatic smoke from his pipe, and saying, 'I warn you not to insult their honour by doubting their courage, manling.'

'Conn Carsten meant no disrespect, Alaric,' said Sigmar.

'No,' agreed Carsten, hurriedly. 'None at all. I apologise, runesmith.'

Alaric nodded and stepped down towards the fire as a dwarf in burnished armour of gold and silver marched from the edge of the hall bearing a long, slender case of dark wood.

'I bring warriors, right enough,' said Alaric, 'but I bring a mightier gift to aid the defence of this city.'

The dwarf runesmith took the case from the warrior, and turned to hold it out to Sigmar. Alaric's expression was hard to read beneath his thick beard, but it looked a lot like sadness, as though he were being forced to give up his most treasured possession.

'I laboured long and hard crafting this in the greatest forge of Karaz-a-Karak,' he said. 'Use it wisely, my friend.'

Sigmar undid the golden clasp securing the case, and lifted the polished lid.

Cold silver light spilled from the fur-lined interior. and the fierce beauty of the object within stole Sigmar's breath away.

It was a sword, but what a sword it was!

Its blade shone like captured moonlight, its edge keen enough to cut the veil between worlds. Etched runes ran along its length, carved into the very heart of the blade. Sigmar had never seen a more perfectly forged weapon.

'Is this…?' whispered Sigmar as those of his friends that could stand gathered around him.

'Aye,' said Alaric. 'The first of the runefangs. Take it.'

Slowly and with reverent care, Sigmar reached out and lifted the sword from its case. Its hilt was silver, the handle wrapped in the softest leather, and the pommel stone a nugget of smooth gold. In the wake of Black Fire Pass, Kurgan Ironbeard had promised him a mighty blade for each of his kings, and Sigmar had never held a sword so fine. The runefang was light, yet perfectly balanced, the work of a master craftsman at the peak of his powers.

The sense of connection he felt with the blade was incredible. It was akin to Ghal-maraz, but this was a weapon crafted for a man's hand and forged for a spirit that endured for a fleeting moment compared to that of a dwarf.

'Does it have a name?' he asked, turning the blade and letting it capture the firelight.

'Not yet,' said Alaric. 'It will earn one in battle, but that is for you to choose.'

Sigmar spun the sword, feeling the blade cut the air like the sharpest razor, and shook his head. The sword was magnificent, a work of art so awesome that it seemed an insult to its perfection for his crude human hand to even touch it.

'No,' said Sigmar, turning to face Pendrag. 'This is not my sword to bear. We fight in defence of Middenheim, and its count is in need of a new weapon.'

Sigmar reversed the blade and offered the handle to Pendrag, feeling the sword's approval of his act. Pendrag looked from the runefang to Alaric. He too shook his head.

'No, I can't,' he said. 'I am not worthy. You are the Emperor, it should be yours.'

'I already have a weapon gifted to me by the king of the mountain folk,' said Sigmar, holding the magnificent blade out. 'Take it, for it is yours to bear, my friend.'

Pendrag took the runefang from Sigmar, and the light that flowed from the blade bathed him in pale luminescence, like the moon of a winter solstice. Sigmar turned to Conn Carsten, the normally sour-faced Udose warleader smiling and full of wonder.

'Still think we are doomed?' asked Sigmar.

Conn Carsten shook his head, and said, 'Not any more.'

THE CITY DID not fall on the first day, and it endured for the next twelve days.

Every day, the Norsii attacked along the viaduct as beasts swarmed up the sides of the Fauschlag Rock. Unnatural storms battered the City of the White Wolf, heaving rainstorms and lightning strikes that levelled whole districts. Doomsayers cried that the gods had turned from the race of man, but as night fell on each day, the defences were rebuilt to face the next attack. After the first day's fighting, there were no bystanders in the battle to save Middenheim. Every living soul within the city bent their efforts to resisting the siege, either as a warrior or in the infirmaries or granaries, or wherever help was needed.

As well as warlike tribesmen, Cormac Bloodaxe sent hideous beasts into battle. Vile, slime-skinned trolls attacked alongside hulking ogres with horribly disfigured limbs and skin like hardened leather. Black wolves ran with the monsters, and red-furred hounds with spiked collars leapt the wall at the head of the viaduct to bite and tear at the defenders, before being cut down by hardened dwarf fighters.

Flying beasts with wide wings swooped over the city, but the foresters of Middenland were deadly hunters, and brought dozens of the creatures down. Soon none dared fly too low for fear of a goose-feathered shaft between the ribs.

The battle beneath the city was no less fierce, with every day bringing fresh attacks up through the tunnels and rocky galleries. Conn Carsten's fears proved as unfounded as Alaric had promised, for the Ironbreakers of Karaz-a-Karak met and defeated every attack. They fought with more than just axes and swords, for Alaric had brought three of the Guild of Engineers' most prized weapons with him.

Called Baragdrakk in the dwarf tongue, each was a bizarre mechanical contraption that sprayed great gouts of liquid flame, and burned the vermin creatures from their lairs in the rock. The fighting in the tunnels was near continuous, and only rarely were any of the Ironbreakers seen above ground.

Sigmar had Alaric spread his remaining warriors around the city to bolster the defences where they were weakest and where the Norsii were sure to attack the hardest. With warriors from the Skrundok clan, the venerable runesmith made his way through the fighting to hammer arcane sigils into the very stones of Middenheim. He would not be drawn on the nature of these runes, but as the days passed, the lightning strikes that clawed at the city grew weaker and weaker until they ceased altogether. With the lifting of the storms, the hearts of the defenders grew lighter, and the oppressive gloom that hung over the city vanished with the brooding clouds.

Sigmar fought in a different part of the city every day, strengthening the spirits of the warriors he joined with his great heart and enormous courage. Where Sigmar raised his hammer, men and dwarfs fought harder and with greater determination than ever before.

Against Cradoc's instructions, Count Otwin took to the field of battle, fighting alongside the King's Blades, and his chained axe was red with blood that could never be cleaned from its edge. Marius also returned to the battle, though Sigmar was careful to position him where the fighting was less intense, for fear the Jutone count's pride might see him killed.

Conn Carsten's Udose fought harder than ever, their broadswords cleaving through the beasts and monsters with a fury borne from the fear of dishonour. No fiercer foe was there than a wronged clansman.

At Sigmar's suggestion, Pendrag also fought in different parts of the city, letting his warriors see the magnificent blade crafted for him by Alaric. Fighting alongside Myrsa and the White Wolves, Pendrag became an inspirational leader of men, and all who witnessed him wield the mighty runefang in battle felt a measure of his power pass to them.

As the days passed and the city endured, hope that a grand victory might be won seeped into every man's heart.

All that came to an end on the thirteenth day.

CORMAC FELT THE blood run down his face, relishing the taste of it even as the stink of dead flesh turned his stomach. He was naked but for a loincloth, and the tanned colour of his skin was entirely obscured by the crusted blood that covered every inch of his flesh. His arm ached from sawing through meat and bone, yet he could not deny the exhilaration that filled him as he stood in the centre of the pit.

The pit was precisely eighty yards wide and eight deep, filled with severed heads to the height of a man's waist. Every corpse that had fallen from the mountainous spire of Middenheim since battle had been joined was dragged here and decapitated. Day after day, Cormac had hacked the skulls from the fallen and hurled them into the pit. Kar Odacen had spoken of a great prince of Kharnath and such a mighty avatar of the Blood God demanded great honour.

The ground underfoot was thick with coagulated blood, and rotting flesh peeled from the skulls of men and beasts alike. Warriors and champions from every tribe surrounded the pit, each with a dagger poised at the throat of his fiercest warrior. Only the most vicious killers would serve as sacrifices, for a sacrifice was not a sacrifice if it was not valued.

Cormac had woken this day with his veins throbbing and his vision streaked with red, as though an endless gourd of blood was being slowly poured over his head. The taste of it was in his throat and a rabid fury filled his heart. He had felt a similar sensation in the tomb of Varag Skulltaker, and he had felt it when Kar Odacen bound the dark spirit to his axe.

Cormac now saw that those moments had been hollow and meaningless, pale echoes of the bloodlust that now coursed through his body. Mighty powers had turned their eyes upon this mortal world with ruinous ambition, and Cormac's heart soared at the thought of being their mortal champion. His axe growled and hissed, the fell spirit bound within the blade also sensing that this day was special.

Today promised bloodletting like no other.

Today, he would fight alongside one of the mighty daemon lords of Kharnath.

Kar Odacen had sought him out at first light, and the moment he caught sight of Cormac his eyes widened with a mixture of fear and awed reverence.

'It is time,' said the shaman.

Word had spread through the camp, and the assault on Middenheim was forgotten as warriors, beasts and monsters were drawn to the pit to witness this great and terrible sorcery.

Alone among Cormac's warriors, Azazel and the Hung had not come to share this glorious moment, for their master was Shornaal, the ancient god most hated by Kharnath. To be a devotee of the Dark Prince at the birth of one of the Blood God's avatars would be suicide.

Cormac had ritually taken the skulls of eight times eight captives, holding their severed heads above his own and letting the blood drain onto his iron-hard flesh. Each baptism had sent his heart racing, and when he dropped into the pit of heads, he felt the *thinness* of the air, as though he could tear down the wall between this world and the void with his bare hands.

The day was silent, no sounds of life or the passage of moments, for the powers pushing into this world were the bane of all living things. Cormac could feel the pressure within his skull, like the coming of a storm. He welcomed it, for this was a storm of blood, a storm of blades and a storm of skull-taking.

He looked up at Kar Odacen, the shaman's wizened features energised by the power being drawn to the pit. Cormac blinked as his vision blurred. The world around him began to turn red, as though his eyeballs were filling with blood. The sensation was not unwelcome. For the first time, Cormac could see the breath of the gods roaring over the earth, clouds of red howling soundlessly around him like smoke in a storm. It touched everything with rage and hatred, pride and glory. Nothing was left without its boon.

The breath of Kharnath was everywhere, in every act of violence, every act of martial pride and every act of spite. Every mortal heart was touched by it, and he laughed as he saw the top of Middenheim was just as wreathed in the breath of the Blood God as his own army.

'I feel it!' he roared, a red fury of power surging in his veins.

Kar Odacen raised his arms, and the red mists gathered around the shaman, drawn to him as he gave voice to a host of guttural, primal syllables that sundered the air with their horror and rage. Instinctively, Cormac knew that these were the first words of death, the sounds of the first murder and the echoes of Kharnath's birth at the dawn of all things.

The shaman nodded, and the champions of the north sliced their blades across the throats of their willing victims. Blood jetted from a hundred opened throats, and the air was rent by howls, roars and cries in honour of the great god of battle and blood. But death alone was not enough, and the blades hacked through sinew and bone to sever each head.

Cormac gasped as the heads were hurled into the pit with him. Ruby droplets spattered him as they bounced and tumbled over the decaying carpet of skulls. The howling red clouds were drawn up into a towering spiral of crimson, like a bloody vortex that reached from this poor, tasteless realm to the abode of the gods.

How Cormac ached to climb to that domain of murder and hew skulls in the name of the Blood God, but this moment was not for him to transcend, but for something far older and far more terrible to tread the soil of this mortal earth.

Cormac felt it pass from its own existence to his, and threw back his head as he welcomed the avatar of Kharnath with a bellowing roar of bloody devotion. The pit began to fill with gore, as though an endless lake of blood was flooding through an invisible tear in reality. Forking traceries of light flashed in the sky and crimson bolts of lightning slammed into the pit. The blood boiled and the earth screamed as something ancient and abominable poured its essence into the world.

The pressure in Cormac's skull intensified a thousand-fold, and he screamed in agony, collapsing into the mass of severed heads that floated in the lake of blood. The jostling skulls and blood swallowed him as his flesh burned with invention.

Too late, he realised his mistake.

His role in this was not to fight alongside a lord of Kharnath.

His role was to become one.

SIGMAR KNELT BEFORE the Flame of Ulric, and knew that this was the last day.

He felt it in the icy fire that chilled his bones, and he saw that same knowledge on the face of the hundred warriors who stood with him in the midst of the half-built temple. Even Wolfgart and Redwane were on edge, sensing that this day was somehow special. Sigmar felt a dreadful pressure on the air, like the last breath before the executioner's axe falls.

Coruscating sheets of lightning danced in a sky the colour of mourning, and streaks of red left blinding after-images on the backs of his eyes. Sigmar's nose was bleeding, and he saw that he wasn't the only one. Cuts and wounds he had received during the fighting bled freely as though freshly sliced in his flesh, and he felt an aching sickness in his soul. He tasted blood and smelled a rank, foetid stench, like an overflowing cesspit in summer. It was the smell of corruption, the smell of things about to die.

'Shallya preserve us, what *is* that?' gasped Redwane. 'Smells worse than a dead troll!'

'I thought it was you, lad,' said Wolfgart. 'You White Wolves look as ragged as Cherusen Wildmen. Proper Northmen you are now.'

'I'll take that as a compliment,' said Redwane, cupping a hand over his mouth and nose.

Sigmar knew that smell, for it had saturated the air in the Grey Vaults. It was the reek of the daemonic. Earlier that morning he had watched a mass of Norsii and beasts gathered around a wound carved in the earth, like a wide pool of blood, and felt the dread power of the Dark Gods being drawn forth.

A column of armoured Norsii warriors was already climbing the viaduct to the half-built towers at its top, but Sigmar was confident that Pendrag and Myrsa could handle whatever the tribesmen could throw at them. The runefang had completed his sword-brother, as though it were a piece of his soul that he had not even known was missing.

'I've got a bad feeling about today,' said Redwane, idly dabbing at a reopened cut on his neck. The White Wolf looked up at the bruised sky and shook his head. 'You remember when we talked about finding a wife? When we marched to Brass Keep?'

'I remember,' said Sigmar, understanding the source of his friend's woe. 'What of it?'

'I wish I'd done something about it,' said Redwane, and Sigmar was surprised to see that the warrior was crying. 'I didn't though. I thought there would be time for that kind of thing later, but there is no later for the likes of us, is there? There's only the here and now.'

'We make of life what we can, Redwane,' said Wolfgart. 'We make the best choices we can, and we have to live with them, good or bad. I'll wager that when this is over, you'll find yourself a good lass.'

'You still think we can win?' Redwane asked Sigmar.

'I know we can,' promised Sigmar.

Redwane sighed, looking over the slate-grey rooftops of the buildings around them to the mighty mountain peaks in the distance that reared to the heavens.

'It doesn't really matter in the end, does it?' asked Redwane. 'I mean, look at the land we call the empire, it's so... eternal, and we're so insignificant in the grand scheme of things. Will it matter if we all die here? Does the land care which king sits upon a throne and declares himself its master?'

'Perhaps not, but it does not change our duty to fight,' said Sigmar. 'We are fighting for the land and everyone who lives under our protection. If we fail, thousands more will die, for the warriors of the Dark Gods will not stop until the whole world burns. Our enemies bring disorder and chaos with them, darkness from the blackest realm of nightmare that will consume all that is good in this world. But you are right, in the end, it does not even matter if we live or die.'

'How can it not matter?' asked Redwane.

'All that matters is that we are here, right now,' said Wolfgart, 'standing against that evil.'

'That doesn't make sense,' replied Redwane, 'and since when did you become a philosopher?'

Wolfgart shrugged. 'I'm not, but I know in my heart that we have to try and stop Cormac or everything we love will be destroyed: Maedbh and Ulrike. If I don't fight, they die. I need no more reason than that to kill these bastards.'

Redwane nodded slowly.

'Then that's good enough for me,' he said.

Though his wounds ached with the promise of pain, Sigmar smiled at Wolfgart's words. Better than any notions of honour or glory, the love of family and the need to protect them was all any warrior needed in order to fight.

Sigmar took a breath of mountain air and tasted bitter, burning metal in the back of his throat. He looked over at the walls of the temple, seeing red smoke hissing from the runic patterns hammered into the stone. Alaric had told him these runes were proof against the sorceries of the northern shamans, but even as Sigmar watched, the stone was disintegrating as though it were no more solid than sand. Only the most dread powers could unmake the runes of the dwarfs, and Sigmar felt an icy hand grip his heart as a shadow passed over the sun and the world was plunged into gloom.

A deafening roar shook the Fauschlag Rock, the scream of a creature older than time and more terrible than any nightmare. Men fell to their knees, screaming and vomiting blood as their every sense was violated by something utterly inimical to mortality.

Sigmar tasted blood and burned meat, wet fur and hot iron.

He looked up and saw the worst thing in the world.

And it was coming for him.

## ◄ TWENTY-ONE ►

# The Last Day

PENDRAG'S SWORD WAS a shimmering blur of silver as it clove through a screaming Norseman's chest. No armour was proof against its edge, and no warrior brought low by its power would live. In the heart of the battle, the Count of Middenheim fought alongside his people; their leader, their hero and their friend.

Count Otwin hacked men down by the dozen with his mighty axe, his muscled form bleeding from a score of wounds, and his face a mask of crimson where his crown of blood pierced his temple. The King's Blades screamed as they slew, paint running from their bodies in streams of sweat and blood.

Resplendent in their orange tunics, the Jutones battled with lance and sword, fighting with a precision lacking in their Thuringian brothers. Marius, though still in great pain from Bastiaan's traitorous attack, stood with his fellow counts, cutting through flesh and armour with elegant sweeps of his eastern cavalry sabre.

Conn Carsten and his clan-kin fought at the viaduct also, all three leaders of men having been drawn to fight together on this last day. Pendrag had welcomed them, understanding on some unknown level that this was where they needed to be. Alaric and the dwarfs were assembled on the wide esplanade, the Grimloks, the Skrundoks, the Gnollengroms and the Grimargul veterans. Front and centre were the Hammerers from King Kurgan's personal guard, and Alaric stood among them, a great runic axe held at his shoulder.

The Norsii attacked with greater ferocity than ever, their war cries more brutal, more hideously animalistic than the howls of the wildest rabid beast. The viaduct was all that mattered now, and the enemy had abandoned their attempts to carry the walls elsewhere. From the edges of the forest, the beasts howled as the men of the north alone fought to break into Middenheim.

A warrior in armour of burnished blue plate leapt for Pendrag's unprotected back, but Myrsa's hammer intercepted him in mid-air. The Warrior Eternal smashed the tribesman aside, sending him tumbling to his death. The two masters of Middenheim fought side by side like brothers, slaying their foes and protecting one another with deadly grace.

White Wolves howled as they killed, the fury of Ulric upon them as they fought to protect the city that shared their name. With their wild hair and brilliant red armour dazzling in the sunlight, they were as fearsome a sight as the Norsii, feral and magnificent.

Pendrag blocked the sweeping blow of an enormous axe and stepped in to hammer his fist at the snarling tribesman. Blood and teeth burst from the warrior's face, though this only seemed to amuse him. The axe came at Pendrag again, and he ducked, bringing his sword up in a whistling arc that sliced his foe from groin to shoulder. The runefang was a weapon beyond compare, its edge sharper than the dawn and lighter than a dream. With its awesome power at his command, Pendrag's wounds and aches were forgotten as he fought with the strength and speed of a man half his age.

How long they had fought for, Pendrag did not know, but they were holding their foes at bay. The Norsii were pushing hard, throwing their all into the fight, but the resolve of the defenders was like iron. Jutones, Udose, Thuringians, Middenlanders, Unberogen and dwarfs fought as one, an unbreakable line of courage that no wild charges of the Norsii could break.

Dreams of triumph filled Pendrag's head, but, like all dreams, they could not last.

As the attackers fell back once more, a monstrous darkness filled the sky, and Pendrag dropped to his knees as blinding pain flared throughout his body. The skin at his neck blackened where the dead king's blade had struck, and blood poured over his silver hand, as though the fingers had been cut from him but moments ago. The runefang tumbled from his grip and he screamed as his body curled into itself in terror. Through tear-blurred vision, Pendrag saw men who only moments before had been fighting like heroes of legend, fleeing from a monstrous shadow that filled the sky with its terrible bulk.

It moved too fast to see, its blood-matted hide reeking of death and ancient rage: enormous wings of darkness, brass and iron, the smell of charred flesh and wet fur.

Blood burst from Pendrag's mouth and nose. He vomited over the cobbles.

The shadow flew over the viaduct, the doom of his race made real, and Pendrag wept as its deathly power washed over him. He scrabbled for his fallen weapon, and no sooner had his fingers closed on the runefang's hilt than the suffocating fear fled his mind. His blade crackled with power, and he felt its ancestral hatred of the enveloping shadow.

The Norsii screamed a name, a vile, filthy sound that clawed at the air like fingernails on slate, but it had no power over Pendrag, for he bore a weapon of ancient times. No matter that it had been newly forged, this was a weapon that had *always* existed. Sometimes as a sword, sometimes a flint spear or bronze-bladed axe, but through all the ages of the world, this weapon and its as yet unmade brothers had always been here to fight the corrupting power of the Dark Gods.

Pendrag stood tall amid the helpless defenders of the viaduct, and the runefang blazed with the purest light, a brightness to conquer the blackest night and banish the deepest of shadows. He thrust the sword to the sky and smote the darkness with its blade. Sunlight broke through as the terrible shadow flew towards the centre of the city, and the warriors of the empire clambered to their feet as the power of the runefang gave them strength.

The Norsii charged, and Pendrag's eyes were drawn to the warrior leading them.

He wore form-fitting silver armour that shone wondrously in the light, and flowing black hair spilled gloriously around his shoulders. The warrior bore twin swords of dazzling brightness and, as he skilfully rolled each blade in his grip, Pendrag was struck by the familiarity of the move. Sigmar had claimed Ravenna's murderer was among the Norsii, but until now, Pendrag had thought that impossible. Clean shaven and pristine, he was monstrously out of place amongst the Norsii, and Pendrag's heart skipped a beat as he saw the image of his old friend Trinovantes in the warrior's face.

'Gerreon,' he whispered.

Though fifty yards or more separated them, Gerreon seemed to hear him, and a smile of breathtaking beauty slid across his face as he angled his course to meet Pendrag.

OF THE HUNDRED men who stood with Sigmar, fully a third dropped dead from terror at the sight of the abomination that landed in their midst. Others fled in terror, leaving only a staunch few able to overcome their fear. Like the darkest desires of men and beasts knitted together in a nightmare, it was a creature of darkness dragged into the light by dreams of blood.

It stood four times the height of a man on back-jointed legs, its body vast and muscled. Sheathed in bronze and iron, its flesh was the brutal colour of charred corpses, and the stink of the grave was pressed into its wiry fur. The blunt wedge of its horned head was filled with serrated fangs, and its eyes were like holes pierced in the flank of a volcano.

Enormous wings of smoking darkness spread out behind it, and flagstones shattered as its enormous weight landed. It clutched a bronze axe in one meaty fist and a writhing whip like a cat-o'-nine-tails in the other. The ends of the barbed whip's lashes ended in wailing skulls that dripped blood from their empty eye sockets.

'Daemon,' said Sigmar, and the colossal beast roared, baring its fangs and shaking the foundations of the temple. Blocks of stone crashed to the ground, and every pane of glass in the city shattered.

'Ulric save us,' said Redwane, his face bleached of colour. As if in response to his words, the Flame of Ulric flared angrily at this violation of sacred space.

'I warned you that you would regret your wish to fight a daemon,' said Sigmar.

'I thought we'd done that in the swamps around Marburg?'

'That was no daemon,' said Sigmar. '*This* is a daemon.'

'How do we fight such a thing?' asked Wolfgart, his sword held out before him in trembling hands.

Sigmar lifted Ghal-maraz to his shoulder.

'With courage and heart, my friends,' he said. 'It is all we have.'

The vast daemon took a thunderous step towards them, its cloven hoof shattering each stone and blackening it with corruption. Sigmar's blood raged around his body, the daemon's presence filling him with anger and the lust to destroy. This was the power of the Dark Gods, and the acrid, bilious taste of it filled his mouth.

Perhaps thirty men still stood with Sigmar, the bravest of the brave, but against so mighty and powerful a foe, there would be few survivors. The daemon's wings flared black, and it was amongst them. Half a dozen men died instantly, hacked down with a single blow of the daemon's axe. Another three were sliced in two by a crack of its whip. Blood sprayed the air and hissed as the daemon drank it in through its furnace hot skin.

It moved like a nightmarish phantom, its bulk shifting and indistinct, as though the mind refused to fasten on its diabolical form for fear of being driven to madness. Sigmar threw himself to the side as the daemon's whip cracked with a thunderous peal, and the stone flags of the temple were torn up like a ploughed field.

Sigmar rolled to his feet as the daemon flickered, and its blazing, black bulk towered over him. The axe slashed down, and he leapt back, the monstrous blade smashing into the ground with the force of a comet. The impact hurled Sigmar back, and more stones came crashing down from the unfinished temple walls. A huge lintel slammed into the flagstones next to him, and he spat rock dust.

Rippling light spilled between his fingers, and Sigmar felt the aeons-long enmity of these two powers, one designed to heal and build, the other to corrupt and destroy. He hauled himself upright over the broken stones of the temple.

The daemon was coming for him.

Broken glass and stone crunched underfoot as the daemon threw back its head and roared, the sound echoing through the city and scraping down every warrior's spine with its primal power. Its hellish bulk seemed to fill the temple, an unholy darkness in a place of sacred power.

A score of men fought to surround the daemon, spears thrusting desperately at its armoured form. Its whip slashed out and they died, their bodies bursting apart in wet rains of blood that were drunk by the creature's axe. Blades shattered on its hide, and a dozen more were slain before the daemon's blade.

Sigmar climbed onto a huge block of stone as Wolfgart rushed at the monster's unprotected flank. His sword-brother's enormous blade slashed the iron-hard flesh of its back-jointed legs, drawing a froth of steaming black ichor from the wound. Wolfgart's sword dissolved in an instant, and where the daemon's blood splashed the flagstones, they were burned to a reeking ooze. A casual flick of the daemon's wrist sent Wolfgart flying. His sword-brother slammed into the stone walls of the temple and did not get up.

'Here I am, daemon!' Sigmar yelled. 'Fight me!'

The daemon heard him and swung its shaggy, horned head towards him. Death lived in its eyes, death and an eternity of suffering and pain. Sigmar's spirit quailed before such awesome destructiveness, but he heard a freezing wind howl in his mind, and winter ice filled his veins in answer to the fires of this daemonic foe.

Redwane leapt in to swing his hammer at the daemon's knee. The White Wolf howled as the iron head of his weapon exploded against the daemon's armour, and Redwane fell back as razored fragments tore at his exposed face. The daemon's fist lashed out, catching Redwane on the shoulder and sending him spinning through the air with a horrific crack of shattering bone.

With a howl of all the wolves of Ulric, Sigmar sprinted over the tumbled stones of the temple and hurled himself through the air towards the daemon. Ghal-maraz spun in his grip as he brought it around in a devastating overhead sweep. The ancient dwarf-forged star metal arced towards the centre of the daemon's face, and Sigmar knew that this would be the blow to end this vile creature's existence forever.

The daemon's fang-filled mouth opened wide, and its whip flicked up, its many lashes coiling around Sigmar like the grasping arms of the monstrous kraken that seafarers claimed haunted the ocean's depths.

They tightened on him like barbed coils of wire and his armour buckled beneath its enormous strength. Sigmar screamed in pain as bony thorns pierced his flesh in a dozen places.

The world spun around him: ground, sky, walls, cold-burning fire.

Sigmar slammed against the floor of the temple with bone-crushing force. Ghal-maraz spun away from him, coming to rest before the Flame of Ulric. The lashes of the whip slithered away like guilty snakes, leaving bloody trails behind them. He heard screams of pain and fear, and rolled onto his back, every nerve in his body shrieking with agony. His arm was useless, and he scrambled backwards on his haunches towards his warhammer.

Black shadows gathered over the temple of Ulric, and the daemon's black outline loomed over him.

The Norsii smashed into the defenders at the viaduct, and within seconds it was clear that the wall could not hold. Enraged by the same darkness that had so terrified the men of the empire, the howling tribesmen killed with savage ferocity and madness, each fighting as though to outdo their fellow warriors.

Swords and axes clashed in desperate battle and scores of men died in the opening moments. The defenders fought for their lives, while the Norsii fought for the chance that their ancient gods might notice their bravery.

Pendrag sliced the runefang through the neck of an armoured warrior, his heavy plates of iron no protection against Alaric's masterful blade. Another blow cut through the helmet of a warrior with golden skin and an oversized axe. His sword moved like quicksilver, cutting and stabbing without pause. He saw Gerreon ahead of him, and the swordsman caught his eye and smiled with feral anticipation of their duel.

The empire line was bowing back from the walls, and for all that Pendrag's men were fighting with renewed courage and determination, he saw that it wasn't going to be enough. The hammers of Myrsa and the White Wolves smashed down time and again, and the Norsii died in droves before this incredible fighting force. The Warrior Eternal was sublime, and the White Wolves fought alongside him as faithfully as blooded bondsmen.

Udose clansmen fought to the battle tunes of their ancestors, the skirling wail of their pipes defying their enemies to silence them. No force but death would dislodge them. The Jutone line had broken in places, and though Marius and his fiercest lancers were helping stem the tide, it was only a matter of time until the Norsii gained a foothold from which they could not be dislodged.

Pendrag moved through the Norsii as though they were no more than clumsy children, leaving his White Wolves behind as he killed without mercy or a second thought. Next to his graceful sweeps and deadly lunges, the Norsii were lumbering buffoons, slow-witted and without skill.

A burst of shimmering silver flashed beside him, and he brought the runefang around in a sweeping block as a glittering blade slashed towards him. He spun around, his sword held out before him, but his battle-fury faltered in the face of this magnificent foe.

'How about you try that pretty little sword against a real opponent,' said Gerreon.

Pendrag tried to reply, but words failed him at the changes wrought upon the man he had once called brother. Gerreon's skin was white, like the finest porcelain, and his hair was darker than the deepest starless night. The sounds of battle faded until all Pendrag could see was the perfect, enrapturing figure before him.

It was the eyes that held him, so full of innocence, yet brimming with cruelty and utterly without pity. Pendrag was enthralled by Gerreon's eyes, appalled by beauty that should have aroused, but instead evoked nothing in his soul but revulsion.

Gerreon's sword slashed for his throat, but the runefang swept up and parried the blow without conscious command. No sooner had their swords touched than the spell holding Pendrag transfixed was broken. The frantic clash of iron and screaming swelled like a tide around him.

'I'll gladly cut you down, Gerreon,' snarled Pendrag, thrusting the runefang towards the swordsman. His attack was easily batted aside, and Gerreon laughed with musical amusement as he bounded lightly from foot to foot.

'My name is Azazel,' said the swordsman. 'Gerreon is dead.'

'Gerreon, Azazel,' replied Pendrag with an angry snarl, 'whatever damned name you go by, I'll still kill you.'

Pendrag attacked again, and Gerreon swayed aside, parried another stroke and launched a dazzling riposte. Pendrag flinched as Gerreon's sword sliced the braids from his beard.

'I do so love your pathetic confidence,' smiled Gerreon, spinning his swords in a terrifying display of skill. 'It's so much sweeter to kill someone who thinks they have a chance.'

'Try your best,' challenged Pendrag.

'Gladly,' said Gerreon, attacking in a furious ballet of blades. Pendrag blocked desperately as Gerreon's swords nicked the skin of his neck, cheeks and forehead.

'Fight like a man!' he roared, blocking another slicing blow. The runefang blazed in his grip, its power surging as it empowered him to fight this dread foe. Pendrag drew on every reserve of courage in his heart, and the runefang steeled his will to resist the dark allure of the swordsman's beauty.

Never in Pendrag's life had he fought with such skill, power and speed.

Instantly he knew that it was nowhere near enough to defeat Gerreon.

'You cannot win, Pendrag,' hissed Gerreon, rolling his right blade around the runefang and slicing another braid from Pendrag's beard. 'You must see that I am far more skilful.'

'Skilful, aye,' said Pendrag, backing away along the fighting step, 'but I have something you don't.'

'Oh,' chuckled Gerreon. 'And what's that?'

'Friends,' said Pendrag.

He relished the look of confusion on Gerreon's face as Otwin's axe swept down and crashed into the swordsman's back. Gerreon was driven to his knees by the force of the blow, his reflective armour intact, yet cracked from neck to abdomen. A graceful sword-thrust struck Gerreon in the chest as Count Marius leapt into the fight.

The swordsman fell against the parapet, his face more angry than fearful. Any normal warrior would have been cowed, but Gerreon's face was alight at the prospect of so many opponents.

'All for me?' he mocked. 'Truly I am blessed to be able to kill you all.'

The Berserker King roared in red fury, his axe sweeping out to take Gerreon's head as Pendrag lunged. The swordsman moved like a cat, dodging Otwin's axe, and blocking Pendrag's attack with an almost contemptuous flick of one of his swords. Marius's cavalry sabre was not intended for duelling, but he wielded its shimmering blade like a veteran fencer. Blood seeped from the knife wound in his side, but only a tightness around the eyes gave any hint of the pain he felt.

The three of them came at Gerreon together, understanding that to face him singly would be to die. Otwin fought with maniacal fury, Marius with calculated precision, and Pendrag attacked with a skill borne of betrayal. Their axes and swords slashed and stabbed at Gerreon, but his twin blades were a blur as he blocked, parried and counterattacked.

He taunted them as he fought, tossing his mane of hair, and flashing them his most winning smiles. Pendrag saw past the trap of Gerreon's wondrous countenance, and it seemed his fellow counts were also immune to his charms. Otwin was too deep in his berserker rage to be ensnared by petty adornments such as physical perfection, and Marius cared only for gold. Neither man craved solace in beauty, and Gerreon's temptations were wasted.

Marius cried out as Gerreon's sword slid past his guard and sliced through his armour, the swordsman's blow seeking out his wounded side. The Jutone count dropped to one knee as Gerreon spun low to stab his other sword into Otwin's thigh. Before Gerreon could twist his weapon free, Otwin thundered his fist against Gerreon's shoulder. The swordsman staggered, but did not release his grip.

The Berserker King reached down and took hold of the blade. Gerreon twisted his grip, and blood sprayed from the Berserker King's hand. Otwin roared in anger, his muscles swelled, and he snapped Gerreon's sword-blade with his bare hand. Otwin fell back with a foot of iron embedded in his leg. Gerreon was left with the broken stump of a sword, and his face twisted in petulant anger.

Pendrag saw his chance, and thrust the runefang at Gerreon's exposed chest.

The swordsman twisted aside, and Pendrag's blade sliced across the mirrored surface of his breastplate before sliding clear. Gerreon threw himself at Pendrag, pulling him close as though for a brotherly embrace.

'Too slow,' hissed Gerreon, and rammed what was left of his broken sword under Pendrag's arm. It punched through Pendrag's mail shirt and ripped into his heart. Blood burst from Pendrag's mouth, and he heard someone cry his name. The runefang fell from his hand, and the world spun in fire as he dropped to the parapet.

Cold stone slammed into his face, and his chest was bathed in warm wetness. The sounds of battle seemed distant and tinny now, as though coming from some far-away place. It seemed he could hear the sound of distant howling, drawing ever closer.

He was cold, so very cold, and he could hear wolves.

They were calling to him.

# ◄ TWENTY-TWO ►

# The Doom of Men

MYRSA CRIED OUT as the silver-armoured swordsman plunged his blade into Pendrag's side. Blood sprayed from the wound as the Count of Middenheim fell, the broken sword still clutched in the hands of his killer. The sky seemed to darken, and Myrsa felt the passing of something precious from the world.

The tableau before him seemed static and unmoving: Otwin with his axe poised to cleave into Gerreon's neck, and Marius with his curved blade thrusting for his unprotected back. Pendrag lay at their feet, but it was the look of loathing and regret etched into Gerreon's face that expressed the greatest sadness.

'Pendrag!' shouted Myrsa, and time caught up with the dreadful moment. Gerreon sidestepped Marius's thrust and bent over backwards to avoid Otwin's axe, which came perilously close to taking the head of the Jutone count. The swordsman threw aside the instrument of Pendrag's death as though it were red-hot, and spun away from the clumsy attacks of his enemies.

His remaining sword hung limply at his side, and Myrsa was amazed to see that he was weeping, as though suffering the greatest pain imaginable. The fighting at the wall still raged around him, and though he never once took his eyes from Pendrag's body, he blocked and parried with magnificent precision.

'You are mine, swordsman,' howled Myrsa, and that howl was taken up by hundreds of throats at his back. Such was the force and fury behind the cries that the surging fury of the battle eased as warriors fighting for their lives turned to seek out their source: the warriors of Middenheim.

They were grim-eyed men who lived harsh lives in the north, not given to open displays of emotion or grief, yet they came with tears in their eyes for their fallen count. The blue and white banner of the city came with them, and Myrsa had never been prouder to call this city his home.

Gerreon saw Myrsa and the warriors of Middenheim coming for him, and shook his head. He threw aside his sword and vaulted back over the wall.

'No!' cried Myrsa, leaping to the blood-slick parapet. Thousands of enemy warriors still pressed up the viaduct, but Myrsa easily spotted the silver figure of the swordsman among the baying tribesmen, a lone figure pushing against the tide of attackers.

'The coward flees!' cried Myrsa, furious to be denied his vengeance.

'Warrior Eternal!' shouted a voice beside him, and Myrsa saw Count Marius of the Jutones pointing to the parapet beside him. Myrsa looked down and saw a dead warrior slumped against the wall. Myrsa stared at the man in confusion, wondering what had attracted the Jutone count's eye.

Then he saw it.

The fallen man's weapon: a crossbow.

Myrsa dropped his hammer and lifted the heavy weapon of iron and wood. He was no expert with a crossbow, but had trained with every weapon devised by the race of man. He slotted a bolt into the groove and pulled the wooden stock hard into his shoulder.

He sighted down the length of the crossbow, seeing Gerreon's fleeing form in the small square of iron that served as an aiming sight. Shooting downhill at a moving target was not easy, but just as Myrsa was about to loose, Gerreon stopped moving and turned to face him.

The swordsman stood motionless, his arms outstretched, and his mouth moved as he said something that was lost in the din of battle. Though Myrsa was too far away to hear his words, he knew exactly what Gerreon had said: *I'm sorry.*

'You will be, you bastard,' hissed Myrsa. 'You will be.'

He squeezed the release, and watched as the iron bolt flew from the crossbow, arcing over the heads of the Norsii towards Gerreon's heart. Myrsa lowered the weapon, knowing the shot was true, and his eyes locked with Gerreon's in the split second before the bolt slammed home.

But it was not to be.

A chance gust of wind or the will of the gods, who could know? Either way, the bolt wavered in flight as its fletching unravelled. Instead of skewering Gerreon's heart, the lethal bolt slammed into his shoulder. The swordsman reeled under the impact, but with a final dejected look of disappointment, he turned and fled down the viaduct, beyond the reach of even the greatest marksman.

Myrsa cursed and tossed aside the crossbow. He ran to where Marius and Otwin had carried Pendrag's blood-soaked body. Surrounded by a ring of White Wolves, Pendrag lay cradled in the Berserker King's arms. Incredibly, he still lived, though blood still pumped over

Otwin's hand despite the fistful of rags held tight to the wound. The fast-spreading pool beneath Pendrag told Myrsa everything he needed to know.

He knelt beside his ruler and friend as Pendrag's eyes flickered open.

'Did… you… kill him?' gasped Pendrag, his lips flecked with bloody froth.

Myrsa struggled to speak, his grief threatening to overcome him. For the briefest instant, Myrsa considered lying, telling Pendrag that he had been avenged, but the moment passed. He was a warrior of honour, and Pendrag deserved the truth.

'No, my lord,' he said. 'I wounded him, but he escaped.'

'Good,' whispered Pendrag.

Myrsa struggled to understand Pendrag's meaning, but simply nodded as Marius knelt at his side. He carried the runefang and held the handle out to Pendrag.

'Your sword, my brother,' said Marius, and Myrsa was astonished to see tears in the man's eyes. 'Take it one last time and bear it with you into the Halls of Ulric.'

Pendrag's hand closed around the leather-wound grip of the incredible sword, his fingers smearing blood over the golden pommel. A mask of peace soothed the lines of pain on his face, and he smiled, as though hearing words of comfort. Just holding the blade strengthened Pendrag, and he looked up at Myrsa with eyes that were clear and determined.

'Warrior Eternal,' said Pendrag, and Myrsa leaned in close.

'My lord? You have a valediction?'

'I do,' said Pendrag, lifting the runefang towards him. 'The sword is yours now.'

'No,' said Myrsa, shaking his head in denial. 'I am not worthy to bear it.'

'Funny…' said Pendrag. 'I said the same thing. But you must listen to me. This is the runefang of Middenheim, and before these witnesses, I name you Count of Midenheim. The sword needs you, and you *must* take it!'

Myrsa swallowed, and looked over at Marius and Otwin, seeking some sign as to what he should do.

Marius nodded and Otwin said, 'Go on, lad. Take it.'

'Heed what it tells you, my friend,' said Pendrag softly, his voice fading.

'I will, my lord,' said Myrsa, taking hold of the runefang, his hand wrapped around Pendrag's as they held the blade together. Ancient craft and skill were woven into the blade's making, and with it came wisdom beyond the ken of mortals.

Pendrag sighed, and his hand slipped from the sword. Tears spilled down Myrsa's face, and the White Wolves howled with grief. Their sorrow lifted to the skies, calling the Wolves of Ulric to carry the spirit of this great warrior to his final rest.

Myrsa lifted the gleaming blade.

'I know what I have to do,' he said.

STANDING AT THE edge of the forest far below, Kar Odacen watched the dark halo around the city on the rock, and knew that its final moments were at hand. He felt every life the daemon lord of Kharnath took, and the pleasure it gained from such wanton killing coursed like the finest elixir through his flesh. It had taken every scrap of his power to summon so mighty a champion of the Blood God, and he had been forced to bind his life-force to it to seal the pact.

Such a bargain was dangerous, but the vitality that flowed from the daemon lord's killing was worth any risk. His mind was clouded with blood, his sight red with the baleful energies of the powerful daemon. The Blood God had no love for sorcery, and Kar Odacen struggled to hold on to his powers in the face of so mighty a slaughter. The present was a blur of blood, and the future a swirling chaos of possibility, so he focused on the past to hold onto his sense of self.

He smiled as he remembered the dawning comprehension on Cormac's face before he fell into the lake of blood that preceded the manifestation of the daemonic creature. Too late, he had realised how he had been manipulated and groomed to become the perfect vessel for the destroyer of men. To think that he had thought that a mere mortal would be the instrument of the Dark Gods' will! The thought was laughable.

Kar Odacen watched the distant struggle on the viaduct, hearing only the faintest sounds of battle. If the men of the empire knew the ultimate fate of the world, they would take their blades to their own throats. The End Times were upon this age, yet it was the doom of men that they could not see the hangman's noose around their necks.

A trickle of bloody saliva dribbled from the corner of his mouth, and he blinked as he became aware of movement around him. He forced his eyes open, seeing the forest beasts with their heads lifted, sniffing the air and gathering in huddled, fearful packs. Kar Odacen felt the urge to kill them all threaten to overwhelm him. The rage of Kharnath was upon him, and only with an effort of will was he able to suppress it.

A pack of beasts with the heads of snarling bears and wolves clustered close to him, pawing the ground and clawing the air. Their fear spread to their twisted kin around the Fauschlag Rock with every bray. Kar Odacen rounded on the nearest creature, a towering brute with dark, reptilian scales and the head of an enormous horned bull.

'What is going on?' he demanded, his mouth thick with the iron taste of blood.

The creature didn't answer, and Kar Odacen tried to draw on his powers to destroy it, but the weight of the daemon lord's presence was too great, and he could summon no trace of his sorcery. The huge beast shook its shaggy head and spat a mouthful of bloody cud before turning and vanishing into the trees. Its pack followed it, and all around the towering spire of rock, others were doing likewise.

'Where are you going?' raged Kar Odacen, but the beasts ignored him.

'They are going home,' said a voice choked with self-loathing behind him.

Kar Odacen turned, and his anger fled as he saw Azazel standing before him. An iron bolt jutted from his pauldron, and his silver armour was streaked with blood.

'What in the name of all the Dark Gods are you doing here?' shouted Kar Odacen. 'You should be atop the city! You carry the walls of Middenheim and bathe in the Flame of Ulric! I have seen it!'

'Maybe one day,' said Azazel, turning and walking away, 'but it will not be today.'

DARKNESS GATHERED OVER the temple, the daemon's outline a deeper blackness against the gathering shadows. Its axe howled with monstrous hunger and its whip wound itself around its arm, the skulls laughing with lunatic glee. Sigmar scrambled away from the colossal monster, knowing he had only moments to live.

The daemon hissed, its breath that of a charnel house, hot and reeking of unnumbered headless corpses. The brass and crimson of its armour was matted with blood, and its black fur stank of burned meat. It stepped towards him like a hunter stalking wounded prey, enjoying the last, futile moments of defiance before stepping in for the kill.

Its eyes fastened on Sigmar, and in that brief moment, he saw the man within the monster, a soul torn apart and used as a gateway for a creature of madness and death to pass between worlds. Somewhere deep in this daemon, Cormac Bloodaxe relished his body's destruction for the glory of bringing forth a mighty avatar of the Dark Gods.

Sigmar's hand closed on the haft of Ghal-maraz, and the shadows lifted as his warhammer blazed with light. He climbed to his feet, and the daemon roared, as though pleased it had found worthy meat at last. Its axe swung for him, and Sigmar rose to meet it.

Hammer and axe clashed in coruscating arcs of crimson, two weapons forged by masters of their art. A thunderous shockwave exploded outwards, smashing the last columns and archways of the temple to ruins. The Flame of Ulric danced like a candle in a hurricane, but it remained true in the face of powers that sought to extinguish its light.

The cold fire flared brighter than ever, and Sigmar knew that Ulric was with him.

'I am ready for you,' said Sigmar, and the daemon raised its axe in salute.

Man and daemon faced one another in the ruins of the temple, the blood-tinted sky like sunset on the last day of the world.

Sigmar charged the daemon, its mighty form vast and terrible, its dreadful axe a weapon to unmake all life. He ducked beneath a killing sweep and smashed Ghal-maraz against the daemon's flank. Brass armour parted beneath the force of the blow, and more of the daemon's black blood sprayed. Where it had melted iron blades and stone, Ghal-maraz was proof against it, and the daemon roared in anger.

Its axe chopped down and Sigmar threw himself to one side. The blade clove the air, but with a dark shimmer, it reversed itself upon the haft and slammed into Sigmar's chest.

All the malice and rage that had gone into the creation of the daemon's axe was in that blow, and it smashed

Sigmar's armour asunder. Runes of protection flared white-hot as they were destroyed by the raw, elemental power of the Blood God, and Sigmar felt the heat burning his skin, forever branding him with the script of the dwarf runesmiths. He felt ribs break and blood burst from his mouth as he was slammed into the fallen ruins of the temple. He fell to the ground beside the Flame of Ulric, still clutching Ghal-maraz tightly as his armour fell from his body in blackened pieces. He rolled onto his side, propping himself up on one elbow as the daemon raised its axe to destroy him.

The sound of wolves echoed through the temple, and the winter wind howled around them. Particles of snow and chips of ice billowed from the fire at the heart of the temple, and Sigmar's chest heaved in pain as the air around him froze. The daemon's form hissed as ice and fire met.

Sigmar knew with utter certainty that this was the breath of Ulric himself.

Just as surely as he knew it was not for him.

He heard a warrior's shout, a cry of loss and rage, courage and devotion, and a silver sword blade burst from the daemon's stomach. Cold fire bathed the blade, its runic surface drawing the breath of Ulric to it in a blinding whirl of ice and snow.

The daemon roared, its essence fighting to prevent its flesh from unravelling in the face of this new power. Sigmar dragged himself to his feet to see the daemon transfixed by a warrior in pristine white armour who drove a dead man's sword up into its unnatural flesh.

White light surrounded the warrior, and Sigmar saw it was Myrsa, the Warrior Eternal of Middenheim. The breath of Ulric was not for Sigmar, but for the hero who had pledged his life to the city's defence. The sword with which Myrsa had impaled the daemon was no longer a weapon forged by mortal hands, but a blinding spike of ice, a shard of the Wolf God's power brought to earth to slay the avatar of its enemies.

Even as Sigmar rejoiced at the sight of Myrsa, his heart despaired. There could be only one reason why Myrsa wielded the runefang.

Moment by moment, the daemon's form wavered and flickered, its will and power to endure a match for the energies that sought to destroy it. This was Sigmar's one chance, and he knew what he had to do. He held Ghal-maraz in the Flame of Ulric, letting the cold fire bathe the head of the mighty warhammer in the power of his god.

Sigmar pulled his hammer from the flames, its entire length rippling with white fire, and ran towards the daemon. He leapt from fallen stone to fallen stone until he was level with the daemon's chest, and hurled himself towards its horned head.

Its eyes blazed, but no daemon-born fury could prevent Sigmar from striking.

Ghal-maraz thundered into the daemon's chest and its darkness exploded into shards of night. Fell powers screamed, and the sky was rent asunder as the daemon lord's body was torn back to the damned realm from whence it had come. Winter storms raged around the fallen temple, and Sigmar was swept up in the tearing, slicing whirlwind of ice and frozen air. His flesh burned with the bitterest cold, but the touch was not unwelcome, its icy bite familiar and divine.

He slammed into the ground, and the breath was driven from his body as the Flame of Ulric surged with life and power. Its fire spread over the ground as though an invisible coating of oil covered every surface. The rocks ran with blue flame and the bodies of the dead leapt with it.

The whole world was afire, and it swept out into the city of Middenheim.

\* \* \*

LIKE A STORM-BLOWN tide, the Flame of Ulric spread through the city, a blazing, seething river of blue fire that echoed with the howls of wolves and frozen winds. It did not burn, yet it roared with the hunger of a mortal blaze, and nothing it touched would ever be the same. A towering pillar of winter fire lifted from the heart of the city, spearing the furthest reaches of the sky and spreading its cold light across the land as far as the eye could see.

The warriors of Middenheim howled as the power of their god touched them, and their eyes shone with the light of winter. Their blades were death, and the Norsii saw the defeat of the dread lord of Kharnath in the cold, merciless eyes of their foes.

At each man's side, whether Middenlander or not, a shimmering wolf of blue fire snapped and bit at the Norsii, tearing open throats, and clawing flesh from bones with ghostly paws. No blade could cut them, no armour could defy them, and the phantom wolves tore into the Norsii with all the power of their master.

Terror overcame the Norsii, and they scattered before the tide of fiery wolves and winter warriors. The viaduct became a place of certain death, with the wolves of the north and the men of the city hacking down their fleeing foes without mercy.

Amid the howls of wolves and the screaming winds, there came another sound, a sound the defenders of Middenheim had almost despaired of hearing.

Great horns, blowing wildly from a host of men.

THEY CAME FROM the forests: the swords of ten thousand men from all across the empire.

From the east came the Asoborns, the Cherusens and the Taleutens. A thousand chariots led by Queen Freya smashed into the Norsii, swiftly followed by the Red Scythes of Count Krugar. Howling packs of Cherusen Wildmen fell upon the scattered beasts and men, their painted bodies glowing in the fire atop the Fauschlag Rock.

From the south came the Endals, the Brigundians and the Menogoths, warriors who had marched day and night to reach their Emperor and fight at his side.

The Raven Helms of the Endals rode down the Norsii fleeing from the viaduct, Count Aldred cutting a path through the northern tribesmen with arcing blows from Ulfshard. Princess Marika rode a midnight horse at his side, loosing arrows from a gracefully curved longbow.

Merogen spearmen drove Norsii horsemen onto the blades of the Menogoths and the Brigundians, and Markus and Siggurd relished the chance to lay waste to their enemies from afar. Ostagoth blademasters cut down Norsii champions with sword blows that were as deadly as they were elegant, while Count Adelhard's kingly blade laid waste to any who dared come near.

Within the hour, the Fauschlag Rock was surrounded by warriors of the empire, and the Norsii were doomed. By nightfall, the Flame of Ulric had retreated to the ruined temple, the winter winds and ghostly wolves returning once more to the realm of the gods.

Only two souls escaped the empire's vengeance: a weeping swordsman in silver armour and a screaming madman whose eyes ran with blood.

They fled into the shadows of the forest, where the beasts were waiting for them.

SIGMAR MET HIS counts at the head of the viaduct.

Krugar and Aloysis stood together, brothers once more now that they had seen what might be lost should their friendship falter. Freya was as magnificent as ever, her golden armour streaked with Norsii blood and her fiery hair unbound. Count Aldred and Princess Marika, resplendent in gleaming black armour, smiled warmly as he approached.

The southern counts, Siggurd, Markus and Henroth, bowed grandly as he approached, their faces haggard from the long march, yet elated to have arrived in time. Adelhard of the Ostagoths swept Ostvarath in a dazzling flourish, ending by sheathing his ancient blade and bowing to Sigmar.

Conn Carsten, though not yet appointed a count of the empire, had earned the right to stand with such heroes, and his normally sour expression was banished in favour of a thin smile at this great victory. Behind them, the pipes of the Endals and Udose entwined in triumphant harmony.

Bloodied and weary, yet no less magnificent, Otwin and Marius held each other upright. They made for unlikely brothers-in-arms, but they had fought and bled at each other's sides and shared great heroism and hardship.

Only one count was missing, and Sigmar's heart ached with his loss.

Alaric, Wolfgart, Redwane and the new Count of Middenheim stood over the body of Pendrag, his fallen sword-brother and oldest friend. All three were hurting, but none would let this moment pass without their presence. Myrsa's face was impassive, but Wolfgart and Redwane wept openly. Even Alaric, a warrior of a race for whom the lives of men were but a brief moment in time, had shed tears for Pendrag.

Sigmar's sword-brother was wrapped in blue and white, for the warriors of Middenheim had fashioned his shroud from the banner of their city, and Sigmar could think of no more appropriate a gesture. Myrsa now bore the runefang, but to honour Pendrag's passing, he laid the mighty blade upon his fallen lord's chest.

Though Sigmar's body was on the verge of collapse, he held himself tall before his counts. To do any less would dishonour the men who had fought and died to win this day.

He tried to think of words that would convey how grateful he was, how blessed with such fine friends he was, but the words would not come. Sigmar stood amid his counts and wept for all they had lost this day, for friends who would never laugh with them again, and for brothers, fathers and sons who would never return to their families.

Count Siggurd stepped forward, his hand on the hilt of his sword.

'I did not know if you would come,' said Sigmar at last.

'You called for us and we came,' said Siggurd. 'We will always come.'

## ABOUT THE AUTHOR

Hailing from Scotland, Graham McNeill worked for over six years as a Games Developer in Games Workshop's Design Studio before taking the plunge to become a full-time writer. In addition to a host of previous novels for the Black Library, Graham's written a host of SF and Fantasy stories and comics, as well as a number of side projects that keep him busy and (mostly) out of trouble. Graham lives and works in Nottingham and you can keep up to date with where he'll be and what he's working on by visiting his website.

Join the ranks of the 4th Company at
*www.graham-mcneill.com*

# THE EMPIRE ARMY SERIES

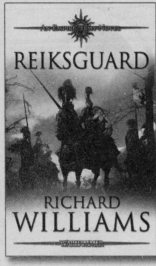

## REIKSGUARD

### RICHARD WILLIAMS

## IRON COMPANY

### CHRIS WRAIGHT

UK ISBN 978-1-84416-726-5  US ISBN 978-1-84416-727-2

UK ISBN 978-1-84416-778-4  US ISBN 978-1-84416-779-1

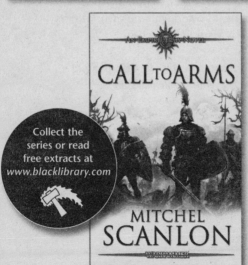

## CALL to ARMS

### MITCHEL SCANLON

Collect the series or read free extracts at www.blacklibrary.com

UK ISBN 978-1-84416-812-5  US ISBN 978-1-84416-813-2